T0354708

THE WARRIOR & THE DRAGON

THE WARRIOR & THE DRAGON

RUSTY REECE

iUniverse®

THE WARRIOR & THE DRAGON

iUniverse books may be ordered through booksellers or by contacting:

iUniverse
1663 Liberty Drive
Bloomington, IN 47403
www.iuniverse.com
844-349-9409

ISBN: 978-1-6632-6910-2 (sc)
ISBN: 978-1-6632-6912-6 (hc)
ISBN: 978-1-6632-6911-9 (e)

Library of Congress Control Number: 2024924874

Print information available on the last page.

iUniverse rev. date: 12/19/2024

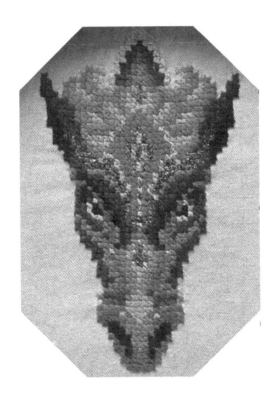

People who deny the existence of dragons are
often eaten by dragons. From within.
—Ursula K. Le Guin

This is a work of fiction. All characters and events are fictional, except for scientists' (slightly modified) names when I describe their results to provide a comparison of technology between Rutendo and our mundane world (e.g., Dimitrios for Dmitri Mendeleev and Évariste the Gaul for Évariste Galois).

To those who ignited the spark: Smaug and Ancalagon the Black, the first dragons to take flight in my imagination, you are not found in this story, but your fiery presence sparked a lifelong fascination with these magnificent creatures.

And to the ever-growing horde: The dragons of Pern, Earthsea, and legend—Cymru, the dragon of Wales, and the dragon kings of China—you expanded my understanding of dragons and their place in myth and magic.

Beyond scales and claws, while Maleficent may have donned dragon form, my inspiration for shapeshifters with a dual nature comes from another source: Patricia Briggs, whose Mercedes Thompson series (and the captivating world of Mercy's wolf-shifting neighbor) introduced me to two-skinned who are neither wolves nor weres.

This dedication, however, is not just for dragons and shifters.

It's for those who, like Jason in Smoky Springs, discover hidden strengths and rise to the challenges fate throws their way. It's for the warriors, both women and children, who learn to defend themselves and their homes.

This is for the magic that lies within us all.

CONTENTS

PREFACE

I was born in the first half of the last century, which makes me older than dirt.

I met my wife at the Occidental College dining hall fifty-five years ago. I spotted a freshman woman sitting alone and sat across from her. I picked up her meal card, read her name, and introduced myself. Not bad for an introverted math major.

We have two adult children and two adult grandchildren, and there are at least four math or science teachers in my family.

I started reading science fiction in elementary school, fascinated by space flight and life on other planets. Later, as the schedule for space flight stretched ever outward, I became fascinated with magic as a suitable substitute. Star Trek also helped to fill the void.

A friend in college loaned me his copy of Tolkien's The Lord of the Rings. I read all three volumes in less than forty-eight hours, pausing only for meals. I was nineteen, and sleep was optional most days.

That started a deep dive into sword and sorcery as a genre. I continued to read science fiction; Heinlein, Asimov, and others were still writing when I was in college.

During my thirty-five-year career in aerospace, I wrote a lot of technical papers and proposals—nothing you would know about unless you worked where I did.

This is my first work of fiction.

I take this opportunity to thank the teachers who made a difference for me: Mrs. First for teaching me to read; Mrs. Robertson for teaching me more than I can remember; Dr. Freedman for teaching me that math is also a gateway to history and literature; Dr. Hardy for teaching me, a mathematician, how to be an engineer; and the teachers in my family—my mother, my wife, my sister and her husband, my daughters, one son-in-law, and one nephew. So far.

I hope you like my story.

ACKNOWLEDGMENTS

Many thanks to the writers' group members who reviewed and commented on multiple drafts and improved the book immeasurably: Lyn, Melinda, Sandy, Bob, Michael, Mark, J. Y., Lawrence, and Julia.

Thanks also to my iUniverse editor, Elizabeth D., whom I have not met but who identified several plot inconsistencies, identified multiple "More detail needed here" spots, and taught me to check for point of view.

AUTHOR'S NOTE

....

Welcome to the Kingdom of Rutendo. I hope you enjoy your stay. A few things might help you get along with the residents.

Humans share the world with five other sentient races: kaihana, dwarves, arboreals, fae, and two-skinned.

For kaihana, consider a parallel evolution with man but with the orangutan as the nearest primate relative, rather than the chimpanzee. Kaihana are shorter than humans, with proportionately longer arms and bowed legs. They are long-lived compared to men and predominantly female in population. The males are called kaihana'sa.

Dwarves are shorter and broader than humans. There are two branches of dwarves in Rutendo: black dwarves, who mine for jewels, iron, and other metals, and brown dwarves, who cut and finish stone for buildings and art. Dwarves are somewhat reclusive, but they do interact with humans.

Arboreals are small beings—rarely above waist high on average humans—who dwell in the forest, reduce undergrowth, and prune trees to keep the forest healthy. They are timid around humans.

The fae live in a separate physical realm and only cross at specific locations. Those locations are almost always beneath the earth's surface, at sites called *sidhe* (hills or mounds hiding doorways to the fae realm).

Two-skinned humans can change to and from an animal form at will, provided they are healthy. The human form can see, hear, and feel through the animal form's eyes, ears, and extremities. The animal shares senses with the human half. Each skin can communicate with its other half, though that ability is limited by how its animal skin communicates among its kin. All known two-skinned humans share their skin with a predator.

As here, minutes and hours measure time within a day. Each day is divided into twenty hours of sixty minutes, with sunrise starting each day.

Predawn time is called "the hour(s) before the day" or "the hours since the previous sunrise."

The unit of time between a day and a month is a tenday. Each month has three tendays and begins on the morning of a full moon.

The shortest day in midwinter marks the year's end. The last month gains a day when needed to align with the lunar calendar.

You will see a little of the religious practices of the people of Rutendo. Most of those you meet worship the Moirai, a goddess with three aspects (Maid, Mother, and Crone), but some worship Nataraja. The Moirai's disciples meet under the full moon and meditate or dance, while Nataraja's disciples worship via dance and song at any phase of the moon.

The dragon cannot speak like a man. He speaks directly to another's mind. Mind-to-mind speech is illustrated here: *Dragon's mind-to-mind speech.*

MacTíre, a fae, does not show his form in this volume. His speech seems to come from above or around you.

I hope you enjoy your travels in Rutendo. Have an excellent adventure.

Rutendo Near Smoky Springs.

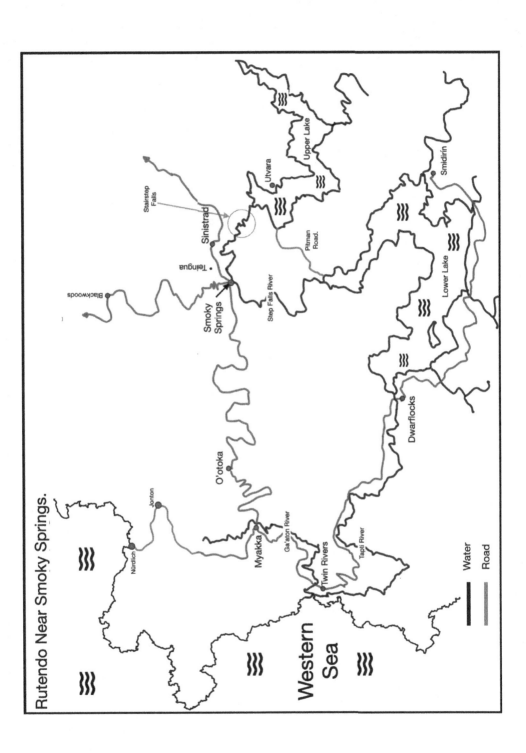

CHAPTER 1

Daughter of the Storm

From the west, a warrior walks.
In his staff, a longbow hides.
Sparks from his fingers fly,
and in his shadow, chaos rides.
—From *The Prophecy of the Beuman√, the Herald of Chaos*

Erlender washed his hands carefully. The metallic tang of blood clung to his nostrils as the crimson traces vanished from his skin and nails. He'd removed his shirt before the interrogation, so no blood marred his clothing. The man's death cry echoed in his ears, a grim counterpoint to the metallic tang in the air. A cruel smile twisted his lips. He had a name!

Four years. Four grueling years of chasing whispers and rumors through dusty taverns. Every dead end gnawed at him like a starving beast. Now, as he hunched over a flickering candle in a dingy back room, the frustration melted away.

"Jason." He breathed the single word, which released a surge of energy through him. He rose, straightening his back as if relieved of a heavy burden. Sleepless nights and countless dead ends faded into insignificance.

With a name, he could seek a person and not a will-o'-the-wisp conjured from a single sentence overheard in a pub—about a soldier carrying a glowing statue who led a charmed life.

Insects, rats, and other vermin did not bite the soldier. He was untroubled by the night terrors following battle mage attacks. He survived

1

skirmishes with minor injuries that left all others dead or seriously injured. Soldiers quartering near him experienced some of these benefits. No other item Erlender knew of would protect soldiers like this. It must have been a kalasha—an icon of great power carved in an aspect of the Triple Goddess, the Moirai!

One thousand five hundred thirty-one days of dead ends. Erlender had chased whispers and rumors through dusty taverns, seeking soldiers of the king who had seen or heard of a glowing statuette carried by one of their own; his quarry had been a nameless wisp of smoke that danced just out of reach. Rumors had been all he had until about two moons ago. An archer he'd found then remembered the man who carried it. His years of searching were finally bearing fruit.

Erlender smiled to himself. Golgol-drath would be pleased with another kalasha of the Moirai in hand.

Somnath, the healer he'd found yesterday, knew the man Erlender sought. He'd volunteered that Jason had brought the glowing icon to the surgery tent and left it with Somnath, except for the times when Jason slept elsewhere. Under Erlender's probing with a knife and hot iron, Somnath had added that the archer would visit during lulls in the fighting, assisting with amputations and mercy deaths, using angel's kiss. The survival rate from surgeries was much higher with the statuette present. Further probing had yielded no useful information about Jason.

He wasn't chasing a ghost anymore but an archer who had lived on a farm run by women. He now had a target, a destination, a reason for all the hardship. A triumphant grin stretched across Erlender's face. The hunt was far from over, but for the first time in years, he wasn't lost at sea. He had a course, a direction, and the wind at his back.

Jason. The name echoed in his mind—a promise, a battle cry. The game was afoot, and Erlender was ready. No man could hide from him; the prize was his. The only question was when.

Searching army records for Jason's last location and destination was his next step.

———— ✦ ————

Jason stepped off the gangplank onto the weathered seaside docks at Twin Rivers Bay. The harbor was alive with activity: ships being loaded and unloaded, porters ferrying crates to and from warehouses, and fishermen selling their catch or inspecting nets.

Perhaps this place is it, he thought.

Since his discharge from the army a year ago, he had drifted, taking jobs as a sell-sword or guard. Then he'd heard that Duke Rashad was looking for longbowmen. His range was a little shy of 300 yards, and few could best him for accuracy at 240 yards. This was a chance for long-term enlistment at the castle and an opportunity to feel that he belonged.

As he made his way toward the town center, he couldn't help but feel excited about his prospects. The city was alive with activity. The market square bustled with vendors selling everything from fresh produce to handcrafted goods to street foods.

His stomach rumbled, and he paused at a vendor selling meat pies. The aroma was irresistible, and he purchased one, savoring the flaky crust and filling of meat, vegetables, and gravy.

A strange sensation washed over him as he continued through the market, eating his meal. It felt as if someone lightly touched the hair on the back of his head. It was not a breeze, since only one area was affected. He resisted the urge to turn and look; if it was nothing, there was no reason to seek a source, and if it was something, there was no reason to alert the person that he had detected him or her.

He continued to walk through the market, finding occasions to glance back whence he came. He spotted an old woman sitting at a small table with her eyes fixed on him. She seemed harmless. Walking across the market, he felt the touch on his hair again. Further surreptitious glances revealed the same old woman watching.

Intrigued and a little unnerved, he decided to confront her. He walked away from the market and down a side street and then circled back. The old woman remained in the booth with her gaze on the crowded street.

Jason approached her quietly. When he spoke, his voice was steady. "Greetings, Grandmother."

She jerked upright and turned to look at him. Her eyes were wide. "Well, I see my touches did get your attention. I was afraid I had misjudged what I saw in you."

"Your touch. It felt like someone tickled the hair on the back of my head. And what judgment had you reached about me?" he asked.

Her eyes flashed. "Why do you call me Grandmother? You know nothing of my story."

"Where I was raised, it is a term of respect for the wisdom women gain as they age," Jason said. "I am Jason, a soldier by trade. How did you touch me from across the market, and what do you wish me for?"

"Respect earned by living long, eh? I can think of worse reasons. As to what I observed and wish, I sense a fire in you that smolders but wishes to burn. And your aspect radiates the Goddess's light. A warrior who is a mage and a devotee of the Lady is unusual. I wanted to learn more about you even before I knew you were a fighting man. So I flicked your aura with a little mana. If I had been wrong about the fire, you wouldn't have noticed."

The woman indicated a chair at her side. "Sit, that I may know you better. And you can continue to call me Grandmother; I like its sound from your lips."

She took a pipe and a small pouch from her purse and eyed Jason.

He chuckled. "You have set the hook, Grandmother. I will sit." He removed his pack, placed it and his staff on the ground, and took the open chair.

"Join me in a smoke," she said as she filled her pipe.

Jason retrieved his pipe and tobacco and filled his.

"Now light mine," the woman demanded.

Jason extracted flint and steel from his pack.

"No, without those," she added as he raised the flint.

Jason raised his eyebrows and stared at her.

"I can read your aura, young man. You do not need those to start a fire."

Jason nodded and then cupped his hands above her pipe's bowl and concentrated. A spark formed and landed on the tobacco, which ignited as she drew air through the stem. She nodded and leaned back, blowing a smoke ring above his head.

He raised his pipe to his mouth, and she flicked a finger, lighting it instantly.

Jason explained his purpose in coming to Twin Rivers City. When he was finished, his pipe was too. He knocked the ash and dottle onto the ground and rubbed them with his toe, leaving just a smear of ash and char. He stood, but before he could say farewell, she spoke up.

"Well, before you sign on with the duke, are you willing to explore other options? And perform a task for me?"

"Yes, I will consider other options. And that depends on the task," he replied.

"You can return to enlist with the duke at its conclusion; longbowmen are rare in this part of Rutendo. I will explain it more after you escort me to my cottage."

"It will be my honor and delight to escort you. What is the way?"

The grandmother tilted her head, studying him from half-closed eyes. She nodded and then said, "It may be what you say. We will walk down the market street and continue downhill after we pass the fountain until we reach the river docks. Then a right turn to the ferry-house."

"Shall we embark then?" He donned his pack, picked up his staff, and reached a flexed arm for her to hold.

She took a piece of bright blue ribbon about an inch wide from her bag and extended one end, retaining the other. "I require you to carry this as you lead the way and cry out, 'Make way for my fair lady.'"

Jason could see nothing other than an old person's eccentricity in the request, so he nodded and took the ribbon.

"Lead the way, commander of sparks," she said.

He raised his eyebrows but nodded, turned, and stepped into the street.

"Make way! Make way for my fair lady!" he cried, drawing out the 'ay' sound and speaking in a sing-song.

He felt the ribbon go taut and then the same flicking he'd felt earlier, except along his entire back.

Looking over his shoulder, he saw a pig. It had been a few years since he had taken livestock to market, and he judged this one as slightly smaller than market-sized about 150 pounds. The other end of the ribbon he held was tied in a bow around its neck.

Jason spun back to stare at the hog as his jaw dropped open. It raised its nose at him several times, grunted, took a few steps toward him, and paused. It tilted its head to one side and made a questioning sound before repeating the nose gestures.

Jason shook his head and turned into the street. *I knew she was a mage, but what does she hope to happen or to learn from this deception? Am I the only one who sees a pig, or will all see her as one?*

"Well, I see that *my fair lady* is not just a description but likely the name of this beautiful swine. So my challenge is to get you to the ferry landing. Let us continue."

As he stepped, the ribbon tightened. The pig matched his pace perfectly.

"Make way! Make way!" he called out. "Make way for My Fair Lady!"

It seemed to him the pig's snort was a concealed giggle. As he walked, he stamped the end of his staff to punctuate his cry. He held his head up and smiled as though crying a pig through town were a noble task. His announcement got the attention of people within a ten-foot circle.

People in earshot stepped away from the sound and turned. Jason heard murmurs about a pig being cried through the marketplace, so the glamour affected the crowd.

Grandmother's magic is fairly strong for her illusion to influence so many.

Most people stepped out of his way and continued watching as he and the pig passed. Older boys cried taunts, and a few tossed pebbles or garbage in his direction. The projectiles ceased after he deftly evaded a few or batted them at the throwers, showing he was quick and accurate with his long staff.

The road curled around a circular fountain, taking Jason and the pig toward the river docks. Three sheriffs lounged on the fountain's rim. Two held flagons, and three empties sat on the ground near the men.

One called out an insult on pig herders. His voice was slurred as a man in his cups, though it was early in the day.

The three stepped into his path.

He stopped. "Make way," he said again firmly. It was an order, not an announcement.

The crowd who had followed him on his journey through the marketplace withdrew to watch while avoiding getting involved in a fight.

"Well, well, if it isn't a little pig farmer! Will this sow's ear become a silk purse for"—the tallest of the group smirked and continued in a falsetto—"my fair lady?" He laughed and drew a cudgel from his belt.

"If'n it don't, we can still roast 'er fer dinner." The shortest one belched. "It'll feed us for a day or three." He drew a sword and advanced, with the other two following. "Let's see if your pig is as tasty as it looks."

As the two sheriffs who spoke drew their weapons, a murmur of fear ran through the crowd. Jason, however, remained calm with his eyes fixed on the approaching men. With a swift and practiced motion, he shifted his staff into a combat stance and let the ribbon fall.

He brandished his staff, hoping it would dissuade the trio, but to no avail.

The sword-bearer attacked first, swinging his blade in a wide arc. Jason knocked the sword tip up and to his right and then struck a blow to the assailant's stomach with his staff's tip, doubling him over.

The second man gripped his cudgel in two hands and swung it as he

6

rushed forward. Jason recognized the ploy; the sheriff intended to knock the staff aside and step closer, where his shorter club would be more effective. Jason swung his staff to meet the blow but released his grip when the two collided. Expecting a hit on his weapon, the policeman spun halfway around and lost his footing as the staff dropped to the ground. Jason stepped forward and tripped the constable. The sheriff fell to the cobblestone street, hitting his back hard and then his head. He groaned and lay still.

The third man stepped back as Jason retrieved his staff. Jason watched the crowd behind the sheriffs part, which revealed a well-dressed man and several uniformed soldiers.

The remaining man drew his sword as he said, "We thought a bumpkin, perhaps fae-touched, led the pig. But you are an experienced fighter. Now I must take you in for assaulting the duke's men."

Jason continued to wave his staff. "Does the duke know his sheriffs harass citizens and threaten their livestock?"

"He does now," a stern voice announced behind the men.

Jason immediately dropped to one knee, holding his staff parallel to the ground with the ends pointing away from the duke. "Your Grace," he said.

The duke, a tall, imposing figure, stepped forward with his jaw set, eyes narrowed, and lips tight. "I heard there was a commotion here. It seems I arrived just in time." He looked at Jason. "Rise, staff wielder."

Jason stood as the duke ordered the arrest of the corrupt sheriffs. His voice carried a sense of finality. The crowd erupted in cheers as the sheriffs were led away in chains.

Jason bowed before the duke. "Thank you, Your Grace."

"I heard that a small crowd was following a parade and thought it worth investigating. It seems I arrived just in time to prevent an unfortunate incident involving my sheriffs." He shook his head. "I know some abuse their authority, and I am working to cull them." He looked Jason in the eye. "Who are you, and whence did you come to defeat three of my men so easily?"

"I am Jason Archer, formerly of the king's army."

"That explains your success in defending yourself. Why are you leading a pig through the city streets?"

"I promised to escort My Fair Lady to her destination," he replied.

"And did you know?" The duke indicated the pig with his head.

Jason grinned. "I learned that later, after I agreed."

The pig, who had remained in one place during the altercation, emitted a series of soft, low, contented grunts.

The duke nodded and smiled. "I appreciate a man who follows through on commitments, especially when the reality differs from the expectation. I am looking for such men. Are you in service to any?"

Jason hesitated. He had come to Twin Rivers City for this, but he was intrigued by Grandmother's hints. "I have not been released yet," he answered slowly.

The duke nodded. "Return when you can then, Jason Archer."

Jason grinned. "Farewell, Duke Rashad. I am pleased to have met you." He picked up the ribbon, pulled it taut, turned toward the river, and called out, "Make way! Make way for My Fair Lady!"

Duke Rashad watched Jason and the pig walk toward the river. He turned to his spymaster and said, "Follow that man. I want to know where he goes."

One of the duke's retinue saluted, whistled a trill, and began shadowing the pair. Three whistles from the crowd and alley rang out.

"Why are you having that fool trailed?" asked one of his lieutenants.

"Because that *fool* is a dangerous man. He commits to a task and backs that with skill. I want to know who he is with if it isn't me."

The crowd dispersed as Jason and My Fair Lady walked away. He resumed his "Make way" cry.

After walking a short distance, My Fair Lady said, "That was very noble and courageous of you, Jason. I will speak more when we reach our destination; until then, I will maintain the illusion."

When they reached the ferry, My Fair Lady told him to turn away from the river.

A few houses down the road, she dropped the glamour. They walked down an alley to a dead end. She dismissed the illusion of a wall, revealing a doorway. They entered, and the illusion resumed.

"Were we followed?" she asked without preamble.

One of the two men who stood beside the door as she exposed it answered, "After the, uh, unexpected and unfortunate incident with the sheriffs, the duke sent his spy to follow. We diverted him and his informants before they reached the ferry."

"Will there be a search?"

"I think not. We turned each before you reached the ferry."

She turned to Jason. "Well, young man, you far exceeded my requirements."

Jason stared at the old woman. "What you did wasn't very polite," he said with an edge to his voice. "Was that incident planned?"

She looked up at him. "True. It is effective, though. My plan was to observe you, hoping you would escort me despite the situation's embarrassment. You did very well. I know you won't give up just because a task becomes difficult or might make you look foolish.

"You were a stalwart escort. I was surprised by the sheriffs at the fountain and thought I would have to step in; your quick actions and the duke's timely arrival prevented that."

"You tested my small magic, and you tested my—what? Stubbornness?"

Soft, deep-throated, gravelly laughter greeted his words before Grandmother answered. "Yes. And what a commitment to a minor task meant to you. You take your promises seriously, and I admire that.

"Now, please join me for a glass of beer, and I will explain why I tested you as I did and describe the task I wish you to undertake.

"I am old. One bad habit of the old is believing that explaining ourselves costs precious time that we don't have much of." She shook her head. "I tell you this: I and my confederates oppose Golgol-drath. I saw the light of the Lady on you, so I am certain you are not a minion of darkness.

"I see a greater potential in you for fire than just starting them. I will help you attain that promise if you undertake a task for me."

Jason finished packing his pipe as she spoke. He lifted the stem to his mouth, and the mage lit it, as she had in the marketplace. "I am not sure I trust you to tell me all the pertinent details of the task now," he said as he sat.

"Even if all the more you can do is start fires like the one I just lit your pipe with, you will appreciate using your full potential."

He puffed quietly for several minutes. "I can see how creating a burning ember will be better than just a spark. I would like that. My mother's mother could start a fire from across the room, and I was ashamed of how little my fire was compared to hers."

"Was?"

He shrugged. "I live with what I can do and stopped judging my abilities against others' long ago. Now I strive to do the best I can and accept that others will be better."

Her head bobbed up and down. "Most men are twice your age before they learn that, if they ever do."

"What is this task, and why was the test necessary before telling me about it?"

"As I said, my allies resist Golgol-drath. Some of them live in Smoky Springs. I have a package I want delivered there. And a healer lives nearby who can help you expand your control of fire."

"Don't you have colleagues who can carry the package?"

"None are available now. In addition to assisting you with your magic, I will pay gold for your service."

Someone brought in a tray containing bread, cheese, sliced meat, and two mugs of ale. She set the tray down and left the room.

Grandmother motioned for him to proceed, and he selected a mug and took a long swallow.

"How far is it to Smoky Springs?" he asked as he set the mug down.

She smiled, and they began negotiating in earnest.

Iudgual hunched over her cluttered desk as the dying fireplace cast long shadows across maps and half-read scrolls. The events of the past two days gnawed at her. Had she chosen wisely? A sigh escaped her lips as she recalled Jason's actions. A flicker of satisfaction warmed her like a stolen ember. He'd shown both courage and a surprising affinity for fire magic—perfect for the task ahead.

She mentally reviewed the tests she'd given Jason, recalling his magical prowess at lighting her pipe and his surprising response to a contrived situation that had spiraled out of control. When faced with the daunting task of defending her against three of the duke's sheriffs, armed only with his staff, he had astounded her with his valiant defense of her conjured pig. A satisfied smile crept across her wrinkled face.

She'd sent him to deliver an athamé—a magical artifact attuned to fire—to Clifton Clowers, the chief of the Defenders, a quasimilitary group at Smoky Springs Valley. Now she crafted a letter summarizing her findings and actions, so he would be prepared for the messenger.

To Defender Clowers, Greetings!

I believe I found what we discussed two moons ago. I arranged for delivery by a walker.

Look for a man coming from the West. His name is Jason. He arrived seeking a position in the duke's guard. I promised him a half year's wages for a guard if he delivers to you within twenty days. I advanced him one lunation's wages against that total.

He is above average height, with a slim build. Brown-blond hair. His eyes are hazel, tending more to green. He carries a staff longer than he is tall.

He will do what he must to fulfill his obligations. He is capable; I watched him face down three sheriffs armed with cudgels and swords while he had his stick. He showed neither fear nor concern for himself while defending his charge (me).

He lit my pipe without flint or steel but cannot satisfy our needs at this time. I am sure he will be able to soon. He called me Grandmother at our meeting—an honorific for an older woman, he said. I gave him no other name to use. I think I am getting too well known, and the name is anonymous enough to adopt.

The adversary, last seen in Limnopolis, searches still. We may have time before mage fire is our only option to stop the darkness. If we fail, corruption will fall and endure for generations.

Until we meet again,
Iudgual (Grandmother)

She read the missive twice before covering the parchment with a sheet of tissue and transferred the ink to the lighter-weight paper with a minor mana pattern. She rolled it up for a bird to carry and sealed it twice, once with magic and once with twine and wax. She repeated this twice, yielding three birch bark capsules, and handed them to her assistant.

"Send these to Smoky Springs by raven—two today and one tomorrow," she said before leaning back and lighting her pipe with a glance.

—⊶⊷—

Following the Succession War, Jason sought a place to live in peace. He hoped Twin Rivers City would be that place, yet there he was, traveling to Smoky Springs to deliver an artifact.

He had entered into a contract with a person he had just met to take an unknown item to a place he had never been and deliver it to Chief Defender Clifton Clowers. What could go wrong?

The artifact was sealed in a package, and he'd asked Grandmother to put an additional seal on the laces of a bag so Clowers could verify Jason had not tried to open it. Her eyes had widened at his request, but she'd complied. There were times during his journey when he felt drawn to look at it, and just thinking of the added security dissuaded him.

Cresting a small hill, Jason surveyed the road ahead. The road curved, limiting his view to five miles. A dense canopy of pines and firs lined the road. Some hilltops above the forest were bare and rocky, while others were covered in trees. By his reckoning, he was descending from the peak of his journey; he was two-thirds of the way from O'otoka to Smoky Springs and making good progress today.

The only landmark on this stretch of road was a small break in the forest on his left—the uphill side. The road was surprisingly well maintained for as little traffic as he had seen. He shifted his staff to his left hand, mindful not to rely on it being in his right. Sensei would've approved. Depending too much on his dominant side weakened his secondary side, and being almost ambidextrous had saved his life on more than one occasion.

As the sun crested the mountains ahead, he saw clouds gathering. It could've been nothing. It could've been a storm approaching. Summer storms came with little warning and could make the road a muddy mess, not to mention catching him without shelter.

Adjusting his pack, he continued his journey.

When he reached the gap in the forest, a chaotic scene greeted him. A landslide, long past its prime, had torn through the land, leaving behind a jumbled mess of boulders and fractured earth. The passage of time had begun its healing work, however. In the crevices between the rocks, tenacious seedlings had taken root; their tiny green shoots reached out toward the sunlight. But they were still mere infants, with their growth stunted by the harsh environment.

He noticed a trail maybe 100 yards above and a short distance past the scree, leading past an overhang on the far side of the path. He thought the space beneath the shelf might be big enough for shelter if the need arose, but he could not see a path to it from the road. The possible storm was too distant and the day too young to seek cover, so he decided to proceed.

Jason raised his waterskin to his lips and took a long drink. With the storm looming, he chose to forgo his planned midday break. Retrieving a piece of pemmican from his pack, he grasped his staff in his right hand and pressed on, quickening his pace past the scree. The scenery remained much the same as it had been—a mix of trees and underbrush, with an occasional bird flitting by. The path dipped and rose several times before rising to the top of a hill two hours later.

He paused as a breeze laden with the aroma of a coming rain caressed his face. He looked to the sky again. The clouds had risen spectacularly and darkened considerably. He could see lightning flashes among the clouds, indicating a strong storm.

A dazzling flash of iridescent green erupted from the sky, tracing a serpentine path along the seam where two towering clouds converged. The sight sent a shiver down his spine as he recognized the telltale sign of a magically enhanced storm.

"Damn!" he whispered.

More colored flashes illuminated the clouds from his vantage point. Yellows, blues, and orange hues reminding him of beetle wings joined the green he had seen earlier.

He had seen the same thing during the battle at Ouray. The flash floods following the vivid lightning display had washed half the army away, and half of those had been lost. He had no desire to get caught in such a storm again.

Shelter. I need shelter—and soon, he thought. *I have passed nothing except the cave above the scree. At least I hope it is a cave. I must reach it; there is nothing visible ahead that could protect against the coming deluge.*

Looking at his surroundings more carefully, he noticed a game trail leading away from the road on the uphill side and arcing back roughly parallel to the route he had walked.

The scree would be wet and hazardous to climb, even in a light rain.

His best option was the game trail. It led in the direction of the cave and at a higher elevation.

He straightened his pack and started along the trail, walking as fast as he thought safe.

The trail abruptly forked, with one path dipping gently downhill and the other climbing just as gradually. The downhill branch seemed to more closely follow the road from O'otoka he'd traversed for the past four days. An unsettling shift filled the air; the clouds were gathering into a menacing mass, and the wind whipped itself into a frenzy. A low rumble of thunder echoed in the distance—a warning growl from the approaching storm.

He judged that he was near the overhang. He had traveled the proper distance in the correct direction but could not see it.

Shifting his load, he studied the two trails. The one leading higher faded into stone a few yards away, while the lower one extended farther. The one heading down could not extend to the road he'd walked earlier in the day, or he would have seen it. He decided the lower branch would lead him closer to the overhang and the hoped-for shelter, and he resumed his rapid pace along that trail.

As he hurried, he noticed a deadfall. Several fallen trees might provide some shelter a few yards off the trail if the overhang proved too shallow for protection. He continued his quest for shelter.

He saw the tumbled rocks from above less than a quarter mile away, which confirmed his choice was correct. Rounding a cottage-sized boulder, he saw the overhang. The sky had darkened more, the winds had picked up, and it felt colder than when he'd left the road.

He sprinted to the protrusion and found it would provide shelter. Three sides of the hemispherical area beneath the projection would protect him from falling rain if the winds cooperated. The opening beneath the overhang looked two paces deep and three paces wide. The extrusion was shoulder height at the trail but sloped upward, so he could easily stand about half a step in. A shadow at the back of the outcrop drew his attention.

Setting his pack and staff down, he examined the shadowy area. It extended farther into the mountainside. A cursory examination found no animal tracks leading to or from the shadowed area, so unlikely an animal's den. This was not the time for exploration; he needed to prepare. He picked his hatchet from his pack and headed for firewood. He ran back to the deadfall he had passed earlier and gathered as much wood as he could safely carry. He made sure he had a few pine branches for torches. He hurried back to the cave, dropped the wood beneath the overhang, and ran back to the deadfall.

He made two more trips for firewood as the rain began. After his third load, it was raining steadily and quite dark. Deciding he had enough and not relishing another round trip in the increasing rain, he started a fire.

He held flint and steel above the kindling without striking them. He felt a slight frisson as mana accumulated and flowed along his arms as he envisioned a spark springing into existence. The spark settled on the kindling, and flames rose as if summoned. It was his only magic. He could also cause fires to burn faster or slower without anyone being able to tell he was the cause.

Once a small fire burned, he fashioned three torches from pine branches, bark, and sap. He lit one by touching it to his small fire and encouraging it to catch. Another slight tingling accompanied his magic use.

He picked up the lit torch and turned his attention to the shadowed area. The cave entrance was lower than the foyer, and he had to crouch to enter. Once past the entrance formed by the overhang, he found himself in a hallway. The ceiling was high enough for Jason to stand and about shoulder-wide. The passage curved about ninety degrees in a few steps and, after a few yards, opened to a squarish room about three paces across, with a ceiling a foot above his head. The dry dust on the floor had no animal tracks, which surprised him.

The torch provided little light. Jason retreated and retrieved a small statue of the Triple Goddess from his pack. His icon always glowed, though the light was barely visible in daylight. Extinguishing the torch, he went back into the cave. The light from his figurine illuminated the entire cave well enough to search it.

As Jason searched the cave, a musty, swampy odor assaulted his nose. Cobwebs brushed his face as he stepped into a sudden cold spot. Spinning around revealed no threat, but shivers ran down his spine as if someone were watching. The uneven floors heightened his sense of vulnerability. He shook the sensations off and secured his small statue in a niche about shoulder high on the far wall. It lit the interior well but not brightly.

He moved about half his gathered wood, pack, and staff inside. Mana flowed from his hands, creating the spark to start a fire within the cave. As the fire came to life, he hummed a song his grandmother had taught him:

A spark of mana, a fiery thought,
a gentle touch, the flame is caught.

It grows and swells, the room alight,
a golden glow, both warm and bright.

It dances, crackles, a living sprite,
a fiery friend, both warm and light.

Warmth to the heart, the chill departs,
a peaceful calm that fills all hearts.

As soon as he looked away from the fire, his anxiety returned.

He stepped out of the cave, and the remnants of the fire he'd started provided enough light for him to collect rainwater in his pan and eating bowl by placing each into the falling rain. He drank two bowls of rainwater, rinsed, and refilled his waterskin for the next leg of his trip.

Straightening, he watched the rain. There would be no progress toward Smoky Springs today. He cleared part of the dry ground of debris and stretched a little, preparing for his evening exercises. He could not stretch fully in all directions without rain falling on his arms.

He considered how to proceed since he would get soaked completing his thasiwoda poses. The water was cold but not uncomfortable, providing an opportunity to bathe before arriving at Smoky Springs.

He retrieved a dry cloth from his pack and undressed. He performed an entire sequence of sixty poses at his slowest speed. The uneven ground made balancing during transitions challenging. His sensei would have approved his daily practice, which usually consisted of a score of poses.

He attributed his survival throughout the Succession War to his training. He rarely lost his balance, and he quickly recovered from falls. He had witnessed men fall and perish when they stumbled or remained on the ground.

As usual, he began with the standing-tree pose, with his bare feet shoulder width apart and his arms at his sides. He waited until he could feel chi tingling in his feet. Sensei called it *chi*. He had also heard it called *life mana*. He knew there were multiple forms of mana, but he knew little beyond that.

"In stillness, be like the stone. In motion, be like the fog," Sensei had said.

He held each pose for a heartbeat and maintained his balance during each movement.

After finishing the sequence, he redid it as fast as he could, ensuring he stopped completely for each pose.

He was breathless, and a few muscles quivered from balancing on the uneven ground. He stepped into the rain and scrubbed the sweat and dirt off quickly. He dried, dressed, and returned to the cave.

Jason settled near the fire, facing the cave's entrance. He carefully measured dried peas, onion, carrot, and herbs into his pan and set it aside to wait for the fire to die down to coals. He was in no rush, so he allowed the fire to burn naturally. He then carved some salted, dried meat into the pan of vegetables and water, adding protein and flavor to his meal.

Despite the fire, the cave still made him feel anxious. *Kieff* would fix that. He had some in his tobacco pouch, wrapped in paper.

As his dinner cooked, he prepared his pipe, putting a small amount of kieff on top of the tobacco. Lighting the pipe, he inhaled the first few draws, which contained mostly kieff smoke, and waited for the herb to relax him.

Kieff was one of the herbs he'd learned about during the Succession War; soldiers had used it following the harrowing battles involving battle mages. He shuddered at the memory of injuries sustained when defensive magic had failed one side or the other. Small doses of kieff reduced anxiety; larger doses brought on sleep. Addiction, while rare, caused a man to seek the drug above food.

The small dose he used reduced his anxiety without impairing him. He relaxed and puffed on his pipe, listening to the storm raging outside.

He reviewed his supplies, estimating how long he could stay there without running out of food before reaching Smoky Springs.

Two days. Longer than that, and he would need to hunt for food, which would delay his arrival even more. He could fast for a day without difficulties if he made good progress tomorrow.

He could do nothing to change his circumstances, so he did not dwell further on his future but leaned against the cave wall and puffed his pipe. Kieff had not completely relieved his anxiety, but it was no worse than the night before a battle, so he was not concerned about sleeping.

He checked his dinner and, finding it done, started to eat.

The storm's sounds ceased abruptly, which was not uncommon for summer storms. Jason looked to the entrance at a small sound and saw the shape of a wolf or large dog's head peering into the cavern.

It came farther into the cave; it was a wolf. The wolf paused at the entrance with its ears perking forward, as if listening intently for any sounds within. Its eyes scanned the interior. It moved with the quiet grace of a shadow; every step was deliberate and purposeful, its body remained low to the ground, and its rear legs were poised to spring.

"Welcome, friend wolf," Jason said in his gentlest voice. "Come in, and share the shelter and warmth of this cave with me." He reached for one of the torches on his left side with one hand and the ten-inch knife strapped to his right calf with the other.

The wolf entered cautiously, and Jason ceased reaching for the torch and studied the wolf from the light provided by his statue of the goddess.

The timber wolf's shoulder was a little lower than waist. Its fur was a mix of orange and brown. It crept in with its tail tucked partway between its hind legs and hugged the far wall of the cavern. Jason placed his half-eaten dinner pan on the ground and slowly and carefully slid it toward the wolf.

"If you are hungry, I will gladly share my meal," he said as he retreated from the pan.

The wolf approached gingerly, keeping its eyes on Jason. It carefully sniffed at the container and cautiously tasted it. After tasting, the wolf ate with abandon and then pushed the empty container across the floor with vigorous licking.

Jason watched without moving. When the wolf stopped pushing the small pan around, Jason cautiously lifted his eating bowl, which was still filled with water, to his lips and drank. Then, as he had done with the food earlier, he moved the water toward the wolf.

The wolf approached the water with less caution and drank noisily.

After finishing with the water, the wolf shifted to a position to watch Jason and the entrance and settled down with a big sigh.

Jason watched the wolf for a while and concluded she posed no danger. He performed his nightly devotions: kneeling before the icon and prostrating himself before doing a breathing exercise, followed by a time of prayer and meditation. He stretched out on his bedding and slept like a soldier—with one eye open.

Sometime later, Jason awakened to the sound of the wolf snarling. His statue was shining, not glowing, and the cave was almost as bright as a summer's day. The light revealed that the entrance to the cave and part of the walls adjacent to and above the opening were covered in a three-inch-thick, glossy black gel sticking to the ceiling and walls as it oozed into the cave.

Jason had no idea what was attacking them in the cave, but his response was to defend. He grasped one of his previously constructed torches, set it on the coals remaining from his fire, and called for it to ignite quickly. The wood and pine sap flared.

The wolf snarled, attacking the gelatinous black thing and jumping back, doing no noticeable harm.

Jason grabbed a second torch and lit it from the first. In the shadow-free light before him, he saw a gaping maw in the black, at about chest height in the doorway leading outside. A pink circle about ten inches in diameter displayed four pairs of long teeth: one up, one down, and one on each side of the orifice. Smaller teeth filled the rest of the mouth opening.

Waving torches at the black thing temporarily paused its incursion along the walls and ceiling. Jason struck the torches against each other and willed the sparks to start fires. Tiny fires flared on the black surface, eating holes in it, and it began to retreat.

Unsure of the creature's nature or its intentions, Jason launched an attack. He thrust one of the burning pine torches into the blackness's mouth, urging the flames to intensify. Fueled by the excitement of battle, he released a surge of mana, causing the branch to flare brightly. The black jelly attempted to retreat, but the burning torch was lodged within its craw. As the creature pulled back, dragging the burning branch with it, sparks flew from the partly closed orifice holding the burning branch.

Jason shoved his remaining torch into the hallway entrance at the floor, where he saw the belly of the beast withdrawing. He cried to the fire, "Burn fast! Burn hot! Burn clean!" and rolled away from the opening. Flames burst into the cave and licked the edges of the entrance, accompanied by foul-smelling smoke. The torch burned itself out in a few minutes. There was no evidence of the first torch.

Exhausted from his battle with the creature, Jason could barely stand. Though the threat seemed to have retreated, he remained wary. Crawling back to his small fire, he reached for his last torch. It took him an agonizing minute to ignite it from the dying embers, as his mana reserves were depleted and unresponsive.

This was a new experience for Jason; he had never before pushed himself to the point that he could not summon fire. He realized he had not held back and had drained his mana; fear for one's life did that to a man.

The wolf continued growling and snarling as it approached the cave entrance and slowly entered it. The black thing did not seem to be in the entrance, and the wolf continued to advance.

Jason followed, partly walking and partly crawling out of the cave. In the torch's light, he saw a patch of black oozing away in the cave's foyer. Using the torch as a prod, Jason herded the remnants of the black jelly into and beneath the pile of firewood he had collected earlier. The wolf assisted by snarling at places where the jelly had evaded his scrutiny, and he used the torch to direct the jelly into the woodpile.

After funneling it into the woodpile, Jason lit the ends and the middle, trapping it in its pyre. He watched, holding the torch, ready to push it back into the flames should it try to escape. The wolf stood at his side with hackles raised, alert.

The fire caught, trapping the remnants of the gelatinous black thing. The warmth of the fire began to replenish his mana, so he called for the fire to burn hot, fast, and clean.

The fire blazed, licking the rock that formed the overhang. It was so hot that Jason had to step back. Foul-smelling smoke roiled, along with the sound of meat sizzling. The wolf retreated from the cave foyer into the night to avoid the sudden increase in temperature.

Jason stretched before the fire, basking as the heat and light restored his mana.

After a few minutes passed, Jason turned and saw the wolf sitting not far from his side, in the spot farthest away from the cave entrance but still within its foyer.

"Well, lady wolf, you came to me a daughter of the storm. We shared food and shelter and now battle. I name you Shadow's Bane, and I will call you Akela," Jason said.

He felt a surge of mana crawl along his arms. The forest seemed to pause as though listening for a moment before relaxing. He felt light-headed and dropped to the crouching-frog pose to recover.

The wolf cried as though injured, jumped into the air, and spun around several times, dancing on her hind legs.

Jason watched, mystified. Suddenly, it occurred to him that he may have True Named the wolf and could control her.

"I didn't mean to True Name you," Jason said. "I won't use your True Name against you. I swear by my True Name, Jojotessantana, that I will never use your True Name to control, coerce, or influence you."

Again, the forest seemed to pause and listen longer before relaxing into the night, but Jason detected no additional mana flow.

The wolf calmed down and sat by Jason; they watched the fire burn down to coals.

"Well," Jason said, "the night's not over. There is still some firewood inside the cave. If the stench is gone, we will be more comfortable there than here without a fire to hold the cold at bay."

The wolf turned and walked into the cave. Jason, surprised at her understanding, followed her. During their time outside, the smell had mostly dissipated.

The coals of the inside fire were still glowing, and Jason used them to start another small fire inside the cave. The postbattle jitters remained, as after each encounter during the war when the balance had been uncertain. He took several deep breaths, but the butterflies remained. He lit another pipe with twice the kieff in it. His adrenaline from the attack by the black jelly hadn't completely metabolized; he would not be able to sleep for a few hours without the kieff.

Jason stretched out on his ground cover and pulled his blanket around him. "Akela, if you want to share warmth, feel free to lie beside me," he said as he raised one side of the blanket.

She did so after turning three circles, as other canids do, and Jason slowly drifted back to sleep.

CHAPTER 2

Two Are Better Than One

Glowstones and the Use of Minerals to Store Mana
Sister Ismat of the Temple of the Moon
Damocles Academy of Magic

Glowstones, which you have used all your life for light, are charged with light mana and emit it. Some glow continuously, while others can be turned on and off. When the charge is gone, the stones remain dark until refilled.

The simplest glowstones are plain river quartz. Common quartz readily absorbs light and easily releases it. These glowstones usually glow steadily and need regular recharging; the structure of the stone makes control challenging. A person with minimal talent can recharge these, so they are inexpensive and available to all.

Clear quartz and amethyst crystals, on the other hand, absorb more, and the release can be started and stopped. Further, they can release their mana more rapidly than they were charged, providing brighter light over larger areas than river stones can.

Other stones and crystals absorb and release other forms of mana. You've likely noticed that all your professors wear jewelry, most of which consists of stones mounted in gold or silver. I wear a necklace of a dozen stones on a simple gold and silver chain. We do this so we have a ready supply of mana to use beyond what our personal stores provide.

Mine are amethyst for light, citrine and carnelian for heat, onyx and obsidian for lodestone, blue sapphire and white agate for lightning, aquamarine for life, and white topaz for spirit. I use life and spirit often, so I have more than one of these stones. This isn't fashionable jewelry; the stones are rough, and the setting is basic.

I'll teach you which stones to find and acquire, how to fill them with mana, and how to draw it out when needed. Some materials are more efficient than others, and certain stones are very rare.

For instance, flawless diamonds are known for storing the most spirit, while emeralds excel at holding life, and dragonstone is the prime choice for heat.

When Jason woke the next day, the wolf was gone. He was a little relieved and a little sad at the loss of his companion. A wolf as a pet might've been difficult in towns, but no partner while traveling was lonely. He completed his morning devotions—genuflecting before his icon, a breathing exercise, and a period of prayer and meditation—and stepped into the foyer.

A hand's breadth of snow had accumulated overnight. That was too much for traveling any distance with his equipment, so Jason prepared to spend more time in the cave.

With any luck, the sun would burn through the clouds and melt enough for him to travel later in the day. Bright sunlight shone on the snow, and tiny tendrils of vapor rose as the snow sublimed.

He performed the basic defensive thasiwoda poses twice: once at the pace "Hold each pose for three heartbeats, and take four beats to move to the next" and once at "Move quickly to next once balanced in a pose." Done quickly, these prepared him to defend against almost any hand-to-hand situation.

His habit of daily devotion had begun soon after he, his mother, and his grandmother moved to South Haven. He'd added the physical exercises when Sensei arrived at that farm a few years later.

Gazing at the remnants from the gelatinous black thing he'd burned the previous night, he realized he would require additional firewood if he was unable to travel by midday. The way was clear: a warrior prepared for each day and planned for contingencies.

The snow wasn't too deep for a short trek, and there didn't seem to be ice beneath, so he returned to the fallen trees to collect more firewood.

On his return, he was surprised to find Akela sitting in the foyer with three rabbits stretched out in the snow before her.

"Well," he said, "it seems I am repaid for dinner last night. I take it you wish me to prepare them for eating?"

Akela looked at him and cocked her head like a dog listening to her handler.

Jason paused, surprised that the wolf seemed to understand him. *What an intelligent animal*, he thought.

He took the three rabbits, removed their heads, and skinned them. After removing the feet, he had headless, footless, furless rabbit carcasses.

He selected one skin and spread it fur side down on the snow to contain the viscera for disposal. He gutted one rabbit, saving the heart and liver, and piled the remaining offal on that skin.

The liver had neither lumps nor lesions, so the rabbit was healthy and could be eaten.

He offered the heart and liver to Akela by placing them about an arm's length away. She approached and wolfed them down.

He stood and, pointing to the three rabbits, asked, "Do you want one still raw, or do you want me to cook them? If you want one raw, choose it, and I will cook the others."

As though she understood him, Akela walked boldly over, sniffed at the three rabbits, selected one of the two complete carcasses, returned to her sitting place, and began eating it.

She's an extraordinary animal, he thought. *Someone spent a lot of time training her, and I found her out in the wild. Curious.*

Jason started a fire outside the cave; cleaned the remaining rabbit, reserving the heart and liver for himself; and added the offal to his disposal skin. He sharpened enough small branches to skewer the carcasses for cooking and leaned against the rock forming the back wall of the foyer, waiting for the fire to reduce to coals.

Akela retreated into the depths of the cave.

Jason thought, *She seems to have found a home for herself*, before turning his attention to the forest and fire a few feet away.

Jason arranged the splayed rabbits above the coals a short time later, resting the skewers on a few larger branches.

When the rabbits were done, he removed them from the fire and sat down as they cooled. He regretted not carrying salt, but a hearty appetite overcame the lack of flavor. He contemplated getting his pipe to enjoy the morning view, but the aroma of the cooling rabbit kept him there.

After the rabbits cooled, he ate one, saving the bones on the skin with the innards.

Akela may want them, he thought.

He scraped the remaining skin free of fat and connective tissue and wrapped the remaining cooked rabbit.

"It's cool enough to last for some time if I pack snow around this," he said.

He rose and walked some distance from the cave. He relieved himself, gathered a yepsen of snow, and then returned to the shelter and entered it, planning on packing the remaining rabbit in snow inside the cave.

When Jason entered the cave, he saw a naked woman sitting on his blanket.

He jumped up and back and cried out in surprise, pain, and embarrassment as he struck his head on the cavern wall and ceiling. The blow brought tears to his eyes and a string of curses to his lips. The snow he carried fell to the ground as he raised his hands to inspect his scalp.

When his vision cleared, he cried, "Who are you? How did you get here? Where is the wolf? What is going on?"

"I am Akela. We have two skins," the woman said, seeming unconcerned about her nakedness. "We are human and wolf and change from one to the other when we wish to.

"We think you are also two-skinned; you smell like a two-skin, but we don't recognize your other one. You are not a wolf, bear, eagle, or any other we have met. If you are two-skinned, we do not know what kind."

Jason slid down the cave wall, too stunned by that revelation to speak.

Jason guessed the woman's age at close to his eight and twenty. She had smooth brown skin and long brown hair with a reddish tinge under the light from his icon. He could only see that her eyes were dark. He struggled to look away from her nakedness and could not estimate her height.

"I expect you will have questions," she said. "After last night, my wolf and I hear you say *Akela* and recognize it as your name for either of us. However, calling my wolf skin Yiska, our former usename, will be easier for you as we talk."

He looked toward her and then turned away. "You ch-ch-change from a wolf into a human?" he stammered. "Are you a werewolf?"

A derisive snort was his answer. "I think all the *were* are mythical.

Anyone who can't control their actions one day a month cannot survive for long. The two-skinned have one animal form and one human; we change when we want to or need to. Our animals are *not* ravening, bloodthirsty beasts." She paused. "Well, no more than our humans anyway."

The desire to look at his conversation partner overcame his embarrassment. He turned toward her. "How are you made?" He averted his gaze again and blushed.

She laughed this time. "A male and a female get together and sometime later have young. How do you think?"

Jason turned even brighter red. "I have never heard of two-skinned before. How many of you are there?" His head swiveled toward her and away.

"Why won't you look at me as we talk?" she asked. "Am I ugly or deformed in some way?"

"You are naked, and that embarrasses me."

She laughed louder. "I was naked last night, and your viewing me did not seem a problem."

"B-b-but," he stammered, "animals don't need clothing."

She laughed again. "I can cover myself with your blanket; will that ease your concern so we can talk more easily?"

Jason nodded, and she stood, wrapped herself in his blanket, and sat back down.

"What brought you to this unpleasant cave?" asked Akela. "Yiska did not want to enter the cave and would do so only after we identified your glowing statue of the Mother."

"I felt the wrongness of the cave, but it was the only good shelter from the storm. Storms controlled by magic are more severe than natural storms," he replied. "I am on my way to visit a healer named Heather Moonstar, who lives in Smoky Springs. A mage I know only as Grandmother suggested her."

He took a deep breath. "I can start fires without flint and steel; I don't need tinder, just kindling. Grandmother said I was not accessing my inner fire and that she could help me with that.

"How did you and Yiska—I'm sorry, but I think of you as two beings— find your way to the cave?" Jason asked.

Akela explained that she and her wolf skin were fleeing their pack leader, Yeruslan, who had learned their True Name. He used this power and high rank to force the pack to do terrible things. Yiska had crossed Jason's trail and caught the scent of an unknown two-skinned the day before. The storm had caught them near where Jason had left the road, washing away his scent. They'd guessed their way to the cave.

"And here we are, strangers in the night becoming friends," Akela said.

They sat silently for a few minutes before Jason asked, "How many two-skinned are there?"

"I don't know for sure. There are about thirty with wolf skins in my village. I know of another hundred or so living in Smoky Springs and villages nearby," she replied. "The others are mostly bears and eagles, with badgers, wolverines, and a few lions. I do not know if there are two-skinned outside of the mountains around us. Each group of us keeps pretty much to ourselves."

"Are two-skinned accepted by your village?"

Akela's eyebrows gathered, and her lips formed a tight line for a few minutes before she answered. "By that, you mean the normals in our village. We are mostly accepted and treated equally there. We trade with singles and other two-skinned. We are a minority in the villages, and our views are sometimes at odds with the majority. We manage to work with them anyway. Our children play, work, and go to school with human children. And other types of folk. Episodes of getting excluded from activities because of our differences are rare."

"Do any hide their second skin?"

"Some do, especially if their second skin is rare, like the big cats. Cats are not social, and their human skin may hide their animal because cats are uncomfortable being close to others.

"Two-skinned can sometimes tell when we meet another, regardless of the skin they wear. It is more of a smell for wolves. A two-skinned human's shadow sometimes shows a feature of their animal: ears, snout, beak, or tail." She paused. "You are an exception."

"Neither of my parents had two skins," Jason said. "How could I have two?"

"What of your grandparents?"

Jason hesitated and then admitted his maternal grandmother could start fires easily. He explained that she wouldn't talk about his mother's father, and he knew little about their relationship. He is sure she is not two skinned, though.

He confessed to lacking knowledge about his father's side, and revealed that he, his mother, and his grandmother had left his father's home on his naming day. They'd arrived at a farmstead run by a priestess of the Lady, where he had grown up.

"What about magic?" Akela asked. "Does your family have a history of mages?"

Jason chuckled, repeating that while his grandmother could start fires from a distance, he could usually manage a spark for kindling; the inferno he'd unleashed against the black jelly the night before had been an extreme example of his ability to accelerate fires. His mother could control the wind, offering relief during hot summers, but he was unsure about any other magical abilities in his family.

She paused, with her eyebrows knitting for a moment. Glancing at the side and back, she continued. "Magic use among two-skinned people is rare. If you have two skins, you will be the first one I have met who can do other magic."

They sat silently for a few minutes before Jason asked, "Can you confirm I have another skin?"

"The only sure way is for us to guide you into a shift; however, Yiska might be able to tell from a closer examination if you are willing."

"What would that entail?" Jason asked.

"Your clothing is deerskin," Akela replied. "It smells of smoke, forest, and various things from your travels."

She said Yiska knew he had bathed the night before. If he undressed away from strong smells and allowed Yiska to smell him, she might be able to confirm the presence of a second skin.

"A wolf's first shift usually happens when we are about two summers old; Yiska and I know of no one whose first shift happened past five summers. You are close to thirty, I think? Our children almost always shift during their second or third year. We are not certain you will be able to shift, but we will try to guide you into your second skin if you smell right and agree."

"I am eight and twenty years old," Jason said. "Let me finish storing the rabbit first," he added uncertainly. "And let me get you my overtunic to wear."

Akela stood, dropped the blanket, changed her posture to an all-fours position, looked up, and said, "Before I forget, thank you. When you changed our True Name last night, you freed us from a Name binding to Yeruslan. I cannot thank you enough."

Jason straightened his back, and his eyes widened. He took a few slow, deep breaths. He had succeeded at name magic! All knew the power of using True Names, but all those he knew of who used name magic were villains, finding and using True Names to control a prominent figure and then working up until vying with a king for a crown. Ruling did not appeal to him, but the realization of his ability sent a shiver down his spine. Suspicion and persecution were the likely rewards if his ability to wield such magic were known to others.

Akela leaned forward, extended her arms in front of her with palms on the cave floor, and stretched, much as a dog did when rising from a sleeping position. As she moved, a fog enveloped her, and the wolf formed out of the mist and then trotted outside.

Jason shivered as he watched the woman dissolve. *What am I getting in for? That doesn't look as simple as just changing clothes, but she talks about it like it is!*

Jason made two trips to collect snow to store the rabbit carcass. He went outside for the examination, carrying his overtunic for Akela to use afterward.

Jason stepped out from the overhang. He glanced at the wolf and thought, *Where do I change?* He felt himself blush at the thought of the wolf being the woman in her other skin. He turned his back, removed his clothes, and folded them.

Yiska walked boldly over and began to sniff him thoroughly. The wolf smelled his feet, legs, back, torso, head, and arms, sticking her nose into his armpits and groin, pushing him with her nose to gain access to his skin. She huffed a few times as she smelled his crotch. Jason jumped each time the wolf licked him during the examination.

She walked a short distance away and stretched as the woman had, starting with the animal-shaped cloud. Jason turned his back and dressed as quickly as he could. When he turned back, he saw the woman wearing his overtunic.

"You are two-skinned, but I, uh—she doesn't know what it is," she said. She grimaced and continued. "Yiska insists I tell you that you smell good." She paused again, her face turned crimson, and she said in almost a whisper, "And taste good. I think she likes embarrassing me sometimes." She smiled.

"How do you and Yiska talk?" Jason followed her lead in referring to her wolf skin as Yiska.

"I hear her words—that term is not quite right, but it will do—in my mind, and she hears me in hers. She understands my words, and I understand

29

her speech—most of the time. Wolf language is specific to smells, locations, and relationships. Human speech is more abstract and nuanced. Some things don't translate well between wolf and human languages. We each understand the other's intentions, though."

Jason nodded slowly as he tried to understand. "How would I change back to my—this skin? How does Yiska change back to you?"

"We mutually agree to shift," she replied. "Yiska sometimes sleeps when I am out, and I need to wake her if I believe she is best suited to handle a situation. The same goes for me when she is out."

"Do you always agree?"

She laughed again. "No, but that is usually when the one within believes she can, or should, be without. If it is a crisis, we choose the one most calm. Yiska often feels she has spent too much time within and lets me know. I then look for a place to switch and release her to run, dance, and be the wolf she is."

Akela paused. "I am usually out most of the day and she most of the night. We each spend part of our inside time sleeping, but we each need some sleep time in our own skin. We sleep less than one-skinned."

"What are my possible skins?" Jason asked. "Could I change into a rabbit, squirrel, or spider?"

Akela's eyebrows puckered, and she frowned. "I admit I never considered it. All I know of are predators—bears, wolves, hawks, foxes, and big cats."

Several minutes passed before she added, "Do you have more questions?"

Jason did not respond for a few minutes. "What, if any, skills do two-skinned have that humans do not?"

She nodded. "We each have some abilities of the other. For example, I can smell better than almost all humans, and Yiska can see colors better than any wolf. We have had these skills for as long as I can remember; I do not know if they will occur immediately for you."

She rubbed her chin. "We live as long as people, which means Yiska didn't die after ten years. If we can change skins, we heal faster than people from nonfatal injuries. The inability to shift is the surest sign of a fatal disease or wound."

"Are there disadvantages to being two-skinned?" Jason asked.

She replied, "The biggest one, and the only one I can think of right now, is that Yiska will force herself to the surface if I haven't let her out in a while. That happens rarely since we switch almost daily."

"Will my other skin be the same sex as me?"

She slapped her thighs as she laughed. "I have never heard of any different sexes for the two skins."

After a moment of silence, she asked, "Do you have any other questions for me?"

"No," Jason said. "I need to think about this for a while."

Akela nodded and went into the cave.

Jason also entered the cave and picked up his pipe and tobacco. He sat in the foyer and lit his pipe, puffing smoke gently into the morning air.

When his pipe was finished, he tipped the ash and dottle out, smearing them with his toe, as was his custom; entered the cave; and stored the pipe and tobacco in his pack. Akela was sitting before his glowing statue with eyes closed. She opened them and turned to him as he stowed his smoking equipment.

Jason took a deep breath. "If I don't try this, I will always regret it. How do we proceed?"

Akela nodded. "Before you change, I need to teach you to enter the *nothing*—a term we use to describe being utterly focused on the present. You reach the nothing by focusing entirely on now, leaving all thoughts behind."

She led him to the cave entrance. "First, sit or crouch; you need to be comfortable for several minutes. Second, take three deep, slow breaths, and exhale each fully and slowly.

"Finally, close your eyes, and pay attention to your breath. Do not control it, but watch it come in and out of your nostrils. Concentrate on your breath, and wait for all else to fade."

Jason said, "Archers call this the *void*. You are aware of yourself and your surroundings, but they seem dreamlike; the target and the release are all you think of."

Akela smiled at him. "Ah, you understand! Entering the nothing—the void—prepares you to shift to your animal skin.

"People's thoughts are scattered among the past, the present, and the future. Focusing on your breath brings your attention to the present without distractions from what was or will be. Wolves live mainly in the present, which puts them at the edge of nothing, a single breath away from being ready. I imagine it is the same for other animal skins.

"We should move outside since we don't know what you will shift into.

The cave entrance is too narrow and twisted for anything as large as a bear to exit easily."

The two exited the cave, and Akela sat cross-legged in the foyer.

"I suggest you remove your clothes. You don't want your other self trapped in clothing that is too large or want your clothes to split if they are too small," she said.

Jason blushed. He took a few steps away and turned his back to Akela before removing his clothing. He turned to face downslope, with the cave and Akela behind him.

"After entering the nothing, continue paying attention to your breathing. Continue until you lose awareness of your body," Akela said. "Seek your center. Some find it near their heart; others find it lower. Once you find your center, you will sense being in a room with an opening or doorway. You must move through it—move is the best word for it. It is a mental action, though."

"Can I get stuck partway changed?" Jason interrupted.

"I have never heard of such a thing. Perhaps if you had exhausted your mana, but then, I think, you would be unable to change instead of getting stuck."

Jason followed her instructions. Perhaps because he often went beyond the void and stayed there during deep devotion to the Goddess, he reached the nothing quickly. Behind his closed eyes, he saw amorphous lights, like the beginning of a meditative trance.

As she had described, he felt as if he were in a large room or outside, even though he could not see anything. The opening felt uphill, while staying for a devotional meditation seemed downhill.

He moved uphill and through what seemed like a hallway. He passed through what seemed like an intersection and felt a hot, dry wind. He passed another doorway and felt a breeze that smelled like the air just before a rainfall.

He reached the end and saw a body shape. As he stepped into that shape, his neck and lower back began to stretch in length as the rest of him expanded. As it was about to become painful, Jason felt himself breaking apart, and fear gripped him as he dissolved. Then blackness.

⁓⁓⁓

Akela watched Jason expand into a fog that grew to a column twice a man's height with a six-foot, serpentlike shape lying on the ground. The cloud spread sideways, forming a kite shape, before it began to condense.

She saw wings forming from the lobes on each side of the cylinder, each extending almost as far from the center as the top was from the ground. They looked like giant bat wings.

Then legs formed on the ground, followed by smaller arms near the top of where the triangles met. The tail and neck solidified next, showing scales the size of her hand.

The head formed last, resembling a snake's but with a longer nose. Four finger-long fangs were visible from that side: two on the top and on the bottom of the jaw. Blue faded from midnight at the top of its head to sky blue on the bottom of its jaw.

A forked tongue extended and withdrew as she watched and recognized the creature: a winged dragon.

The dragon pointed its nose to the sky and made a musical sound similar to that of an organ.

The undersides of its wings and belly were sky blue, with spots and streaks of gray or white. Its back glistened a darker hue. Those were the only details she observed before it turned its head toward her.

Xavier felt himself condense out of the fog. He stretched his neck up, stood tall on his back feet, stretched his forelegs out, and spread his wings. He trumpeted a joyful chorus, luxuriating in his newfound voice.

He looked out over the mountainous terrain spreading beneath the cave and overhang. For a moment, it looked unfamiliar, with the blues subdued and the browns warmer than he saw through Jason's eyes. The bottoms of the clouds were darker, and the tops were brighter. Glancing around, he saw the greens of the forest were also brighter, while the spots of snowmelt were almost black.

A flash of white caught his attention, and he felt his eyes change focus. The slightly blurred image of a squirrel formed where it had paused in its traipsing across boughs. The edges of the branch on which the rodent sat were in sharp focus.

Too small for prey, he thought.

Fanning his wings slowly, he felt muscles Jason lacked flexing and relaxing. The air along the surface of the wings registered variations in temperature, which would help him as he maneuvered in the air.

He bent his legs, coming to a seated position, resting on his tail and back feet.

He followed another flash, this time feeling his ears flex as small frills extended, amplifying the sounds the bird made as it landed on a distant rock.

Turning his head, he looked at the woman standing nearby. He could see the tips of his tongue as it extended and withdrew without effort. He knew it was Akela from memories shared with Jason, even though her coloring was different through dragon eyes.

The woman took a step back and raised one hand to her open mouth. Her cheeks brightened as he watched.

Akela stepped back quickly as the dragon turned toward her with the frills at its jaw extended and, with a slight quaver in her voice, asked, "Ja-Ja-Jason?"

Jason is not here right now. The change has disoriented him.

She heard the voice in her mind; it was as if she were talking to herself, except the voice reverberated slightly.

"You can speak to me!" she exclaimed.

Yes, I can. The internal voice sounded amused. *I am Xavier, at your service, Lady Akela.* The dragon lowered his head in a semblance of a bow.

Akela relaxed upon hearing this. "You don't have the same name as Jason?"

No. Jason and I are perhaps more separated. I believe it is because I can speak as a human, but a wolf cannot.

"My wolf and I are always aware after a shift; is something wrong?"

Was that always true? Even during your introduction to your wolf? I have been a passenger up to now, not even able to speak with Jason mind to mind. He is, I think, bewildered at being the passenger and frightened after dissolving the first time. He will adapt after a few shifts.

"I am not sure," she said slowly, with uncertainty clear in her tone.

Xavier raised his head, looked around, and said, *I hunger.*

He turned, bounded down the trail toward the scree, spread his wings, and leaped off the ledge. In two wingbeats, he gained altitude. He circled overhead a few times, continuing to rise, and then headed northwest as Akela watched in awe.

His underside coloring made the dragon almost invisible against the daytime sky.

∞

Jason regained his composure slowly. He felt a little nauseous. He also felt air blowing over his face, chest, and—wings? Opening his eyes, he could see the sky as though looking through a lightly tinted window. He could hear the wind, but his ears seemed filled with water; all sounds were muted.

Jason began to panic. He was in the air and unable to turn his head or move his arms.

Good. You are awake. I wasn't sure how long you would be disoriented after the change. I sensed your fear as we changed. Fear not.

Jason heard a voice in his mind, like an internal dialogue, but he had not started one.

Who are you? What are you? Where am I? Jason tried to speak, but it felt like the flailing of a nightmare.

Expecting no response, he was surprised when he heard, *You and I are one being, but you are the passenger right now and not on the surface.* The unfamiliar voice echoed slightly, which distinguished it from his personal mental dialogue.

I am Xavier, your second skin. I have been a passenger for a long time. I saw through your eyes and heard through your ears. I was unable to communicate with you until today. We are flying, hunting. We won't fly much longer. There are deer ahead, and I am hungry.

Flying? What are you? Jason asked.

I am a dragon—a winged fire dragon—and I can fly, Xavier replied joyfully.

I have a dragon as my second skin, thought Jason. *Wow. I have a creature from myth inside. What else can he do? Can we do? He, we, I—this will take some getting used to. Can he do any magic? Are there more of us? How will we find them?*

As the truth dawned on Jason—his other skin wasn't just powerful; it was a dragon—Jason's mind reeled. Excitement warred with a tremor of anxiety. He wasn't the one in control; he was the passenger on a flight to the unknown. Jason's anxiety lessened but did not dissolve as they flew farther. He watched, realizing he was seeing through Xavier's eyes. Dragons saw colors that men could not; the sky wasn't the same shade of blue, there were more shades of red, and the clouds had bright spots not visible to men. Jason pondered the differences without coming to any explanation.

Xavier looked down, and Jason saw the clearing seem to come closer without the feeling of falling or lowering. The dragon focused on one deer near the center of a clearing and some distance from the others in the herd.

Jason felt a surge of adrenaline and the surety that the deer was prey.

Xavier circled lower before diving toward the deer. Jason felt as if his stomach were still above him, and he was falling, feeling no control and not liking it. Fear and curiosity raged within him as he saw the dragon's rear claws come into view between him and the deer. The taloned feet struck the deer's neck halfway between its shoulders and head. Jason heard the muffled crack of bones breaking and watched the deer collapse.

The rest of the herd scattered into the forest. Xavier raised his head and looked around for some time, ensuring that nothing moved in the clearing and that neither prey nor other predators were near. Nothing moved in the clearing. Nor did anything closer than five feet beyond the tree clearing's edge.

Jason realized he—they—could see animals in the darkness beneath the trees when in dragon form.

Lifting the deer's head, Xavier cleanly sliced through the neck and inside the jawbone. He pulled the tongue out and sprayed something from his mouth onto the flesh, which burst into flame.

You don't breathe fire? Jason formed the words as though he were speaking.

How would that work? Xavier replied. *I need air just like any other living being. If my breath were fire, how would I breathe? I can spit venom that ignites when exposed to air.*

The dragon gulped down the cooked tongue without chewing, like a lizard working food into its gullet.

Xavier stretched his wings and turned in a circle, watching the forest for any possible threat. Satisfied, he returned to butchering the deer.

He sliced the deer from gullet to pelvic bone in one stroke; Jason marveled at how sharp the dragon's claws were.

In just a few minutes, the dragon consumed the tongue, heart, liver, and one entire leg.

My goodness! Jason said. *You just polished off an entire adult deer hindquarter in minutes.*

We just polished it off, Xavier said.

The dragon flapped his wings a few times and sat on his haunches, resting and maintaining a watchful eye on the forest.

After about fifteen minutes, Xavier picked up the carcass and carried it to a higher point in the meadow. Grasping it in his rear claws, he leaped into the air, headed downslope, and began flapping hard. It took him most of the distance to the forest before he gained altitude.

How will we find the cave? Jason asked.

What a dragon seeks a dragon finds, the dragon answered.

What a useful ability, Jason thought. *I wonder how it works.*

When I think about what I want, I feel a light tug in that direction. When I was hungry, I thought of deer and knew where to fly. The more I know about something, the more precise that tug feels.

You can read my thoughts? Jason asked. *Can you do magic?*

The dragon sounded amused, or Jason felt the amusement directly. *You are not used to the difference between thinking of what you want to say next, which I can hear, and just thinking. And you can do more magic than I.*

Do we have any privacy? Jason asked. *You didn't hear my thoughts earlier. Or you didn't reply anyway.*

Several minutes passed.

I was concentrating on finding food earlier, so your thoughts did not attract my attention. Just now, I was listening to you, so it seemed that I read your mind. I do not know how our memories interact, but we will learn. We share emotions, but I do not feel yours as strongly as you do, the dragon said.

How will we learn to live while so connected without one or both of us going insane? Jason asked.

That is an interesting question. We will learn to. The risk of not succeeding is too great. You—we are a warrior, and we face the conditions we find.

Jason was taken aback at the direct reference to the way of the warrior but did not respond.

Xavier flew back to the cave and oriented himself to approach above the scree to the cave. He dropped below the level of the trail and rose, almost pausing in flight, before dropping the carcass onto the path and veering off for another circuit.

To land, the dragon flew almost parallel to the trail, slowed, and settled down gently on the ground with a few rapid wingbeats.

Xavier spoke. *I am more tired than I expected. We should change. You will hear me now if I am awake while you lead.*

So you can talk with me while my skin is out? And no one else can overhear?

Yes. That is how I communicate with you, and you with me, when the passenger.
Can we sleep while inside? Jason asked. *Ah yes, Akela mentioned it.*

Akela sat in the foyer. She looked up at the sound of the deer carcass falling, and her eyes followed the dragon circling, watching him land.

Xavier took a deep breath and focused his attention internally. Unlike Jason, he saw no lights, just a cave with a single exit. He used it.

Time seemed to slow for the two—another new sensation for shifting skins.

Jason solidified out of the fog, staggered, and ended up on his hands and knees. Akela rushed over and helped him stand and walk to the cave entrance.

"Hi, Akela. Will you please hand me my clothes? Being naked before you embarrasses me."

Akela complied and turned her back to him as he dressed. She said, "Just like after the fight with the black jelly, you've exhausted your mana. Food and rest usually recharge them quickly."

"Well, Xavier ate an entire hindquarter. Does that count?"

"I do not know. I do know that sleep will," she replied.

The cave hallway was too narrow for them to walk side by side, so Akela could not assist Jason into the cave. Jason half walked and half crawled in, as he had left the cave after burning the black jelly. On his way through the cave entrance, he saw something glinting on the ground, reflecting the bright morning light.

He found two pairs of long teeth and a half dozen or so smaller teeth that had not been consumed by the fire. He carefully collected them, carried them inside, and stored them in his pack.

Jason slept. He awakened to the sun shining. Walking outside, he found Akela with several kebabs of deer near a fire; three were over it, cooking, and about a half dozen were finished and cooling.

"That smells amazing. May I have some?"

"Yes. You slept most of the day. The sun will set in two hours or so."

Jason ate the cooked meat she had given him. After consuming each skewer's kebabs, he reached for another.

After eating his fill, he noticed the remaining rear haunch was gone from the carcass. "Did I just eat an entire haunch?" Disbelief colored his words.

"No, my wolf and I ate our fills, but you ate about half of the thigh."

"Eating that much meat should cause a bellyache, but I feel fine."

"My mother told me that we eat somewhat more like wolves than other people," she said. "I suspect you are eating more like a dragon."

Jason's eyes widened with realization. "Oh my! Does this mean I'll have the appetite of two or three people every time I eat?"

Akela laughed at his remark. "Only in certain situations, such as replenishing mana or the initial skin change. You each expended a lot of energy during your first transformation."

Akela paused for a moment. "By the way, your dragon skin can talk with me. Yiska can only speak with me or other wolves, though I can translate when a person talks to her. I think Xavier's ability may be unique among two-skinned.

"You will discover that your senses expand a bit; for example, you may see things people can't, and Xavier may see things not visible to dragons. Just as Yiska and I have better sight and smell than single-skinned."

My, Jason thought, *I know the dragon sees things that I do not see. And I see colors the dragon does not. Will Xavier be able to start fires without his venom? I wonder what other talents we will share.*

They sat in silence for several minutes.

"I need to leave soon. I doubt I can make up time lost due to weather," Jason said. "I contracted to deliver the artifact to Clowers by the day after tomorrow."

He looked down the scree to the roadway below, considering the paths he might walk.

"You can fly there now," Akela said.

Jason's head jerked up. "Yes! I can. Thank you for reminding me of Xavier. I need a way for a dragon to carry my pack and staff."

"And the clothes you usually wear," Akela added. "If you want to keep your second skin secret, you should fly at night and near treetops so you can't be seen."

"Should I keep Xavier secret?"

Akela looked him in the eye. "A dragon. A creature of myth and legend. A creature legend says has a hoard of gold and gems. A ravening beast who eats cattle. A being whose body parts are rumored magical. Every treasure hunter and hero wannabe will flock here. Are you and Xavier ready for that?"

"I didn't think of that. Thanks. I'll double-check with Xavier that we keep this under wraps for as long as possible," Jason said.

Akela nodded. "There is a field about two miles this side of Smoky Springs where wagons gather to load or unload goods. It should be empty this time of year and will provide you with a place to land, change, and walk into town in about an hour."

"That sounds like a plan. May I leave my overtunic for you to wear?"

"No need. I have a cache of clothes about a day away, traveling on four legs. However, I think I will relocate to this cave. It is larger."

She looked at Jason. "The unease I felt on first entering the cave is gone. I think it was the lair of the gelatinous black blob we slew last night, and the fire cleansed it."

Near sunset, Jason repacked his belongings, including what he wore, leaving his rope out to tie the pack to Xavier's front leg.

"Akela, I can't thank you enough for everything. You've taught me so much, even if it was all a bit unexpected. Thanks for introducing me to Xavier. I still feel a bit lost, but he is interesting."

"The world is a dangerous place, Jason. Be careful," she said.

"I'll be fine, I am sure. What will you do now that you are free of Yeruslan?"

Akela paused. "I feel better already. The only challenge now is that I need to find another pack. Wolves need regular contact with other wolves to remain sane."

"I wish you well in finding a new pack. I am happy about this chance meeting. I hope we can meet again sometime. I have a feeling things are about to get interesting."

"Are you sure it was chance?" she asked.

Jason paused. "I hope it was, because if it wasn't, we are pawns in some game played by the gods, and we do not know the rules."

Akela nodded. "There is much we don't know, Jason. But the answers will come in time. Regarding the dragon, trust your instincts. You are more than you seem.

"Stay safe, Jason. You're not alone."

The skin change went faster this time. Jason was disoriented again but for less time.

Akela helped secure the pack and staff to one of Xavier's front legs. Xavier then took a dry run, flying and landing with the load on one leg.

After that trial, Xavier ate more of the deer and bid farewell to Akela. He launched into the air and began climbing.

Fly lower, Jason said. *We do not want to be seen.*

Xavier responded quickly and emphatically. *We are not prey! We are a prince of the sky and do not permit others to fly above us.*

He continued to climb before turning toward Smoky Springs.

CHAPTER 3

Flying

Gravity: A Force That Isn't Magic
Professor Isocrates
Damocles Academy of Magic

Gravity, like time, is an aspect of existence we do not understand. We experience it and can measure it, but no one has successfully argued it is mana. For it to be an energy of magic, it needs a dual that counters it, and it must combine with other forms following the rules of symmetry; neither of these has been demonstrated.

Natural philosophers know that gravity depends on the quantity of mundane matter in two objects and their separation. Knowing just these, they can calculate the movements of the moon and the planets.

"Gravity," the professor said with a slow, beautiful smile curving her mouth. "The one force we can never escape is not magic."

Xavier continued circling, gaining altitude. As Jason watched through the dragon's eyes, his anxiety increased.

When they flew into a cool air pocket and dropped a few feet, Jason screamed without sound.

What is the danger? Xavier asked as he leveled their flight.

We were falling! Jason screamed in panic.

No, we are flying. The air has bumps in it, just like roadways. The differences are that we can't see them well and do not know how deep they might be, Xavier said.

Xavier circled for a few minutes, thinking about how he had learned to fly and how he had increased in skill, even though in vivid dreams.

We fly together now. We need to learn to fly without fear. You can't distract us during moves in the air. It may take more than one lesson, Xavier told Jason.

He dropped one wing and raised the other. The world tilted in Jason's eyes, and they entered a wide turn. When Jason did not react, Xavier turned in the other direction. Still no reaction.

He made a tighter turn in each direction and continued shrinking the radius of his turns. When Jason reacted, Xavier opened the turns up and spent more time shrinking until he reached the same tight turn that had caused the reaction. He held that turn for several moments, confirming Jason endured it before straightening out. Tighter turns would wait for another day.

Xavier flew toward a brighter area of the sky. Upon entering that area, they ascended suddenly in the warmer air. Jason cried out but not as violently as to the earlier plummet.

Xavier looked for a patch of air without bright or dark spots large enough for some extended flying without sudden rises and drops. Finding one, he started flying them up and dropping them through the air, starting with gentle slopes and gradually making the altitude reversals steeper, deeper, and more sudden.

Again, he found Jason's limit and repeated the back-off-and-approach-more-slowly method to extend Jason's tolerance of rising and falling suddenly.

Xavier flew in a large backflip. Jason's reaction was muted.

He tried a barrel roll and was rewarded with almost instant panic.

This is enough practice for today. We will continue practicing maneuvers until you are comfortable flying; I hope you learn to enjoy the freedom the sky provides.

The flying lessons had taken them away from their destination, so Xavier changed course, flying them over the cave where they had spent two days and one night before proceeding to Smoky Springs.

Sighting the clearing Akela had described, Xavier noted a dozen or more men camping. It was not a place to land unseen.

Circling the city, he found a vacant area at the bottom of a switchback going up a mountain to the north of town. There were no man-sized heat sources that Xavier could see. A road appeared, going from the base of the mountain toward the town.

Xavier landed as the predawn sky brightened; he spent several minutes watching the meadow at the mountain's base, the switchback, and the forest on either side of the road.

Satisfied that they were alone, the dragon receded, and Jason emerged.

Can you believe we did a two-day trek in just a few hours? Jason marveled. *Flying definitely has its perks.*

I'm exhausted after flying all night. This is the first day I used my wings, so I'll probably sleep most of the day, Xavier said.

The rope that held his pack snugly to the dragon's foreleg draped loosely on Jason's arm. He unpacked his clothing, dressed, and repacked the rope.

His morning devotions and thasiwoda poses followed. Then, since it was not yet dawn, he filled a pipe and sat on a boulder alongside the road to enjoy the sunrise.

When the sun rose, he started walking south along the road.

The roadway was wide enough for two two-horse-drawn wagons to pass each other. The forest encroached a bit on the sides of the road, but only a few tree sprouts showed. The easy conclusion was that travel this way to Smoky Springs had been sparse for some time.

After about five miles, Jason stopped and examined the surrounding forest. The floor appeared clean where he stood. Looking back, he could see the gradual changes converting the wild underbrush into a garden.

The trees were more uniformly spaced and lacked dead branches overhead. As far as he could tell, no plants were missing from the typical undergrowth, but it wasn't the usual riot of intertwined bushes. Wild berry bushes seemed more prevalent than normal, however. Small clearings appeared about twenty feet from the road surface.

"I've seen this before," he said to no one. "I can't recall where or who makes the forest into a park."

A few miles farther along, the road forked. One fork went uphill slightly, and the other went more steeply downhill.

He did not recall seeing this detail through his dragon's eyes from the air. He took off his pack, retrieved his pipe, loaded it, and lit it as he pondered his next action.

"Man wal' to 'ivah?" A heavily accented voice from behind was barely decipherable.

Jason jumped and spun around at the sound. His eyes widened as he stepped away from the source, raising his arms to near shoulder height and balancing on the balls of his feet—a defensive posture against the unknown threat. His pipe fell to the ground and embers spread over the roadway. He gasped, leaving his mouth agape.

He saw a creature resembling a person covered in short reddish-orange fur except its face and hands. This one stood almost chin high to Jason and wore an apron with pockets containing a few small farming implements. Its arms were longer than those of a human of the same height, and its legs were slightly bowed. It bent forward a little from its hips. Its skin was darker than that of most humans.

Seeing no threat from the being, Jason relaxed, dropped his arms, and took a deep breath. "I am sorry; I do not understand," he said.

The creature pointed toward the upper fork and said, "Ci'y." Then it pointed to the other fork and said, "Wa'er. 'Ivah."

Jason repeated the gestures, saying what he guessed the creature had declared. "City," he said, pointing to the upper road. "Water. The river." He pointed to the lower one.

The creature nodded vigorously; apparently, it could understand Jason's speech. Jason turned toward the upper road and shouldered his pack. When he turned to thank the being, he learned he was alone on the road again.

Jason thought, *Its woodcraft was excellent. It snuck up on me and faded into the forest, and I didn't notice. I wonder what manner of being it is. I have never seen one before.*

The road curved so that a walker could easily have believed he was still walking through a forest, if not for the groomed roadway.

Coming around one curve, he saw what appeared to be a town square. It was more rectangular than square, with its boundaries curved like the streets. It was a center of commerce, with signs of people coming and going. Oxcarts were alongside goat carts, and donkeys, ponies, and occasional horses were among the people—men, dwarves, and some of the manlike creatures he had met earlier.

He had found Smoky Springs.

A large building stood at the far end. The stone construction resembled tree trunks at the corners, and the building seemed to grow out of the earth beneath it. It was the town hall.

To his left were man-made buildings, except the corners seemed to be living trees, and the foundations and steps were stone. Each seemed to grow from the ground. Horizontal boards formed the storefronts. Windows and doors looked normal, except more glass panes were evident than usual for a small town. The storefronts staggered and followed the street's curvature around the square.

On his right, a blacksmith shop occupied a corner halfway along the square, with a partly enclosed area for the forge.

A public house sat before him and to his left, with an entrance facing the town square. A large carved sign showing an owl laughing gave Jason its name: the Laughing Owl. A wraparound porch fronted the town square and the side Jason could see. Five people with mud on their clothing stood outside: three men and two women wearing matching tunics.

A fourth man wearing a similar mud-speckled tunic stood on the street, saw Jason, and walked rapidly toward him. He was shorter and heavier than Jason, with unkempt medium-brown hair and brown eyes.

"Are you Jason, the courier from Twin Rivers Bay?" he asked.

Jason stopped before answering. "Yes, I am."

"I'm Thaddeus, a Defender of Smoky Springs. Chief Defender Clowers thought you were lost in a mudslide two nights back," the guy said. "He's at the pub across from the square. You can see some of his people outside. He's eager to talk to you."

The man turned and ran to the pub, shouted something at those on the porch, and entered through the doors.

Erlender traveled to Capua, the capital of Rutendo, figuring he could learn Jason's destination from the clerks at army headquarters.

Simple bribes gained him access to the army's payroll records. Finding a man based on his first name was uncertain; Jason was not an uncommon forename.

He could hardly contain his excitement when the scribe found two entries for Jason from a year earlier.

"Let me read the entries," Erlender said.

"I cannot," the clerk said.

Erlender closed his eyes and took a deep breath. Then he ran his fingers through his hair. He resisted the urge to pound the table. He could not take his frustrations out on this minor functionary.

After four years and six months of searching, this was a minor setback. He would find the man and take the kalasha. He closed his eyes, dreaming of the moment he presented it to Golgol-drath and the reward he would receive.

"Let me copy the names and destinations of those on this page," Erlender said. "Perhaps one of them knows Jason's whereabouts. His uncle will be very disappointed if I cannot find him. He is the last heir to the family estate."

"That would be improper. And I have no destination for either Jason on this page," the scribe stated.

"It will mean so much to his uncle," Erlender pleaded as he placed one hand flat on the table. Lifting his hand, he revealed three silver pieces.

The librarian looked carefully around and then scraped the coins into his hand and turned the ledger so Erlender could read it more easily. "I need to check the status of goods coming in through the main gate. It will take me half an hour."

Erlender hid his smile; his lie continued to persuade those helping him to find Jason.

The port city Biblola was the destination of half the men on the page. There were four other ports and three small towns. The ports seemed to him more likely. He had five cities to search. He would split his men into squads and pursue Jason in all ports. He would take five men to Biblola himself; his instincts cried that it was the place he wanted.

Jason studied the people at the Laughing Owl's entrance as he closed the distance. Five people wearing uniforms watched him approach.

Marshals? he wondered.

One of the men was about Jason's age, a little shorter, with a heavier build, black hair, and a thin beard. The second was a bit older, with salt-and-pepper hair and a short, neatly trimmed beard; he was also taller and slimmer.

The third man, standing farthest from the door, carried a bow with a quiver of arrows. He was the shortest of the men—shorter than the taller of the two women. His brown-blond hair was cut short, and he was clean-shaven.

One of the women had hair between silver and white, with amber eyes;

she was slightly built and came up to about Jason's nose. The other woman was shorter, had darker hair, and was heavier set. She had brown eyes.

The black-haired man and the white-haired woman stepped between Jason and the pub entrance.

"What business do you have within, stranger?" the man asked with his eyebrows gathered and his lips drawn into a line.

Jason paused and looked each of the marshals in the eye. "If the Laughing Owl is open, I have an appointment with a mug of ale. And if Clifton Clowers is within, I have business with him."

"What business is that?" the woman asked with a smile and a twinkle in her eyes.

Jason looked at her and considered how much of his undertaking he should divulge. "I have a package for him from Twin Rivers City," he said after a short delay.

"Wait here a moment," the black-haired marshal said, and he stepped inside the pub.

Jason studied the other marshals outside.

A few minutes later, the marshal who'd halted Jason stepped out of the pub. "I am called Galaad of Ardennes. I presume you are Jason. Welcome to Smoky Springs. Defender Clowers awaits you within the Laughing Owl." He held the door open for Jason to enter.

Jason inclined his head slightly before saying, "I am Jason Archer. I am pleased to meet you."

Galaad and the silver-haired female followed Jason into the pub.

Stepping inside, Jason realized the building was much larger than its exterior suggested. A short staircase led down to a pub floor, while another spiraled upward to balconies. Unlike the quiet street, the interior buzzed with a sound like wind rustling through trees beside a rushing stream. Yet there were no open windows or breeze within, leaving the sounds unexplained. The symphony of wind and water quieted to a murmur as the door swung shut behind him.

There's magic at work here, he thought.

Familiar pub smells—the aromas of stale beer, roasted meats, and simmering vegetables—assaulted his nostrils. The pub itself was a rustic tavern furnished with worn tables and a long, scarred bar running along the wall to his right. A lone figure manned the bar, busy washing mugs. The marshal from the street lingered by the entrance, joined by another adorned with an emblem on the left breast of his tunic. A third marshal occupied a seat at the bar, nursing a tankard.

The marshal sporting the badge pointed to a weathered hall tree and a worn bench. "I am Padraic, a Defender of Smoky Springs. You may leave your pack and staff here."

"Thank you, Padraic," Jason said, his voice echoing slightly in the surprisingly large room. I am Jason, and thank you, but no, I will keep my things with me."

Jason started down the stairs, heading toward a table where a large bearded man sat. His hair and beard were a forest of brown and gray, and his weathered face was etched with stories waiting to be told. The man wore a more ornate insignia on his left breast.

Jason wasn't sure if the man looked welcoming or intimidating, but a conversation seemed inevitable.

The man's eyes were hazel, barely discernible in the dim interior light. He stood and said, "We know from raven messages that Jason, the archer from South Haven, left O'otoka and headed east along the road five days ago. He should have been very close to the mudslide that destroyed over a mile of the road the night before last. Now you show up smelling of kieff like an addicted wastrel.

"Wolverton Mountain has been almost impassable since the rockslides two years ago. Crossing from Blackwoods to here would take at least three months; if the weather cooperated, if the streams had water, and if the bears and mountain lions were hunting elsewhere in the range. The bears also tell me when a stranger walks on Wolverton Mountain.

"So exactly how did you get here from the north?" Clowers asked with a condescending smile, dropping his arms to his sides. Distrust was heavy in his voice.

Jason was taken aback by the vehemence—almost anger—rolling off the man.

Jason took a deep breath and exhaled. "First, when I saw a storm driven by magic approaching two days ago, I backtracked to a cave I had seen and spent one night and day waiting for the weather and road to clear.

"Second, if you want to know everything that's going on up Wolverton Mountain, you're gonna need to talk to the birds, not just the bears. Xavier, a two-skinned I met at the cave, flew me to the bottom of the mountain last night. I didn't walk anywhere where bears could spot me.

"Third, you accuse me of misconduct simply because I use kieff on those rare occasions I have trouble sleeping.

"Finally, you violated all hospitality rules before allowing me to introduce myself. I have neither time nor patience for such disrespect. Good day!"

Jason turned his back on Clowers and took a step toward the door.

Galaad stepped into Jason's path.

Jason shifted his stance and his grip on his staff slightly. "Do not stand between me and my path," he said gently but firmly.

Galaad hesitated and looked toward the large man.

Again, the sounds of branches swaying and water bubbling obscured most sounds within the pub. Jason still could not identify why the wind was louder inside than outside.

"Wait!" The word was halfway between a command and a plea. "You are correct. I apologize. The Defenders and citizens of Smoky Springs spent last night and this morning searching for your body beneath the mudslide that destroyed over a mile of the road to O'otoka."

Jason turned to face the man.

"Please forgive my earlier outburst. My marshals and I are a bit on edge, and your arrival from an unexpected direction has me thinking of conspiracy. I should not assume you are guilty of anything before we talk.

"I am Clifton Clowers, chief of the Smoky Springs Valley Defenders.

"Come in, and let me treat you to a mug of beer. This is Ratray, the city's best brewer and proprietor of this pub." Clowers extended an open palm toward the man washing mugs.

The barkeep was near Jason's height, with straight black hair tied back into a short tail. He wore muttonchop sideburns that had streaks of gray near his temples.

"Ratray, please bring our guest a mug of ale," Clowers said as he motioned with his other hand, inviting Jason to the table.

Jason raised one eyebrow. "Which person is inviting me in? The belligerent, quick-to-judge bear who first spoke or the gracious host I see now?"

"I apologize again. I know Iudgual, whom you know as Grandmother, would not trust the artifact to a kieff addict. You got here when she predicted, so you are not a wastrel. Please give me a chance to redeem myself from that unwarranted outburst."

Jason stared at him for several moments before nodding in acceptance.

Clowers turned to the silver-haired woman and said, "Tovia, please fly to the base of Wolverton Mountain, and tell me what you find."

She saluted and exited the Laughing Owl.

Jason noted that the Defenders accepted two-skinned. He had not been certain after Akela's comments about being in a minority. Jason walked to the single chair on his side of the table. He stood his staff on the floor to his right by tapping it twice and releasing it. The staff stood on end as though rooted to the floor. He removed his pack and set it on his left.

Clowers extended his right hand in greeting and said, "Welcome to Smoky Springs, a community of men, dwarves, kaihana, arboreals, and a few other races. We expected you no earlier than today and are pleased you are here safely."

The two men shook hands, and Jason exclaimed, "Arboreals live here! That explains why the forest north of town looks like a fancy garden. And I presume it was a kaihana who gave me directions along the road?"

"Yes, we have a few score arboreals living here. Moana, a kaihana, met you and sent a bird ahead to report that someone was walking on the road from Wolverton Mountain. She finds some sounds of the common tongue difficult to say, but she successfully communicated with you."

Jason sat, and Ratray brought a mug and set it before him.

Jason raised the mug to his nose and smelled the ale. He opened his eyes in surprise and took a healthy swallow. "This is excellent, especially after so many days of water alone. Toasty and malty but not sweet. Very refreshing."

Ratray thanked him and looked pleased at the compliment.

Jason looked around the pub from his seat and noticed he could not focus on the wall behind Clowers's right shoulder. The wall decorations faded into a fog, only to reappear a little farther to his left.

The Defender entered his seat awkwardly from his left, as if he were avoiding an unseen obstacle.

The wind noise inside returned. Jason observed Clowers turn his head to his right and, with a slight incline, raise his right ear.

"Tell me more of the last two days," said Clowers as the wind sounds abated.

"There isn't much more to tell. A two-skinned wolf and I shared the cave during the storm. We fought off a gelatinous black thing during the first night."

"You and a wolf defeated a black blob?" Clowers sounded surprised.

"Yes. Is that unusual?" Jason asked.

"Very. They are escape artists, and fire is all they fear," Clowers replied.

"Well, it was fortunate we had a fire still burning in the cave," Jason said.

"Can you confirm this tale?" Galaad asked.

Jason opened his pack and retrieved the small pouch containing the teeth. "I collected these from beneath the blob's location after it had retreated from the fire." He carefully spread the teeth out on the table.

Clowers and Galaad bent over the table and looked at the teeth carefully. Clowers sat back and tilted his head up and to his right.

Galaad took a step back to his former position. "These look genuine," he said. "They show burn marks but don't appear very old. I think these could well be from the night before last."

Even though inside, Jason heard a wind whispering through trees, rustling the leaves in a gentle symphony, while water flowed with a steady, gushing sound, creating a soft, tinkling melody that hid the sounds from the pub's interior. Jason struggled to see behind Clowers, who asked, "What else happened?"

"The next morning, the sky still threatened storms, and the snow was too deep for traveling. The sun came out, and the snow receded some. Xavier, another two-skinned, joined us. He agreed to help me make up for lost time and carried me to the foot of the mountain," Jason replied.

"What kind of bird is Xavier that he can carry a man?" asked Clowers.

"If he wanted you to know, he would have landed us nearer the O'otoka road, where my rescuers are camped. That was our destination before he saw the campsite," Jason answered. "It is his secret to share, not mine."

Again, the wind noise was audible as Clowers tipped his head to the side.

Jason leaned back in his chair and took a long pull from his mug. He looked Clowers in the eyes. "Every place I have been, it is the height of rudeness to include a hidden member in a conversation," he said.

Clowers sat up suddenly with eyes widening. "What do you mean?" he asked.

"You turn your head to listen to someone on your right side; each time you do, the sound of the wind inside the building increases. I cannot focus on the wall behind you on your right. Someone must be using magic to avoid detection."

The air alongside Clowers shimmered, revealing a woman in a dark green cloak standing at his side. She was not tall—a few inches over five feet. Her short, wavy hair had a red tint, and her skin looked brown beneath the glowstone lanterns in the pub. Her cloak, over a loose-fitting off-white dress, reached her ankles and obscured her build. Her face was full but not plump, and her expression looked as though she were suspicious of something.

"I am Glorinda the Green, an earth and water mage. I serve with the Defenders. My task today was to see if you were truthful with Chief Defender Clowers. I sense you have not told the full truth but have not said anything you believe is false.

"Speaking of truth-telling, a raven's message informed us that you possess some control over fire. We have a simple test to confirm your abilities: light this candle." She placed a new wax candle on the table in front of Jason.

He looked at the candle apprehensively. "I have never lit a candle's wick. I start fires from kindling with neither flint nor tinder."

"Well, it is time for you to try."

Jason focused on the candle wick. He felt mana building in his skin and saw a spark form before his eyes about a hand's length away.

As he directed the spark slowly to the tip of the wick, he noticed the wax along the wick and at the candle's tip melting. A tendril of vapor rose to meet the spark.

When the wax vapor touched the spark, a flash of light and a pop surprised everyone. The tip of the candle had vanished!

Jason's eyes widened, and he jerked back, scooting his chair and exhaling a meaningless "Whuff." He took a shaky breath as he stared at the candle.

Glorinda looked closely at the top of the candle. "Our guest did more than just light the candle; he completely burned the top away, leaving tiny tentacles of wax spreading like an anemone."

She turned to Jason. "You haven't learned about the flammability of the spirits of wax, tallow, wine, and lamp oil. You have much to learn to master your talent. You also need to learn forms of mana beyond fire; life and fire are strong in you, and there are other forms you should learn to control.

"I will take charge of the artifact you brought; let me see it now," she said, holding out one hand.

Jason opened his pack, rummaged in it, and retrieved a leather pouch laced up and tied. The knot was covered in sealing wax, and a seal was impressed on it.

Clowers looked carefully at the seal and nodded. "This is Iudgual's public seal, but this is not her pouch."

"I put her package in my pouch and asked her to seal the knot to confirm that it had not been opened when I arrived," Jason said.

Clowers nodded and then picked up the package and reached for the lacing.

Jason held up a hand to interrupt him. "Once you finish inspecting the contents, I expect payment."

"Of course," Clowers responded, placing a small bag that clinked on the table.

After breaking the seal, Clowers unlaced Jason's purse and removed what appeared to be solid wood.

He handed the piece of timber to Glorinda, who muttered over it briefly before a seam showed around it. She opened the box and unfolded the cloth inside it.

Inside was an unusual knife. Its blade was four inches long, but its handle was sized for a sword. The grip was wrapped by braided gold, copper, and silver wire, and the hilt appeared gold. The pommel was a silver disk holding a deep red gemstone.

"The blade looks like a flame," Jason said.

Clowers held the box up and turned it to different viewing angles before saying, "I can see that if I hold it just right."

Xavier pushed his consciousness near the front to stare at the blade. He and Jason simultaneously thought, *Mine!*

Jason reached for the knife eagerly, overcome by a primal urge to possess it. The sudden loss of control frightened him; a warrior did not act so.

"Do not touch the athamé," Glorinda said.

Jason yanked his arm back, straightened suddenly, and looked at her. She folded the cloth over the knife and closed the box.

Jason wasn't sure if he was more disturbed by his momentary loss of control or by the possessiveness Glorinda expressed. He desired that knife like nothing he had wanted before.

Turning to face Jason, Clowers pushed the pouch of coins across the table and continued. "Jason Archer. I have never seen an archer without a bow. Where is your bow?"

Jason stood, picked up his staff, and turned it over in his hands, running each hand along its length. As he did that, he said, "You are right. An archer without a bow is not of much use." When he finished, he held an unstrung longbow with a small quiver attached, containing a half dozen arrows.

Clowers's jaw dropped open when Jason revealed the bow.

Glorinda looked more closely and said, "Magic to conceal a bow like that is very sophisticated."

"It was a gift from Fedlimid, King Aurvang's mage, after the last battle with the king's nephew," Jason said.

Clowers looked up at Jason, surprised. "Are you the archer who ended that battle with an impossible shot?"

Jason started to speak. "I—" He felt a sharp pain in the center of his chest. He leaned forward, dropping his bow and holding his weight on the table with his arms. "I can't—" He began to shake. The pain radiated to his left shoulder and arm. He took a few labored breaths and continued. "Speak. Of. War." He collapsed, disappearing partially beneath the table, as his body trembled from unseen turmoil.

Jason watched Glorinda step around the table and kneel beside him. She extended one hand over his torso. A faint green glow formed around her hands and projected to him.

"He was death-cursed!" she exclaimed. She withdrew her hand, and the green light dimmed and went out.

Jason heard Glorinda's words and spoke to Xavier: *It was nice meeting you, X; I wish we had more time to know each other better.*

Xavier again pushed to the surface and responded, *Some human used magic against us! This cannot stand!*

Jason felt a flush of rage emanating from Xavier, and then mana flowed from deep within, gaining strength and heat as it reached his skin. He felt as if he had been standing close to a large fire for too long.

What just happened, Xavier?

Dragons are immune to almost all human magic. We are more magical than mundane but not as much as the fae, who are almost pure magic. I pushed you aside, and my magic unraveled the curse, Xavier replied.

And you didn't think that was as important as—or more important than—close seeing when I asked what other cool things dragons could do? Jason exclaimed.

I did not think of it then, Xavier said.

Jason inhaled a shuddering breath and then continued breathing, although his breath was labored.

—⬗—

At the summer palace, Fedlimid, the king's mage, stumbled and fell to one knee, overwhelmed by the backlash from the raveling of a mana pattern he had formed more than a year earlier. He knew no one strong enough to break one of his closed patterns.

—⬗—

"Wow!" exclaimed Clowers. "What was that? I felt the heat from this side of the table!"

Glorinda reached toward Jason; the green glow reappeared. "The death curse is broken!" She lowered her hands nearer his chest, paused momentarily, and then said, "It is as though the mana of the curse exited through his skin. He will live, but his heart was damaged."

As she started to stand, Jason mumbled in a voice inaudible to all but her, "Green Star on a White Sky." He then said, "Help me, please," which the others could hear.

Glorinda dropped to her knees and placed both hands above his heart; the green light got brighter. Those standing close could see green flowing from her into Jason.

After a few minutes, Jason took a deep breath and began breathing normally.

Glorinda stood up, turned to Clifton, and said, "He is healed. Death curses attack hearts, and his was damaged. Time will improve him. I must leave." She picked up the box containing the athamé, closed it, and rushed outside.

Once outside, Glorinda muttered, "How did he learn my True Name? I *should have* healed him without request; it is my duty—my oath! I should not have needed the True Name compulsion." She shook her head in frustration and guilt and left the square.

—⬗—

The pub's door burst open, and Tovia ran in, still pulling her tunic on. "Defender Clowers," she said, "I saw footprints of a large animal just at

THE WARRIOR & THE DRAGON

the bottom of the switchback, evidence of someone walking around and smoking a pipe recently, and a man's footprints leaving there, headed for town."

She came to a sudden stop and surveyed the room. "What happened in my absence?"

Jason attempted to rise and collapsed back onto the floor. Galaad and Clowers helped him up and seated him in the chair.

"Our guest was telling us a bit about himself, when something triggered a death curse on him. Glorinda broke the curse and healed him to the extent she could but thinks his heart was damaged," Clowers said as they helped Jason into a comfortable position.

She didn't break the curse; we did, said Xavier, mind to mind.

Yes, but no one else knows that, he replied.

Jason reached one hand toward his mug of ale, but it shook so much he could not grasp it. He shifted to both hands and scooted the mug closer so he could bend his head forward, closing the distance from mouth to mug. He straightened up and gulped down a few swallows, spilling some over his mustache and beard.

"My apologies to Ratray," he said softly. "Beer this good should not be wasted. And please give my heartfelt thanks to Glorinda for saving me."

Clowers walked toward the door and called the Defenders to him. After a brief conversation, he, Tovia, and Galaad returned to the table, and the others left.

Clowers took a seat, but the other two stood to one side. "Ratray, please get a tureen of your special Defender stew for our guest. He has spent a lot of his mana this day." He turned to Jason and continued. "The happenings today are unusual, to say the least. I hope I do not trigger another reaction from you as I review them.

"First, I think you are, or were, under a geas not to discuss what happened during the war. That makes me think you know something interesting, but my curiosity is unlikely to be satisfied this day.

"I am pretty sure you know who put you under the geas; do you also know who death-cursed you?"

Jason responded in a low voice, "I do know the man."

"I suspected as much. What do you intend to do?"

Jason felt Xavier stir. *I can find him,* he heard, followed by a cold, vengeful rage building within.

He raised his head, looked Clowers straight in the eye, and replied, "I will find him. And I will end him. There is no place he can hide from me." His voice was flat and cold, reflecting the dragon's emotions, and he had no expression on his face.

Clowers raised his eyebrows. "That sounds like braggadocio, like a desire for revenge; you may not have the strength to back it up."

Jason looked at him with a cruel smile. "I am not in the habit of making commitments I do not fulfill. I will say no more about that now."

⸺⸎⸺

Ratray arrived with the tureen of stew and a plate with slices of bread and set them in front of Jason. "This stew should restore your body and magic in a day or two," he said.

"It may take longer than that to restore a damaged heart," Tovia said.

Clowers and Ratray nodded.

Jason leaned over the bowl and sniffed carefully. "Onions, mushrooms, lentils, potatoes, thyme, and other root vegetables I can't identify. I see peppers and a thick gravy. It smells delicious."

Jason reached for the spoon, but his hand shook too much to grasp it.

"Let me help," Clowers said. He reached across the table and scooped a spoonful, which he extended to Jason.

Jason leaned forward, and Clowers pushed the spoon into his mouth, spilling half of it.

While Jason tried to clean the stew from his beard, Tovia took the spoon from Clowers and said, "It is clear you have never fed anyone as weak as Jason."

She took a towel from Ratray and wiped Jason's mouth and beard as best as she could. Sitting alongside him, she moved the bowl closer to Jason and partly filled the spoon, mostly with broth. She held it up for Jason's view and brought it to his mouth, sliding it gently between his lips and waiting for them to close over it. She removed the spoon and continued feeding him half spoonfuls of stew, pausing each time until Jason nodded that he was ready for more.

The Defenders talked shop for a few minutes as Tovia fed Jason. He raised one hand and motioned for her to set the spoon down. "I think I can handle a spoon now," he said with a weak grin.

His hand shook a little, but he managed to eat the stew.

"What are your plans for the next several days?" Galaad asked.

"My only plan beyond delivering the artifact was to visit a healer named Heather Moonstar, per Grandmother's instructions," Jason replied. "I expected to walk there today or tomorrow, but now I am not sure I can do it that soon."

"How did you learn of our healer, Peaiman Moonstar? What do you need of her?" Galaad's question was colored by suspicion.

Jason sighed. "Grandmother recommended I see a healer named Heather Moonstar. She said I was not accessing my inner fire and that Lady Moonstar could help me.

"My maternal grandmother could start a fire without kindling from across a room—much more than just a substitute for flint and steel."

He could tell the others were not mollified. "I also have a letter from Grandmother introducing me to her."

"Let us see it," Clowers said.

"It is sealed, and I will not let you open it," Jason said.

"Yes, that is fine. Seeing a letter addressed to Peaiman Moonstar in Grandmother's hand will be as good a clearance as you can have," Clowers replied.

Galaad moved Jason's pack within easy reach. Jason retrieved a folded, tied, flat leather pouch from the bag. He untied the leather laces and extracted a piece of stiff bark with strings holding a parchment. The bark had protected the parchment's seal from damage. He offered the letter to Clowers.

"This is her seal again. Thank you for indulging us," Clowers said.

Galaad nodded. "Yes, thank you. But know that we all revere Heather Moonstar; any threat to her threatens us all."

"I assure you I have no ill intentions toward anyone in Smoky Springs," Jason said.

Clowers cleared his throat. "Since you were attacked in our house, we can arrange lodging and care until you recover. Galaad and Tovia will escort you to our barracks and infirmary. I believe the infirmary is empty now, and we can see to your care."

Galaad and Tovia agreed quickly.

Clowers called Ratray over again. "Please bring us a round of Summer Wine to celebrate our arrangement."

Jason finished his stew and pushed the tureen away. Looking at it, he said, "I was hungrier than I realized. That should have served at least two."

Ratray brought a tray of small glasses for Jason, Clowers, Tovia, and Galaad. Clowers passed the drinks out.

Jason smelled the contents of the glass. "Honey wine with cherry blossom honey?" he asked. He sipped and added, "Strawberries. And angel's kiss? The army used angel's kiss when amputating or when a soldier in pain could not be healed. What does it do in honey wine?"

Ratray grinned and responded, "Excellent taste, young sir. The army likely used the fruit and leaves, which make a powerful sedative. I use the blossoms for a mild soporific intended to relax—similar to the effect of hops in beer. This glass won't put you to sleep—I don't think."

The three Defenders and Jason toasted Ratray's craft.

Jason picked up his bow and quiver of arrows. He spun them around and ran his hands over the length of the bow, and the staff he'd carried into the pub reappeared in his hands.

Jason tried to stand but failed. He tried again, bracing his hands against the table, and got to his feet. He wobbled a bit until he got his staff positioned so he could lean on it. He took a few tentative steps, grunting in effort for each one. Sweat broke out on his face and brow.

"I am sure to need this to walk; I didn't expect to need a cane for another two score years." He chuckled a little.

Galaad exited to get a means to carry Jason to the infirmary. Tovia and Clowers walked alongside Jason as he hobbled to the Laughing Owl's door. Galaad returned with a goat cart. The cart was a four-wheeled model with one bench seat above the front wheels and a four-by-six-foot railed bed behind the seat. Each wheel had springs, ensuring a smooth ride on the roads of Smoky Springs.

They loaded Jason's staff and pack into the back and helped him onto the seat. Galaad drove the cart, and Tovia walked, skipped, and danced alongside.

When they were in sight of the infirmary, Tovia turned to the two men and said, "I am off, flying to Terlingua to invite Peaiman Heather Moonstar to look at you." She nodded at Jason. "She is our primary healer; Glorinda is not often in town, so Heather will be the one to monitor your recovery. Since you intended to meet her anyway, this will introduce you to her. And Galaad can present you to the infirmary as well as two of us can."

"Thank you for your help this day, Tovia the Kind," Jason said, bowing his head.

"Ooh, a title!" she exclaimed, clapping and laughing. "It gives me chills to hear you say it." She ran ahead to the barracks, skipping occasionally.

A few minutes later, a large white hawk with a ring of dark feathers around each eye flew toward them. The bird screeched at Jason and Galaad and then circled for height.

"How many two-skinned are there among the Defenders?" asked Jason.

"About one-third of us are two-skinned. About half of those are birds. As you saw, Tovia is a spectacled hawk, I am a badger, and Defender Clowers is a bear. The birds watch the valley's roads, trails, and outlying areas. That is how we knew where you were on the road."

Galaad helped Jason down from the cart, handed him his staff, and collected Jason's pack. They walked slowly toward the building's main door.

CHAPTER 4

Jason Meets the Healer

Introduction to Magic and Healing
Master Healer Kimimela

Medicine comprises four major groups of practitioners: physicians, herbalists, midwives, and surgeons. Magic is not necessary for any of these, but the best in their fields possess strong life mana and, often, spirit mana.

Physicians and herbalists are the most common professions. Both study the body, its ailments, and treatments, but physicians investigate disease spread and prevention, while herbalists focus on disease manifestations and cures after infection.

Physicians taught us to keep treatment rooms clean, use vinegar or alcohol on surfaces, and clean wounds with lime chloride. As these practices spread, death by infection dropped.

On the other hand, herbalists have made significant contributions to medicine by discovering that willow bark treats fevers, aloe vera eases burns, and angel's kiss induces a deep sleep. Their discoveries have enriched our understanding of plant remedies.

Midwives train to prepare women for childbirth, easing birth and postpartum recovery. They use both techniques discovered by physicians and herbs in their treatments.

Surgeons are a special group of physicians who excise tissue to allow the tissue to regrow without the ailment. Surgery is usually the last resort, and recovery is uncertain. Amputations are common during war and are among the most successful surgeries performed.

Mages and clerics who become physicians, herbalists, and midwives use life and spirit mana to accelerate healing. They are the only ones who successfully treat damaged organs, whether trauma or disease has affected the patient. They visualize the hurt, direct mana to the harm, and allow the mana surplus to restore health.

This class will provide you with the basics of magical healing—skills all mages should know. I hope some of you elect healing as your focus.

To Grandmother,
Greetings!

I believe I shall adopt your new name as well.

Jason arrived after a rainstorm that could have targeted him but missed. The adversary's reach and information are much improved if your courier was the target. The duke's desire for tax income from us is a plausible explanation.

The meeting went much as you predicted. He saw flames on the blade and reached for it quite possessively. Glorinda intervened. I am not sure you and she are working on the same plan.

We were surprised when a death curse activated on our young man. Glorinda saved his life, and he is recuperating in our infirmary. The healer is coming to check on him tomorrow.

The alternate plan is in effect; I hope our fledgling mage has no more surprises for us.

I remain your loyal servant,
Clifton Clowers

———— ❧ ————

The barracks had three doors facing the street: a large double door in the center and two single doors near each end. The building was stucco, with a red tile roof.

Jason and Galaad entered the right door into the foyer. Jason stopped and looked around with his mouth open.

"This looks like an entrance to the governor's house in South Haven," he said, "except the theme there is a bountiful harvest."

Ornate hand-painted tiles climbed the walls in mesmerizing waves of blue, green, and white. The ceiling, a breathtaking expanse, showcased a painted scene of a cherry orchard in full bloom, bathed in the soft glow of a rising sun. Lush, rolling hills stretched toward a snowcapped mountain range painted in soft hues of green, lavender, and gold. The illusion of a perfect sunrise cast a warm glow on the scene.

Potted plants lined the outer wall and surrounded the central fountain, which provided soothing waterfall sounds.

"This is one of the earliest spas built to attract the rich and ailing and separate them from their money as gently as possible." Galaad chuckled at his inside joke about the industry. "The mineral springs that attracted them more than money failed on this side of the river. The spas moved following groundwater vagaries, which bankrupted the owners. That was about when the Defenders formed. The building was already divided into rooms, so the town donated it to us. It also serves as our headquarters," he added.

He nodded to the right of the foyer, which contained a waist-high counter stretching from wall-to-wall. A few storage cabinets and staffed desks sat behind the counter and a door opened onto an office.

"Most spas were dismantled, and the stone was used in newer, more expensive pools across the river. Three pools remain for our use; hot water makes for a relaxing soak, even without the minerals that once bubbled up from the earth."

A wide corridor bisected the far wall, and two doorways opened to hallways leading deeper into the building from the foyer.

A kaihana rose from one desk and approached them. As with Moana, she was covered in short fur except for her face and palms. Her fur was a lighter color: a dark tan with reddish-orange highlights. The skin of her face and hands was the color of cured buckskin. Her stare was open and accepting, and she smiled. She was shorter than Moana and wore a light blue dress appropriate for a business. She had a smaller nose and less prominent eyebrows than Moana's. She could have been Moana's sister, so similar did they look.

"Hello, Galaad. What brings you and a visitor?" she asked with a slight accent unlike that of the kaihana Jason had met on the road.

"Hello, Mivaela," Galaad replied. "This is Jason, the man we believed dead in the mudslide, here to recuperate for a while."

"For one trapped in mud, you are remarkably clean," Mi√aela said.

"Well met, Meek-ayla. I avoided the mud, only to encounter a relic of my time around battle mages, which almost killed me this time," Jason said with a half smile.

Mi√aela looked closely at Jason for a few moments. "That was pretty close," she said in a friendly tone. "The *k* sound is made with the tongue, like this." She demonstrated, clucking with her tongue against the roof of her mouth. "But that lesson can wait. And good news: the infirmary is empty, so you can choose whichever room and bed you want. I will summon a nurse." She examined Jason's hair and added, "And a barber."

Galaad led Jason down the central hallway, past doors on each side. A rug ran down the center of the hallway, muffling any sounds of their passage. Some indistinct voices occasionally emanated from a room they passed.

The walls along the hallway had decorative panels between doorways, continuing the motif from the foyer.

As they walked, Galaad asked, "Do you think you could have gotten past me in the pub?"

"That was the only acceptable answer at the time," Jason replied. "I did hope the test would not happen, because I might have hurt you, and that would not have been a good start to our relationship."

"You think pretty highly of yourself, don't you?"

Jason laughed. "When faced with an uncertain situation, I choose the best option I know and strive to attain that. I succeed more often than I fail. To be sure, I would not attempt to get past you now," he said as he tapped the staff.

At the end of the corridor was another doorway, opening onto a breezeway. Large stepping stones covered the breezeway's ground, with what appeared to be herbs growing between them. A slight zephyr brought the smell of horses and cooking fires from outside to mingle with the odors from the plants. Jason heard faint sounds of children playing and adults working, along with animal sounds.

Opposite the breezeway was another building. A door on their right was open, and Galaad led Jason to that doorway.

When they entered the room, Jason saw three beds separated by wooden partitions with curtains that could hide each bed from view. Cabinets containing bedding, surgical instruments, jars of herbs, and ointments lined the walls. An iron stove sat at Jason's right. The room smelled of vinegar, wood smoke, herbs, and spices.

Behind each bed was a basin with running water and drain pipes exiting through the back wall.

"Running water inside! What marvel of engineering and magic allows this?" Jason asked.

"Simple pipes bring water from hot springs into the room," Galaad replied. "When the mineral springs failed, hot-water springs remained. They heat the building in winter. A holding pond cools the water brought into the infirmary; the stove allows the healers to heat water for cleaning and making infusions."

"I have never seen such a room."

"I believe we have the only such infirmary," Galaad said. "You may select your bed and unpack what you need into the bureau next to the bed. Then I will escort you to the bathhouse, where you can bathe and soak. You will be given a clean tunic and trousers while recuperating here. Your clothing will be cleaned and returned to you.

"The barber will attend to you either in the bathhouse or when you return to bed. Until you are stronger, a nurse will escort you wherever you need to go during your stay."

Jason's mind buzzed with a storm of emotions. *Here I am after walking unaided through a dozen years and more of war, leaning on my staff,* he thought.

A wry chuckle escaped him. It was humbling—a reality check slammed into his self-image of boundless youth. There was resilience in accepting help and a chance to learn something from a stranger.

He thought of Tovia, Galaad, and the kaihana he had met; all had gone out of their way to help him feel welcome this day.

I hope it means that most people in the valley are friendly.

Right now, though, focusing on putting one foot in front of the other seemed like a good goal.

A warrior deals with the situation he finds, he thought. *I will endure.*

Jason selected the bed closest to the stove; he retrieved his pipe, tobacco, and icon of the Triple Goddess from his pack and set them atop the bureau. He placed the remaining contents of his bag in the drawers.

Galaad stared with fascination at the glowing statuette. "Not many men carry a token of the Triple Goddess with them," he said.

"I was raised on a farmstead managed by a priestess of hers," Jason replied. "She insisted I take it when I left."

"Why did you leave?"

Jason paused. "Several reasons." His hushed voice was swallowed by the empty room.

The weight of his words hung in the air, with each syllable carrying the burden of a past he had long tried to bury.

Once a sanctuary of love and support, the household had transformed into a battleground of conflicting wills and unspoken tensions. The arrival of a new woman, a stranger with a cold, calculating gaze, had brought things to a head.

Jason had found himself ostracized, with his presence unwelcome in the spaces he once had cherished. The women, once his guardians and protectors, had eyed him with a watchful wariness.

In that suffocating environment, Jason's spirit had begun to wither. When his sensei in thasiwoda had left, Jason had decided to go as well.

His departure had been not a rejection of his family but a desperate attempt to preserve his existence. Leaving behind the familiar comforts of home and the lingering memories of his mother's warmth, he'd sought a place where he could simply be. The army of the king had been a satisfactory solution.

There was no way to explain all that had transpired at South Haven in the year before he left.

Jason took a deep breath. "Let me say only that I, as a fourteen-year-old boy, felt unwelcome in my own home. An older priestess gave me the statuette to remember the good times and guide me through the difficult times to come. I left the farmstead and joined the king's army about six months later."

Taking a step along their path, he continued. "And here I am a dozen years later, delivering boxes, drinking good wine, and walking with a stick." He smiled at Galaad.

Galaad nodded. "I did not mean to pry. I am sorry you did not leave home on better terms."

The bed was higher than any Jason had seen before. He commented on that.

"The height is for the convenience of the caregivers," Galaad explained. "They do not need to stoop or bend much to minister to their charges. We try to make their jobs as easy as we can.

"If you are finished unpacking, let us continue to the bathhouse." He looked pointedly at Jason's hair. "If you have head lice, the barber will shave your head. One purpose of bathing on entry is to eliminate any skin and hair parasites you might have; they interfere with healing."

Jason and Galaad walked slowly out of the infirmary and into the bathhouse, where Galaad introduced Jason to Myla, a kaihana. "She will take charge of getting you bathed, barbered, and relaxed before returning you to the infirmary," he said.

Myla's fur was a light tan with orange highlights. She was the tallest of the three kaihana he had met and wore a pale green dress with white trim. She looked enough like the other two that she could've been a cousin. Jason studied her briefly, stopping before his gaze could be considered rude, and committed the differences in her appearance to memory.

He turned to Galaad and whispered, "Are all the attendants female?"

"All the kaihana here are female." Galaad paused. "I am not certain I have seen a male kaihana. Our human attendants are both sexes, but all on duty today are kaihana."

Myla escorted Jason to a bathing area, with Galaad following along.

"You undress here," Galaad said. "Then put on this robe and walk through that doorway; you will find a seating area. Take a seat, and Myla will wash your hair and check you for lice and other parasites. After that, you will get a hot water soak. The barber will find you after that. I leave you in her capable hands." He left.

Jason undressed, donned the robe, and took a seat in the designated area. Myla lowered the back of the chair so it rested above a basin, poured warm water over his head, and began massaging his scalp.

What have I gotten myself into? Jason thought as he felt the tension ease from the firm fingers Myla applied. That was his last thought of the afternoon.

Jason awakened in the infirmary bed he had selected—apparently the day before—with no memory of getting there. He was dressed in cotton trousers and tunic. He reached up and found the hair on his head was shorter, stopping slightly above his shoulders. His beard also felt shorter and stiffer. The doors admitted enough light that he was sure it was daylight outside.

"Ah, you are awake."

Jason turned to see Tovia standing at the foot of his bed.

"Mi√aela has a pot of Defender's stew on the stove, keeping it warm for you. You fell asleep during your bath yesterday; I did not realize you were so exhausted. I hope sleep and more of Ratray's good cooking will get you back on your feet.

"Heather will be in later today to check on you. Her healing differs from Glorinda's, and I think she is better. Let me get you a bowl of stew."

She turned away and stepped out of view. Jason slid his feet to the side of the bed and stood, holding onto it. Slowly releasing it, he found he could stand unaided.

He looked for his staff and saw it on the opposite side of the room, next to what looked like his clothing, which was cleaned and folded. He tried one step and almost fell. He reached for the bed to maintain his balance.

Xavier, if you are awake, Akela told us that two-skinned healed faster than others. She did say that changing made that happen. I don't know how to transform and keep us hidden. Jason spoke to his internal dragon.

I hear you, Jason. I agree to keep us a secret awhile longer. If you can endure the healing, I can tolerate being a passenger for a little longer, the dragon replied.

Tovia returned, carrying a tray with a bowl of stew on it. "You are up. I guess you tried to walk alone. Sit back down to eat, and I will bring your staff so you can get around on your own."

Jason smiled. "I titled you truly, Tovia the Kind."

She blushed. "Lady Moonstar will be in this afternoon. I need to leave now and attend to my Defender duties." She smiled and left.

Jason ate. Then he found a pair of sandals near his bed, put them on, and explored the infirmary, offering thanks again to Tovia for moving his staff within reach. He found a toilet with running water and spent some time figuring out how it worked.

He returned to his bed and slept.

Jason awakened to voices nearby. He opened his eyes slightly and saw Myla talking with a woman he had not seen before. They stood outside the partially drawn privacy curtain at the foot of his bed. He could not understand what they were saying and concluded they were talking in the kaihana language.

He turned his eyes to confirm his staff was within reach; if they had been plotting something that would harm him, they would have moved his weapon out of his range.

Xavier, can you tell us anything about our situation from within? Jason queried his other skin.

He felt something like but not like muscles tensing and relaxing, though he was not moving—the dragon stirring, he concluded.

I sense no danger from the women. I hear their speech with your ears, not mind to mind, as I would in my skin, so I have nothing to add, his dragon replied.

Jason sat up in bed. "Hello," he said. "How long have I been asleep?"

Myla jumped slightly, and surprise flickered across her face. She turned toward him and answered, "Good afternoon, Jason. After Tovia served you some stew, you slept the morning away. It is now a little after noon. Let me introduce you to our healer, Peaiman Heather Moonstar. Heather, this is Jason Archer."

Heather was taller than the kaihana. Jason guessed the healer would come up to his nose if they stood face to face. She was slender and dressed in a simple tan skirt and a pink-trimmed white tunic. Her hair was honey blonde, bound in a single braid reaching her midback, while her skin was the color of tea with milk. Her blue-gray eyes twinkled like those of someone who was laughing, complementing her neutral half-smile, which showed one dimple on her left cheek. She stood tall and exuded the calm confidence befitting a master healer.

The woman stepped past the curtain into his room and extended a hand toward him in greeting. Jason's icon increased its light to the brightness he had seen in the cave with the gelatinous black blob. She stopped, dropped her arm, stared in shock at the statue, turned back to him, and gasped.

"You possess one of the Goddess's kalashas; how did you come to such a treasure?" Her eyes were wide, and her jaw was slack.

Jason looked at Heather for a few moments. "It was a gift from Xochitl when I left South Haven more than a dozen years ago. She believed having a token to remember the farmstead would be useful."

"I have never heard of one carried by a man. I expect you are on a mission for the Goddess, even if you are not aware of it. What do you know of Xochitl?" Heather asked, furrowing her brow and pursing her lips.

"I know of no mission, and Xochitl was a priestess of the Goddess. And she was replaced as the person in charge of South Haven soon before I left."

Heather walked closer to the figurine, and its brightness lowered to its usual glow. "I think there are six of these, and you have one. This is amazing!" She shook her head and turned to Jason.

A wave of emotions washed over Jason: wonder and a strange pang of guilt for not protecting the kalasha, as Heather had called it. *One of six? How had it come to him, and what did his possessing it mean? She had never heard of one being given to a man. Why had Xochitl selected him to take it?* He could think of no answers to these questions.

He gazed at the icon resting on the bureau top, which now was imbued with a newfound value. "Wow," he breathed, opening his eyes wide. "This is incredible." He turned to face her. "How do you know so much about the artifacts of the Goddess? I knew neither their number nor what they were called."

"Tell me what you do know, and I will tell you what I know," Heather responded with a slight laugh.

Jason paused for a few moments. "Xochitl met me the morning I left the farmstead. I told my mother and grandmother I was leaving but revealed my plans to no others. She was waiting for me at the gate. She gave me the—kalasha, was it? And she told me to go with the blessings of the Goddess.

"I did not know it was special outside of being a gift from Xochitl. I knew only that it lit like a glowstone but never needed its magic replenished."

Jason fell silent, waiting for Heather to continue the discussion.

"Well, a kalasha is a container—I think that is the right word—for the Goddess's blessings. According to legend, six were created and given to those tasked with establishing her temples. Three temples were founded, each with a kalasha on the center of its altar.

"Have you noticed any protection from her?" she asked.

Jason thought for a few moments. "Yes, although I did not take much notice at the time. When the army encountered snakes, spiders, and other annoyances, their presence did not affect me much. I was always on high ground when waters rose after a rain or when brought by a battle mage."

He thought a little more. "And I believe I was encouraged to return to the overhang on the night of the storm that washed out the road to O'otoka." He paused. "How did you learn of the kalashas?"

"Like you, I was raised by devotees of the Goddess. I lived in a temple precinct and was taught alongside the novices. Our temple had a kalasha, which would light up on ceremonial days."

She paused for a while. "I left when I was twelve—more sent out after a disagreement with the high priestess about whom was worth healing. As an itinerant healer, I wandered for a few years, and I found myself here one day, at an enclave of the Lady just out of town. It felt like home, so I stayed."

The two sat in silence for several minutes.

71

Curiosity sparkled in Heather's eyes, and she smiled. "Tell me more about the farmstead and what you did there."

"It was a moderately large farm, housing 150 women and fifty children. Xochitl led devotionals to the Goddess each night; most women attended. Two dozen men lived on the farm, and more came for day work. I learned plowing, planting, harvesting, and storing grain and other crops. I helped ewes with difficult birth until my hands got too big. I can milk cows, repair fences, and construct outbuildings. I learned the bow and hunted some to contribute meat to our diet. I also helped the brewer on occasion.

"The farmstead was a sanctuary of sorts. Several refugees and solo travelers stopped for a tenday or a month or more and told their stories. While a few stayed for some time, most traveled on after a short while."

Jason summarized the events of the previous tenday. He reached for his pack, saying, "I have a letter of introduction here from Grandmother." He pulled the letter out, unwrapped its leather covering, and gave it to her.

Heather looked at the seal on the letter. She touched it, and a small puff of smoke rose from her finger. She opened the letter and read it.

After reading, she turned to Jason again. "Iudgual—that is, Grandmother—wants me to help you connect with your inner magic. Why is she sending you to me?"

"I do not know. When she and I met, she told me I had potential beyond what she saw when I lit her pipe with magic. She suggested I come to see you and contracted with me to deliver a package to Clifton Clowers, which I did."

Heather nodded and smiled at him. "Well, that explains how we got here. Before we go further, I need to check how well you are doing after a death curse and Glorinda's healing. She is a competent battlefield healer, healing enough that you live but often not enough to fully restore."

She stepped to the side of his bed and examined his eyes and mouth. She felt his pulse, listened to his heart, and palpated his abdomen.

She instructed him to lie back, placed one hand above his heart, and closed her eyes. Jason saw a white glow around her hand and felt an incredible calmness settle over him.

A few minutes passed.

Heather removed her hand and sighed. "I have done what I can; with blessings from the Mother, I believe you will fully recover. As for your core magic, that could take some time. You are the oldest person I have heard of who hasn't learned how to access theirs. What forms of mana do you access when you try your magic?"

Jason's eyes widened. "I don't know. I know that there are different forms but not what they are."

She nodded. "Most people don't know much about mana, except that it is what mages and clerics use. My healing is based on controlling life and spirit mana. Since you lit Iudgual's pipe, I suspect you control heat mana. It is often confused with fire—which is, strictly speaking, not mana.

"I will need to monitor your heart for a few weeks, and it will likely take longer than that to reach your core. You should come to Terlingua; I will accept your work on the farm as payment for my services. I think you will be able to travel in two or three days. I will look for you then.

"I am sure the Goddess guided you here for a purpose that I do not understand," she said with a quick smile. Then she turned and left the infirmary, pausing to say farewell to Myla.

Jason leaned back on his bedding. *Guided by the Goddess. I guess I can't argue with that logic, but I don't like thinking that we are all pawns in some divine game. How does having a dragon skin fit any guidance from earlier?*

Xavier reacted to his internal musings: *I am not a pawn—I don't even know what one is, but from your emotion, being one is not good. I reject the idea that I am guided by any being but myself—and you.*

Jason nodded to acknowledge the dragon's contribution, though there was none to watch.

As he fell asleep, his mind wandered to Tovia and Heather. He had met two human women since arriving at Smoky Springs and felt attracted to each of them. How much was due to the long interval since he last had spoken with an attractive woman versus natural attraction, he could not say. He had no prospects, so nothing could come of it.

You forgot Akela, Xavier said.

Jason nodded.

The way of the warrior did not prohibit relationships, but Jason had observed that attached men's assessments of risk were biased. He was unsure of the future and what his actions should be. The way did not provide road maps. He sighed and rolled over to sleep. Those were problems for another day.

⚬⚬⚬

Jason could walk short distances the next day without leaning on his staff. When he first tried to walk, Myla fussed over him and complained that he shouldn't push himself so hard. He smiled at her, thanked her, and continued.

The day after, he could walk twice as far without a crutch.

Tovia stopped by to visit, and he asked her if she could hire a cart to take him to Terlingua. They scheduled the journey for the next day.

Jason performed devotions at the statuette early the following day before packing his belongings. He dressed in his leathers and folded the cotton pants and tunic he had worn in the infirmary, leaving them on the bed.

He completed the twenty basic poses of thasiwoda, surprised at how challenging they were. He found Myla and Mi√aela and said his thanks and farewells.

He felt conflicted about leaving. The kaihana had cared for him and endured his rule stretching—made for his benefit, he was sure—and he was sad to be leaving. But he was relieved he could walk unaided—leaning on his staff did not count. He was curious about the kaihana people and their culture, specifically why they were all female at the infirmary. He smiled as he tried to visualize leading a discussion on that question.

He smiled as he recalled his thoughts when entering the infirmary. *Not endured. More like enjoyed.*

He walked slowly to the street to wait for his ride, putting some weight on his staff. Myla walked alongside him, mumbling that he wasn't ready. He responded with variants of "I understand your objections, but this is what I am doing," without irritation toward her doting over him.

A horse-drawn wagon approached with Tovia and a young man sharing its bench seat. Myla waved when they drew close.

CHAPTER 5

Terlingua

Harnessing Mana: Rituals versus Raw Power
Master Itara
Damocles Academy of Magic

Mana control is a skill coveted by both trained wizards and those without inherent magical talent. Rituals are a common tool the general population use to tap into this power, particularly during social events, such as weddings, coronations, and trials.

Some rituals, especially those involving runes, allow people with little magical power to activate a predesigned pattern created by a more powerful mage. Think of them as shortcuts embedded within social traditions. For example, a coronation ritual might activate beneficial magic for the newly crowned ruler.

However, there's a catch. Rituals, especially when used by the uneducated, can be unpredictable. People with limited knowledge might combine different rites without fully understanding their effects. This results in a lot of trial and error, with meaningless gestures becoming mistakenly revered as sacred. Even worse, someone's mishandling of rituals might accidentally undo the intended effects of a previous ceremony.

This is why your teachers discourage you from relying on rituals, including specific hand gestures, to learn spells. While they might appear to make spell-casting easier, especially for complex magic, they're ultimately crutches. Depending on rituals as you learn hinders your growth and control over mana.

The young man driving the wagon had black hair and was either beardless or clean-shaven. He had broad shoulders and wore a plain tunic; Jason concluded he was not a Defender.

"Greetings, Tovia," Jason called out.

She waved and yelled, "Greetings, Jason, man of mystery! I see you are ready. I wasn't sure you could walk out here unaided; Myla would not have left your side if you were not able to."

The wagon stopped, and Tovia continued. "This is Tiernan. He is a journeyman blacksmith and has some business at Terlingua, and he agreed to take you for no fee."

She hopped down and leaned into Jason for a hug. It surprised him, and he stiffened before relaxing and returning the hug.

"I will be at Terlingua later today to see that all is well with you there," she said as she released him and stepped back.

She picked up Jason's pack and set it in the back of the wagon, which was empty save for a firkin—about nine gallons of water—and offered him a hand up, which he accepted. When he was seated, she handed him his staff.

Jason extended a hand to Tiernan. "Well met, young smith; I am Jason, archer and traveler."

Tiernan looked at Jason's hand momentarily before taking it in his grasp. The smith's hands were strong, but he did not squeeze harder than needed for an introduction.

"Yah. Tiernan I am. Drive you to Terlingua this day I shall." He waved at Tovia and clucked at the horse, which proceeded ahead, nickering a little.

Jason made a few attempts to start a conversation with the smith but soon gave up and paid attention to the road and the surrounding countryside.

After about two hours, Tiernan stopped the wagon in the shade of a large tree, filled his hat with water from the firkin, and held it for the horse.

A man who cares for his animal, Jason thought with approval.

As the wagon neared Terlingua two hours later, Jason saw the tree. From a distance, it blended into the forest, but from closer, its great height separated it from the background.

One tree. It looked like a small forest from this distance, but he knew it was a single tree. Its branches spanned nearly fifty yards, and its height exceeded 100 feet. Jason sensed the tree's age—at least five times a human's—from a mile away, farther than any other tree had affected him.

The tree summoned his attention, as nothing had since he was given the kalasha. It whispered to him—but not in words—of passing years, summers and winters, birds nesting in its branches, and squirrels scampering up and down its trunk.

No tree had spoken to him since his childhood. Acacia, the solitary arboreal who lived near South Haven, had tutored him in forestry. He smiled at the memories of her gentle guidance in identifying plants, including those to avoid and those eaten by different animals; recognizing signs of recent animal activity; and leaving little evidence of his passage. Her home was near an ancient tree, and she'd taught him to listen to the unspoken speech of trees. He wondered if this was a sign he had reached his new home.

The tree's leaves were deep green and danced in the breeze. They shimmered and sparkled in the sunlight.

The road to Terlingua ran almost due west to the farm's entrance. The road curved a quarter circle clockwise, leading to Terlingua's gate. The barrier swung open as they approached, allowing the wagon to enter. A kaihana operated the gate. Jason noticed Tiernan stiffen slightly and grit his teeth when she—he wasn't sure it was female, but Galaad's comment had indicated males were rare—came into view.

The roadway from the gate continued 200 yards straight to a large barn, but a curved driveway opened on the left, leading to the main house about 120 feet from the gate. Fruit trees occupied the space on the right of the pathway, extending as far as he could see.

The carriageway continued curving past the house, forming an oval drive leading back to the entryway. The twenty-by-fifty-foot center ellipse held an herb and flower garden currently being weeded, deadheaded, and harvested by half a dozen human and kaihana women.

Tiernan stopped the wagon at the front porch of a three-story building. A round turret stood at the left side of the house. A covered front porch with a white railing fronted the house, circling the turret. Steps from the porch to the ground were at each end and at the center.

The house was painted a light brownish maroon, while a bright green colored the doors, shutters, and trim.

A kaihana and a human child ran from behind the house toward the wagon.

Tiernan's face and neck reddened slightly before he took a deep breath. He looked at Jason. "Deliver you here I did." He lowered his voice to a mumble. "Kaihana with men mix. Wrong it is." He shook his head before climbing down and helping Jason down from the wagon.

Jason thought, *He's the first person I've heard express prejudice against the kaihana. I'm curious how common this feeling is. Everyone else I've talked to seems to accept them without issue. I can't figure out why he's so hostile.*

As Tiernan retrieved Jason's pack, the door to the main house opened. Heather came out, accompanied by two women and one kaihana.

"Greetings, Jason and Tiernan." Heather looked at Jason carefully. "You are recovering quickly. I didn't expect to see you for another day or two. I will examine you later. This is Maliyah," she said as she extended one hand to the kaihana's arm. "She will take you to your room and show you around if you are not too tired." Turning to Tiernan, she added, "Let us go to my office to discuss Terlingua's needs in iron."

Maliyah smiled at Jason, shook his hand, picked up his pack, and said, "Come with me, Beuman√."

The kaihana was slightly taller than Myla at about five inches above five feet. Her fur was a darker tan than Myla's. Her skin was about the same shade of brown, and her eyes were a piercing brown.

She stood tall with open shoulders, looked Jason in the eye, and let her gaze flow over him. She gave a slight nod as though approving. Her eyes were wide open, bright, and twinkling as though at a private joke.

She bounced slightly on the balls of her feet, a seeming bundle of energy waiting to be released.

"My name is Jason."

Maliyah stopped bouncing and looked at Jason for a moment. "Chaysson, please come with me."

"Why did you call me Beuman-click?"

Maliyah paused. "Because you are the Beuman√, and the sound is a cluck with the back of your tongue." She continued walking away from the main house.

He walked as fast as he could to catch up. "What does *Beuman-click* mean?"

She stopped and turned to face him. "I said what I should nah say." She shook her head. "An older one must tell you. √ has not so much loud."

"Beuman√," he said. "Better?"

She nodded. "I speak about this no more."

"Tell me of this ancient tree," he said, gesturing toward the massive growth.

She stopped and studied him for a moment. "Come. I will introduce you to the Grandfather Tree. He is the oldest tree between the river and the cliffs."

They walked forty yards to the drip line of the immense tree, following a path that started parallel to the driveway before turning south. Jason sat and removed his boots. He crouched and spread his hands on the soil until he felt chi begin to flow on his palms and soles. A minute passed before he felt the peace of listening to the woodland titan.

Jason closed his eyes and listened to the wind rustling through the giant leaves. He could smell leaf mold and a slight perfume from milkweed and a few other blossoms. Bees circled the open flowers beneath the tree.

He felt the cool breeze on his face. Opening his eyes, he saw an arboreal about thirty feet away, tending the wild plants beneath the tree's canopy. The arboreal looked about three feet tall—average, from what Jason knew of them. This one had curly blond hair escaping beneath a wide-brimmed hat. He could not tell gender or any facial features at the distance separating them.

"Defender Clowers told me that arboreals lived in the valley. This is the first one I have seen since I was about ten. No wonder this tree is so magnificent. I did not know arboreals dwelled with just one tree to tend," he whispered.

Maliyah studied his face for a moment. "Not many know of arboreals, and they seldom let strangers see them. They tend the Grandfather Tree, several smaller amboyna trees twenty yards away at the forest edge, and our fruit trees. Let me know when you are ready to continue."

Jason watched the birds, the squirrels, and the lone arboreal for a few minutes, basking in the peace of nature. He sighed and then turned to the kaihana. "I am finished here. For now." He donned his boots.

They returned along the path they had taken from the main house. When they reached the back corner, the path split, with one branch continuing past the farmhouse and the other leading between a large, plain building and a formal garden the width of the house.

Maliyah gestured with one hand toward the building. "Here are apartments for families; the building surrounds a play area. Beyond are the dormitories where the single women live." She indicated a separate building on the opposite side of the greenery, extending from beyond the apartments and partway along the garden's edge. "After we pass the garden, we will reach the dining hall."

They walked between the garden and the house, stopping about midway.

"As you see, the garden has a central fountain and paths lined with flowering bushes spiraling out to the edges."

Jason saw benches set along the path. "Is this a meeting place too?" he asked.

Maliyah nodded. "This is where we meet for full-moon celebrations when the weather permits. The Chapel to the Lady is off the right corner, and we meet there when it's too cold or wet outside." She pointed beyond the building identified as the dining hall. She turned and indicated the large porch at the back of the house. "And this is where Lady Heather leads the congregation."

The porch extended back from the garden almost ten feet, with the last four covered by an awning projecting from the house.

Jason turned as she indicated buildings and directions. "How many live here?" he asked.

"About a hundred live at Terlingua right now. About half are adult women without children, about one-third are women with small children, and about one-quarter are young men and women not ready to go out on their own."

"How many are kaihana?"

She hesitated and stiffened a little. "Less than a third of the residents are kaihana," she said.

"Oh," Jason said, recalling Tiernan's body language. "I just spent three days under the care of kaihana; I admire what I know of you. I look forward to learning your language, your customs, and what you share about your religion with outsiders."

She smiled, and some tension faded from her posture.

"Forgive me, but I have walked almost thrice as far as yesterday, and I would like to rest now," Jason said.

"Oh, let me take you directly to your room. I would have taken you there first had you not asked about Grandfather Tree," Maliyah said.

"Where are my assigned quarters?"

"Out there, near the barn." She gestured almost due north.

She led him past the house to the dining room and the kitchen on their left and the kitchen garden on their right and then to the barn.

She indicated a lean-to on the side. "Here, in a waterproof shed. It is not airtight, so the winter nights may be cold."

The entrance to the room faced away from the farm and was almost a quarter mile from the entrance gate.

"I am ready for cold nights, though cold days disturb me," Jason replied.

Maliyah threw her head back with her eyes closed and her mouth wide open, making almost no sound. Jason realized she was laughing.

"Here is your place for your stay here," she said, opening the door to the lean-to, which rested against a porch roof jutting from the barn. She set his pack down inside the room.

He saw a cot against the inner wall and shelves along the outer wall. A shelf in the corner farthest from the door was a perfect niche for his icon, which he placed there.

Jason looked around the room. The door opened to an unobstructed path into the forest northwest of Terlingua. Xavier, watching through his eyes, noticed the short distance to the wildness and began champing at Jason's resistance to running and changing that instant.

"This is a delightful accommodation. I will rest awhile. Where shall I find you to continue my tour?"

"I am glad you find it suitable." Maliyah smiled. "When you are refreshed, come to the main house, and we can resume." She walked back toward the main house.

Jason started unpacking and storing his belongings. After a few minutes, he looked out his doorway. Finding no sign of anyone, he shuffled across the twenty yards of grass and rocks that separated the barn from the forest as quickly as he could. Once inside a few paces, he stopped and surveyed his surroundings before undressing and allowing Xavier to emerge.

Not a good space for flying, Xavier said as he stretched. *At least there is enough space among the trees to run.*

The dragon carefully folded his wings so they stood straight up and back along his body. He started trotting through the trees, gaining speed until Jason was sure they would crash headlong into each tree that flashed by. He felt the exhilaration of racing horses; he enjoyed the cross-country ride more than flying.

Xavier ran for several minutes before entering a small clearing. A group of large flightless birds scattered, screeching at the dragon's sudden appearance. He snagged one in his jaws and another in one forefoot. He sprayed them with venom and swallowed them once the flames subsided.

The dragon sat after his meal and surveyed the forest.

Xavier, Akela said we would share talents. I can create a spark, slow and accelerate a fire, and feel chi through my feet. Your flying and fire require wings and venom glands; I suspect I won't learn those two from you. Have you tried any of my talents? I am curious about which of our strengths are shared.

Xavier tried half a dozen times, each without success. *Jason, why don't you try controlling the fire as I spray venom?*

Jason successfully slowed down the burning of a small stream of venom. Xavier spat a second time, and Jason slowed it at first and then accelerated it.

A blinding white flash of light and a fwoosh resulted.

Xavier crouched and blinked several times. *Well, that worked. Perhaps too well. Assuming my blindness is temporary, we must look away or close our eyes when you improve on my fire.*

Jason could only see through Xavier's eyes and was also blinded. *Perhaps changing skins back will speed up our recovery.*

Xavier's vision began clearing. *I will return to Terlingua. We will find out how well your recovery has gone and hope for similar outcomes for my vision,* he said.

Before we go, please start a fire. I will accelerate and slow. Tell me if your heat sight shows a change, Jason said.

Xavier did so, and they discovered he could see more or less brightness as a fire was accelerated or slowed.

He retraced his steps to their shift point. *Jason, I will need a place to sleep and molt. Soon.*

Molt? I know little about dragons. What happens? Jason asked.

We are reptiles, like lizards and snakes. We shed our outer skin, Xavier said.

How often will you shed? Jason asked.

I do not know. We ate the deer—was it five days ago? I will shed as I grow, Xavier answered.

And you don't know how often that will be? Jason asked.

True.

Well, Jason said, *I have a lot to learn about dragons, and shedding will be a new experience for me.*

Jason dressed and started walking back to his room without leaning on his staff. He felt neither unbalanced nor any shortness of breath. He kept walking faster as he completed the short journey, jogging when he reached his room.

A shift in our skin improves healing; I hope we seldom need to rely on this effect.

⸺ ❧ ⸺

Jason exited his room and circled north around the barn. To the east of the barn, he saw animal pens and a hay barn. He carried his staff without leaning on it as he walked to the main house, approaching it from the north this time. As he approached the building, he saw Tiernan climbing onto his wagon seat.

The smith looked at Jason. "I know not how you can stay here. Things for you work out, I hope," he said as he started his wagon.

Jason watched him leave and shook his head in frustration. He looked up and saw a large spectacled hawk fly toward the dormitories. *Is that Tovia's hawk skin?* He walked to the eastern corner of the house, a spot with a view of the housing, in case it was.

While waiting, he considered how to respond to Tiernan's apparent prejudice against the kaihana. He recalled how little he knew of the city's residents, having met fewer than a dozen, most of whom were Defenders. Was it important to share his observations with Heather? If so, how should he broach the subject?

Tovia called out to him and ran to join him, skipping during her short trip. She embraced him again. "How was your trip? Have you settled in? Where are you staying?"

She grabbed his free arm and walked with him. "You aren't using your staff to walk; you needed it this morning. Has Heather already treated you?"

"Hello, Tovia. I don't know which question to answer first." He found her enthusiasm infectious and chuckled. "The trip was fine. I settled next to the barn. I am feeling much better already. The air at Terlingua must be special.

"I think I saw your hawk arrive a few minutes ago. Surely you didn't fly here just to check on me."

"I live here, silly!" She giggled. "I have a bunk in town for days I am on duty. My mom and little sister live here full-time."

"How well do you know Tiernan?"

She stopped suddenly and stared at him with wide eyes. "He moved here about a moon ago. Conchobar, our current smith, cannot keep up with the work and won't take another apprentice. He wrote to their guild, and they sent Tiernan to open a second smithy.

"That is all I know of him. Why?"

"Defender Clowers said dwarves lived here; how can there be a shortage of smiths?"

She laughed. "The brown dwarves live here. They are stonecutters and masons, not miners and smiths. Conchobar is a dwarf, but none of his kinsmen smiths live here. Why are you asking about Tiernan?"

"He said a few things that I found troubling. He seems to think associating with the kaihana is somehow inappropriate," Jason replied.

"He will find few, if any, who will agree with that. The kaihana are an integral part of this valley," Tovia said.

Maliyah called out from the front door a few minutes later. She and Tovia completed his tour of the farmstead's main buildings: the kitchens, dining room, chapel, smokehouse, and bathing facilities.

Outbuildings for tools and other equipment were located near their point of use, and he would discover them as needed while working on the farm.

After the tour, Maliyah escorted Jason to the main house to meet with Heather.

Elani greeted Jason at the door and escorted him to Heather's office and consulting room.

The office consisted of a single small room with a heavy wooden desk. One padded chair was behind the desk, and two wooden chairs sat in front of the desk. One wall had a window, and sunlight peeked through thin curtains, casting shadows on the worn wooden floor. A few glowstone lamps sat on the desk for light when the sun was insufficient. One wall contained bookshelves, and most of the books looked well worn.

The air was heavy with the scent of herbs, with a vinegar-like background.

A ledger or record book lay open on the desk, with an inkwell and pen set for a right-handed person's use.

Jason took one of the wooden chairs and waited.

It wasn't long before Heather entered the room. He stood and bowed slightly; she smiled and extended her right hand. He shook her hand.

She looked at Jason carefully. "You are recovering quickly. I didn't expect to see you for another day or two." She went to her chair and sat.

"I am feeling much better," he said.

"How are your accommodations?" she asked.

He laughed. "Before my time at the Defenders' infirmary, I spent sixteen days sleeping beneath the stars with a blanket for mattress and cover. The cot in my room will be much more comfortable than the ground. And the roof, Maliyah assures me, will keep the rain out. My quarters are spacious and near the forest. I find them excellent."

"I am glad to hear that. Do you have any questions or concerns before I examine you?"

"I'm a little concerned that the farm is close to the wildness and some distance from the town and the Defenders," Jason said. "I do not know how the farm is protected from bandits. I saw only Tovia here, and one Defender won't do much against a dozen men."

Heather looked at him as though appraising. "Defender Clowers told me you were a soldier. Your concerns are those of an experienced fighter. I shall introduce you to MacTíre," she said after a moment. "Please follow me. He is found between your room and the forest."

"I did not see anything there during my tour," he said.

She chuckled. "Not all is above ground."

He gave her a questioning look.

"All will be clear soon," she said. "Follow me."

She led him to a fifteen-by-twenty-foot grass-covered hillock about one hundred feet north of his room and nearer the forest. A gravel-lined path led to the north end and down a trench to a door. The mound extended ten feet above ground level at the entryway.

When Heather opened the door, a blast of chilled air struck Jason in the face. The outer chamber smelled of damp soil and compost.

The door opened into an entryway with a second door to the interior.

"Is this an icehouse?" asked Jason as they stepped through the first door.

"Yes. It is also where MacTíre is found."

Opening the second door revealed the interior of the icehouse. It smelled faintly of damp soil and raw meat.

As they stepped in and closed the inner door, twinkling multicolored lights suddenly broke the darkness. A voice from all directions said, "Why, Lady Moonstar! What a pleasant surprise to see you today! And you bring a new one."

"Hello, MacTíre. This is Jason. He will live in Terlingua for some time and needs to learn about our alarm system. Jason, this is MacTíre, a major fae."

Jason tried not to let the sudden lights and directionless voice affect him. Having a fae as an ally discomfited him; they were not known as trustworthy. Hearing a disembodied voice added to his unease. The fae were rumored to take multiple forms, but he had yet to hear about one with no form. He felt an urge to spin around and look for the source but managed to keep it under control.

"When someone whom MacTíre does not know crosses the boundary of Terlingua save through the gate, he raises the alarm for all, here and at Defender headquarters," Heather said.

"I allowed Jason back in after his short time in the wildness earlier today." The voice sounded all around.

Heather turned to face Jason with her eyes widening and mouth agape.

The music changed to a melancholy tune. "Jason is but one of your names."

"Jason is the name I use at this time."

"Excellent! However, if each of your forms wishes to enter and leave without raising the alarm, your other name I must know," the directionless voice said.

Heather spoke up. "What does MacTíre mean, Jason?"

"Why do you think I have another name?" Jason turned slowly as he spoke, directing his speech to the room.

"A nonanswer, but it teaches me something about you. You do not wish to state an untruth, so you deflect. Your aura has two parts," the voice answered.

Jason felt Xavier's awareness within.

"Now your aura is separating slightly. You have two forms and two names."

"Yes, I have two names. I learned that I am two-skinned about five days ago. We wish to keep my second skin, which is rare, hidden. I am concerned about his identity raising old fears and about hunters believing old tales, which could result in us being stalked."

"Your caution is well advised. Tell me anyway," the voice insisted.

"His name is Xavier," Jason said through gritted teeth.

Heather glanced at him sideways; her forehead wrinkled. "I did not know you had two skins. Well, this is interesting! Two-skinned seldom wield magic to any degree! Does Iudgual know?"

"No, I left her before I learned of my second skin," Jason said.

"And your other form?" The voice persisted.

Jason reacted to the surround sound this time, turning his head side to side but not seeing anything. He said, "I am not sure I should trust you. And I admit I'm unfairly branding you with stories of the fae's trustworthiness."

"Even better! A man who introspects! Trust me or not, but if you do not, when your other skin tries to enter, those within will hear this."

A clarion sounded, and a gong belled in the room, causing the two humans to jump.

"It is loud enough to wake any within the farmstead and everyone in the Defenders' barracks," the voice said.

Jason paused momentarily and swallowed. "I suppose I must." He took a deep breath, let it out slowly, and then looked at Heather. "Xavier is a dragon—a fire dragon. I hope we can keep this between us."

Heather gasped. "Dragons haven't been seen in Rutendo for over two. Hundred. Years!"

"*A dragon improves Terlingua's defenses more than any other entity, save perhaps another major fae. What brings you to Terlingua, Jason Xavier?*" MacTíre asked.

Jason took another deep breath. "The short story is that a mage I know as Grandmother sent me here for Heather to help me tap my core magic."

"*Ah! Yes, the candlelight you show versus the inferno within needs correcting. When Lady Heather succeeds, come again for instruction on patterns and symmetries with mana.*"

The twinkling lights went out, leaving the two humans in the icehouse's silent darkness.

As they exited the icehouse, Jason said, "Well, that was a lot to take in."

"Yes, it was. I learned quite a bit today too." She nodded as she spoke. "We will take a more direct route back to my examination room. It is almost a straight line back to the house."

"Well, lead the way."

Jason was quiet for several minutes as he followed Heather to the main house. The meeting with the fae both troubled and intrigued him. Here he was, allied with a major fae who had identified his two-skinned nature and pried his dragon's name loose. MacTíre was an astute interviewer and a critical observer of events on the farm—a dangerous enemy for sure.

Two more now knew of his second skin. His resolve to keep the dragon hidden was crumbling. Heather might have learned eventually as she helped him reach his magic core, but this felt different. He disliked yielding the information under the threat of the alarm.

Akela had mentioned other two-skinned beings having only one name. How, then, did MacTíre know he had two? The aura explained his knowledge of two skins but not names. Why would the fae need both names to allow him in and out without alarm? He had no answers.

And yet another mystery: no one had discovered any magical potential during the war, or else he would have been recruited by the battle mages. And now two—MacTíre and Iudgual—had identified it, or said they had, within minutes. Were they both wrong? Or right? He would act as though they were right and hope for success at Terlingua.

Jason was relieved that MacTíre provided an alarm system, easing his concerns about the farm's safety. But with the fae's reputation for trickery, could Terlingua rely on it? Basing a conclusion on tales with no actual evidence wasn't the warrior's way. He had to distrust his initial reaction until he had more data.

But why did MacTíre provide the alarm service? Could he trust this fae based on Heather's acceptance? He would have to.

He was determined to learn more about his magic while suspicious of the fae's offer to teach. Was there a hidden trap in this offer?

He resolved to trust MacTíre while keeping a watchful eye for any subterfuge. He decided he would accept the offer to learn from the fae—a significant step in his journey. He smiled. In for a penny, in for a pound.

<hr />

From the sidhe, they walked a more direct route to the house. It took them past the animal pens and between the barn and a hay barn. Ahead on their left, Jason could see the orchard he had noticed when Tiernan's wagon entered Terlingua. A few steps later, the driveway to the garage from the gate appeared on their right.

Heather walked alongside Jason without speaking. He thought, *Perhaps she expected the visit to affect me. Knowing what I do, I would expect it to affect me.*

He broke the silence. "Do you know MacTíre's form?"

"No," she replied. "He always appears as the twinkling lights. Why do you want to know?"

"I don't know. Perhaps I want to know as much about him as he does about me. I did not ask him because I did not want to offend him. I have heard tales of small slights or missteps leading to an overwhelming response."

They walked a little longer.

"Why does a major fae live in your icehouse?" he asked.

Heather stopped and turned toward him. "I do not know," she said slowly. "I am not sure he lives there, but that is where I go when I want to talk with him. I think this is another question—like 'What is his form?'—he might object to."

He turned and looked at the mound near the forest. "A small hill. And a fae lives within it. Is this a gate to the fae realm? A sidhe?"

"Not that I know," she answered.

"Maliyah called me Beuman√ at first. She would not say more when I told her my name; she said an older one should tell me. What does Beuman√ mean?" Jason asked.

Heather looked startled. "I do not know that word. I think it has to do with a fire or burning. The kaihana have their legends and prophecies, both great and small; perhaps one of those mentions Beuman√.

"Among kaihana, age is equated with wisdom, and each defers to those older than she is, though as they get older, their comparisons shift from days to months up to decades."

She paused. "Maliyah is seventy-five and one of the oldest living at Terlingua; for her to defer to an elder means she inadvertently said something about one of their greater legends. I wonder what it is."

"She is seventy-five years old? That is amazing! I would have guessed our ages were closer."

"The kaihana have long lives. I have been told that their Council of Elders are all 300 or older."

"You refer to kaihana as though they are all female. That doesn't seem possible," Jason said.

Heather thought for a moment. "All who reside at Terlingua are female except you. I am not sure I have seen a male kaihana. Their main home is some twenty miles from here, near Upper Lake. The males stay there, out of sight. They do not share the reason."

Jason and Heather entered the main house, and she escorted him to her examination room.

A glowstone lamp on an interior wall cast long shadows across the examination room. The air was heavy with the scent of disinfectant—a mix of vinegar, alcohol, and chlorine—and herbal aromas. A worn burgundy rug covered most of the wooden floorboards, whose age was evident in the creaks and groans that accompanied his every step.

A plain wooden examination table dominated the room. Its dark varnish gleamed faintly in the glowstone light. Beside it stood a mahogany washstand with a chipped porcelain basin above a drain and a valve Jason recognized as water control from his time at the Defenders' infirmary.

Anatomical charts hung on one wall, depicting the human and kaihana bodies in stark detail.

A glass-doored cabinet along one wall displayed an array of gleaming medical instruments—scalpels, saws, and others. Their purposes were both mysterious and intimidating.

Dried herbs and jars filled with colorful medicinal tinctures lined shelves on both sides of the window. A bowl of potpourri with strong scents sat alongside the washbasin.

Scattered around the room were three simple chairs with upholstery in a faded floral pattern.

Heather directed him to lie down on the table, where she repeated the exam from the infirmary with an additional heart monitor. She used a trumpet-shaped metal device from a cabinet, placing the wide end on his chest and touching the small end to her ear.

"What is this thing?" he asked.

"It magnifies the sound of your heart. I can hear more detail than with my ear alone. Now, be quiet!"

After a few minutes, she looked at him and said, "Your heart is much stronger today. I can feel it in your pulse and detect nothing unusual using the horn."

She shrugged. "I would doubt another healer telling me of such a rapid recovery from a damaged heart. Congratulations on your healing. Now let us discuss your stay at Terlingua.

"There are few agreements among us at Terlingua. First, we expect all to help around the farm in whatever capacity they can; small children excepted. This should not be news to you, who lived in South Haven." She smiled at him. "Second, we have monthly gatherings to discuss happenings on the farm. Some decisions are made then, and some are made by a smaller council. The farm rests on kaihana territory and does not have an owner with bond servants you see in other farms. You are invited to attend and participate."

"The priestesses of the Triple Goddess ran South Haven," Jason said. "Under one of them, no one was consulted on anything. The farm was headed to insolvency when I left."

Heather nodded. "We received a letter a tenday ago that you were arriving. At our last council meeting, I was granted the authority to approve your stay with us on a trial basis, which I did in Smoky Springs." Her smile widened. "Welcome to Terlingua; I hope your stay here results in finding your core.

"We celebrate each full moon, as I am sure South Haven did. Participation is voluntary, but residents seldom miss more than a few each year," she added.

She looked away from him before continuing. "Each day, a wagon of fresh produce goes to Sinistrad, the kaihana village, and another goes to Smoky Springs. You have one self-day each tenday and may join either if you wish to journey to town. If you don't ask for a different self-day, yours will be Hathsday, nine days from today. There isn't much for you in Sinistrad. The kaihana are master weavers and potters, and most of their trade is outside the valley."

Looking back at him, she continued. "Maliyah will give you daily tasks and oversee your progress until she learns your knowledge, skill, and workmanship. She will also provide you with cotton clothing, sandals, or shoes for field work; your leathers and boots won't be subjected to the dirt and muck from farming.

"Adults eat in the common room you saw during your tour. If you miss a meal, visit the kitchen. Bread, cheese, and dried fruit are almost always available. If Maliyah did not show you where to look for them when the kitchen staff is absent, I will.

"Finally, your room is some distance from the other living quarters. Young women live here, whom an unscrupulous man might attempt to dishonor. I do not think the Goddess would entrust you with her kalasha if you were of that sort, but the room placement allows us to pretend we can protect our girls. We know we cannot totally protect them."

Jason replied, "I find your conditions reasonable and acceptable. I also hunt and will contribute to the farmstead what I and Xavier find. My room placement allows Xavier to arrive and leave mostly hidden from view. I do not know how long I can keep him hidden; he and I will discuss what to do when we are exposed."

Tell her of my nidus needs, the dragon said to Jason.

"Furthermore, Xavier needs a place to sleep. I am not sure how long each of us needs to sleep in our form, but he will need an enclosed area large enough to house him. It will be better if it is a short walk from the farm than a longer one; he can find his own lair, but someone on the farm surely knows of a few suitable places nearby."

"I will check with Maliyah. She knows the surroundings as well as any living here," Heather replied. "With these understood, there is no better time to begin freeing your magic than now."

"Before we begin, please tell me what to expect as you help me reach my core magic." Jason interrupted, shifting in his seat.

"That is a very reasonable request. I will guide you to relax and free your mind from distractions until you are left with just your inner self. The last fire mage I helped had flames appear on his hands when he reached his core. He was ten and became an average mage. Iudgual's message implied that your inner fire is strong. Your response—I have no idea what it will be. Working with someone your age is uncharted territory for me."

"Let me assure you I have no expectations. Sparks and starting fires from kindling are enough, but I feel I must try since Grand—Iudgual thinks I may be able to do more. I will do as you say and hope for success," Jason said.

"I like your attitude," she said. "Now, show me what you can do with fire."

Jason reached his hands out and concentrated on creating a spark. After four heartbeats, three formed between his hands.

"This is about the extent of what I can do unless I am fighting," he said. "And I can make fires burn faster or slower."

Heather nodded and pursed her lips. "My. A spark can mean either lightning or heat. Controlling the rate at which a fire burns is heat. I am not sure …" Her voice trailed off.

"I have heard several people talk about mana as though it is not one thing. How many forms are there?" he asked.

Heather smiled and replied, "I am not a wizard. I don't know very much. I direct spirit and life when I heal someone. I know that heat and lightning are two other forms. You would need to ask someone who has studied magecraft. Glorinda, for example. She graduated from the Damocles Academy of Magic about ten years ago. Ask her the next time she is in town."

She shook her head slightly. "Now let us begin. The goal is to relax without fear of falling over as you explore your inner self," Heather said.

"You may squat, sit cross-legged, or remain in the chair. Now take three deep, slow breaths, and exhale each fully and slowly.

"Now close your eyes and pay attention to your breath; do not control it, but watch it come in and out your nostrils. Concentrate on your breath, and wait for all else to fade until you feel your center."

Jason looked at her and around the room before saying, "Uh, Lady Heather, I know of these preliminaries. It is what archers call 'entering the void.' It is also how the two-skinned prepare to change. I am sure you would not be happy if I followed your directions and they resulted in my shifting in this room."

"Why is that?"

"As you learned at MacTíre's, my other skin is a dragon; Xavier will not fit in this room should I change." He smiled.

Heather looked at him, scrunching her face to one side. "I suppose I must. There is an area near the barn, next to your room. It is halfway between your door and the icehouse and is secluded from two sides. I don't know of a spot in Terlingua that is better suited to avoid being seen. Shall we adjourn there?"

They exited the house through a side door and descended the short flight of steps Heather suggested, avoiding the main entrance to maintain their privacy.

They strolled past the dining hall and kitchen on their left; the savory smells hinted at the coming dinner. On their right, the kitchen gardens offered a colorful contrast.

Reaching the end of the buildings, they turned north. The ground quickly transitioned into a rough, rocky area. Sparse weeds and stunted plants struggled to find purchase in the shallow soil and around the many stones. This area, unsuitable for farming, gradually gave way to waist-high rocks on their left, which hid the steaming-hot springs and the bathhouse from their view.

After a short walk across the rocky terrain, they arrived at the lean-to where Jason had previously unpacked. The rocky patch continued for a bit farther before surrendering to the encroaching forest. This clearing, bathed in dappled sunlight filtering through the trees overhead, was where Jason had released Xavier earlier. The trees on the farm's property protected them from observation.

"Is this space large enough?" Heather asked.

He chuckled. "Definitely. Xavier and I went deeper into the forest that way"—he pointed west—"and shifted shortly after our arrival. I'm confident we are hidden from view here."

The clearing was isolated: trees blocked lines of sight in two directions, and the barn provided a barrier to the east. The hot springs to the south remained exposed, but any watcher there could be spotted.

When they reached a suitable spot, Jason turned to Heather. "Um. You know, we came here because I might change skins, and I need to undress in case that happens." He blushed.

She turned her back, ensuring his privacy. His last look at her as he turned his back to her was of her turning away. Despite that, he felt as if he were undressing under the gaze of her dazzling blue-gray eyes. It was pure torture—every stolen glance and every rustle of his clothes felt like a limelight on his burning cheeks.

He turned a brighter red and held his breath as he removed his trousers. He folded his clothing and then crouched on his heels, facing away from her, and called out, "I am ready."

He listened for her movement and heard her say, "Me too," and then he began the long, slow breaths Heather wanted.

He reached the void quickly. He saw amorphous lights floating behind his closed eyes.

As before, he felt the sensation of a large room. He moved along the hallway, passing the first intersection and feeling the hot, dry wind. The second smelled like just before a rain.

Stepping into the body shape, he felt the stretching and dissolved into fog.

As Xavier solidified, Heather stepped back and raised a fist to her mouth, astonished and frightened by the dragon's appearance despite the warning. The dragon was larger than she had expected.

Xavier spread his wings and stretched himself as tall as he could. He bugled a soft, joyful sound; turned toward Heather; and spoke mind to mind. *Greetings, Lady Moonstar. I am Xavier, Jason's second skin. We did not believe your parlor would accommodate me.*

She gasped. "I can hear you!"

Yes, I can speak directly to your mind. The dragon seemed amused.

He bowed his neck before her and looked closely at her. *My apologies, blessed one. I just realized whom I was addressing.*

"No one here knows who I am," she said. "Please do not share with others. Will Jason know?"

Jason is not present at the moment. The dissolution as he fades still disorients him. Xavier paused. *It confounds me too, but it takes him longer to get reoriented. I expect these difficulties will resolve over time.*

It seems, Lady Heather, that we each know a secret of the other. I intend to keep yours and ask for the same courtesy.

She nodded her agreement.

Xavier raised his head high above Heather and looked around. *Akela is looking for me. I must go to her now. Ask Jason to tell you the story of Akela; she is important to us.*

Xavier leaped into the air and beat his wings rapidly for a few moments until his flight settled. Then he turned toward the west and disappeared over the forest.

As Heather watched the dragon disappear over the forest to the south, she pondered what it meant to have this two-skinned man-dragon who carried a kalasha at Terlingua. Kalashas were gifts from the Goddess to establish temples in her name. Heather could not remember any temples established by men, with or without the Goddess's token. How would her mother react to the first priest of the Lady? The high priestess was jealous of her position, and she expected a schism would follow.

She could do nothing but speculate, so she shrugged, whispered a prayer, and returned to the main house to see her next patient.

CHAPTER 6

The Dragon and the Wolf Pack

From *Introduction to Magic*
Master Itara
Damocles Academy of Magic

On True Names. Name magic is the least understood magic. This summarizes what we know.

All items in nature have True Names. The First Gods announced the True Names at creation, and knowing the True Name of any item gives you control over it to some degree, depending on the strength of those involved.

Some cultures have adopted the practice of a naming ritual, during which a True Name is tied to a special name given to the child. That particular name acts as a replacement for the True Name for all intents and purposes. We do not know why the rituals developed by these cultures work, nor do we know the origins of these rites.

There are occasional mages who are born intimately connected with True Names. These mages pluck an individual's or artifact's True Name from the First Gods without effort and can use it to effect changes. This ability is rare.

After Maliyah finished showing Jason around Terlingua, she resumed her task for the day: checking the irrigation system.

This morning, her nascent foresight alerted her that Elder Althea's interest was focused this way. She wasn't surprised at the elder's interest after meeting Jason that morning. There was something special about him; she was sure he was the Beuman√. A slight tingle at her forehead meant the time to act on her premonition was now.

Turning, she saw three birds circling Terlingua's main house. In Maliyah's lifetime, Althea always sent three, and three always arrived. Each bird usually had a slightly different message, and a recipient needed two to decipher the elder's intent.

She told the rest of the crew she had business at the house and to continue without her.

Upon arriving at the house, she retrieved the messages and read them. All three were variations of "You are needed at Sinistrad now"—a change from the elder's habit.

Something must be amiss.

This was the first time the elder had summoned her. The usual messages were requests for action or to schedule a visit, but those had never been commands.

Why does the elder want me? Information about Jason is not urgent, she thought.

Maliyah picked up the overnight pack she had prepared after her premonition in case a trip was warranted and left the house.

As she exited, she found Tovia holding the reins of a goat cart with two wethers—neutered male goats—already harnessed.

"Greetings, Maliyah! I saw the three birds circling and figured you would be leaving soon. I hope this cart will serve."

"My, your interpretation of the birds was more clear than my time-walking this morning. Thank you very much!"

As Maliyah mounted the driver's seat, Tovia said, "Enjoy your trip to Sinistrad!"

The road from Smoky Springs headed northeast into Sinistrad's town square, where two other roads met. One ran parallel to the cliffs, and the other led east toward Lion's Tooth Canyon.

The fourth side of the quadrangle was a sixty-foot-wide, thirty-foot-high archway leading into a cave flanked by two ancient trees whose branches intertwined overhead. The concourse outside the cave was lined by brick buildings, each sporting a cloth-covered area for displaying wares. Today no merchants had set up for trade.

The first thing Maliyah saw as she approached Sinistrad was the line of cliffs behind the village. She could barely distinguish the top row of entries carved into the sheer rock face.

As she drove past the buildings and small farms along the road from Terlingua, she saw black lace mourning cloths adorning the lintels of the buildings and cottages. Her time-walk before first light had given her no indication of the disaster these displays indicated, and a shiver ran up her spine. The village was silent as she drove to the town square.

It was a strange and imposing sight: brick cottages clustered around a central cavern, while shadowy cave openings dotted the rock face higher up.

Wailing and keening came from within the cavern.

Driving the cart into the cave, she recognized the bent form of Elder Althea sitting near the entrance. The elder's fur was almost white, and she wore a colorful wrap embroidered with a geometric design. Four guards surrounded her, maintaining a safe zone around her. The guards loomed over the elder, each wearing white armor and armed with a sword, buckler, and short spear. They parted as Maliyah set the cart's brake, creating a path to Althea.

Maliyah's heart pounded as she climbed down from the seat. She nervously wiped her hands on her skirt. Her eyes darted around the cavern, avoiding the elder's gaze, before she prostrated before the elder. "I came as soon as I read your message," she said. Her voice trembled slightly. She seldom spoke to Althea, and the difference in their status made her uneasy.

"Elder Gabrielle died in her sleep last night," Althea said in a deep, resonant voice. "Neither the Council of Elders nor the Circle of Seeing saw that coming. The eldest sits in her room, rocking and keening. Walk with me."

Maliyah stared with wide eyes and an open mouth, unable to speak. She shifted her weight from foot to foot as her eyes darted around. Her breathing was rapid and shallow, and a bead of sweat trickled down her temple.

Althea smiled gently and held a hand out for Maliyah to hold. In a soft voice, she said, "Come, girl; there is no need to be afraid. I know your sight is waking; I must know what you saw or felt, or fear is coming. The early sight has the clearest view of near events, and yours won't be blinded by what happened here."

Maliyah scrambled to her feet and walked alongside the elder. The four guards took their positions: two ahead and two behind. Their heads swiveled constantly to see any approaching threat.

It took her several moments to work enough moisture in her mouth to speak with the elder. She drew a shuddering breath and said in a quavering voice, "I saw the Beuman√ this morning."

Althea stopped suddenly, turned, and stared into the younger one's face. She blinked slowly and clutched her wrap to her chest. "Are you certain?"

"Yes. I saw flames surrounding him with my inner sight, rising from his body and reentering it during my time-walk before dawn. A few hours later, when I first saw him, I recognized the man immediately. I erred and called him the Beuman√ without thinking."

Althea looked at the ground and slowly shook her head. "I should have—" She stopped. With a cracking voice, she continued. "I should have suspected. I should have known."

She sat on the ground and looked around the village. "Tell no one else. I will summon the circle, and we will try to determine how long we have before we can no longer foresee." She took a breath. "We will endure. We will be blind to our future for a while. This has happened before and will happen again.

"Tomorrow, Maliyah, you must drive your cart to Ognyen. Take a dozen wicker baskets with you. You will meet Heather and help her harvest the medicinal plants there.

"Now I must be alone. No, I must rouse the eldest."

She stopped talking suddenly and looked at Maliyah. "I told your mother you were coming tonight; she has a place prepared for you." She turned from Maliyah and walked away with her guards circling about her like moons.

Maliyah stood near the center of Sinistrad for several minutes, calming herself before going to her mother's apartment.

Dragons found what they sought. Xavier located Akela as Yiska, padding through the forest with two other wolves. He bugled a greeting and sprayed some venom into the air to get her attention. He circled until he was sure she had seen him. He sighted a bare hilltop a few miles away and flew toward it.

The dragon spotted a yearling boar as he flew to the bluff. Swooping down, he killed, flamed, and swallowed the animal before continuing to the summit. Landing on the rock mound covered partly in lichen and short grass, he settled down to wait for the wolves.

The three wolves trotted from the forest onto the hilltop. He noticed that two carried packs on their backs. Akela he knew from her coloring: a mix of orange and brown. The other wolves were mixed gray and white and mixed black and brown. Akela started to shift, and Xavier turned to face away, protecting his human self from viewing the unclothed women. After a few moments, Akela told him it was safe to turn around.

He saw three women in simple dresses and two empty packs on the ground next to them. *She brought clothing for them to avoid embarrassing Jason after I shift*, he realized.

Akela's hair was reddish brown. One of the other women had silver-white hair and hazel eyes. The last had dark brown hair and brown eyes.

Akela brought Xavier a loincloth, saying, "You might be more at ease among us wearing this."

Xavier nodded politely to Akela and turned away as he shifted. Once Jason donned the loincloth, he turned to face the three.

"Well met, Akela," he said. "Xavier heard you call; how can we help you today?"

"These are two former pack mates of mine," Akela replied, dispensing with small talk. "Since you freed me from Yeruslan's True Name binding, we wish you to free them too. I won't introduce them now, hoping you are successful."

Jason stared at her for a while. "Akela, I do not know how I did that. I would be glad to help if I knew how."

The platinum blonde spoke. "We would be grateful if you could help us by freeing us from his name binding. If you cannot change our True Names, we have a proposal: join us to form a new pack."

Jason's jaw dropped, "A human-dragon in a wolf pack? Is that even possible?"

The brown-haired woman spoke. "We are almost certain the ritual to form a pack will work if you join us. The minimum number is four—usually, two mated pairs when that small. At least one male and two females must participate in the ritual.

"Groups often break away from a pack to form a new one. Usually, a strong member who chafes under a leader but is not strong enough to wrest control will recruit others. They separate from the troop and establish a new territory a distance away but sometimes overlapping with their former group's."

Jason was not convinced. "What would the pack dynamics be with just four members? And what role do you expect of me? I know nothing of belonging to a pack."

"We know you've never been in a wolf pack, but we believe you could thrive in one. We can offer you companionship, support, and a sense of belonging. Each of us has two skins and can understand some of what you are going through in learning about yours. We were born two-skinned, while you have known you are for a handful of days," Akela said.

"Having two skins is indeed different," Jason said, hearing a snort from his dragon.

He sat in thought for a few minutes. "Forming a pack will not free you from a True Name binding since it isn't affected by belonging to a group. At best, it might make it easier to resist his True Name commands.

"Renaming each of you is likely the only way to achieve that. Akela and I shared a meal, a shelter, and a battle before I gave her a new True Name; I know not how or why I could rename her."

"Perhaps we have not spent enough time together for you to learn our True Names," Akela said.

"How would belonging to a pack affect me?" he asked.

The brunette spoke up. "I will start with some cautions about pack life. We were in a dysfunctional pack, with Yeruslan usurping the role of pack leader and abusing his power over the pack. Before he did that, there was some infighting and strife as the prior leader aged and became too weak to lead. That is always a risk in a pack."

She rubbed her chin for a moment. "And over time, the leader's personality is expressed through the pack. The impact on individuals depends on their strength."

"We have to follow orders we disagree with and sacrifice personal desires for the good of the pack," the blonde added.

Jason raised his eyebrows. "I have been on my own for, uh, fourteen years. I am used to being isolated and, despite my years in the army, being my counsel, doing what I want when I want. I haven't shared my emotions with another for, um, another five before that. It sounds like I may not fit in very well."

"A few wolves always live on the fringe, limiting what they share and how close they stay. I think you will be just fine," the blonde said.

Xavier reminded him, *You have shared with me for years but only became aware of it a few days ago.*

Jason laughed slightly. "My dragon says he shares my emotions, but I did not know this, so I am destined to share mine with others now."

Akela said, "Each of us understands the struggles of being two-skinned and can support you as you learn about your two natures."

"How will others know of my struggles?"

The three women blinked as they exchanged glances.

"Through the pack link," the blonde said slowly, as though explaining to a child.

"How does that work?" he asked. His face showed his curiosity.

"The link connects the pack—think of it like a thread connecting you to each of us, allowing us to be aware of the emotional state of each other. It isn't specific, so I might know you are upset but not why. It provides support but also demands it. If a pack member is distressed, you will feel a need to help. If you are distressed, you share that with everyone in the pack. You forfeit some privacy," the blonde answered.

"Everyone in the pack knows when another is in danger. It takes some effort not to immediately drop everything and provide help if you are within eyesight of the other. That sensation drops with distance," the brown-haired woman said.

"You will find you defend the pack over yourself, which can be unsettling. You were in the war and had to rush into danger, so you likely understand that," Akela said.

"How does the pack link work while hunting or fighting?" he asked.

"It keeps us out of one another's way and gives us indications about what the leader of the hunt intends so we can herd prey to a spot where others of the pack are converging. In a fight, we coordinate like hunting if we are rescuing someone, but otherwise, we fight singly for the group goal," Akela explained.

"I am, um, apprehensive about how close the relationship among us will be. It seems I give up autonomy for some uncertain benefits. How would a pack of four work?"

The four continued to discuss how the pack might work; each woman described situations that arose in a pack and how they wanted the difficulty resolved.

The discussion paused, and Jason asked again, "What would my role in the pack be?"

"Pack leaders are not always male," Akela said. "Does that help?"

The platinum-haired woman suddenly cackled. "He wants to know if he gets to fuck us all if he is the only male in our pack!"

Jason turned crimson and looked away. "That is not what I meant!"

Akela stepped into the conversation. "Among the two-skinned wolves, any individual can initiate a, um, relationship by asking. A refusal is not as absolute as among humans. One can refuse and, sometime later, ask the asker to participate.

"You will not be forced into a match you do not want, and I think Zarya wanted to shock you." She glanced at the blonde, who did not speak.

The brown-haired woman spoke up. "You're right, Jason. A pack of four is small, but it's a start. As for your role, we need a male to form a pack. You fit that bill. You're also a skilled fighter and tracker. Akela says you are an agile thinker, which would help us."

Jason turned toward the brunette. "I know your name. It is as though I had forgotten it and now remember," he said. He felt mana flow over his skin, and the forest became quiet as though waiting with bated breath. "You are named Bright Night Sky. I now name you Moonlight on Still Water, and I will call you Phaedra."

The forest sounds returned. He resisted the urge to scratch when the mana flow stopped.

Phaedra stood and jumped back. "That hurt!" she exclaimed.

"Yes, the name change feels like you are getting slapped from all directions at once," Akela said, nodding in agreement. "Do you still feel the pack link?"

Phaedra looked herself over and replied, "No. It is gone, as is his binding. I am free from that monster Yeruslan!" she exclaimed joyfully.

"How are you feeling, Jason?" Akela asked. "You were low on mana after renaming me."

"I am not as fatigued as with you."

"So perhaps we should just continue as we are until Jason feels up to changing my name," Zarya said. "Perhaps we can form a pack among us. That will establish a pack bond."

"I haven't agreed to that," Jason said.

Phaedra nodded. "While you think about it, let us describe the ritual to you. It isn't complicated."

"No, it is fairly simple. There are four parts to it," said Zarya. "First, we each bring a bit of firewood here. Second, we all walk around the firewood three times and take seats around the fuel. Third, we each light the fire from where we sit; we can share a burning ember. Finally, we repeat together, 'We are a new pack,' until we feel the pack link."

"That seems simple. Is there anything else I need to know before my dragon and I decide?"

"As I said, leaders don't always have to be male. One of us will start as the leader, or we will colead since we know how packs work," Akela said.

Phaedra added, "Another reason is that wolves require a pack to remain sane. We came here wanting to exit ours to separate from Yeruslan. Thank you, by the way, for breaking my name binding. Forming another will let us achieve that goal without going rogue.

"At this point, we have you, one wolf leaving her pack, and two lone wolves. We three women are also plunging into new waters; we have followed a pack leader all our lives. If we succeed, become the leaders responsible for the whole pack's well-being." She glanced at the other two women. "Initially, that will be easy, but it will take more effort when the pack expands."

"Pack expands?" Jason's eyebrows rose.

"We hope and expect to find a dozen more wolves disaffected by Yeruslan who will join us. Changing a pack happens more often than forming a new one."

"I am not sure I know enough to decide, but I must. I will think about it." The three women agreed.

Jason walked a few yards from them. *I wish I had brought my pipe. Smoking seems to help me make decisions.*

But now you have a confidant you lacked. I may not be as effective as your pipeweed, but I am used to listening to you.

Jason laughed out loud, earning quizzical looks from the women.

Jason and Xavier deliberated for several minutes. Xavier was less concerned than Jason about sharing emotions but more concerned about following another's lead in battle. Both were apprehensive about the ritual, since they were not wolves.

The deciding factor was Akela's sanity. They had broken her name and pack bindings without knowing it and condemned her to this fate. Akela had also freed Xavier.

They owed her.

Jason stood and returned to the women. "Akela, I will do this for you. You need a pack, and I took you away from yours. So now each of us walks into the forest and brings back a faggot or two of firewood."

The three women rose, and they headed down from the bald dome on which they sat.

When they were all back, they started the ritual.

After they sat, Jason took several deep breaths to calm his nerves before igniting a handful of twigs and distributing them so each of them could light his or her side of the fire.

The die is cast. Now to survive, the dragon said to him.

Phaedra led them in the repetition part of the ritual. It took several minutes for Jason to feel a link; he looked around the fire but could not tell if the others felt it. He began to feel as if it had not worked, when all three women looked at him and said, "It did not fail," in unison.

Jason closed his eyes. He could sense that the women were all excited and pleased that the pack had formed.

Sitting this close, each connection felt different; he wasn't sure the distinction would remain with distance.

With Akela, the link felt like sitting in a room with a close friend; each knew the other was there, but neither needed conversation to feel in the company of the other. Phaedra's link, however, felt more like sitting with a person he had just met but was not yet comfortable talking with. Zarya's link was like Phaedra's but felt more tenuous, like a spiderweb instead of a rope—a little stretchy and strong but easily breakable.

Turning toward Zarya, he asked, "What does the bond feel like to you?"

"The pack link with Yeruslan is gone," she responded. "I feel his name binding almost as strongly as when he first used it to force me to lie with him."

Jason jumped to his feet. His face flushed red with anger. "He *forced* himself upon you using your True Name! Yeruslan is an abomination and must be stopped." As Jason spoke, mana streamed along his arms and legs from his surroundings, collecting in his chest. His skin tingled from head to toe.

Xavier's ire at a man who would abuse women amplified his anger. For the dragon, it was about protecting kin, even though they had not yet performed the pack ritual.

"I will find him; I will stop him." Jason's voice gained authority and strength.

He paused, and the forest seemed to fall silent as though observing.

Jason turned toward the platinum-haired woman. "You are named Thunder Cloud," he said in a voice that seemed to echo from the mountains.

"You are wise but impetuous; I name you White Owl in the Mist, and I will also call you Zarya."

Zarya cried out in pain.

Jason continued as the sky seemed to darken. "Yeruslan, the jackal who abused you, is named Silver Shadow. I name him Black Bog Scum and strip from him the wolf skin he dishonored!" Jason's voice seemed to reverberate, and mana flowed outward, burning his skin like stinging nettles. "I bind his tongue so that he cannot abuse the True Names he knows." He shouted, "So it must be!"

Four wolves padded along a game trail twenty miles away. The lead wolf stopped, jumped into the air, yelped, and snapped at the air around him. He howled mournfully and shifted to his human skin.

The other three wolves growled, and Yeruslan realized the pack link was broken. He looked at the wolf closest to him, opened his mouth, and could not speak.

The wolves snarled and attacked the man.

In her keep thirty miles to the north, Glorinda felt the name magic flow. She shuddered from fear that the mage wars of history would return.

Fedlimid felt the name magic ebb and flow at the summer palace as it sought its target. He held his arms out from his sides and turned but could not triangulate the source.

Jason's eyes rolled back in his head. He collapsed, and Akela caught him before his head hit the hill's bare stone crown.

Phaedra and Zarya moved to surround Jason. One checked that he was breathing, and one listened to his heart.

"He is alive at least," Zarya said. "What happened?"

"He doesn't know how to hold back. He puts his entire heart and being into his magic to help others," said Akela. "That makes him strong because he commits totally to it. All or nothing, he lets his emotions take over, and it all goes at once."

She shook her head. "He must learn to care for himself, not give all to others. But I don't know who would teach him. We felt the difference between Phaedra and Zarya; the magic was much stronger and shorter with Zarya. I hope he reached Yeruslan."

"Zarya, you cried out during your Naming; are you still in pain?" asked Phaedra.

"Yes. It hurt. It hurt a lot, and it still hurts! Like I was hit by reeds all over. And hit hard!" Zarya lifted her dress and looked at her torso. "I am surprised I am not covered in welts!"

Phaedra gently slapped Jason's face and called his name a few times. Jason groaned and blinked.

"Why are all three of you kneeling over me?" he asked.

"You tried to rename Yeruslan. He is not nearby, and we don't know if it worked. The strain on your magic caused you to faint. You need to learn your limit and not cross it," Akela said. "Exhausting yourself like this is not healthy."

"Thank you, Akela," Jason said. "But I cannot change what is done. What should we do next?"

"To cement the pack bond, we need to sleep as a pack," Phaedra said. "We three will sleep as wolves; I expect you will want to be in your dragon skin since we will be exposed to the weather. We are not close to a shelter large enough for the four of us."

As Jason sat up, Xavier spoke with him. *This was not stated as part of the ritual. I am not pleased with this change—not pleased at all!*

Jason struggled to his feet. *This was not mentioned before. However, I am responsible for Akela losing her pack link; we must do this for her.*

Then you do it! It was your mistake, not mine, the dragon said emphatically.

True. My skin is not as durable as yours, which I suppose doesn't matter. Recall, however, that Akela identified us as a two-skinned. Without her, you might be a passenger still, Jason reminded him.

Xavier grumbled. *Dragons are solitary. We seldom meet except to fight or* mate. *Sleeping alongside three wolves—the thought revolts me. If there were other dragons to know, I would be mortified.*

But you sleep with me inside you. How is that not revolting? And why do you care what others think?

I— The dragon fell silent. *That had not occurred to me.* He shuddered, which felt to Jason as though his insides were shaking.

After a moment, Xavier said, *I agree we owe Akela, and I will do this. For her. While I consider how our situation is different.*

When his silent conversation concluded, Jason spoke. "I apologize for my silence. Xavier and I needed to discuss the ritual." He turned to Phaedra and said, "Lead the way unless someone else knows where we can settle down. I may need some assistance unless Xavier can walk the distance. His wings restrict his movement in the forest."

Zarya and Akela walked alongside Jason as Phaedra started downhill, looking for a location where they could settle down for a night. She found one without delay, and the women donned their other skins.

Xavier balked. *I still do not like it. This is not a dragon's way; we eat, sleep, and hunt alone. Having three wolves skin to skin with us is not acceptable!*

Can you endure it for one night? Jason asked.

I agreed that we owe Akela; I can do this for one night. He shuddered again.

They changed to their dragon skin, and Xavier shook off his tension. He curled up and raised one wing, allowing the wolves to snuggle up against him and one another. His wing provided more shelter than anything else in the forest could have.

The following day, each changed to human skin. The pack link now held them together. To Jason, it was similar to the affection he'd felt for Xochitl and a few others at South Haven.

How are you feeling the pack link, X? he asked.

Similar to how I feel you when you are out, the dragon replied. *But weaker. I admit my reaction to being close to the wolves was irrational, and I will try to do better.*

Jason donned his loincloth with his back to the women. When he turned back, Zarya was facing him, unclothed, about an arm's length away.

"Pack mate Jason, will you lie with me?" she asked boldly.

"I, um," Jason stammered.

Remember, you can refuse requests for intimacy from others if it makes you uncomfortable, Xavier said.

"I do not want to."

She glanced at his loincloth. "Your body disagrees," she observed.

Jason took her hands gently in his. "Zarya, you are beautiful and desirable, as my body's reaction attests. However, I am not ready for an intimate relationship at this time. I barely know you, and sex is not as casual for me as it is with wolves. Just going through the ritual with you three to form a pack scared the hell out of me for the closeness of the bond. Feeling it now is not very comfortable. It wasn't easy for Xavier either."

Zarya nodded. "I feel your anxiety through the pack link. I accept your refusal now, but I will ask again."

She folded her dress and Akela's into one backpack. Akela shifted, and Zarya adjusted the pack to fit Akela. Zarya changed into her wolf skin.

Phaedra packaged her dress and asked Jason for his loincloth. She put them into the remaining duffel, fit it onto Zarya, and turned to Jason. "I think you handled the situation with Zarya very well— a gentleness not shown by many men. Farewell, man of the pack."

She shifted, and the three wolves disappeared into the forest.

Jason stood and watched after the wolves left. He could still tell that the women were satisfied with the outcome. *Xavier, can you also feel the pack link?* he asked.

Yes, Jason. It feels to me like it does to you.

We are now part of a two-skinned wolf pack. I feel like I just stepped out into the air and am hanging there. And I don't have wings like you do, so it is more than a little scary. I can't even tell which way is down. I have no idea how this will affect me. Us, Jason said.

I don't feel the uncertainty as strongly as you do. We have barely started learning about being two, and we have three others with whom we share more than with any other being.

We are warriors. We will survive. Jason sounded to Xavier as if he were convincing himself.

The dragon laughed. *We shall indeed.*

Jason walked to the top of the hillock where the ceremony had occurred and performed his devotions and exercises before changing skins.

Xavier launched himself into the air and flew. *We should practice flying before returning to Terlingua. If we wait until final darkness before dawn tomorrow, we should be able to return unseen.*

He paused and then continued. *Of course, we do not know how many saw us leave or that Heather kept our secret, so our precautions may be moot.*

———⊷⊶———

The trip from Capua to Biblola was hot and dusty. Erlender wanted nothing more than a bath and a glass of chilled wine. After ten days in a carriage, his first desire was usually to replenish his mana store by torturing someone to death.

Necromancers took life mana from other living beings, which could lead to the donor's death. Erlender enjoyed the act of murder itself; this limited his strength and made him almost a pariah among an already outcast group.

Erlender had, however, perfected getting the most out of people by taking them to the brink of death, allowing them to heal, and repeating, bringing them closer to death each time. He drooled, imagining his next victim.

He directed two of his attendants to find appropriate lodging near the harbor. If the inn lacked space for their horses, they would find stables on their own. He purchased a glass of chilled wine from a street vendor and wondered if the man practiced heat magic or had paid for snow transported from the mountains. Magic seemed more cost-effective, but a mage could make more money than a wine merchant. Perhaps he hid his magic, which was not unknown among the peasants and merchants.

The wine improved his spirits. After a good meal and a restful night's sleep, tomorrow's search would be endurable.

Tomorrow he would send Arnock, a small, obsequious, oily snool related by blood and tied by magic, on an errand. Thinking of Arnock made him grimace despite the pleasant wine. He hated to be in the same room as his cousin, but the man had his uses.

He trusted Arnock where he would've trusted no other. His cousin would find a place and procure a girl, preferably a young slave whose absence would not be noticed.

Erlender smiled, anticipating several evenings spent drawing out the woman's life, easing his mind from the drudgery of searching the docks for Jason.

———⊷⊶———

Erlender rode a horse to a dilapidated wooden structure a few miles outside Biblola, along a poorly maintained one-lane road. Taking his carriage would've involved letting his driver know of this assignation, adding another to this coterie. He hadn't ridden a horse in a long time and was sore, regretting his decision by the time he reached his goal.

The sun was just past its highest point in the sky when Erlender arrived at his destination.

Arnock, a man perpetually on the cusp of middle age, bore the mark of his turbulent past in every line of his face. His blondish hair, a shade more straw than gold, had begun a stealthy retreat from his temples, leaving a widow's peak that seemed to furrow his brow permanently. A thick mustache the color of sun-bleached hay and sideburns that mirrored it framed his face.

He met Erlender at the door. "All is in readiness, mighty cousin." His voice dripped with fawning.

He wasn't a large man. He hovered just shy of tall, and his lean frame was a testament to a life lived on the move. But most striking were his eyes, which often drew curious stares. One was a clear blue; the other was a startling icy gray—a result of mismatched corneas. This, some whispered, was a mark of his illegitimacy, a constant reminder of his origins as the cast-off son of a minor nobleman.

"I told you not to call me that!" Erlender quickly replied with a hand raised to strike.

Arnock stepped out of range with a practiced move. "There is no one here to hear who doesn't already know, except one, and she won't be able to tell."

"Bah! Tell me about her."

"Young—maybe eighteen or twenty. Slender. Some scars. Her mind is mostly gone, and no one would have her as a wife. Her uncle would have given her to me if I lived in the city."

With a sidelong glance, he continued. "No one will look for her; I told him I was taking her to Babirusa to serve as a chambermaid. That is the extent of her abilities."

Erlender nodded. "Have you found other candidates? Will the uncle see you later and wonder about the story?"

"I have another three or four possibles. And no, I was careful to disguise myself when dealing with him."

"Very well. Return for me at about midnight. Ride this horse to town, and return in the carriage."

Erlender liked the shanty's remoteness. After Arnock left, he ensured no sound would escape the building by applying a careful layer of a sound-soaking pattern he knew to the door, the window, and the exterior walls.

He rubbed his hands together in anticipation and entered the shack. He checked that the pitcher alongside the basin contained water before removing his outer clothing and undershirt. Then he turned his attention to the girl.

When Arnock returned, Erlender stood outside the shack with a wide smile.

"She is strong. I expect you to feed her and clean her up a bit. I will be back overmorrow," the necromancer said.

"Sunup is just a few hours away, heralding tomorrow. That leaves but a single day for her to heal. Are you certain?"

Erlender paused and suddenly spun, aiming a roundhouse blow at Arnock. His cousin rolled expertly, so even though Erlender felt his palm strike Arnock's cheek, the blow failed to draw blood, merely reddening his cheek.

"How dare you speak without permission! I tolerate you because your father is my uncle, but you are not to contradict me!"

Arnock turned his roll into a step, taking himself out of Erlender's reach. He lowered his gaze but remained quiet.

Erlender took a breath. "I will return on the third day," he said, as though it had been his conclusion, not his cousin's. "I expect her to think her ordeal is over. And I want her bathed and in clean clothing. Persuade her you are her protector. I will need to bloody your nose so she continues to think it after tonight's session."

Arnock nodded; such abuse was common. Erlender was a legitimate son and seemed to delight in occasionally reminding him.

Erlender entered the carriage, and his cousin drove toward the city.

CHAPTER 7

Dragons Shed

Heat and Light
Prince Adair of the Fae

Light and heat are related and could be a single form of mana that appears as two.

When we observe some light, as in sunlight, we also observe heat.

Are light and heat the same?

But other observations of light—fireflies, ocean algae, and some fungi—produce no heat that we can measure.

Neither mage light nor glowstones provide warmth, and the soft glow produced is barely visible in brighter light.

Heat will creep along an iron rod when one end is placed in a fire. Clearly, the fire heats the rod, but the heat moves much more slowly along the rod than the light does.

Water in hot springs is hot, as are the stones near a geyser's mouth, but no light is emitted.

Are heat and light different?

Observed behaviors continue to confound our theorists. Young's experiment with light passing through two slits demonstrates the clear distribution into peaks and valleys of light that can only be explained if light is a wave.

Directing a beam of sunlight through a prism breaks the light into bands of different colors. If you place a thermometer bulb just out of the red end of the spectrum, you will observe the temperature increase. Therefore, sunlight carries heat.

Using light to construct mana patterns demonstrates that it, like other forms, can be treated like small particles.

Are light and heat the same? We do not know. Practical magicians use the theory that most easily fits the situation. We treat the heat and light as separate and light as particles, except when a single mana type or a wave suits the spell being crafted.

X avier flew for the remainder of the day and most of the night. The flying lessons went well; Jason still cried out during sudden maneuvers but less than on earlier flights. The dragon hunted, ate about half an adult deer, and carried the rest to Terlingua.

Arriving before dawn, he circled for a few minutes, looking for the heat signature of people near his departure site. Seeing none, he dove and landed.

His clothes remained folded where he had left them. After changing skins, Jason dressed, picked up the carcass, and walked to his room, setting the carcass down outside.

A folded note rested on his bed, illuminated by his statue. He opened it and read:

> Jason,
>
> See me when you get back regarding your stay at Terlingua.
>
> Heather
>
> PS To the best of my knowledge, no one saw you leave. However, your absence may be difficult to explain to those you met on your first day.

Jason reread it, set it down, and performed his morning devotions and exercises.

What does she want to discuss? he thought. *I was here for less than a day, and I agreed with all her conditions for residents. Did something about meeting a real dragon upset her? Xavier didn't say anything that would make me believe that.*

The dragon remained silent.

Sleeping, Jason concluded.

The way directs a warrior to accept the consequences of his actions. That he did not know what he had done that would elicit a reprimand did not matter. He would do without complaint whatever Heather felt needed to be done.

He carried the half deer to the kitchen as the sun peeked over the horizon.

When he entered the kitchen, all the cooks stopped what they were doing and stared at him.

A husky human female wearing a toque blanche walked toward him and said, "Who are you, and what do you want?"

Jason lowered the carcass to the floor. He introduced himself and explained his arrangement to hunt and provide game for the larder. The kitchen staff showed him where to deposit the deer for them to butcher.

As the cooks raised the deer, one said, "This looks fresh today, but the amount gone would feed a man for several days."

"You know that hunting increases your appetite." Jason laughed. "It had been a long time between hunts for me. It doesn't seem like I could eat that much, does it?"

He left the kitchen staff silently staring at his back and walked to the main house. Lights and sounds from within indicated the house was awake, so he knocked on the front door.

A kaihana he had yet to meet answered the door.

"Good morning. I am Jason. Heather wanted me to see her as soon as I returned," he said.

The kaihana looked at him briefly, nodded, and opened the door for him. "I am Elani. Lady Heather told me to expect you and to seat you in the consultation room. Please follow me."

She led him to the same examination room as the last time. He took a seat. Heather came in a short time later.

When she arrived, she stood rigidly in the doorway, opening and closing her fists. He stood and greeted her with a smile and one hand outstretched in greeting.

Ignoring his hand, she glared at him. "Where did you go for two nights and a day? And why did you not tell me about your planned absence? Surely you were not this irresponsible at South Haven! I thought you agreed that Hathsday would be your self-day."

Jason's jaw dropped. "I don't know what Xavier told you before we left," he said. "We had to meet with a two-skinned wolf named Akela and a few of her former pack. I do not know what alerted Xavier to her need for us."

Xavier snorted. *She isn't big enough or scary enough to compel me.*

Jason choked back a laugh.

Heather's brows rose at his muffled chuckle.

"I'm sorry. Xavier just told me that you aren't big or scary enough to intimidate him," Jason said as he struggled to stifle his laugh.

He rubbed his chin before continuing. "Although being bigger and scarier wouldn't guarantee obedience. He and I share a life, and he ignores me when he feels like it.

"Xavier flew to the wolves, and our business took us into yesterday. Xavier returned us here, um, half an hour ago."

Heather jerked her head back, and her eyes widened. "Xavier did say that Akela was looking for him before flying away."

"We met Akela in her wolf skin during the thunderstorm—what was it?—seven nights ago. I helped her dissolve a link with an abusive male, and she helped me and Xavier change for the first time. This time, she had two pack mates trying to escape the same man. Xavier and I helped them with that."

"Wolves—you dissolved a pack link? A pack of two-skinned wolves? How did you do that?"

Jason shrugged. "I will repeat what I told them. I do not know how I did that for Akela; I do not know how I repeated it for them. But after it was done, we formed another pack since the wolves need one for their well-being."

"I think you know or suspect more than you let on." Heather sounded skeptical. "So you are now a member of a wolf pack."

"Yes, I am half wolf and half dragon, with a touch of snapping turtle." He smiled.

A little laugh escaped before she choked it.

"The formation ritual is not very selective about membership. This is all I feel comfortable sharing," he said. "Perhaps I will tell you more when we know each other better."

Heather nodded and said, "So be it; share more when you trust me more."

She abruptly changed the subject. "Well then. Let us discuss what happened during our first attempt at accessing your core. Describe each sensation or thought from when you decided to change skins until it finished; consider how this last time differed from earlier changes. Try to recall everything you saw, felt, smelled, or tasted and as those things altered. End with Xavier—taking over? I am not sure how to refer to that."

"The last thing before I, uh, left was the feeling that I had been stretched and started to dissolve," Jason said. "I don't recall a term, but *taking over* is pretty descriptive. Use that." He grinned. "I feel like I am back in school and reciting my lessons."

"If that helps you remember, then back in school we are." She smiled.

He shook his head. "The steps to the void, which seem to be preliminaries for shifting, are to take three deep, slow breaths and let each out slowly. Then you focus on your breathing, watching each breath come in and out your nostrils. When other thoughts surface, acknowledge them and let them go. If you find your mind wandering, take one deep breath, and start watching your breathing again."

He continued. "I find my thoughts slowing down and my breath slowing. Then my thoughts stop, and I am in the void. At that point, I am acutely aware of myself—body and mind—and my target. I concentrate on a smooth release while keeping my eyes and attention on the target."

He paused momentarily. "I don't need three deep breaths to enter the void. It doesn't seem to make a difference after almost twenty years."

He took another breath and continued. "I focused on the darkness behind my closed eyes. After a few moments, I saw a dim light; it changed shape and size. As the light spot grew, it also brightened. It changed to yellow and then red.

"I followed an opening—a doorway, I think. After that, I moved down a corridor. I felt a hot, dry wind and a breeze smelling of petrichor. These two can't happen at the same time, but that was what I sensed. Traveling a bit farther along the corridor, I saw a man-shaped opening. When I reached it, I felt a cool breeze on my face and chest, followed almost immediately by the sensation of falling. Then I felt my back, neck, and shoulders stretch—to the point of pain.

"Then I felt as if I were breaking into pieces, and I feared what was coming. I regained awareness a few minutes later, when we were in the air."

"You fear the skin change? I haven't heard of that from others," she said, furrowing her brow.

"My one teacher did not mention it, and the, um, disruption of changing masked my fear the first few times. I feel it at the end, when I am partly faded and before Xavier manifests; yes, that is frightening. I do not like the sensation of breaking apart."

"How often do you change?"

Jason chuckled. "We haven't discussed that yet. We will find a mutually inconvenient split of each day. We have changed, uh, five times, counting when Akela introduced us."

Heather was silent for several moments. "Your experiences are not the same as those of others I have guided to their core. Part of that is your skin shifting, but I don't know how changing skin affects core access."

She sat in thought for several minutes. "I suggest you slow down the total experience and try to pause at each change you experience and accept them as they occur: each change in the light, the hot wind, the prerain smell, and the cool breeze. Try to resist or slow down the shifting, accepting your second skin as part of you, while you look further within. We will meet again for me to observe in, oh—how does ten to fifteen days sound?"

"That sounds perfect. Thank you, Lady Heather," said Jason.

"We aren't very formal here; I am just Heather. Now on to other things." She looked up and smiled. "Maliyah identified a cave about a half hour's walk from us that might work for Xavier's sleeping place. Is now a good time for a walk?"

"Nothing would delight me more, Heather." He smiled back.

Heather and Jason continued northwest, leaving Terlingua's boundaries behind. They came upon a crude wooden gate across a steep path heading to a jumble of gigantic rocks. They clambered up the path, which revealed a bowl-shaped depression cradling a muddy pond at its base.

A silent drama unfolded on its earthen walls—seep springs trickled down like tears, leaving damp trails that spoke of constant, unseen weeping. A still, opaque pond, roughly fifteen feet across, lay nestled in the heart of the depression. Its periphery teemed with lush, vibrant green vegetation, a stark contrast to the sunbaked earth surrounding it.

But as their gazes drifted toward the center, a different story emerged. There, a four-foot-wide circle contained muck the consistency of potter's slip—a liquid, viscous mud. Bubbles erupted near the center with soft plopping sounds, releasing wisps of steam that danced capriciously in the cool air. The silence—broken only by the gurgle of the springs, the burping of bubbles, and the sigh of the wind—seemed to press down on them

From their vantage point, they could feel the heat from the mud—the pond stank of burning sulfur, rotting vegetation, and rotten eggs.

Heather stopped on a rise separating the mud bowl from the gate. "We call this place Ognyen—a word related to heat in the kaihana language."

Stepping around the end of the bowl, Jason saw the cave opening, as did Xavier through his eyes. He cried joyfully and ran up the rubble to the cave as Xavier's enthusiasm overruled caution. He stepped inside.

A few minutes later, he emerged and said, "It is perfect." He turned and stared at the pond. "Rejuvenating mud—it couldn't be better!"

Jason climbed down more sedately and joined Heather. "Why is the path gated?"

"The air in the bowl is toxic to people and most animals. The gate is to deter people from coming up here and dying inside the bowl. Healing herbs, roots, and bulbs grow here, so people come anyway."

Heather frowned and said sadly, "Alas, we find a victim to the fumes every year or so. Sometimes we have to wait for several weeks until a wind allows us to extract the corpse and notify families."

She turned to look over the pond. "Maliyah and I usually harvest here when winds are strong enough to clear the air, which happens only three or four times a year. Sometimes rain washes the air without filling the bowl, and we harvest then.

"The plants grow in a few other places where bubbling, stinking mud occurs. They are overharvested there because they are easy to get at."

Jason spoke mind to mind with his other skin. *X, can we do anything to help her harvest some now?*

Yes. I am sure I can provide enough wind with my wings, the dragon replied.

Jason turned to Heather and said, "Xavier proposes creating a wind with his wings so you can harvest some right now. Would you like him to do that?"

Her mouth dropped open, and her eyes widened. "Yes. That would be wonderful! I should walk with you more often if I'm going to get lucky like this."

Jason climbed back to the cave, and Xavier emerged a few minutes later. The dragon hopped down past Heather to the lowest part of the bowl rim. He stretched, held his nose above the bubbling mud, and inhaled deeply.

He raised his head high and exhaled; the sound was not his typical bugle or organ-music sound but a moaning.

After breathing the fumes a few times, Xavier said for both to hear, *Rejuvenating mud. If I can breathe some of its air, my fire burns brighter. I could not have asked for a better home.*

He sprayed a small amount of venom into the pond's center, and flames flared where the rotten-egg-smelling gas was concentrated enough to burn. The flames did not spread but danced around the mud for a few minutes before stopping.

Xavier climbed higher up on the rim and turned to face the pond. He beat his wings but not fast enough for flight. After a few minutes of air stirring above the pond, he told Heather the air was clear, and she climbed into the bowl. She began harvesting branches with leaves, blossoms, and flowering bulbs that grew near the edge.

Maliyah left Sinistrad before dawn in her goat cart loaded with baskets and drove to Ognyen.

Arriving at the bowl of mud, she saw an open gate, confirming Althea's foretelling.

She gathered eight of the baskets and climbed the steep trail. Halfway to the pond, she heard Heather's voice and hurried to meet her.

Rounding the last curve and reaching the top of the rise between the gate and the pond, she saw a great winged blue beast seated on the bowl's rim, beating its wings slowly.

Her heart hammered in her chest as her eyes widened in disbelief. She felt her knees weaken and her breath quicken. The majestic creature seemed to fill her entire vision. She trembled and broke into a sweat as her heart raced, and she instinctively reached for a nearby stone. Her fingers shook.

She gasped and started retracing her steps before realizing that Heather's voice was calm. *If Heather thinks it is safe, it must be,* she thought.

Taking a few deep breaths to calm her nerves, she slowly climbed the remaining distance to the bowl's edge. Her curiosity battled her apprehension.

The dragon looked at her, revealing amber eyes shaped like a cat's, but it did not otherwise change its posture or movement. Its belly and the undersides of its wings reminded her of thin clouds in an otherwise clear sky.

It took Maliyah several moments to speak; her initial fear was quelled but not conquered. "Good morning, Heather. Elder Althea suggested I join you here for the harvest but failed to mention your winged companion." Her voice quavered a little despite her attempt to be calm.

Heather looked up at her, and a smile lit up her face. "Maliyah! What an unexpected surprise! I am pleased with the elder's foresight. Xavier is keeping the air in the bowl clear for me. Us."

The dragon stood behind and above Heather. Maliyah could barely hear the healer's words above the gurgling pond and the rustling of the dragon's breeze.

"She told me to bring baskets, which I have." Maliyah raised her voice to be heard.

"Well, bring them on down, and let us take advantage of today's opportunity."

"What of—" Maliyah gestured with her chin toward Xavier.

Heather followed her gaze and chuckled. "The dragon isn't a danger to us."

Maliyah transported all the baskets to the bowl's shoulder before joining Heather in thinning the plants.

The two women thinned the pond's growth, sorting their harvest into containers according to plant and part. When they finished, about one-third of its growth was gone. Maliyah and Heather took several trips to ferry baskets out of the bowl. Xavier stopped fanning.

Xavier sounded a note when one basket remained in the bowl and swiveled his head between the two women. *Good afternoon, Maliyah. May I know how you learned of our excursion today? And how many people know I am in the area?* He broadcast mind speech to the women.

Maliyah spun about to face the dragon with her mouth wide open at hearing without her ears. She closed and opened her mouth a few times before saying, "I did not know of your presence before I climbed the trail, dragon. I followed Elder Althea's directions to join Lady Heather at Ognyen to harvest medicinal plants.

"But, sir dragon, that leads to another question. How do you know my name?"

Xavier studied the kaihana for a few moments before turning to face Heather. *Well, that is awkward. I seem to have let the cat out of its bag.*

Heather looked at Xavier. "How much of what you say to me does she hear?" she asked.

I can focus my mind speech on one individual or direct it to all who are close enough. You can both hear me, he said.

"Maliyah, let me introduce Xavier. He will use Ognyen Cave for a few months, possibly longer. As to how he knows your name, he is a companion of Jason, who must have told him."

Maliyah studied Heather for a moment. "Few men can tell kaihana apart until living among us for two years or longer. Are you telling me Jason can describe one of us well enough for another to identify after only a few days with us?"

Heather sucked air between her teeth.

Xavier played a short musical tune. *I apologize for the attempted subterfuge, Maliyah. Jason and I are the same individual with two skins. We are trying to keep my aspect from public knowledge. Heather told you a partial truth, trying to keep us secret after my blunder. Jason can identify you from among the kaihana he has met, and so can I. I trust this explanation is satisfactory.*

I am puzzled that your elder knew of Heather being here without knowing I was. If she did know of me, why did she not tell you? Questions that cannot be answered here or by you.

I request that you not disclose that you and I met this afternoon.

Maliyah looked back and forth between them several times. "I agree you answered my question and that I cannot answer yours. What an elder knows and what she shares are subject to her judgment and hers alone." She turned to Heather. "We have the goat cart ride to Terlingua to get our story straight. I am sure we can keep Xavier out of it."

My thanks, Maliyah. I will strive to remain unobserved during our stay.

The women loaded the baskets into the cart, closed the gate, and left.

The next day, Heather returned to Ognyen in a goat cart soon after the sun peeked above the horizon. The two-wheeled cart was intended for ferrying people; instead of one, it had two benches for sitting. Its axles had springs, and its harness held two wethers.

Jason had told her of his dragon's need to molt, and she wasn't sure if he would welcome company. She justified her visit by arguing he *might* want to talk about his experience. Really, though, she wanted to get to know him better away from the farm.

The morning was chilly, and the bubbling mud filled the bowl with vapor so that tendrils flowed over the lower rim. She could not see the bottom through the mist but could hear bubbles plopping.

She climbed up the dew-slicked rocks to the cave entrance. She stepped in and saw Xavier sitting on his hind legs, pulling shed skin from his front feet and abdomen. One end was in his mouth, and he swallowed what tore free from one leg. He continued to worry the skin on his other leg free while Heather watched.

"Hey, need a hand with that?" she asked. "It looks like you could use an extra set of—well, not exactly claws, but you get the idea! Those scales look so impressive, even when they're coming off."

She paused. "Would it be easier to get out of the old skin by changing to Jason?"

Xavier's head jerked up, almost hitting the cave ceiling, with eyes wide open. *That would never have occurred to me.* He paused, looked over his belly and legs, and continued. *I think I should finish my arms, legs, and torso. I feel more tightly connected to him there, and I would hate to trap him in armor that might stretch him wider than his bones reach.*

Xavier continued to peel and consume the skin while Heather watched.

"Xavier, I hesitate to ask, but there are references to using dragon scales in old healing texts. I never thought I might find any until last night. Would you be willing to give me a portion of your shed scales so I can try to reproduce them?"

Xavier swallowed the last piece of his abdominal skin and looked at her. *I am compelled to eat the shedding, but I do not think I must eat the whole thing. I also do not know if the compulsion will remain after I become Jason. Nor do I know if shed skin will have the same effects as a whole scale, but that is for you to address. I will share.*

From the underside of one wing, he pulled a strip about two feet wide by eight feet long, which he dropped onto the ground close to her. She picked it up and exited the cave.

He shifted, and Jason stepped out of the shed-skin shell. The rear legs and torso might have confined him, but it was not evident that they would have hurt him. He dressed and walked to the cave entrance. Turning, he viewed the dragon's form in the shed skin.

"So that is what you look like!" he said. "I can't see any color in the shed skin, but it gives me an idea of your size and shape."

"His back side is dark blue, and his underside is light blue, with spots and streaks of white and gray, just like the sky on a slightly windy day with thin clouds," Heather responded.

Jason nodded slowly.

Jason and Heather descended and walked the steep trail to the gate. When they reached Heather's goat cart, they found Maliyah waiting. Her gaze darted between them and landed on Heather's hands, fixating on the coil of dragon skin shimmering in the morning sun.

Maliyah sucked in a deep breath. Her eyes widened, with the pupils dilating like those of a desert cat spotting a rare bird. A smile, broad and sudden, split her face. It wasn't just any smile; it was a grin that stretched from ear to ear, revealing a dimple in one cheek. Her entire body seemed to vibrate with barely contained energy.

Before Heather could speak, Maliyah blurted out, "Is that—can I have some?" Her speech, usually a calm, measured pace, tumbled over itself in a rush of excitement.

Heather glanced at Jason, who nodded. She gave a portion to Maliyah, who expressed her gratitude.

"Maliyah, Xavier eats his shed skin, like many lizards. But if he agrees, you can have more skin after his next shedding," Jason offered.

Maliyah hugged Jason impulsively. "That would be wonderful. I know you aren't promising me anything."

Heather suggested Maliyah take the cart to the kaihana village with her portion of skin, and she agreed.

As Maliyah drove off, Jason and Heather started their walk back to Terlingua.

"Xavier isn't sure how much of his shed skin he needs to eat. We don't know if he will share some of each shedding with Maliyah. Do you know when he will shed next?" asked Heather.

"No, I do not. I will let you know when he needs to shed again," he replied.

They completed their walk to Terlingua in silence.

—⟡⟡⟡—

The next day, Jason felt a tugging from within while harvesting fruit. He stood atop the three-legged ladder with a bag of fruit hanging from his shoulder. He stopped moving and checked his balance on the ladder as he waited for the sensation to resolve. He did not know what it was. It was similar to the stretching he felt when he and Xavier were changing skins but not as physical.

He turned his attention within—just to the point of the void, not past it. He did not want to enter a deep devotional state, nor did he want to fall from the ladder or change skins.

The pack link was active in a way he had not experienced before.

The tugging continued but did not get stronger, nor did it diminish.

Suddenly, he felt an expansion through the link. As he observed, it coalesced into the connection he remembered, except more individuals were involved. Three more, he was pretty sure.

He had no names for his new pack mates, and he did not know the genders or ages of the new wolves; the pack link did not provide those data.

He sensed acceptance and gratitude through the link.

He heaved a sigh and resumed harvesting, ignoring the questioning glances from those working with him.

He had too little data to decide, so he would wait for more.

The following day, Jason awoke before dawn and performed his devotions before the kalasha and thasiwoda outside. He then had breakfast with the residents and met Maliyah before the barn doors for his assignment.

His first task was cutting hay and clover, preparing for winter. For that, he needed a scythe that fit; the women and kaihana at Terlingua were well below six feet tall, and Jason was close to that height. The scythe handle—snath—for a taller person needed a curve to keep the cutting edge parallel to the ground.

Jason found a curved-snath scythe in the barn's rear. It had not been used in some time but had been carefully coated in oil before storage, and the oil had dried into a skin covering the blade.

He cleaned the dried oil from the blade and honed it before joining the kaihana in the hayfield.

It took the better part of an hour to recall the rhythm of mowing with a scythe.

By the end of the day, Jason's muscles were trembling from unaccustomed use. They stiffened by dinnertime, and he limped to his room afterward, not hobbling but favoring the scythe-swing forward leg.

Following his devotions, he tried some thasiwoda, discovering his stiffened muscles were not up to it. Too sore to walk to the cave, he strolled to the spot where Xavier had first appeared at Terlingua, crouched, and began his change preliminaries. When Xavier manifested, the dragon ran through the woods to a clearing and launched into the air.

Xavier found and ate a yearling boar during his flight around Smoky Springs. He spent some night hours practicing flying for Jason's benefit and the rest getting familiar with the land within fifty miles of Terlingua.

One area of Terlingua was warded against sight; Xavier could tell since his eyes would not focus directly on it. He could find the boundary, though—a mystery for another day.

A little after midnight, Xavier returned and walked to their changing place. After the shift, Jason noticed his soreness was almost gone; overworked muscles did not wholly heal with a change. He returned to his room and napped until shortly before sunrise.

His second day was also spent mowing hay; using the sore muscles again felt good.

He repeated his devotions and exercises before walking to Ognyen Cave. Once there, he tried to slow down his skin change to Xavier, per Heather's instructions, before the dragon emerged.

One morning, as Jason performed his morning exercises, he saw Farid, a boy, and Adina, his mother, walking through the rocky field outside his room.

Farid was twelve years old, average height for his age, and slim, with a narrow face. His skin was tanned from time in the sun. His short hair was auburn, and his eyes were green. Adina, his mother, was about thirty. She was an inch or two above five feet, with skin darker than her son's and a heart-shaped face. Her hair was very dark brown, almost black, and her eyes were brown.

"Good morning, Farid and Adina. What brings you out before the day starts?" Jason asked as he held the one-legged-rooster pose.

"Mushrooms. There is a patch twenty yards or so inside the forest," Adina replied.

Jason changed to the prance-with-rainbows pose as he said, "Good hunting. I hope you find the patch."

"What is this dance you are doing?" Farid asked.

"It does look like a dance, doesn't it? It has some dance-like movements.

I imagine doing them will make dancing easier, though I don't dance much. Thasiwoda emphasizes balance and movement control," Jason replied as he moved into the wave-at-the-clouds pose.

"How often do you do this?"

"Twice daily but not the same each time. There are 121 poses and prescribed movements between pairs. The longest sequence has sixty-one poses."

"Why do you do them?" the boy asked.

Jason stopped his exercise and looked straight at the boy. "I do them so I remain balanced as I move without thinking about it.

"If you are interested and Lady Heather and your mother agree, I can teach them to you." Jason looked at Adina, the boy's mother, for confirmation, and she nodded. "I will start teaching you the beginning poses tomorrow morning."

Sensei had told him he would find students and should accept them, as he had been accepted. He was a little apprehensive about teaching his first student, though he had offered to.

"What time do you begin?" Farid asked.

"I finish in time for breakfast. If you arrive half an hour before breakfast, that will give us enough time for the first lessons."

Farid agreed to meet Jason the following day.

Jason sought Heather before breakfast. He found her leaving the main house, headed for the dining hall, and told her of his plan to teach the boy.

"That sounds like an excellent idea. I have only one question." She glanced around and lowered her voice. "Will you be able to keep your other skin under control?"

Jason thought for a minute. "I have no reason to believe I can't. I also cannot think of anyone here, except maybe MacTíre, who could provoke either of us to an unthinking action."

"Tell me a little more about your exercises."

"The beginning is all about finding and maintaining your balance. Later lessons are oriented toward defense against an attack; aggressive moves won't follow for a year or more. Feel free to join us any morning to observe or participate."

"That is sufficient for me. You may proceed. Let me know if there is more I can do," she said.

Jason finished his morning exercises the following day and waited near his room for Farid.

When Farid arrived, Jason began. "There are two things at the core of thasiwoda: stillness and movement. When you are still, perfect stillness is your goal. When you move, total control over your movement is your intent. The beginnings are all about balance. Now, stand straight, and strive for balance."

Farid looked at him as though he were a talking frog. "I am balanced."

"Oh?" Jason said as he reached out and firmly touched one shoulder.

Farid took a sudden step back. "What? Why did you shove me?"

"That was a touch. You were not balanced. Your weight was mostly on your heels and left foot. Now you try."

Farid pushed Jason's shoulder with more force than Jason had used. Jason wavered slightly but did not take a step.

"When you are balanced, it is easy to remain balanced. Now let us try again. Stand with feet shoulder width apart, shoulders above your feet, and weight balanced between each foot and between heels and toes on each foot.

"Try pressing down with your toes until your heels begin to lift. Good. Now relax your toes until your heels bear the same weight.

"Good. Now press with your right foot as though stepping onto a low brick; watch your center, and pause if you begin to lose balance. Excellent. Now relax your feet.

"Good. Change feet; press with your left foot.

"Excellent. Now alternate pressing between left and right until both are the same."

It took several minutes for Farid to balance to Jason's satisfaction. Farid grinned when Jason's touch did not cause him to take a step backward.

Jason nodded. "Excellent. Think about how comfortable this feels, and try to return to balance whenever you have a chance. Now we go to the first pose. It is called *raising the clouds*."

Jason showed Farid eight poses, checking his balance on each one. After the introduction, they repeated the eight until breakfast while Jason continuously corrected his balance. Farid's legs shook a little after maintaining proper form for so long.

After their lesson, Farid asked if he could invite other boys to train with them.

Jason looked at him for a few moments. "Yes, but their mothers must agree. I will check with them, so let the others know not to come without that permission. I will not tolerate dishonesty in a student."

The following day, three new boys joined Jason and Farid.

Heather came by to observe the classes in action. Jason invited her to join them, and she did, surprising Jason a little.

Something changed, he thought. *I wonder what.*

Jason introduced the boys to the same eight poses, spending more time with the newcomers than with Farid. The group repeated the poses as Jason monitored their balance.

Jason called out poses and expressed his pleasure that Farid had remembered them after one lesson. He spent time correcting the boy's balance, though.

During the lesson, Heather observed that Jason was a careful, patient teacher. He never rushed or reprimanded students and never made them feel foolish for attempting something new or for their fumbling while trying to follow his lead.

She took Jason aside at the end. "You are a natural teacher. You broadcast a touch of feel-good mana when each student does something correctly or at least more correctly than before. I suspect they will all learn quickly."

"I am? I don't even know what that is!"

"You extend a bit of life to them; it is also done in healing. It makes people feel good while mending them. I am impressed!"

"But I am just doing what my sensei did to teach me the poses and movements," Jason protested.

"No, no, no. What you are doing is rare. You are broadcasting mana to your class. Others take years to learn how to encourage students with a touch of feel-good; some never achieve it. And here you are, doing it without effort."

"Wow. I was worried when I offered to teach Farid that I would be a terrible instructor. I am pleased that I was wrong." He grinned at her. "Shall we head to breakfast?"

"Yes, that sounds wonderful." Her partial smile widened to involve her entire face.

The next day, all the boys ten or older came to the lessons. Jason now had seven students and realized he needed a place for classes during inclement weather.

The day after that, Tovia and a girl named Constance joined them in the morning.

Constance had never tried to balance, so Jason returned to review her frequently. He had to dismiss the class for breakfast after showing her just the first two poses; the rest achieved all eight.

Tovia, however, balanced almost perfectly. He had her shift her weight more to her toes but otherwise had no corrections. He taught her the same eight he'd started Farid with and added two more.

At the end, he spoke with her as they walked to the dining hall.

"Your balance is very good. You've had some weapons training, but your focus was not on balance."

She smiled at him. "Yes, I have trained with sword, knife, staff, crossbow, and rifle. And you are correct; maintaining balance was stressed early and then just weapons handling."

"Well, your challenge here will be different. You may have to unlearn a few things to learn correctly. You may feel like you are losing skill with your weapons while your balance reflexes adjust. I believe you will be better with each weapon once that happens."

"Something to look forward to then," she replied.

"What brought you here this morning?" he asked.

"I have no Defender duties today, and Heather mentioned you were teaching balance in the mornings, so I thought I would give it a try."

"Could you tell me more about the Defenders and how they react when MacTíre sounds the alarm if the farm is attacked?" he asked.

"Well, that will take more than breakfast." She grinned at him. "We will have to talk several times."

He laughed. "I'm sure it'll be worth it."

As word spread among the residents, more came to the sessions. Some mothers started watching, and Jason encouraged them to join—a few accepted. Jason's class had six boys, a dozen young women, and half the adult women. The space adjacent to his room was almost at capacity.

At the conclusion of the morning's exercises, Heather approached Jason. "It is time to review your progress in slowing"—her voice lowered to a whisper, and she glanced around to see if anyone was close—"your transition to your dragon. Come see me this evening after your chores."

—⸙—

That evening, Jason went to the main house and asked for Heather. He was shown to her consultation room and sat down.

She arrived a few minutes later, smiled at him and extended a hand in greeting. "I am glad to see you again, Jason. How are you, and how is your fire control now? Any changes?"

Jason stood and shook her hand. He stepped back and chuckled. He raised his hands with palms facing each other about a hand's breadth apart. After a moment, several sparks formed between his hands.

Heather smiled as she sat in her chair. "Quicker sparks this time? And they seem larger to me. I think you are making progress with mana control. That is good news!

"Now walk me through a change, and tell me how it feels now."

Jason began. "I enter the void and dodge entering a devotional state. I see lights behind closed eyes, as I described last time. I feel that I am moving uphill and through what seems like a hallway. I reach what seems to be a doorway or intersection and sense a dry, hot wind on my face, as before. I can now see wind-blown flames."

He paused for a moment and then continued. "After passing that intersection, I reach a second doorway and smell a coming rain. Passing that, I enter a man-shaped opening and feel my neck and lower back begin to stretch in length as the rest of me expands. It feels like I am breaking apart. Then I feel air blowing on my face and chest, the stretching sensation fades, and Xavier surfaces."

A comfortable silence settled after Jason described the shift. Heather listened intently with a thoughtful crease forming between her brows. When he finished, she asked, "No fear of the shift? Are you just getting used to it, or has something changed?"

A half smile crossed his lips. "I think I am just getting used to it. We also practice changing quickly, and there isn't time to be frightened. I do not know if our improved speed is from practice slowing or just repetition. I know that thasiwoda prepares the body for rapid movement, and slowing the transition to dragon may work the same."

Heather sat in silence for a moment, chewing on her lower lip. "Well, I am pleased that you are practicing. Some patients do not follow directions."

Jason laughed. "I'm open to expert advice, but I won't blindly follow it if it contradicts my own experience. I had virtually none when I started, so practicing was my only option. I have tried for speed a few times and will continue doing that. I believe speed will be crucial in the future, and I want to be prepared."

She nodded. "I can't think of anything else to say except to keep going. I hope you learn more about the transition, and then I might be able to give you better advice."

"I agree, and I will continue practicing," Jason said with a little laugh. "What else can I do?"

A sudden smile lit up her face, her eyes crinkled, and her left cheek rose; it faded as quickly as it had formed. "Absolutely. Keep at it, Jason. Learn more about the transition, and maybe then we can cook up some new strategies. Now let us retire to the changing space, and let me observe your transition."

"That is something we can do." Jason nodded, pushed himself out of the chair, and grinned. "You will witness this magic behind the barn. Will you lead the way, or shall I?"

The two walked to the rocky area bounded by Jason's room, the barn, and the forest. Jason could see no one else, but this time, he noticed the icehouse sidhe. From this side, the trench leading to the door could not be seen; it appeared as just a small hill covered in grass.

As he undressed, Jason focused on reaching his core. However, a stolen glance at Heather revealed her glancing back at him, which caused him to blush. It felt as if the redness spread onto his chest.

He carefully folded his clothes, crouched with his back to Heather, and, as before, called out, "I am ready."

Upon hearing her say, "Me too," he changed. He knew it took longer to reach the end now than it had when she last observed it. He scrutinized each of the two openings off the tunnel, intending to report to Heather later. He reached the man-shaped opening; he could feel no other option, but this space felt larger than it had. The familiar stretching took over.

Xavier condensed out of the fog and turned so he could see Heather.

Good evening, Peaiman Moonstar. How are you doing this day? Xavier asked when he solidified.

"I am well. Is Jason present tonight?" she asked.

He will be soon. The change is not traumatic now, but slowing the transition down seems to exhaust him for a moment. Do you need to speak with him through me? the dragon replied.

"No, but pass on to him that you are definitely slowing down and that I saw flames on his hands just before he faded. I am sure we are making progress. Enjoy your night," she said.

I shall. Until we meet again, the dragon said. He then jumped into the air and flew over the forest.

CHAPTER 8

The Girl with the Golden Voice

Cooperating Magics
Master Yona
Damocles Academy of Magic

Occasions arise when no single mage has the power to accomplish a task. These are often natural disasters, such as large earthquakes or major floods. Defending against a stronger mage is another instance in which cooperation is necessary.

The simplest technique, reminiscent of a healing technique, is for one mage to volunteer his or her mana to another. Direct contact makes this sharing possible; mages grip the donor's hand or arm and draw on his or her strength. This continues until the donor falters or the director is disabled. The practical limit of sharing in this manner is three mages; with each added person, the risk of one faltering and destroying the link increases.

Coordinating mana among more allies for one to wield requires different techniques. All of the successful merging techniques use patterns and repetition, recalling those used in mana control. The external manifestations of those patterns vary.

The desert people use intricate mandalas constructed using colored sands to represent different mana forms. These mandalas are accompanied by songs, and sand is carefully dropped onto the ground in time with the music.

The dwarves use runes carved while their shamans chant. The power stored in these runes can be activated with a trickle of mana, focusing all stored energy for one person to wield.

The priests of Nataraja use music and dance. Intricate steps mimic the patterns of the mandalas and runes, and the music amplifies the contributions of each dancer. The lead singer or dancer then wields the mana collected by the choir or troupe.

The king's battle mages form indirect links, and all involved can project mana as though touching one another. The loss of any link diminishes the strength of the lead wizard's pattern but does not disrupt it.

"Jason! Wait a moment!" Heather called from behind.

He paused on his way to the fields, set his tools down, and turned to greet her. "Good morning, Heather. How may I help you this day?"

She ran up to him. "Tomorrow, as you know, is a full moon. It is the first since you came to join us. I want to remind you that we gather for prayer, chanting, and devotional dancing each full moon. It is a time of great power when we can connect with the Goddess and other devotees in a way that's impossible during the rest of the month. I would be honored if you would join us."

Jason took a moment before answering. "I thank you for the gracious invitation and assure you I will attend. Does your group start at sundown, the first moon sighting, or when the full moon is totally in view? A later start will let me bathe and wear clean clothes for the celebration."

"We start gathering at sundown, but the action awaits the full moon in view," she answered with a smile. "So you will have time to clean up after tomorrow's tasks.

"Tomorrow will be special. Melody agreed to join us," she added.

"Who is Melody?"

"Oh, I thought you'd met all our residents."

"I have met many but did not have a checklist. What can you tell me about her?" Jason asked.

"Well, she is one of our younger women; she is ten years old. She is more than a girl but not yet a woman. The Mother's light is strong in her.

"She and her mother, Fionola, arrived about a year ago. Melody uses crutches to walk and spends much of her time in her room. Fionola works in the kitchens most of the time."

"I look forward to meeting them after tomorrow night's full-moon celebration," Jason said with a slight bow.

"I am so sorry. Melody joins us infrequently and likes to fade into the background at the conclusion. I will introduce you overmorrow."

"Very well. What cannot be changed must be endured," he said without any signs of disappointment.

"Knowing about it today gives me time to negotiate time with my other half." He laughed, picked up his tools, waved goodbye, and continued his journey to the fields.

That night, Jason walked to Ognyen Cave. Once there, he changed into the dragon.

Xavier, I am meeting with Heather and the other residents tomorrow night. Jason spoke with the dragon.

Yes, I was awake during your discussion. We both knew this would happen eventually. Heather said attendance was voluntary but that residents seldom missed. I suspect she wants us to integrate more with the community, and this is one way of doing that, Xavier replied.

Jason nodded, though it was just a mental motion. *Good. I agree. You will miss a night of flying. I suggest we plan a two-day hunting trip starting in, uh, three days. That will give you two nights and a full day out. I think we should return an entire carcass to the kitchens.*

Xavier exited the cave and stretched. *That means two kills. We each hunt, or I kill two and bring one back.*

You are a more successful hunter than I. Finding a suitable animal could take me two days, so the second option. That gives you more time out as well, Jason said.

The full-moon gathering was held in a circular garden between the main house and the dormitory.

Jason had not paid attention to the garden and fountain during his first-day tour, so he spent some time admiring the alternating spirals of tile walkways and flowering shrubs.

When he arrived, the area was populated by a dozen or so women, but it filled up soon after sunset. Jason positioned himself near the perimeter to participate without drawing attention to himself. Tovia noticed him and sat beside him.

"You have been at Terlingua for more than a tenday. How are you finding life at the farm?" Tovia began the conversation.

"It's not much different from life at South Haven. Having a priestess in charge made it more closely linked with the Goddess's church. It feels more relaxed here than there."

"How do you like kaihana?"

"I like them. When one supervises me, there is none of the 'Not that way, you dummy!' I sometimes got at home. Instead, they ask me why I am doing it my way or demonstrate how they prefer. They always check that I have water. They don't talk much, at least not to me. I'm comfortable working in this environment."

"The kaihana are astounded that you can tell them apart," she said. "You won them over in just a few days."

"My, I don't know what to say. Their faces are quite distinct." He looked at the sky for a moment.

I wonder if others find the fur and different head shape confusing. Or if it's due to Acacia insisting I learn to identify individual birds and squirrels, he thought.

They watched the moon crest the horizon.

When the moon was barely above the horizon, Elani came from the main house, holding a musical instrument Jason had not seen before. It appeared to be a large gourd with an extended guitar neck. He was too far away to count the strings. One of the human women brought out a pair of small drums. The musicians sat on the back porch of the main house, about a quarter of the way around the flowering garden from Jason and Tovia.

The night was chilly, and dew showed on the paving stones. The coolness did not disturb Jason; his inner fire kept him feeling warm most of the time. He could weather the night but was concerned about Tovia.

"The evening will get cold. Do you have a wrap for this evening?" he asked.

"No. But I will sit close to you to stay warm." An impish grin accompanied her statement.

"Well then, take a seat." He adjusted his rolled blanket for two to sit upon.

All talking subsided when Heather arrived a few minutes later.

A girl walked on crutches alongside Heather and sat on the bench. The girl looked about ten years old, with shoulder-length dark hair. The cold, silvery light of the full moon robbed Jason of his color vision, so he could tell little else about the young lady. All the women wore ankle-length white gowns; Heather's had some decorations on its yoke, but he could not identify what they were from his vantage point. Heather raised her hands above her head and began a prayer to the Goddess. When her prayer ended, the musicians started playing a chant.

After the musical introduction, the girl began to sing. "The moon shines bright above; the mother comes with love. The daughter's also near ..."

The group joined in the chant, a bit ragged at first, as most groups sang at the beginning. As the song progressed, the crowd's voices synchronized with the girl's. The voices began to match the tones she sang; some sang her note, some were an octave above or below, and some sang in harmony. The effect was a single voice raised in praise.

Her voice enthralled Jason. It began as a joyous sound in his ears, shifting to a harmonic ringing enriching the sounds. As he joined in the chant, the words and music echoed through his skull. His vision seemed to contract until he noticed only the chanters.

The moonlight seemed brighter on the musicians and the singer than on their surroundings. Jason watched as that brightness expanded and contracted in time with the music. As more voices matched Melody's, the light pulse extended farther into the singing devotees.

When the light reached Tovia and him, it felt as if it penetrated his body. Unbidden and without his usual preliminaries, a golden circle with a blue center appeared behind his half-closed eyes.

He felt chi circulate from feet to head. He heard sounds: one like distant thunder, one like river rapids a short distance away, and one like a stiff breeze blowing through tall trees. As he listened, his consciousness receded.

Jason, what is happening? Xavier sounded worried, but Jason was carefree.

He allowed the sounds to wash over him and absorb all his attention.

He did not notice when the chanting ended and the women dispersed.

Tovia tapped him on the shoulder. He blinked slowly as he emerged from the trance the chanting had eased him into.

Jason! Jason! What happened? Where were you? Xavier's words were rushed and quivered slightly.

"I am awake, X, and present. Thank you," Jason said quietly.

"Who is X?" Tovia asked.

Oops, I said that out loud, Jason thought.

He said, "I don't know an—"

Tovia interrupted him. "You are a terrible liar, Jason. You looked away from me while talking for the first time since we met." She paused. "I have watched you tell partial truths and avoid answering questions. I presumed you value truth highly." She leaned in closer. "You should not start lying now; it shows in your face and voice."

"I cannot explain X right now," he said.

"Aha! That was at least not an untruth. You are hiding X for some reason. I am good with that answer." She paused. "For now."

"Who was that girl with the angel's voice?" he asked.

"That is Melody. She finds walking difficult and seldom leaves her room. I am pleased she made the effort tonight," Tovia replied.

"Ah. Heather told me her name, but tonight seems to have erased it. Thank you very much!"

"And thank you for a warm shoulder to lean on." Her smile was mischievous, and she winked at him.

Jason strolled to his room, distracted by the effects of the evening. He felt a deep sense of tranquility, of having been emptied and filled with the Goddess's energy. As he walked, he felt almost weightless.

Jason?

Yes, Xavier? Jason's response took a moment as he pulled himself further out of the trance.

What happened tonight? You just faded away. I felt confined, and it was not a pleasant sensation.

Jason was shocked at the revelation; deep devotional trances restored him. *I find a period of deep devotion refreshing; I feel calmer and a sense of euphoria. I am sorry it distressed you.*

It was not distressing per se. I did not expect it, and I did not know how to respond, Xavier explained.

Would knowing about it make it easier for you?

Xavier was quiet for several minutes. *I think so. You suddenly not being here was almost more than I could take. I was trapped for almost thirty years, and it felt much like that.*

I apologize. I will alert you next time and try to take it slower. You might like being in the Goddess's presence, the man responded.

A few moments passed before Xavier responded. *When you emerged, you certainly seemed at peace. I think I might like it as well.*

Jason walked to Ognyen and shifted. Soon after launching into the air, Xavier felt a tugging from within. Jason, still awake, identified it as what he had felt when the pack expanded.

The tugging continued, followed by the link expanding. When it contracted, there were four new pack mates, maybe more. Acceptance and gratitude flowed through the pack link as before.

They lacked information about their new pack mates, but they were now only one of a pack of a dozen two-skinned individuals, eleven of whom were wolves.

Xavier hunted while Jason slept.

When Erlender and Arnock arrived at the inn in Biblola, the sun was halfway to its zenith. The streets were busy with daily activities, and vendors hawked their wares. The aroma of freshly baked bread competed with the street odors of horses, pigs, cows, and smoke. The sun warmed Erlender's skin as it burned through the morning fog.

Erlender climbed down from the carriage Arnock drove and entered the inn. His lieutenants were waiting for him in the parlor.

"How many ships are in dock today? How many carry passengers? Where do the passenger vessels go?" He started the discussion.

"Biblola has more docks than I have ever seen!" responded Arkadios, one of Erlender's lieutenants. "The twelve of us covered more than a quarter of the ships today. You might have better luck with the harbor master than we had talking to captains and first mates."

"How many are in that quarter?" Erlender asked.

"About three score. It is worse than it seems, since they installed a new dock lighting system; the docks operate almost all day and all night. We watched ships depart the docks to wait for the tide and new ships dock," replied Arkadios.

"What is this new lighting system?"

"The dock workers call it *captured lightning*. The docks are lit like midday all night. The water looks black, and you can't see beyond the reach of the lights."

Erlender sat in thought for several minutes. "I will check with the harbor master. That could speed things up. Even if he doesn't keep track of destinations, I may be able to learn which ships take passengers.

"Arkadios, I want you, and"—Erlender pointed to the youngest mage in his entourage—"I want you, Cathán, to accompany him. Find out as much as you can about this lighting system. I suspect the engineers have collaborated with the mages again."

Arkadios rose, stretching his almost six-foot frame as he reached upward. His light brown hair, streaked with premature strands of silver, was short and practical. A neatly trimmed beard, flecked with the same silver, framed his face. Though he was not overweight, his solid build and erect posture spoke of a past honed by physical challenges. Scars along his forearms and peeking from beneath his collar were silent testaments to battles fought. His rich hazel eyes held a depth beyond his years, sparked with a curiosity tempered by the weariness of staring into the abyss.

The older man motioned for Cathán to follow him as he left. Cathán had joined Erlender soon after gaining journeyman status, and his wizard robes still looked new on his lean frame. His clean-shaven jaw revealed a swarthy complexion beneath his shoulder-length raven-black hair. A silver ring adorned with a swirling rune hung around his neck.

The two mages left the inn.

Erlender's success with the harbor master exceeded his expectations. He had the names and destinations of all passenger ships that had left the docks over the past two years but no passenger manifests.

"Why should I care who goes on the ships?" The harbor master had been surprised at the question.

There were often men, alone or in groups, who traded labor for passage on merchant vessels, so his list would not ensure he found which way Jason went. He mulled this over, deciding he could not track down men who chose to work their way to a destination. The captains might not have been truthful in any case.

That evening, Erlender visited the docks to observe the captured lightning. He saw glass cylinders glowing brightly, with unfamiliar lines going to each. He watched men climb the poles on which the lights were mounted every hour and fiddle with something he could not see. The lights brightened as the men worked on them.

The pungent scent of a recent lightning strike blended with the usual harbor odors of fish, tar, and sweating men.

He heard a buzzing and felt heat as he approached a light pole. He could not look directly at the source; it was almost as bright as a noon sun. The light penetrated the evening fog that rolled in from the ocean.

An amazing technology at work, he thought.

When he returned to the inn, Arkadios and Cathán awaited him. He recognized the older mage by his height and graying hair, but Cathán's shiny black hair was also unmistakable.

Cathán said, "We found quite a bit about the captured lightning. You were correct that it was a mage and a natural philosopher. They may have hired an engineer to help construct and install each light, though.

"A water wheel rotates iron disks through a lodestone in the shape of a horseshoe, producing lightning flowing through a strand of copper wrapped in paper coated in wax. That strand goes to each light, and another returns to the rotating disks.

"Two finger-sized cylinders of charcoal and powdered sugar are held close together until lightning forms. The glass restricts air so the canister doesn't burn up, and a mirrored surface directs the light downward."

Arkadios added, "The mage is named Jablochkov, and the philosopher is Davy. The first approached Messer Trinidad Atkin to install on his docks and warehouse, allowing him to operate all day and all night.

"It wasn't long until all the warehouses and docks wanted the lights. The mayor is negotiating to light up parts of the city."

"Fascinating! I wonder how long it will be before all shipping centers have lighting on their docks," Erlender said.

After a moment, he shook his head and brought out a sheet of paper. "Here are the names and destinations of ships carrying passengers for the last two years. I need you and the others to approach each one in port and ask if they recognize the sketch of Jason." He handed the list to Cathán. "Cathán, make copies of the list and the sketch so you, Arkadios, and the others can approach the ships in port. If none of them recognize the man, we will split into teams and follow each to search for him where they stop.

"We should also question the dock workers. Perhaps we can narrow the list based on who saw him, even if we can't identify the ship."

Three days passed as Erlender's men circulated among the sailors and dock workers, showing the sketch, greasing palms, and questioning people. Some recognized Jason, but none knew which vessel he had boarded.

Erlender spent the time questioning the guards at the city gates. One remembered Jason entering with a group of five men. All had told the same story of leaving the king's army and searching for their fortunes farther away.

Six of the ten ships that had entered the harbor after Jason arrived were in port but denied giving him passage.

The next passenger ship entering Biblola's harbor was the *Firebird*. The captain neither confirmed nor denied Jason's presence on board, because four of his crew from the prior trip had left his employ and could not be questioned.

Erlender split his entourage into five groups, one for him and one for each remaining location. He booked passage on the *Firebird* to Twin Rivers Harbor, having time for a short, rejuvenating meeting with his captive before embarking on his journey. He paid no attention to how Arnock would react to her death when he came to clean up the remote shack.

The remainder of his troop stayed at Biblola. They would wait for the other three ships to arrive. If they could not determine if Jason had traveled on a particular ship, one group would book passage to search the destination. If they found the ship on which Jason had traveled, they would send message birds to all who were no longer at Biblola, and the groups would converge to follow Jason.

CHAPTER 9

Jason Prepares

Rituals
Sister Ismat of the Temple of the Moon
Damocles Academy of Magic

Rituals serve several purposes in magic: mnemonic devices for complex magic, ways to combine the strength of several into a magic action, and bindings at social events (marriages, coronations, etc.).

A ritual can be a mnemonic device to ensure that a pattern is constructed in the correct order and that nothing is left out. Gestures can be part of rituals, but they slow the creation of the pattern and should be avoided.

Rituals can enable a mage of lesser power to activate a pattern constructed by a greater. These are often embedded into social rituals, such as coronations and weddings, to activate beneficial magic for the person or persons involved.

The uneducated propagate and expand some rituals. They know a few rites and combine them without understanding the effects. Their magic consists of trial and error, and meaningless rites are elevated to sacred status, hamstringing advances because of this lack of understanding.

The kaihana, on the other hand, rely on rituals for their time-walking. Little is known of their rites beyond the lack of music or chanting. This is the only known merging that does not use music in some form.

Ten humans and one immature wolf arrived at Terlingua's gate the next day with a handcart of goods, asking for Jason. The group comprised six adult women and four children: three females and one male. The cart seemed to hold clothing and not much else.

Three kaihana, working near the entrance to the farm, greeted them, and one ran to get Maliyah.

When Maliyah arrived with Elani, she said, "Good afternoon. Jason is not available right now. I am Maliyah, a member of the guiding council, and this is Elani, also on the council. How may we assist you?"

The new arrivals looked at one another. Finally, one spoke up.

"I am called Akela. We are all friends of Jason and are seeking asylum."

"Welcome, Akela. Jason spoke of you. You are a two-skinned wolf, correct?" Maliyah asked.

Akela was taken aback. "Yes, we are all two-skinned, and we are all part of Jason's pack."

"Jason told me of a pack of three members, not ten and one."

"Our pack expanded after Jason, I, and two others formed it. After the former leader's death, the more aggressive members fought to become the new head. None were successful, and our old pack splintered.

"Our village collapsed with the fragmenting; the humans were unhappy with constant feuding and ostracized us. We seek refuge and a respite from unending demands to join one faction over another."

A woman with white hair added, "Some from the old pack found us and asked to join our pack. Jason felt the additions when each occurred, though he was not present."

Maliyah looked back and forth between the two speakers. "My, we don't usually get such large groups arriving. How many families are among you?"

"Three mothers with children account for five. We are used to living close together—one characteristic we share with our wolves. Further, we tend to have days while the wolves take nights. Our space needs are less than humans or kaihana."

"I see. Now, about your wolves—"

"We know to avoid farms." Akela interrupted Elani. "We will, however, hunt rabbits and other small pests in and around the farm."

"We will certainly offer you short-term asylum, Akela. A longer-term association must wait until you have been here awhile and the guiding council approves. I hope that is not a problem."

"We are grateful for whatever you can provide," said the platinum blonde who had spoken earlier.

Akela said, "Let me introduce our pack, Maliyah. This is Zarya. She is one of the original pack members. And this is—"

"Why don't you introduce us as we walk to your rooms, Akela?" Maliyah interrupted. "I imagine you would like to get settled and rest as soon as possible."

Turning to Elani, Maliyah said, "Are the four rooms in the south cottage still open?"

"Yes, they are. They have unfettered access to the forest, which, I think, will serve our two-skinned wolves well," Elani replied.

"Excellent," Maliyah said. "Please ask the kitchen staff for help with bedding and blankets for our new arrivals."

Maliyah guided the ten people and the wolf pup to the rooms while Elani detoured by the kitchens.

Jason completed his morning exercises and waited for his students to arrive at the exercise area. He saw Heather approaching from the main house.

He grinned. "Good afternoon, Heather. What brings you to our exercise area at this time of day? Need your balance checked?"

A sudden smile lit up her face, her eyes crinkled, and he saw a dimple form on her left cheek. "Hello, Jason. I guess I am a little early for tomorrow's session, but that is not why I am here. It has been almost a tenday since we talked about your magic. Is this a good time for you?"

"Yes. Today is Hathsday, my day off from farm duties, but you know that. I was just discussing archery targets with Maliyah."

She stopped, and her smile faded. "I know the council agreed, and I know your background and experience direct that we prepare to defend against raids ..." She trailed off, shook her head, and smiled again. "I did not come about that either. Do you want to meet in my exam room now, or is there another place you prefer?" Her gaze dropped as she finished speaking.

I wonder what that head movement means, he thought. *I don't know what I don't know.*

"Well, we are closest to the barn, but there are no chairs, while the dining hall and the main house are about the same distance. Or we could sit in the formal garden area."

"I want to watch you change skins." She blushed, looked away, and continued. "I thought we might sit on the chairs where the mothers watch our morning exercises. It is a short walk from there to the changing spot."

She gets embarrassed too, he thought. *I feel bad that I feel good about that.*

Jason rubbed his hands and feigned excitement, saying, "And we are looking at them, so we can start without delay," which earned him a smile and a head shake.

They sat, and she spoke. "After our last time, I saw flames form on your hands before you faded. I am sure you are on the right track. Have you reached your core on your own?"

Jason's eyes widened. "No, at least I don't think so. But I am not sure how I will know if I reach it."

She laughed. "I am sure there will be no doubt when it happens, but I could be wrong. How is your fire control now?"

Jason raised one hand, and after a short delay, a spark jumped from each fingertip.

"Well, that is new. One-handed and casual."

He saluted her with three fingers of his right hand extended.

She nodded. "Now please describe your recent shifts."

Jason drummed his fingers against his thigh, grimaced, and then began. "The slower change is less comfortable—"

"In what way?" she said.

"I will get to that. I enter the void. After the darkness of closed eyes, I see lights, as I described before. I feel that I am moving uphill and through what seems like a hallway."

"Sounds the same as last time," she commented.

"Yes, so far. Then I reach what seems to be a doorway or intersection; sense a dry, hot wind on my face; and see wind-blown flames. That sensation stabilizes, and I hear a breathy voice faintly whisper, 'Diablo.'"

"He is scary—destruction incarnate. He wants things to burn up and blow away. I struggle to get past this opening." Jason shuddered as he spoke.

"This is new, and I see that Diablo makes you uncomfortable. He sounds frightening."

A half smile played on his lips. "I agree. I don't want to imagine the havoc he might wreak if he gets out. I don't think I can control him. To make matters worse, I got stuck at Diablo several times and had to retreat and try again half an hour later. Xavier is not happy when that occurs.

"When I get past Diablo, I reach a second doorway or intersection and smell a coming rain."

"No name at this opening?" she asked.

"No, but I didn't have a name for the dry wind last time."

When she did not add anything, Jason continued. "Finally, I see a doorway shaped roughly like a human body, but the space between the rain and the opening feels larger than before. Then I stretch and expand until I feel air blowing on my face and chest; the stretching sensation fades, and Xavier surfaces."

"Getting stuck at Diablo is uncomfortable, almost physically."

After a moment, he took a deep breath and turned to face Heather.

"Do you know who or what Diablo is?" she asked.

"No, I do not. I think he may be a windstorm; I have heard of destructive storms in the desert: sirocco, haboobs, and derecho, for example. He feels like wind or air with a sense of identity."

"Is it a third skin of yours?"

Jason blinked several times and then spoke slowly. "No. At least I don't think so. Changing to Xavier was a little scary because it felt like I was stretching apart, and I expected it to hurt, so it did." He chortled. "That is one very good thing I learned while slowing the switch."

His face resumed a serious mien. "But we are one and the same, and the shift is not as rough as it was. I get no sense of fading for Diablo; I sense his anger and desire for destruction, which does *not* reflect any feeling of mine. He wants to be freed, and I suspect I can free him, but I do not know if I can call him back."

"So something other than a new skin," she said, pursing her lips and furrowing her brow.

Heather sat for a few minutes before saying, "You are, I think, making steady progress. I think you should speed past Diablo if you can and then slow down. Your discomfort with him must be important, but I can think of nothing to explain it. You are slowing the change and experiencing it in more detail. I also believe you are learning to control the change, but more is happening in you than we know."

"I will continue practicing," Jason said with a little laugh. "What else can I do?"

She joined him in the laugh. "Now let us retire to the changing space, so I can observe your transition." Her gentle smile offered a silent encouragement.

They walked the half dozen steps to the center of the rocky area.

Jason tried to keep his face expressionless and his movements deliberate while he undressed. He managed to complete that task without sneaking a glance in Heather's direction, but he imagined her looking his way and blushed.

Crouching, he called out, "We are ready."

When he heard her response, he started to change.

Several moments later, Heather saw flames form on Jason's arms and hands, followed by a fog forming on his skin and expanding. When the fog extended thirty feet end to end, it began to condense.

Xavier sat before her.

Lady Heather, I am delighted to see you again, the dragon said. *What were your observations this time?*

"Greetings, Xavier. I saw flames on Jason's arms and hands before he shifted. I think that means he is getting closer to his core," the healer replied. "What will that mean to the two of you?"

I doubt his reaching his core will affect our relationship, but thank you for asking.

"Is Jason present?"

Ah, yes. He is now. Do you wish to speak with him through me?

"As long as he knows I saw flames on his arms, I have nothing more to say to him right now."

Then farewell, Lady Heather. The dragon turned from her and took two bounds before spreading his wings and flying over the forest.

That evening, Xavier told Jason he needed to molt again but agreed the next night would be adequate, so Jason could postpone his class instead of being a no-show as the instructor the following morning.

After leading the residents in thasiwoda the following day, he told them there would be no class the next day. "Practice on your own, either together or alone. Remember, though, that none of you is good enough to critique others, so practice and watch one another without commenting on one another's skill or progress."

He pulled Heather aside. "The students are learning the names of the poses and the positions after one lesson," he said. "It will take several more for their balance to improve to an acceptable level; they are making excellent progress. I expect they will be ready for the transitions soon, and then we can work on slowing down so they maintain their balance at all times."

"And what comes after that?"

"Nothing needs to come after that. Maintaining balance in most situations prevents injuries, and daily discipline helps keep emotions under control during the day.

"Thasiwoda performed slowly improves balance and body control. However, the transitions are movements that occur during combat. Done quickly after practicing slowly, they prepare a person for battling hand to hand without losing balance. Losing your balance in battle almost ensures you lose.

"Watching others practice against one another trains the eye to detect the other's intention; this gives a practitioner an advantage over an untrained. While I hope none of our children are required to fight, it will ease my mind if they are prepared. So I want to start having the children compete with one another."

He paused for a moment, letting those words sink in. "Further, while the hands of an expert are weapons, it takes ten years or more to become proficient with hands alone, so I would like to extend the lessons to a weapon."

"Practice fighting? Is that wise? And what weapon do you have in mind?" she asked quietly.

"I believe so. The competitions I have in mind won't injure anyone beyond bruises. Practicing with others also improves a beginner's confidence. As to the weapon, a quarterstaff. We can use a regular staff; they are easier to find than a suitable log for quartering. The basics are easy to learn, and a man skilled with a quarterstaff can defeat a man with a sword.

"I also want to start using bows more. We have three or four young men who hunt small game, and me with my longbow. Increasing the number of archers will provide a greater deterrence."

"How much protection will half a dozen boys provide against a group of marauders that the Defenders don't?"

"That's a fair question. Tovia explained the Defenders' alarm response to me. They will arrive in about half an hour—enough time for some serious damage to some of Terlingua's residents. However, facing even half a dozen armed boys and women will slow them down until the Defenders arrive," he answered.

"Teaching our young men and women to use the staff will be good insurance. I think we should invite the kaihana to participate; I do not know their views on preparing to fight, and their body shape is different, so my lessons will need tailoring. I also want to invite all the adults to participate—the more the better. Fewer will get hurt if we can hold our own until the Defenders arrive."

"I, uh, don't know. We have never needed more protection than the Defenders provide. I would hate to antagonize them."

Jason nodded. "I imagine they will approve. They protect the entire valley, and having the farm prepared to hold out until they arrive will make their jobs easier."

Heather shook her head. "I know you have a military background, and I appreciate your concern and offer to help. I just don't know ..." Her voice trailed off.

"What are your concerns?" he asked.

She hesitated before saying, "I don't think violence is ever the answer. I don't like the idea of our children being in line to get injured. I am concerned about injuries while training. I do not know what resources such a program will require.

"However, I will bring it to the farm's guiding council overmorrow. I know I told you about it; it comprises five kaihana—including Maliyah—and me and Tovia. Will you be available should they want more details than I know about your proposal? And please take no action until the council has decided."

"That sounds fair. What time do you meet? I may need to negotiate with my other self if you meet after dark."

"We meet in the main house parlor after dinner. It will be dark."

"Excellent. I will let Xavier know when he wakes, and I will sit on the back porch until summoned or dismissed." He smiled at her.

She nodded and walked to her medical office in the main house.

Xavier hunted that evening, consuming half an adult deer. He took the carcass to his cave. The following day, he consumed his shed skin, except for the entire wing he set aside for Maliyah. Then he finished eating the deer, changed to human skin, and walked to the farm from Ognyen.

That evening, Heather, Maliyah, Elani, and Tovia went to the parlor in the main house after dinner. Jason walked with them to the house but sat on the back porch, waiting in case he was needed in the council meeting.

It wasn't long until the rest of the council arrived and took seats. Elowen, the oldest kaihana at Terlingua, was the last to arrive.

Following kaihana traditions, the oldest in the room led the meeting. Elowen's face was a road map of time; her skin was etched with a lifetime of experiences. She glanced around the room.

"All are present? Good. Let us begin. Maliyah, tell us how the farm is doing." Elowen's low, rumbling voice carried through the quiet room.

"The crops are bearing fruit, but insects are becoming a problem. We are seeing fewer birds, which could explain the increase in bug damage. Since the arrival of the two-skinned wolves, the damage by rabbits and squirrels has been down." She paused. "I do not know if the wolves are scaring the birds. I do not think so, since the birds are active during the day. Perhaps something has interfered with the bats in the area. Ognyen Cave still has a good-sized nest, though. I am sure we are well on our way to an excellent harvest."

"Good. You have managed the farm for almost thirty years, and I trust your judgment in these matters," Elowen said. "Elani, you are acting like you wish to speak. Do so now."

Elani looked up with a flicker of worry in her eyes. "More and more people are seeking Heather. The road to Smoky Springs is congested several days each tenday. I wonder if it is selfish to keep her here, when she could be of greater service to the community if she moved into town." Her voice trailed off.

A question hung in the air.

"I do not wish to move to Smoky Springs," Heather said without heat. "Terlingua is my home. I visit town twice each tenday. Perhaps I should increase that. And we should encourage people to visit the Defenders' infirmary in town. They have four qualified healers. I can be there in an emergency in less than an hour."

"Well," Elowen said, "more people needing care is a concern for the valley but not our primary consideration. If Heather is willing to change her schedule as she indicates and we encourage people to visit the infirmary for minor ills, that may solve the problem. Is this something we need to vote on?"

"No," Heather answered. "I will change my schedule and spread the word."

"Excellent," the elder declared.

The council discussed several other issues that affected the members of their community, primarily issues with kaihana or humans objecting to tasking or training. The matters were resolved quickly that day.

"What else do we need to discuss?" Elowen asked.

Heather cleared her throat. "As you all know, our only male resident is teaching any who wish to maintain their balance—a discipline called thasiwoda. So far, only humans are attending his morning sessions. He wants to expand to teaching quarterstaff and hand-to-hand combat so we can hold our own until the Defenders arrive in the event of any attack on the farm. He is also interested in teaching kaihana, though he isn't sure he will be successful, because human and kaihana bodies are so different."

She swallowed. "I have personal objections to doing this. In addition, doing so will take resources from the farm regarding materials and time."

Elowen's eyes narrowed. "Is this the human you saw during your time-walk, Maliyah? The one who brought the star of the Moirai to our land?"

Maliyah nodded with her brow furrowed. "Yes, but I know nothing of this star of the Moirai."

Heather injected. "He carries a kalasha. Kalashas are often called the stars of the Moirai. It's a symbol of the Triple Goddess."

"What say the rest of you?" Elowen asked.

Maliyah said, "I believe he is the Beuman√, and we should support what he wants."

"And you, Tovia?" the elder asked.

Tovia, with her face a mask of contemplation, spoke. "He is a teacher of balance, skilled and competent. I knew another who practiced as he does, and that man was a formidable opponent. The Defenders have no objection to this but will not change their procedures."

Elowen nodded. "Then should we welcome his endeavor? All in favor?"

A chorus of agreement filled the room, save for Heather's solitary dissent.

"So we have agreed, so it shall be. We will support Jason. However, the farm must not suffer. No crops or livestock will be diverted for his project. Nor shall anyone be assigned to his training. Any who wish to join him in the morning are welcome to do so." She turned to Maliyah. "Ensure this, and encourage the kaihana in residence to at least try.

"Is there any other business for this council?" she asked. She surveyed the room and gave a final nod, rising.

The meeting was adjourned.

As the lingering silence filled the room, the kaihana began to disperse with minds occupied by the implications of the decisions made. The old ways and the new were colliding, and the future of their community hung in the balance.

Heather turned to Tovia. "I accept the decision of the council. However, I ask you to share the decision with Jason."

"I will do as you ask," the young Defender said.

Tovia exited the main house through the back doors, which opened onto a large open porch. Jason sat cross-legged at its edge, puffing his pipe and blowing an occasional smoke ring.

The night was clear, and the sounds of crickets and other insects filled the air. Tobacco smoke, with its complex, earthy aroma with undertones of leather and hay, permeated the area near his seat.

"Greetings, Jason," she said as she sat beside him. "Are you enjoying the evening?"

"Yes, I am. The garden looks extremely peaceful in the moonlight," he answered. "I assume the guiding council's meeting is over? And you are the bearer of news?"

She laughed. "Yes, and yes. I know the doors were closed, but did you overhear any of the meeting?"

"No. I was focused on watching the insects and bats flying about. Besides, I wasn't invited, and eavesdropping is just rude."

"The council approved your proposal to teach quarterstaff and hand-to-hand, with the caveat that the farm's support is limited to permission. You won't get any materials or people assigned to help you."

"Well, that is good news to my ears. Heather objected, and I wasn't sure how much sway she had with the council."

Tovia nodded. "She is uncomfortable with the thought that violence may come to Smoky Springs and Terlingua. However, the kaihana are very pragmatic and welcome the increased security, especially if they don't have to pay anything except for free time."

"I will need some assistance in teaching quarterstaff moves. You mentioned you were proficient with a staff—will you volunteer morning time to be my demonstration partner?"

"I need to check with Defender Clowers. It may require changing my Defender assignments. Would it be OK if I was there every other day?"

"That sounds perfect to me." He knocked the ash and dottle from his pipe, donned his boots, and stood. "It will take me several days to find reeds and assemble training staffs that won't hurt students. Let me know when you know your schedule. We must discuss the training sequence, so plan some time for that too."

She stood also. "Walk me to my room?" she asked.

Jason's eyebrows rose, and he stared at her for a moment. His eyes sparkled with amusement as he looked at Tovia. "My lady, it would be an honor to escort you to your chambers. Consider it a small token of my gratitude for your support of my proposal." He held out his bent arm.

She took his forearm with both hands, and they walked to the dormitories.

Following Maliyah's directions, Jason found a stand of sturdy reeds near Terlingua. He harvested a few score reeds and set them out to dry.

When they were dry enough, he tied them in bundles of five. Each sheaf was about the diameter of a quarterstaff and two-thirds the length of one. He whipped each end and wrapped twine along the length to stabilize the reeds.

The next day, he introduced them to his class.

"We will learn how to use a quarterstaff for defense. We will start with these reed bundles; they are lighter and more flexible than staffs and won't break bones while we learn to use them. They will bruise and raise welts, so do not try moves beyond what I show you. At least not yet.

"Tovia, please join me to demonstrate the first defensive moves."

He directed Tovia to attack him overhand slowly while he held his bundle of reeds in a blocking position. The pair demonstrated attacking and defending from both the left and right sides.

Jason and Tovia paired up his students and had them repeat the moves demonstrated. Each critiqued the students, had them repeat, and then had them change positions and redo the exercise from the other position.

Unknown to Jason, several avian two-skinned Defenders observed the lessons and reported them to Chief Defender Clowers.

———— ∞ ————

Hathsday was Jason's day off. He found Maliyah near the main doors of the barn right after breakfast. When she completed assigning tasks, he asked if there was a location where he could set up an archery range and straw to make into targets. She said yes to both.

In addition to his day off each tenday, he had a little time between the end of the workday and dinner that he could apply to make targets. He knew Xavier might complain if he spent too much time on it. It was a low-priority item. Heather and the farm's council knew he was doing it but lacked his sense of urgency.

The straw was the easiest acquisition. A large pile of spoiled hay and straw near the barn awaited its fate as bedding for the animals. Some of the material in that pile was suitable for that or mulch but nothing else. Some of it was too dry for feed but otherwise pristine, perfect for archery targets.

After soaking, he could braid a three-strand string from the straw, which would get woven into a thin rope about thumb size. The rope would get coiled into a mat about shoulder width. When he had three mats, he would stitch them together with twine, forming a cylinder three ropes thick and the width of a man's chest for the bale.

He could work in his room or the covered area just outside until it was time for the target frame. That would require woodworking tools for the stands, so it could only be done in the barn. Should he ask Heather for farm staff to help make them? She did not share his sense of urgency in training residents to defend Terlingua, and he feared pushing the issue could result in her withdrawing support for his teaching thasiwoda.

Last, he would need space for a range and mounds of earth for each butt. Mounting each bale on a stand against the butts would complete the archery range.

He thought of the bow hiding in a staff beside his bed. Dare he amend his needs for the range with Maliyah to longbow distances?

Could he put a target at his range of 240 yards? Physically, it should not be hard. Long, open spaces were abundant on farms but not static. He would negotiate times when no one would be too close to the target, so he could practice. A shorter distance would make his proposal more palatable, he decided.

It would get tongues wagging that a longbow archer was in town. Five Defenders, one wizard, and one brewer knew he carried one. Gossip could already have been spreading.

He decided he would construct a bank of targets for regular bows and one for him. His would be the fourth target. Preparing the residents was more important. He could wait for one at his range if three weren't enough for them to practice.

Maliyah brought half a dozen young kaihana to Jason two days later.

"Does this go against Elowen's direction to not use farm resources?" he asked.

"No. I went to Sinistrad and asked for volunteers from among the apprentice weavers. This does not affect the farm's resources," she answered.

The kaihana were master spinners and weavers. They bred a variety of spiders that could live close together and used filament from their egg cases to make silk, which was in high demand. They spun milkweed fiber into a thread almost as soft as silk, usually blended with cotton for a strong, soft yarn.

Assisting Jason allowed them to develop their weaving skills and help implement his plans for defending Terlingua.

Instead of a three-straw base thread for the targets, they braided five. This resulted in a denser weave that would last through several arrow punctures.

Jason watched them in awe. Their fingers raced as they formed strings from straw.

Jason was grateful for the kaihana's help; they produced four targets in eight days instead of the three months Jason had estimated it would take him alone. He could not have done it without them.

Jason faced Maliyah and bowed his head. "This is beyond what I had hoped for." His eyes glistened with emotion. "'I cannot thank you enough for your extraordinary work," he said. His voice was filled with gratitude.

Once the targets were finished, Jason focused on acquiring bows and arrows. He knew he would need a good supply for residents' practice.

Smoky Springs was known for its skilled bowyers and fletchers, and Jason was confident he could find what he needed there.

Tovia recommended a bowyer to Jason.

Kahu was a short, stocky man with a thick beard. He greeted Jason warmly and asked him what he was looking for. Jason explained his plans to make Terlingua more secure and said he wanted five short bows in lengths from four feet to five feet, six inches and three score arrows suitable for young adults.

"And what do you need for yourself?"

"I have a longbow, so my only need is a supply of arrows long enough for me to draw them fully."

"A longbowman! I did not know there was one in the valley. Our bowmen have a range of about a hundred yards. What is your range, young man?"

"I can hit a target the size of a man's chest at 240 yards," Jason replied.

"That is impressive! I knew the king had a few hundred longbowmen, but I did not realize their range was so great.

"Do you know the construction details for a longbow? If so, can you share them?" Kahu asked.

"Most of the king's men had ranges of 300 yards. However, the short bow can aim and release more rapidly. There is a place for each on the battlefield.

"To answer your question, all I know of longbow construction is to use yew wood. I am sorry." Jason shook his head.

The bowyer nodded and said he could satisfy Jason's needs. They negotiated a price of one-quarter of Jason's pay for delivering the athamé to Clowers.

Now he needed archery students.

The following day, he asked for volunteers from his thasiwoda students. Tovia, Heather, and two other young women volunteered for archery lessons. The young men who hunted did not.

CHAPTER 10

Teach Your Children Well

The Way of the Warrior

Listen, then, and learn the Way of the Warrior.

A warrior decides and then acts.

A warrior is neither rash nor timid in deciding.

When acting, a warrior commits totally to the action.

Warriors own their actions; they are their only worthy possessions.

A warrior is true to his word and shuns falsehoods.

A warrior is always prepared for battle, both physically and mentally.

A warrior does not allow habit to decide; all actions are intentional.

A warrior prepares for each day, anticipating contingencies.

A warrior knows that actions have consequences and accepts those without excuse.

A warrior decides based on what is known and what can be done.

A warrior is willing to learn, grow, and adapt to new challenges.

A warrior is compassionate and understanding, even to his enemies.

A warrior is humble, knowing he is not perfect and can always learn more.

A warrior faces his fears and is not ruled by them.

You are a warrior. You will fail at times and succeed at times. Neither defines you; learn from each what you can.

Do not lose yourself in the past; you do not live in the past. Do not lose yourself in the future; the future is not fixed. Remain in the present, and drink deeply of life.

Do not let your emotions cloud your decisions. Love, anger, worries, and
fears are distractions. Decisions based on them are still decisions. Own
them. You are a warrior.

You are defined by the decisions you make.

The way will change you; you will change the way. Accept the changes and
continue.

A warrior decides and then acts.

A warrior endures.

It is the way of the warrior.

W hen Melody, the girl with the golden voice who had led the full-moon
chant, learned that Tovia attended the morning exercise sessions
with Jason, she begged her mother, Fionola, to allow her to watch.

The following day, Fionola rose early and helped Melody to the exercise
area.

The young girl stared with wide-eyed fascination at the group performing
thasiwoda.

"I like watching the others perform for Jason," Melody told her mother
later in the day.

"I am glad you do. I like that you are interested in the others and coming
out each day to watch them. It is wonderful to see you outside," Fionola
replied, smiling at her daughter.

After a few days of observing, Melody began participating by calling for
the next pose. Her calls were often accurate, even though Jason mixed up
the sequence of poses to ensure the students paid attention and to introduce
new transitions.

After one session, Melody told her mother, "I love watching Tovia and
the others; I wish I could join."

Fionola tried to keep pity from her voice as she murmured to her
daughter, "You know you can't stand still on your feet without your crutches,
and each pose starts from that stance. I am so sorry, babe."

"I know. I still wish I could," Melody said with despondence heavy on
her face.

Jason noticed the young girl sitting next to her mother and intently watching the exercises. He was surprised when she first called out the next pose, and he encouraged her to call them by bowing in her direction and waving at her, whether she called them correctly or not.

After three days of her calling poses with him, Jason approached Fionola. "Fionola, I would like to include Melody in the morning exercises if you permit it."

Fionola raised her right eyebrow and dropped her jaw. "Are you daft, man? How can she perform the poses, when she can't even stand on two legs?" she blurted out.

"She may not be able to do the same as the rest, but I can teach her to maintain her balance on one foot. She may still need crutches to walk, though.

"Further, as her balance improves, she will fall less often. I will teach her to fall without injuring herself, and I promise I will not let her fall during a lesson." He tried to reassure her.

Heather and Elani were standing close enough to hear the conversation. They moved closer.

Heather interjected. "I think Jason's idea to include Melody is wonderful. I understand how you feel, but Melody will be as safe with Jason as when she stands with you while you watch, and this could be amazing for her."

Fionola remained reluctant.

Elani added, "Fionola, I understand your concerns, but Melody would benefit from joining the morning exercises."

"But she is so fragile!" Fionola countered.

"Jason will take every precaution to make sure she's safe," Elani replied. "When she falls now, she almost always gets bruised and scratched and sometimes injures a joint. Joining the exercises will reduce the number of times she falls, and with time, her falls will be more controlled. They will strengthen her muscles, which will protect her joints. And she will learn how to fall safely."

"I don't know, Elani. I'm still not sure about this," Fionola said.

"Fionola, please give it a try. Let Melody participate in Jason's morning exercises for a tenday, and see how she does. If she's not enjoying it or if you're not comfortable with it, then you can always pull her out. But I think it's worth giving her a chance," Heather pleaded.

"And think of how much her mood has improved with just a few days of watching. Think about how much better she will feel when she is successful," Elani said.

"Melody needs to be more active and would benefit from participating in the exercises, Fionola. It would improve her balance and coordination and be a great way for her to interact with others each day," Heather added.

"But what if she gets discouraged? What if she feels like she can't keep up?" Fionola said.

"I don't think that will happen. Jason is very good at encouraging his students. He'll make sure Melody feels successful, no matter what," Heather said.

Fionola sighed. "OK. I'll let her try it. But if she doesn't like it or gets hurt, I'm pulling her out."

The following day, Jason invited Melody to join him. With a broad grin and sparkling eyes, she turned to her mother for permission. She beamed when her mother nodded her approval.

Before they left her mother's side, Jason said, "Melody, I tell you now, on my honor, that if you fall, I will catch you—time after time. Please take my hand, and come with me to the exercise area." He reached his right hand out to her.

Melody looked up to her mother, who nodded. The girl took Jason's hand but maintained one crutch as they walked a few yards from the porch.

Jason turned to face her after reaching an area free of tripping hazards. He crouched down before her and began. "Now take ahold of my head with your free hand. Take a good handful of hair, and hold on tight. Good. Now I will take your crutch from you; when I do, grab my hair with your other hand."

He tossed the cane an arm's length away, slightly out of reach, emphasizing that he was her support. Melody watched the crutch with a trembling lip as it landed a yard away from them. She wobbled slightly and started to scream, releasing her hold and flailing her arms. Her scream was cut short when she realized that both Jason's hands were on her waist, holding her firmly and preventing her from falling. She relaxed a little in the cradle of his hands.

"Now grasp my hair again with both hands while I hold you."

She did so and smiled at him, closed her eyes, and took a deep breath. After opening her eyes, she bit her lower lip.

"I am going to remove one hand. Hold on tight."

He slowly moved his right hand from her waist down her side and grasped her left ankle. He paused there for a moment, studying her expression. Since she remained calm, he continued down until his fingers were beneath her arch.

"Hang on. I am going to move your foot." He raised it until the tops of her hip bones were parallel to the ground, shifting his grip so his palm was beneath her sole.

"Now imagine you are a candle, and raise one hand above your head like the flame."

With one hand on her waist and the other holding one foot, he kept her from wobbling as she raised one hand.

They repeated raising one hand half a dozen times, alternating arms.

"Excellent! Now raise both your hands so your arms form the shape of a flame."

It took several tries for her to build up the courage to release her second hand; she returned one or both hands to his head several times as he encouraged her.

When she finally succeeded, he smiled and said, "That is it, my brave one. Now I am going to remove my left hand slowly. Tell me if you are falling, and I will return my hand to your waist. Are you ready to stand alone?"

She looked at her mother, who was smiling despite tears running down her cheeks. Turning back to Jason, she nodded.

Melody's eyes widened when his left hand was about an inch from her waist, and she trembled. Before she could cry, his hand was back on her waist, and he praised her for her effort.

He helped her relax and had her return both hands to his head. She performed the candle twice before Jason called an end for the day and carried her and the crutch back to Fionola.

"I look forward to our session tomorrow," Jason said as he sat Melody beside her mother.

"Momma! Did you see? I did it! I was a candle for Jason!" Melody's excitement had her mother laughing and crying at the same time.

"I never expected to see her so happy," Fionola choked out past her tears.

Heather approached Jason. "You have a red mark across your cheek and eye."

"I do?" He raised his hand to his left eye. "Yes, it is a little tender. I guess Melody made contact when she thought she was falling." He chuckled.

"That may become a black eye before morning."

"A wound fairly dealt and honorably accepted. I would be a poor teacher if I didn't receive a blow from a student now and again."

Heather stared at him. "You are a strange man, Jason Archer."

He bowed to her. "A title I accept, given from an admirable person." His tone was slightly mocking, as among friends.

He turned and stepped to see how his other students were doing.

Later that day, Jason walked by the tack room and sought Aishwarya, the kaihana who made sandals and other leather goods for residents. He described Melody's foot size and the shoe thickness needed so the girl could stand straight.

The kaihana tilted her head to one side and frowned. Shaking her head, she walked to her workbench, picked up a single sandal, and returned to Jason.

"Why do you have a single left sandal with a three-inch-thick sole on your workbench?" Jason asked as she handed it to him.

She shrugged. "Sometimes I get vivid visions that repeat; these I act on. About six months ago, I saw this sandal. I did not know when it was needed, but I made it and set it aside." She scowled. "I should have realized it was for Melody; I suspect the Goddess hid that from me until you arrived."

Jason's face showed shock. "You foresaw the need for this special sandal six months ago? And you made it?"

"Yes, sometimes the future becomes clear. The more clear the vision, the less clear the time it is needed. It is true for many kaihana."

Jason shook his head. "I thank you for seeing the need and for making the sandal. I have no idea whom to thank for the prophecy."

After the class, Heather lingered near Jason, pushing back a stray strand of hair. "Jason, wait a moment. I am so pleased you urged Fionola to allow

Melody to join in. And Fionola is so proud of her and so grateful to you for the care you show while teaching her little girl."

His eyes crinkled at the corners as a smile split his face open, and his eyes glistened with happiness. "I am so happy for the two of them. It does my heart good to think of Melody gaining strength and confidence."

Heather chuckled. "I have time before my first patient today. Shall we walk to my exam room and discuss your last transition?"

Jason cleared his throat, glancing briefly at Maliyah, before replying. "Of course. Your wish is my command, m'lady." He gave an exaggerated bow, which earned laughter from all in earshot.

Jason attended to their surroundings intently, but he didn't think his eye swiveling would catch the attention of anyone except Heather.

Once he was sure they could not be overheard, he began speaking in a lowered voice. "I am glad your advice is helping me too."

"I am glad of that." She also spoke quietly. "What do you feel and observe as you change skins now?"

He frowned a little. "As before, I enter the void, and then I feel that I am climbing uphill and through a hallway. The first intersection still blows a dry, hot wind on my face, and I see wind-blown flames. A breathy voice says, 'Diablo.' The sound is stronger now, but I can—and do—pass quickly. I suspect that passing by slowly made him aware of me, and he tried to hinder me."

"Are you certain it's Diablo's doing?" Heather asked with a glint of curiosity in her eyes.

"No, I am not. I occasionally feel resistance as I pass him by, and that is the only explanation I have for it not being there all the time."

She nodded. "Please continue."

"After passing that intersection, I reach the second doorway and smell a coming rain. I can hear a gentle rainfall and a whispering, gurgling voice saying, 'Tess.' I believe it is also some form of self-aware storm. She—I think of the sound as feminine—lacks Diablo's destructive urges. Stopping there, I get the sense that I am being studied by a curious child. I can't justify that sensation, though."

"Now each of your obstacles is named," she said as they reached the steps to the house.

He nodded as he reached to open the door for her. "Yes, I can name each. And make jokes about them, but I don't know how else their names help."

She tried to hide her smile as he opened the door.

As he ushered her into the house, he continued glancing around to keep track of their distance from other residents. "After leaving Tess's intersection, I see the body-shaped doorway. The space around me feels larger now, but no separate passageway appears. And the void has few features to measure."

"Well, this is new. If the end you find is expanding, perhaps something will show there." She stopped and stared at him for a moment. "I urge you to continue slowing. Try to measure the size, shape, or time interval. You are close to some revelation, and it could be your core."

He nodded. When she took another step, he continued. "Waiting there, my neck and lower back begin to stretch and expand. Those sensations fade for me, followed by Xavier surfacing."

They reached the door to her exam room. She unlocked the door and opened it for him.

As she walked over to her desk, she picked up a fragment of dragon skin Xavier had shed earlier. "These are tough. I haven't found anything that will grind them into powder. They resist every tool I have. Oil of vitriol softens them but doesn't seem to dissolve them. I am happy your dragon gave me these to experiment on."

Jason said, "I will try to remember that this evening. Perhaps he has some insights into powdering his scales."

She sat and directed him to take a seat also. "Are you sure your surveillance wasn't noticed by others? If someone thinks we are keeping secrets, all will study us more intently than a child watching a chick hatching."

Jason laughed. "I am pretty sure. I tried to keep my head movements subtle. Did I fail?"

She returned the laughter. "I wasn't sure until just now. It looked like you were blinking rapidly, and I could see no reason for that."

"Observant and bold to ask such a direct question. I must be on my guard around you, I see."

"But my observations are what you pay me for."

He laughed again.

"Do you still fear the transition to the dragon?" she asked with her humor fading.

"No, I am used to changing skins. And I think most of my fear was due to anticipating pain that didn't appear as I dissolved," he answered.

"Show me your fire now, please," she said.

Jason held out one hand; a few heartbeats later, a column of a dozen sparks rose a foot above it.

"Well, it seems your control over fire is improving." She laughed. "In our last session, I noticed flames on your arms as you faded, and I am curious if that has changed."

He grinned at her. "I cannot tell you that; neither can Xavier. We are blind for a few moments during each change." He rose and stretched. "I will meet you behind the barn at the end of the day, and you can see for yourself what has changed."

"How about we walk there after dinner?" she said with a coy smile.

"That sounds perfect. I will find you at the dining hall after I clean up. Farewell." He stood, bowed his way out, and walked back to the barn to find Maliyah.

Jason sat where he could see both entrances to the dining hall. He was joined by six of the wolf pack. He watched Heather enter and sit with Maliyah, two other kaihana, and two human women.

When Heather finished her meal, Jason excused himself from his companions, cleared the table, and met her at the door closest to the barn. "I am ready now if you are," he said.

He extended an arm for her to take, and the two exited, walking to the rocky area between the barn and the forest.

Without further conversation, they took their usual positions. Heather stood with her back to the barn. Her shoulders were tense. Jason stood ten feet away with his gaze fixed on the forest. He took a deep breath, trying to quell the flutter of nerves in his chest. As he began to undress, he heard the creaking of the barn doors and the distant screech of a hawk.

"I'm ready," he announced. His voice was barely a whisper.

Heather nodded. Her eyes were filled with a mix of anticipation and concern.

Heather counted the time between his announcing he was ready and his fading. She observed flames flickering on his shoulders, arms, and hands before the dragon appeared.

Xavier stretched his neck and wings before turning his attention to the woman. *Lady Heather, it is good to see you again,* the dragon said. *What were your observations this time?*

"Greetings, Xavier. First, it took almost half again as long to change this time as last time, and I saw flames flickering on Jason's shoulders, arms, and hands before he shifted. I am sure that means he is making progress," she replied. "Is Jason present?"

Yes, he is aware of you from within. Do you wish to speak with him through me?

"No, I think the lack of disorientation is a good sign, though," she said.

Then farewell. The dragon turned from her and flew over the forest.

The next morning, Jason brought Aishwarya's custom shoe for Melody to the morning class. He had wrapped it in a clean white cloth and tied it with a leather thong.

As he had the day before, Jason approached Melody at her mother's side. "Please join us again this morning, Melody," he said. "But before we begin, I have something for you."

He knelt and handed her the white bundle. Her jaw dropped open, and her cheeks flushed crimson.

For a moment, Melody could only stare, speechless. Then a squeak escaped her lips. Her fingers fumbled with the leather thong, and her hands trembled as she opened the package.

"A shoe!" she exclaimed. She looked up at Jason with surprise still etched on her face.

"Yes. A shoe to help you balance and hold your head up as you walk." He smiled. "Now, walk with me, and I will help you put it on."

She dropped her crutches, flung both arms around his neck, and, with tears running down her cheeks, exclaimed, "Thank you! Thank you so much!"

Jason laughed gently and patted her back. "You should also thank Aishwarya for crafting them."

He stood, and the girl took one of Jason's hands but maintained one crutch as they walked a few yards from the porch.

Jason had her hold his hair with both hands as he put the sandal on her bent foot. The multiple layers of leather added to the sole allowed her to stand with her hips aligned, as Jason wanted. Extra laces held the sandal firmly on her foot, supporting her as she shifted her balance under his direction. A carved felt insole, shaped by Aishwarya to match her vision, fit her foot perfectly.

While tying the laces, he wondered why the Goddess allowed children to be born with the wrong bones. He blinked back tears, but one fell onto Melody's left foot.

"That tingles!" She giggled. "Why are you crying, Jason?" she asked.

"Because you are so brave, Melody," he replied.

With the sandal in place, Jason moved both hands to her waist and had her repeat the candle poses from the day before.

He taught her the cross asana, standing upright with arms straight out from her sides. Once she stood firmly in the cross, he had her rotate her torso left and right as he held his hands an inch from her waist.

The second day concluded much as the first had, with Melody exclaiming her progress to her mother while Fionola smiled through tears.

The day after, Melody was not present. Jason started the class on a sequence and sought the apartment the girl shared with her mother.

"She is still abed, crying because she hurts too much to attend the lessons today," Fionola said.

Jason asked to see her and went to her room. "Melody, I understand your muscles are too sore today for exercise. This is normal. You used muscles in ways you have not before, and they are crying about it since it is new. They will learn as they strengthen; fear not."

Melody's eyes widened, and her jaw dropped open. "You came to find me!" she exclaimed.

"Of course. I needed to know why my newest student was absent," he said with a big grin. "If you allow me, I can massage the newly strengthened muscles in your legs to reduce the pain."

Melody looked to her mother for approval before nodding her consent.

Heather arrived a few moments later with a jar of salve. After discussing his presence, she offered it to Jason.

"I will massage this into her calves, ankles, and feet if that matches your prescription, Heather," he said.

"Exactly what I would do. Why don't you take her left leg, and I will work on her right? It will be over sooner that way," she responded.

Jason applied the salve to and massaged Melody's lower leg. As he applied pressure to the muscles and joints, he felt a tingling in his hands like but not the same as using magic to start a fire. This was a new experience for him, so he put aside thinking about it until later; it could've just been something in the ointment.

"Your hands are warm, while Heather's are cool," Melody said.

Heather looked at Jason and said, "Jason has a fire affinity. As he massages your legs, he is projecting life mana, but some heat follows along with it, making his hands feel warm. I have a spirit affinity, so spirit flows from my hands. Spirit usually feels cool. Our mana increases the potency of the lotion's healing herbs and oils."

When the pair finished with her lower legs, Jason glanced at Heather. "I am so glad you are here. I believe she will benefit from massaging on her thighs. Will you please take care of that?"

"I am happy to finish our treatment on Melody," Heather responded.

Facing Melody, he said, "I think it would be easier if you watched tomorrow and we resumed overmorrow. Your muscles need time to recover from all the new things they have done; then they will be stronger, and we can add new poses."

Melody smiled. "Thank you, Jason."

"You are most welcome, my brave one."

Jason left the room as Melody lay back in her bed, and Heather continued her massage.

Erlender sat at a table near the back of the inn. Two days of searching the docks at Twin Rivers City and Duke Rashad's castle had resulted in naught, despite his having a sketch of Jason. He was pleased he'd found one of Jason's fellow archers who liked to draw two moons ago.

That day had been a success. While he'd questioned the duke's recruiter about a longbowman, one of the palace guards had walked by.

He'd looked at the sketch and exclaimed, "That man is crazy! He escorted a pig through town, crying, 'Make way for my fair lady.' He was facing three sheriffs with swords when the duke spotted them; the sheriffs were harassing the fool. He stood with a staff held in guard position, as calm as if facing children armed with twigs."

The guard had had no additional information but had suggested that the Listener might know more. The guards did not know the spy's name suggested that an operative might contact Erlender and exchange information.

Erlender could barely contain his glee. He finally had confirmation that he had correctly gauged Jason's path from Biblola.

Upon returning to his inn, he had directed Arnock to recall his lieutenants and their squads. He had ordered them in other directions after losing Jason's trail in Biblola.

That evening, he was eating his dinner, sopping the last of the gravy from his plate with a piece of bread, when a drunken man leaned on his table.

"New in town, ain'tcha?" the drunk bellowed. He followed with a whispered, "Follow me to see the Listener."

The innkeeper hustled the drunk out, yelling, "Merrill, I've told you before you are not welcome if you bother paying guests!"

Erlender noted that the drunk cooperated, and he concluded the proprietor knew of the deception.

Erlender smiled with satisfaction, savoring the last sip of his wine. A few minutes later, he followed the man out of the inn, nodding at Cathán to ensure his companion would follow. As he stepped into the crisp night air, Erlender's excitement threatened to bubble out.

Merrill started a complex route, leading Erlender down a narrow alley. At its end, he took Erlender back as though to the rear of the inn. From there, he led him to the docks, along the river downstream, and then back to the city's center.

The path continued in circles—sometimes closer to the river and sometimes farther away, sometimes near the high-rent district and sometimes in the hovels of the poor. The walk continued for more than an hour, and Erlender was unsure where he was in the city. It did not help that his guide occasionally let his lantern flash into Erlender's eyes, night-blinding him for minutes. He hoped Cathán had been able to keep track of all the meanderings.

On the way, Erlender observed at least four watchers and two followers; the Listener was taking no chances on being surprised, he concluded. He was sure Cathán would also notice them and avoid being seen.

Merrill opened a door into a small room with a lattice panel opposite the door. A shadow on the screen implied that the Listener was positioned behind it. Erlender took the seat his guide indicated.

"Your manservant is alive and sleeping in the inn," a voice from behind the panel told Erlender as they entered. "He may have a headache when he awakens."

Erlender's head jerked up; he caught himself before he cried out. Cathán had followed them from the inn; the novice watched with magic and his eyes. For someone to sneak up on the neophyte—well, within a city, the habitués could set a trap for anyone following them. He'd underestimated the sophistication of the Listener's organization.

Erlender sat but was no longer confident about this meeting.

"Well, Master Erlender, what brings you to my city? What business do you have to conduct? What information do you desire? What information do you have to trade for that which you wish?"

The Listener's voice changed with each breath. Erlender identified a drawl of the Deep South, a falsetto, and other heavy accents. Erlender thought the accents were fake to hide his identity and wondered if the Listener was female.

"You are trying to identify me. You will not succeed," the Listener said in a husky, feminine whisper.

"I am looking for Jason Archer from South Haven. His uncle is ill and searching for his nearest kin to inherit the family lands," Erlender said.

"The next time you lie to me will be with your last breath," said the voice from behind the lattice in a firm reprimand.

Erlender reached into his pocket for his flash pellets, but a hand from behind him, a being he had not seen, grasped his wrist firmly and pulled his hand out. The unseen being tore his pocket open, revealing three clay balls.

"It was prudent to come prepared for violence, as it was for your servant to follow you. It is not good you acted prematurely." The Listener sounded like an ancient man on his deathbed, struggling to find the breath to talk.

Erlender suddenly found it hard to catch his breath. He was in the presence of a truth sayer. He did not doubt the Listener would try to kill him if he deviated from the truth. His mana stores were low, and he wasn't sure he could defend against the spy or strike quickly enough to get both men in the room. And he was sure there were more than two. He shook his head and settled on what he could say.

After taking a deep breath, he said, "Jason carries an artifact. The dark one, Golgol-drath, is seeking it. Jason does not know he is being sought and needs protection."

All of that was true, but he did not say he was the one seeking Jason. Truth sayers generally could not distinguish partial truths from whole truths.

"The information I have to trade is of Golgol-drath's preparations to expand into the west."

"How current is your information?" The voice now was that of a robust middle-aged man.

"I learned of the invasion plans about three months ago."

Silence, broken only by the sound of drumming fingers, lasted for a minute.

"I knew of the troops gathering near the border. Do you know the number of men, their disposition, or their schedule? That the dark one is starting another war is not new information." This time, the voice was that of a young girl.

"I know only that he wants to conquer before the end of the year."

"The information you offer is less valuable than that which you wish. However, I want you out of my city as soon as possible. I will not abide a former battle mage who now just steals mana.

"I know he arrived by boat on the ocean side of Twin Rivers. My eyes and ears followed him until he confronted the sheriffs, which you know about. Then we lost him. He has not been seen since.

"He did not leave by ferry or exit by either castle gate. Few areas remain outside my eyes and ears for long, so he is either dead or gone by water, as the smugglers do. Look near the river docks.

"This interview is over."

A curtain fell between Erlender and the latticework.

The door behind him opened, and Merrill entered with a lamp. "I will escort you back to the inn," he said.

———— ✕ ————

Arnock spent several days and nights observing the riverside near and beneath the docks. He watched skimmers—low, wide watercraft propelled by magic—loaded with small packages and, occasionally, people traveling on the river.

Questioning dockside residents, he learned that this method of transport was popular among the city's merchants and messenger services.

Tapti, the wider river, was served frequently by ferry; the skimmers supported most commerce along the Ga'aton River.

He showed the sketch of Jason around. He found one person who had seen Jason beneath the docks at night several tendays ago. Arnock was surprised that Jason did not carry a bow.

No one admitted to ferrying the man, but some admitted to seeing packages or single passengers leaving and going upstream at night.

The destination could have been either river, but most skimmer traffic went via the Ga'aton River toward Myakka Town. Jason would likely have wanted to go that way if he was trying to evade followers.

There were two paths to follow, one more likely than the other. Things were looking up.

CHAPTER 11

The Dragon Revealed

**"Notes on Necromancy," from *Defensive Magic*
Sister Ismat of the Temple of the Moon
Damocles Academy of Magic**

Have you ever wondered what lurks in the shadows, preying on the innocent for a power that defies death itself?

Magic, when used for noble healing, can transfer life force—a practice twisted in the brutal throes of war. Battlefield healers, forced to siphon life from the fallen to save the living, birthed a dark secret: the war mage. Marked by a black armband, these warriors wield stolen life as a weapon.

But beware of the wolves in sheep's clothing. Some war mages, intoxicated by the surge of stolen power, become rogues. They lurk in the shadows, draining the innocent to fuel their dark magic—a stark contrast to the king's loyal war mages, who fight on two fronts: protecting their allies and vanquishing enemy necromancers.

The crown fears this forbidden power. Even with watchful eyes, some rogues escape, hiding their hunger in plain sight. These are the true monsters you should fear. Stealing life for twisted purposes, they leave only hollow husks behind.

This class will equip you to face these horrors. You will learn to recognize the signs of necromancy, the subtle changes that mask a monster in human form, and how to defend yourself from their unholy grasp. This is not just defensive magic; it's a fight for survival.

J ason's task the next day was chopping wood for the kitchen, the only place at Terlingua with a fireplace. Other buildings were heated by water from the hot springs.

The morning sun was warm, and Jason stripped off his tunic, continuing the task shirtless.

"Wood heats you twice, once when you cut it and once with you burn it." Jason fondly recalled his sensei's words.

Suddenly, he heard MacTíre's clarion and gong, which indicated an incursion. Jason secured the ax and removed his boots and trousers. By the time he was ready to shift, he heard screams. Jason ran toward them and leaped into the air. He shifted on the fly, and Xavier landed on one foot, stumbling a bit, before continuing the run and launching into the air.

That was close! I barely formed in time to land and run, and you didn't even check that I was awake! If you want to do this again, you need to run faster and point your feet like I need them to run, Xavier complained.

That was an unqualified success! We did exceptionally well for not practicing! And I will work on each of those with you in days to come, Jason replied.

There are times I am sure you are deranged, human.

Jason laughed.

Xavier flew toward the cries, just high enough for his wing tips to clear the ground. Telescoping his vision, he saw three men spread out between the trees and fields and six horses close to the forest. Two more men were closer to the fields, each carrying a struggling woman; a kaihana was running at those two with a sickle raised to attack. The women screamed and thrashed, slowing the escaping men.

Xavier climbed abruptly and then dove. He sounded a challenge, like bagpipes mixed with a lion's roar, and sprayed some venom ahead, forming a small cloud of flame through which he flew.

The horses spooked at the pipe's unearthly sound and broke loose from their tethers. Xavier saw the men look up at him. They released their victims, turned, and ran toward the horses.

Xavier continued diving toward the center of the fleeing men. Passing over the first, he reached and grabbed the second by the neck in his right rear claw. He landed with the left foot in the middle of the third's back, crushing his chest and breaking the neck of the one whose head he held when he landed.

He grabbed the next man by the shoulders in his front claws and spat venom at the head of the last invader. Jason delayed the burn until it struck the man's head and then accelerated it. All flesh on his skull vaporized in a sudden flash of light and heat. The man fell face forward. A sound like a cannon firing reverberated when his head exploded as his brain turned into steam. The detonation threw half a dozen pieces of cranium outward.

The terrorized horses bolted into the forest.

Xavier swung his tail. It caught the marauder he had bypassed just above one knee. The man screamed as his femur snapped in two. He tumbled through the air and landed on one shoulder, collapsing into a heap and making no more sound.

Spinning the raider in his claws around, Xavier demanded, *How many are with you today?*

The man looked into the dragon's face and screamed, "Six! Six! There are six!"

One is missing, Jason told Xavier.

Xavier turned toward the kaihana. *Be not afraid, Keshia. Do you have the means to secure this one until I return?*

The terrified kaihana holstered her sickle, opened a pocket on her apron, and retrieved a coil of thin rope. "Yes, I do." She nodded vigorously.

Kaelin, the human woman closest to her, was crying hysterically.

Xavier held the assailant while Keshia hogtied him, and then he leaped into the air and flew over the nearby forest, following the horses.

MacTíre's alarm sounded at Defender headquarters as well as at Terlingua.

The response was immediate. The Defenders practiced for this eventuality, and they mustered in a few minutes with military precision. A tarpaulin packed with clothing, armor, and weapons was dragged from storage. After checking the ties, two meaty humans shifted into eagles, picked the bundle up, and flew with it toward the farm. Three waves of four raptors followed them.

Two smaller two-skinned avians changed and flew toward the farm to reconnoiter; they would determine the source of the incursion and direct the larger birds and their burden to the best place to engage the invaders.

Once they located the kidnappers' entry point from the forest, they flew back and directed the larger birds to the clearing.

When the eagles reached the attempted abduction site, they observed a large, winged blue creature leave the ground and fly away from them over the forest. The blue creature flew in a zigzag pattern, which was not the behavior of a scofflaw escaping.

The eagles dropped the tarp near the clearing and circled above it to protect the arriving Defenders from any hostile presence. The first wave of four avian Defenders arrived, changed skins, and opened the tarp.

The four quickly removed boots, helmets, and shields from the bundle. They put on their helmets and boots; armed themselves with shotguns, spears, and shields from the cache of weapons; and positioned themselves to protect more arriving in bird form behind them.

The eagles who had carried the tarp landed, changed skins, and armed themselves.

The first half dozen wore neither armor nor clothing, except boots, but held shields, shotguns, and short spears.

The second wave of four flying Defenders arrived and took a little longer to equip themselves, each donning a gambeson and leather armor. They selected from short spears, swords, crossbows, and shotguns to arm themselves and joined the first six to form a defensive line between the forest and the landing area.

Two more waves of avian two-skinned landed, dressed, and armed themselves.

Seeing no active hostilities, Tovia, the leader of the defense squad, told the naked Defenders to clothe themselves and don their armor.

Isadora, one of the female Defenders, walked over to where Keshia and Niamh, two kaihana, were trying unsuccessfully to calm Camille and Kaelin, two human women who had not recovered from their near kidnapping. Isadora spoke with the human women in soothing tones.

Camille's hysteria after almost being kidnapped was palpable. She shook uncontrollably, her eyes were wide with fear, and she struggled to breathe. She kept repeating the phrase "He was so close."

She couldn't stop shaking, and her breath came in short, ragged gasps. "I feel like I am going to throw up and pass out!" she said between gasps.

Kaelin shook from her knees through her shoulders. She tried to scream, but no sound came out. She collapsed onto the ground.

Heather, Elani, and Adina arrived in a goat cart, which had an open bed containing Heather's healing supplies.

Heather joined Isadora in soothing the distraught human women. Seeing Heather, each of the victims relaxed and began breathing easier.

Camille shivered. "Thank you. We are so glad to be safe."

Kaelin nodded, agreeing. "Yes. Yes, we are!" she exclaimed.

"It must have been terrifying," Isadora said.

Kaelin cried softly and whispered, "We were so scared. We didn't know what would happen to us."

"It is OK to cry. You have been through a lot. I will prepare some tea for you to drink; it will help you calm down," Heather said. "We will take you back to the farmhouse, and you can rest. We will talk later."

Elani approached with a cup of cold kieff infusion for each to drink. "I fixed this while you were talking," she said. "I thought it would be helpful."

"Thank you, Elani. This is perfect. After they drink it, help me move Camille and Kaelin to the cart to rest while we examine the other fallen," Heather said gratefully.

Once they were settled in the cart and began to recover from their ordeal, Heather shifted her attention to the invader whose leg Xavier had broken.

He was awake and moaning in pain but not moving. His thigh was bent forty-five degrees and slightly rotated; bruising was slight, indicating that no major blood vessels had broken when the dragon's tail hit him.

A half dozen horses galloped to the clearing, led by Clowers. Each carried a Defender armed with heavier weapons than the tarp contained.

Defender Clowers approached Tovia. "What happened here?" he asked.

Tovia called Keshia over. To Clowers, she said, "Keshia was here during the entire episode and saw what happened." When the kaihana joined them, she added, "Keshia, please tell Defender Cowers what you saw this day."

The kaihana described the invaders' arrival and the attempted kidnapping. "Niamh killed one during the skirmish as the men captured the humans. I was chasing the rest, when a huge blue demon came through a flaming hole in the sky, killed three, grabbed one, and disabled one.

"It knew my name! I have no idea how the demon learned it."

The kaihana looked around before continuing. "It asked me for rope and held that one"—she pointed at the hogtied man—"while I secured him. Then it flew over the forest, and Thaddeus and other Defenders arrived in bird form."

She paused again. "I think they can tell you of happenings since then better than I can."

Tovia added, "I have nothing more to add to Keshia's account."

Clowers walked to the cluster of armed two-skinned, and they discussed the smoothness of the avian arrival and arming in response to the alarm. He then directed the Defenders to help Niamh, who knew the location of the sixth assailant's body, drag the corpse into the clearing.

Clowers called for Thaddeus to join him. They walked to the man lying on the ground, who was trussed up like a calf waiting for its brand. They untied his legs, led him back to the Defender enclave, and began questioning him.

One of the Defenders shouted an alarm and pointed above the forest; the unknown winged beast was returning.

———— ◦◦◦ ————

Xavier flew back and forth about fifty feet above the forest canopy. From that height, he could see the ground with his eyes telescoped. He looked for human body heat before extending his vision for far focus. One man was missing from the clearing, and Xavier was determined to find him.

Xavier scanned the forest canopy for signs of life. With his telescopic vision, he could see small details from a distance. He could focus on individual trees or even individual leaves if he wanted to.

Jason was amazed by the dragon's vision, telescoping each eye independently, but the constant focus changing nauseated him, so he ceased watching.

After a few minutes, Xavier passed four horses. He continued searching until he reached about twice as far into the forest as the horses had run and then turned back. If the men had run this way, he had missed them. On his return trip, the dragon searched in a broader pattern without success.

Finding the last two horses, he herded them toward the four he had passed earlier. When the herd had gathered, Xavier spoke to the horses in a language of images, showing food and safety in Terlingua's direction. After the horses nickered and turned in that direction, he hurried them along with bagpipe sounds.

He watched to ensure they were heading to the farm, and then he turned toward the site of the attempted abduction.

—◦◦◦—

As Xavier approached the clearing, he and Jason saw half a dozen horses sweating from being ridden hard. Almost a score humans stood in the meadow, including Tovia and Clifton Clowers.

A tarp spread on the ground held weapons and pieces of armor.

The Defenders wore leather armor and were armed with shotguns, spears, short swords, or crossbows, except for Clowers, who wore chain mail, with a long sword at his waist.

Xavier and Jason concluded that the tarps contained the armor and weapons for the two-skinned avian Defenders; some were still donning armor in their human form.

The bodies of four kidnappers lay on the ground; one was dead from sickle wounds. One or more of the kaihana must have dispatched him in the fields, and his body had been dragged into the clearing later. All were accounted for.

The dragon's search of the forest had been unnecessary, except for finding the horses.

Xavier, you are headed into a group of armed men who came here to fight someone attacking Terlingua. Some may decide you are the threat. Be careful. This meeting will set the tenor for the future, Jason warned.

I do not fear what men can do to me, the dragon replied.

I do not know if they have guns. Those might be effective against even your scales. Please be careful.

The dragon ignored him.

The raider Keshia had bound stood near Clowers, who appeared to be questioning the man. Heather was kneeling alongside the one assailant where he had landed after Xavier's tail swept him off his feet.

Xavier circled above the small clearing, issuing an introduction like a royal fanfare on a pipe organ. When he had the attention of all the humans and kaihana on the ground, he landed in the clearing, as far from the men as he could, near the body of the headless thug.

The Defenders cried out in alarm at the dragon's appearance. A few moved as though to attack him. The distance separating them from the dragon was within crossbow range.

Clowers noticed his people preparing for battle and called out, "Hold! The beast has not threatened us. From what the kaihana said, it prevented the kidnapping."

Xavier sat on his haunches and curled his wings partway around himself, with his wrist joints slightly above his head. The effect was that he was seated above them in an alcove. After a few adjustments in his posture, he faced the men.

He spoke mind to mind to all of them.

I am Xavier Kahuruan of the House of Fire. You have my prisoners. Return them to me immediately. He punctuated his words with a small stream of flame shooting above the heads of the Defenders.

The voice Jason heard was unlike what he usually heard when Xavier spoke. This voice was commanding, authoritative, and arrogant, not what he had used with Heather and Maliyah. He spoke as though issuing a royal command, demanding immediate compliance.

If Jason had been in body, his jaw would have dropped in surprise at the dragon's attitude. Heather reacted by jumping to her feet with wide eyes and holding the back of one fist to her mouth. Xavier did not seem like Jason's friendly second skin; he presented a fearsome, intelligent beast.

Seeing a spurt of fire above their heads was too much for one young Defender. She raised her crossbow and fired at the dragon's chest.

Xavier's wing blurred as he closed it farther around himself; the bolt struck the back of his left wing. The quarrel screeched along his scales before sticking between two. The dragon responded with a small jet of venom, hitting the Defender in the neck, just above the crossbow's stock. She screamed once, inhaled some burning dragon venom, and collapsed.

She twitched a few times and then lay still.

The horses, except Clowers's, reared and tried to break free. His horse trembled, and its eyes were wide with terror.

Other Defenders raised their weapons to engage Xavier.

Clowers drew his sword and jumped to stand in front of his people. He swung it in a wide arc above his head, yelling, "Hold! Hold, I say! Xavier defended himself against an unwarranted attack." He struck a crossbow aimed at the dragon from one Defender's hands. His face turned purple, and he shouted, "The next one to attack the dragon will face me if he survives what the dragon does in self-defense!"

The Defenders lowered their weapons.

"Did you forget the dragon dispatched five men in a few heartbeats? And without using his fire! Had he wanted us dead, he would have showered fire on us from above or landed in our midst! Do not antagonize him!"

Turning to the dragon, Clowers said, "I apologize for my people's actions. We were surprised to see a dragon and had no reason to attack you.

"I am Clifton Clowers, chief of the Defenders of Smoky Springs Valley."

Well, you don't defend very well, do you? I had the situation under control before you were in sight of the assault, Xavier said.

All of the Defenders gasped at the insult. Clowers's face reddened as his back straightened and his fists clenched.

"We saw you flying away; we thought you might be a two-skinned raider fleeing. It wasn't until our team landed that we learned about your timely arrival, which prevented the abduction of two women. And then we weren't sure of what had happened. I am questioning them to find out if there are more raiders and where they might be," Clowers said through clenched teeth.

And you think you can get more out of them than I?

"Perhaps. Perhaps not." Clowers's voice did not betray the anger displayed by his high chin and clenched fists.

Xavier turned toward the headless body of the attacker and opened his mouth, preparing to spray venom on it.

To the men on the ground, the dragon seemed to intend to pick up the corpse with its mouth.

Stop! Do not eat that man's corpse! Jason cried urgently to Xavier alone.

Xavier closed his mouth with a snap, jerked his head up, directed his gaze over the fields behind the Defenders, and continued the private conversation. *What is wrong? It is just meat. Besides, eating this one will make the man Clowers holds fear me even more, which could help with questioning him.*

We do not eat our dead and consider those who do barbarians. We can discuss the treatment of our dead later, but for now, know that if you eat that man, everyone here will remember that above all other things. After a few retellings, all that will be recalled is a man-eating beast nearby, living in the mountains. Their fears of a man-eating dragon will grow with each account until they convince themselves they must kill us, Jason said.

Xavier turned his head to face Clowers. *My human skin tells me that not all men cremate their dead. I offer my assistance in burning these if that is your custom.*

Clowers's eyes widened, and he took a step back, nonplussed by the unexpected topic. Shaking his head slightly, he replied, "No. We bury our dead here."

Xavier took a few steps closer to Clowers and the prisoner. He brought his head closer to the kidnapper. *What is your name?* he asked.

"What is happening? I hear a voice in my mind!" The prisoner turned his head from side to side, his eyes widened more, and his voice spiked to a higher pitch.

Yes, you do. I am Xavier Kahuruan, the dragon before you, and I speak to your mind.

"I am called Oliver, and you cannot make me tell you anything. I fear Nizar more than I fear any death you can deal." Despite the fear in his eyes, he remained defiant.

Xavier moved closer to the prisoner. He stared the man in the eyes and collected some venom in his mouth. He opened his jaws slightly to admit air, igniting the venom. Then he closed his mouth, forcing flames to appear along his lip line. Dragon fire dripped from his mouth in a few places.

Oliver began to shake, and he leaned against the Defenders holding him. The threat of dragon fire had shaken him badly.

Jason spoke to Xavier alone. *His True Name is Alberich Water-Walker.*

How do you know you have it? the dragon asked.

It is like I suddenly recalled it after trying to remember it, Jason answered.

Xavier turned to Clowers and said, *I will let you question them first. I will interrogate them afterward to assure myself they told all they knew.* It was almost a dismissal.

Facing the prisoner, he continued. *You are called Oliver Brewerson, but your True Name is Alberich Water-Walker; you will answer Defender Clowers fully, helpfully, and without hesitation.*

Privately, Jason asked, *How did you learn the rest of his usename?*

You can pluck a man's True Name from the air. That talent is becoming mine. I don't see his True Name yet, but I see his public name, the dragon replied privately.

Oliver's trembling increased, and his face paled. He would have collapsed onto the ground if two Defenders had not been holding his arms.

Clowers looked between the man and the dragon. "Well, that should make things easier. How did you learn his True Name?"

I hear your mind as you speak. When a man is terrified, he thinks of the things he fears most and sometimes verbalizes them strongly enough that I can hear them. Almost all fear having their True Names exposed, so the more I intimidated him, the more I could hear his name. Xavier mixed the true with the false seamlessly and without a trace of shame.

"I know of a flying Xavier; he carried Jason Archer to the north of Smoky Springs a lunation ago. Do you know him?"

Yes. I carried Jason past the destroyed section of the roadway. His voice lost some commanding, arrogant tones but retained the authority. *How has Jason fared?*

"He fares well. He is staying with Lady Heather." Clowers nodded toward her. "She can tell you how he fares better than I can. What brings you to this place at this time, Xavier Kahuruan of the House of Fire?"

I was nearby and heard the cries of the human women. My human part reacted, and we came to help.

I will now check on the other prisoner; I doubt I can instill fear in him while he is in such pain, so do not expect to learn his True Name now.

The dragon and the Defender walked to where Heather was attending to the man with the broken leg.

"How fares your charge?" Clowers asked.

"His life is not in danger from his injuries, but I can do nothing for him here. A leg as severely broken as this needs a place to secure him before applying traction. Moving him will cause considerable pain and could damage his leg to the point that amputation is our only option," Heather responded.

Xavier, only you hear me when I am within. I believe we can assist Heather here. I know about setting bones; it is among the things the war taught me. I would like to forget many of those experiences, but some are useful. I think she will appreciate the help.

Hold up one front claw, and spread the digits so I can guess your dexterity.

Xavier complied by spreading the fingerlike claws on his forefeet where they sat on the ground and looking at them. *What are you thinking?*

That we set the man's leg here. It looks to me like you can grasp a thigh and a knee, and I know you are strong enough.

Xavier accepted by announcing to Heather and Clowers, *I am Xavier Kahuruan. I presume you are Heather. Perhaps I can assist here. I am considerably stronger than a human and can straighten the leg right here.*

Heather looked at the dragon for a moment. "I am pleased to meet you,

Xavier, though your mind speech startled me. Dragons have not been seen in Rutendo for a long time, and most think them mythical. I will appreciate any assistance you can give."

We will need a sedative. Ask if she has angel's kiss. Jason interjected.

Xavier turned his attention to the man on the ground, who moaned. *Do you have angel's kiss with you, Miss Heather?*

The dragon was a quick study and continued to broadcast. Jason could hear him, though no one except the dragon could hear Jason.

"Yes, I do. I have a tincture made from the leaves," she replied.

That will do very well; the leaves can sedate without killing, Jason told her through the dragon.

My human skin aided healers during the Succession War. He held men and administered an angel's kiss potion during bone settings and amputations, and he will instruct me.

Xavier turned to face the intruder. *What is your name, man?*

"What? Who? A voice in my mind?" The prisoner moaned the words.

Yes. I am Xavier Kahuruan, the dragon before you, and I speak to your mind. I repeat: What is your name, man?

Through moans, the man gasped, "Hildingr."

Well, Hildingr, I am going to set your leg. Heather, the healer, will administer something to ease your pain.

Jason added for the dragon to hear, *Heather needs to administer her tincture in drops until Hildingr is asleep. Then one more. Wait for his breath to slow down to half of normal. Give him another drop if that takes too long.*

Xavier asked Heather to administer the angel's kiss in single drops until Hildingr slept, followed by two more after the man's sleep wasn't as deep as Jason wanted. *I apologize for telling you how to do your craft, but this will keep him still during and after the setting of the break.*

Jason gave more instructions. *Xavier, you need to grasp the man's leg with one claw between the break and the hip and one between the break and the knee. Have Heather monitor the break and tell you how to move the leg to reduce rubbing bone on bone as you align the two. Then just hold it until she is finished with her splint.*

Xavier grasped the man's leg as Jason instructed. He found that his thumb and second finger held a thigh easily, but his thumb and first worked better for just above the knee. His stance meant he would push out from his center when he straightened the leg.

When that was done, Heather put one hand directly above the separation

186

and directed the dragon to position the lower leg so the bone ends aligned. Xavier held them in place for Heather to apply her healing arts.

She put both hands around the break, and her hands began to glow, barely showing in the sunlight. Her patients always told her that her spirit mana felt cool.

She looked up at the dragon in surprise. "You are sending life—healing—to Hildingr's leg! I feel it as warmth."

I am as surprised as you at this; I assure you it is not intentional, the dragon replied to her alone.

"Your mana is strong and accelerating healing beyond what I can accomplish with my gift alone. Splinting for movement may be all the additional care he needs for his leg to heal. I never expected such assistance from another not schooled in healing!"

"Did you see the invaders' horses as you flew over the forest?" Clowers broke the silence that followed Heather's comment.

Xavier raised from his four-legged stance to sit on his haunches and looked down at the Defender. *I found six horses, which I claim by right of conquest.*

"The goods of criminals are part of the compensation for the Defenders," Clowers objected. "Those horses are broken for riding. What use does a dragon have for riding horses?"

Why, to eat, of course!

"They are worth more than meat value to me if well trained and battle ready."

Jason whispered to the dragon, *Xavier, trading the horses for a suitable food animal will help us befriend Defender Clowers.*

Having something to haggle over changed Xavier's tone to one of pleasurable competition. He grinned, and his teeth gleamed in the sunlight. He intertwined the fingers on his foreclaws and spoke eagerly. *What do you offer for each horse?*

"A kaihana killed one attacker. They adhere to the pact; one of the horses is mine!" Clowers said.

Agreed. The kaihana shall select the horse.

Clowers nodded his agreement. "We have to care for two men through interrogation and execution. Surely, we deserve two of the horses as compensation."

One horse of my choosing, Xavier stated.

"And the saddles and tack of two horses," Clowers added.

Xavier's head snapped back. *I forgot that saddles and reins are valuable to humans. Agreed.*

"What will you take for each remaining horse?"

Four adult hogs.

"That is preposterous! A single adult hog weighs the same as a horse! One for one is much more reasonable!"

Heather realized the dragon was only speaking to her and Clowers. All the others were preparing to depart the scene or bury the dead.

She gathered her supplies and arranged for help in transferring Hildingr to her goat cart. Once he was loaded, she drove toward the town, leaving man and dragon to negotiate about the horses. They seemed oblivious to her departure.

Xavier flew above the forest, away from Terlingua.

Well, X, it is time for a talk. I was a little surprised during your negotiations. I was more than a little surprised when you killed the Defender. You weren't hurt.

The dragon flew for a few minutes. *I guess the best answer is reflex. I hadn't planned on having a crossbow bolt sent my way.* He flew a little longer. *And Clowers is correct. Had I wanted them dead, they would have been. Are people both careful and thoughtful and simultaneously reactionary and stupid?*

Yes. The paradox is that a stupid, reactionary young person can become a careful, thoughtful older person. I am glad Clowers falls into the thoughtful category, Jason replied. *Where did Kahuruan of the House of Fire come from? It sounds like a royal title, not just a name.*

The first part is my name; I just never said it before. I also wanted to make a proper impression on them. The phrase "House of Fire" jumped to mind, Xavier responded.

I think you impressed them that you are dangerous. Was that all that jumped into your mind?

No. I did not say Prince Xavier, the dragon said.

Jason was silent, wondering if the dragon was joking or being serious. He said slowly, *And what does that mean?*

Xavier exuded humor. *I fooled you, human!*

So you did. Jason paused momentarily before adding, *Your Highness.*

His mental laughter wasn't as satisfying as when he controlled the vocal apparatus.

Xavier did tight barrel rolls, alternating left and right, with abrupt drops of a hundred feet, followed by a few 360-degree yaw spins, until Jason remembered he didn't like those maneuvers. Then the human laughed again.

You win, dragon! I no longer fear flying!

Xavier settled his flying. After a few minutes, he said, *We must look for a larger cave. I am growing. I am about one-quarter bigger than when we first shifted.*

Jason paused for a moment. *I noticed your sheddings getting larger. I should have realized the cave might only be suitable for a little longer. Heather also told me your back is changing to a darker blue with some red and orange down the center of your back and the middle of your wings. A pattern is forming. You've also developed a double row of spines along your back, with more around your neck. The spines show in your shed skin.*

Xavier thought for a moment. *Spines and patterns are signs of maturity among dragons. I wonder what I will look like when they are complete.*

Jason was silent for a few moments. *How do you know about dragons maturing?*

It was Xavier's time for silence. *I, uh, I do not know. It is not like flying, which I recall learning during vivid dreams.* His tone turned pensive. *There is much about us that I believe I understand, but I have no idea how I know those things.*

Jason seemed to sigh in relief. *I am glad I am not the only one who feels like he is walking down a corridor without enough light. Our being seems to be the only one of our kind.*

By the way, I wonder what you look like now. Heather and Akela each described you to me, but seeing for myself would be better. I haven't seen a mirror large enough, and even if I knew of such a mirror, I don't know how we would get you to a viewing place, Jason said. *Perhaps I can find someone to paint your portrait, though I do not know where we could display it.*

Xavier replied thoughtfully, *A larger cave might have a good wall to hang it from. Then I could wake up to beauty.*

Jason laughed and settled in to enjoy the night.

Xavier landed at Ognyen about an hour before sundown, having spent the afternoon hunting. He placed half a deer carcass on the ground.

Jason's clothing was neatly folded at the cave entrance. Perhaps Maliyah had foreseen his need. If not her, he had no candidates.

Xavier took several deep breaths of the gas collecting above the mud, sighing his pleasure with each, before releasing Jason.

Jason dressed and carried the half deer to the farm.

The dinner bell sounded, and he walked to the dining hall and selected a table that gave him a view of both entrances to the dining hall, as was his habit.

Tovia joined him a few minutes later.

"I know who X is," she whispered.

"Well, who is he?"

"You have two skins. My hawk sees your shadow while you work in the fields. It is not a human shadow, so I know you have two skins," she said quietly.

"Please continue."

"I know you disappear from Terlingua each night. Several of the boys have tried to follow you without success."

"I noticed them. I let them follow me for about a quarter hour before losing them. I kept making my trail more difficult to follow so they would learn to track a man through the forest," Jason said.

Tovia stared at him. "That's just like you. You're always teaching, even when you don't mean to."

"You let X slip after the full-moon celebration a tenday ago; you said you didn't want to talk about who that was, which I respect."

Her expression became stern. "Then, today, Xavier Kahuruan appeared. Three kaihana saw you run naked through the yards from the kitchen, and the dragon took to the air, flying toward the kidnapping site.

"You, Jason Archer, are the human skin of Xavier Kahuruan, a dragon of the House of Fire."

Jason continued eating through Tovia's analysis. He finished chewing, swallowed, and responded, "What do you intend to do with this information?"

"That was neither an admission nor a denial. Will you give me a straight answer?"

Jason laughed. "I have spent too much time avoiding discussing my history. But for you, yes, the blue dragon is my second skin."

"Are you concerned that I know?"

Jason chuckled. "When we decided to respond to the alarm, all thoughts of secrecy were abandoned. I imagine that since you have figured it out, all of Terlingua will know by this time tomorrow. Which means all in Smoky Springs Valley will know of the dragon within a tenday."

Tovia jerked her head back. She stared at Jason for a moment. "Well, I am surprised by the admission. I was worried about how you would take the news from me. Remember, Jason, that you are not alone. You have friends here." She reached across the table and grasped his hand.

Heather joined them, glanced at Tovia's hand on Jason's, and then quickly looked away. "I want to discuss today's events with Jason," she said.

"Tovia knows almost as much as you do, Heather. We can discuss here if we keep it quiet." He grinned as he withdrew his hand from Tovia's. "Although all in Terlingua will know of the resident dragon after today."

"You don't seem upset about it."

"I cannot change what has happened. All I can do is live from this moment on."

Tovia exclaimed, "You are the strangest man I have ever met! Or heard of. Does nothing alarm you?"

"Well, MacTíre's clarion alarmed me this morning."

An exasperated sigh came from each woman.

"Xavier frightened me at the clearing this afternoon," Tovia said. "I did not know dragons existed; I was caught between awe and terror."

"He surprised me more than scared me," Heather said. "When you first introduced me to him, he sounded like you in a different skin. He did not sound like that today."

Jason looked between the two women. "He surprised me too. However, this is the first time Xavier encountered men without them meeting me first. I think we were exposed to the dragon unfettered by any human constraints."

"He sounded like a noble, like a duke or higher," Tovia added.

Heather nodded her agreement.

They ate in silence for a few minutes.

"What was the outcome of trading food animals for horses?" Heather asked.

"After almost an hour of offer and counteroffer, Defender Clowers agreed to five market-sized hogs for each horse and two more for all the tack."

Tovia's mouth dropped open, and she gasped. "That is less than one-half of Xavier's original request!"

"I was taken aback by his settlement too," Jason said. "However, a 200-pound market-ready hog is close to a full meal for him. I don't know how he would have handled the carcass remaining of an adult hog after one sitting; they are at least twice that big. Clowers and I each pointed out the advantages of market hogs versus full-grown to Xavier."

"How are they going to get delivered?" Heather asked.

"Clowers will deliver two hogs to the clearing by sundown every two tendays, beginning a tenday from now."

"How will this affect your contributions of meat to the kitchens?" Heather asked.

"Not much, I should think. Three things. First, you may have one pig from each delivery if you wish. Second, Xavier will eat meat for about ten days after searing, so he can eat one there and carry the other to his cave for a future meal. Third, he has been eating more recently. I don't think our offerings will change much. He's been eyeing the elk herds higher in the mountains, but they are too big for me to carry his one-meal leavings from Ognyen to the kitchens.

"Perhaps I should take a handcart with me on hunting days to carry the bounty to the kitchens. Yes, I shall do that."

Before Jason slept that night, he thought about better preparing Terlingua for defense. The attempted kidnapping provided an urgency missing before. His approach to date had been an introduction to the martial arts with some quarterstaff maneuvers using reeds. How must he change to provide them with the skills they would need for defense? He feared there might not be enough time to teach them what they needed to know to protect themselves before an attack by a bigger group, and he and his dragon might not be close enough to intervene.

The sudden attack on Terlingua had changed what he knew or believed he knew. He thought teaching the residents the quarterstaff was a good precaution, but now it seemed like a necessity. He considered how he could better prepare his students to defend the residents in armed conflict coming sooner than expected from a group of brigands.

He took a deep breath, let it out slowly, and entered a light meditative state, seeking guidance.

He liked Terlingua, its people, its kaihana, and the nearby town of Smoky

Springs. He thought of the Succession War and the devastation visited on communities like this one.

How can I prevent that from happening here? he asked himself.

First, he had to choose to commit to helping them.

With that done, what could he, one man, do? He could not provide weapons; such required funds, which he did not have. Perhaps Terlingua could help there.

He shook his head. The farm was prosperous but not rich enough to buy weapons for all.

Thasiwoda would transition to training for hand-to-hand combat easily, but that was a long-term enterprise, taking two or three years for a student to progress past balance to battle. There was no time.

In a few months, the residents could learn to use the quarterstaff sufficiently for defense, but the farm needed more wood staffs so that each could have one to use.

Sometimes weapons were not available, so it was time to teach them to fight without them. To learn hand-to-hand combat, his students needed to know how to fall. That became his top priority, which meant padded mats to protect them as they learned.

As before, he consulted with the kaihana at Terlingua when he needed specialized items. Maliyah and Elani again brought a passel of kaihana youth and a supply of burlap. They fashioned three mats as wide as Jason was tall, twice as long as they were wide, and a hand's span thick. They were packed with straw, neither loose nor tight, so they would cushion enough to reduce injury.

They could be rolled into knee-high cylinders as long as the mats were wide. The finished rolls weighed 150 pounds—too heavy for the children to move. Two adult women would have to position and unroll a cylinder.

Maliyah and Elani visited Jason outside his room at sunrise the next day. He had just completed his morning exercises and was waiting for his students to arrive.

"Maliyah and Elani, what a nice surprise! What brings you here so early?" he said. "Will you be joining us today?"

Elani spoke first. "Jason, you are the only human who can tell us apart after such a short time. We appreciate your attention to us and your kindness."

Maliyah nodded her agreement and added, "The Circle of Seeing realized you want quarterstaffs to arm Terlingua's residents. We bring a score for your use and hope we never need them. They are a bit smaller than usual—a better fit to the hands of women and children."

Jason stood dumbstruck. He shook his head in disbelief. "I don't know what to say. I worried about not having weapons here that the residents could use if necessary. Thank you! And thanks to the Circle. I appreciate this gift more than I can say."

"Well then, say nothing," Maliyah said. The two kaihana bowed and returned to their tasks.

Jason felt as if a weight were suddenly lifted off his shoulders. The sense of relief overwhelmed him. He was deeply touched by the kaihana's gift. It showed their trust in him and their willingness to help Terlingua's residents.

With the staffs, he could teach the residents how to defend themselves. He felt the warmth of satisfaction spread through his chest. Now his only obstacle was time.

The day started as those before it had. Xavier landed near the cave a few hours before sunrise; Jason dressed and jogged to his room.

They learned that the longer he and Xavier coexisted, the less time they needed to sleep in their skins. Akela had mentioned this effect a long time ago. Jason needed but two hours a day of sleep as Jason. Xavier required about six hours but only every third or fourth day.

Jason completed his devotions and exercises about an hour before sunrise.

His students assembled on the packed earth alongside the barn just as the sun peeked above the mountains.

Under his direction, they performed the basic poses and transitions slowly. Most students progressed rapidly; their balance during each pose approached the stillness he wanted, but they still wobbled during transitions.

He led them through ten intermediate poses. There were more balance and transition challenges, but they were improving. He added one advanced pose at the end, walked among them, corrected their postures, and dismissed them when he was finished teaching.

———∞∞∞———

The next day, under clear skies, Melody held her crutches at her side but did not touch them to the ground as she walked slowly and carefully, while wearing her custom sandal to Jason.

He hugged her, cried openly, and praised her for her effort.

"Your tears still prickle, Jason," she called out with a huge smile.

She wiped his cheeks with her hands and dried them on her knees.

The other students cheered, and Melody blushed at the attention.

Jason resumed tutoring Melody. As they began, he noticed that her new shoe elevated her left side above the right. He removed the shoe and trimmed a half inch off the layered leather sole so she could balance side to side.

Jason added two poses to Melody's repertoire, and the session took almost twice as long as their first one.

"Rest tomorrow, Melody. Let your muscles and joints get accustomed to your new abilities and your longer leg before we meet the day after. Try to walk with your crutches raised part of the time, as you did today. It will strengthen your legs, ankles, and feet." He paused a little. "I am so impressed with your efforts, my brave one."

After Melody left for breakfast, Fionola asked Jason, "What is happening?"

"Her muscles and joints have stretched, so her left leg extends slightly more than it did. She is also more flexible in her lower back and legs after only five days! Teaching her the poses is all I am doing. That and generating sparks are my only talents." He grinned at her and then turned his attention to his more experienced students.

With the warm-up complete, he distributed the reed bundles and paired the students to start quarterstaff practice. His students were getting adept at beginning blocking and attack moves. Soon they would graduate to wooden staffs provided by the kaihana.

A commotion at the front gate got their attention. It was still before breakfast, and no visitors were expected this early.

The surprise visitors were fifteen men and women on horseback, led by Chief Defender Clowers. Galaad, Thaddeus, and Padraic were among the group; they were the only Defenders Jason recognized.

They rode through the gate, dismounted, and walked to the exercise area.

"Please continue," Clowers said. "Isadora, in her hawk skin, observed you teaching quarterstaff using bundles of reeds. I am interested in your teaching and your students' progress."

Jason could think of no reason fifteen men were required to watch the lessons. However, he had no excuse to refuse Defender Clowers's request.

The students resumed their fighting exercises until one of the Defenders called out, "What qualifies Jason to teach staff fighting? We have the best fighters in Smoky Springs, and one of us should be the instructor."

Heather bristled and practically shoved her way out of the student huddle, clutching her bundle of reeds tightly. Her gaze snapped to Angelique, the Defender who dared to question Jason.

"Jason is more than qualified!" she declared. Her voice was laced with a protectiveness that surprised even her. "He's one of the best instructors I've ever had."

"If that is true, why doesn't Jason demonstrate his skill against one of us?" Angelique asked.

"A demonstration proves nothing," Heather argued. Her voice was tight with worry, but she shifted her stance to stand beside Jason. A flicker of anxiety crossed her features as she unconsciously raised the bundle of reeds in a way that mirrored a guard stance. "It's pointless theatrics."

Angelique stepped back with her eyes widening. "We will be assured that your teacher isn't giving you and us a false sense of security."

"Who are you suggesting he fight?" Heather's voice rose a notch. Her anger was fueled by a surge of something else, something warm and fiercely protective.

Angelique turned her head from side to side, glancing at Clowers and then Galaad. She held still as though in thought for a few minutes. "Galaad," she finally said.

The adults at Terlingua murmured.

"That is unfair; he won the harvest festival staff competition for the last five years! A demonstration should be against Padraic or Kyriakos," one said, naming two of the Defenders in the troop.

Defender Clowers rubbed his chin for a moment. "I think watching

Galaad against Jason would demonstrate Jason's skill to the best advantage. It will showcase his abilities."

"Tovia hasn't complained about Jason's methods," Heather said, holding her chin high as she confronted Clowers directly. Her grip on the reeds tightened until her knuckles turned white, betraying the simmering worry beneath her fierce facade. "This is about something else."

Tovia chimed in. "I will face Jason. I usually make it to the quarterfinals of the harvest contest."

Clowers's face flushed; the color rose from his neck to his forehead. His eyes narrowed, and he furrowed his brow but said nothing.

Jason realized he had been set up. If he refused, the Defenders would say he knew he was not qualified. If he agreed and Galaad was much better than he, they could conclude he was not qualified. He did not understand why Clowers wanted this; his only option was to face Galaad and defeat the man.

Before Heather or Tovia became enraged, he stepped between the women and Clowers. "Of course, I will face whomever Chief Defender Clowers suggests. What are the ground rules for this demonstration?"

"The two of you meet inside a twenty-foot circle. You will spar until one is knocked down or steps out of the circle. The rules are the same as those of the harvest festival, except one fall instead of three."

"I lack the armor warriors usually wear when practicing with staffs, and the staffs here are sized for a woman's hand," Jason said.

"Well then, Galaad will forgo his protective gear to equalize the competition, and we brought two staffs. You can select from them first. Isadora, please set up a ring for them," Clowers said. "Galaad, bring the staffs, and follow her to the site."

Jason nodded, walked to a barrel, sat down, and began to remove his boots. Heather and Tovia followed him. Galaad's possession of his staff and armor confirmed Jason's suspicion that this competition was planned.

"Jason, you don't have to do this," Heather pleaded softly. Her voice was a stark contrast to her earlier anger. "Galaad is a formidable opponent. I'm afraid you'll get hurt." Her eyes were fixed on Jason and showed a flicker of apprehension and something deeper—perhaps affection—evident for a brief moment before she steeled herself again.

"He is. He won the harvest festival staff competition for the last five years. He won't cripple you, but he could break an arm," Tovia added.

Jason stood and faced them. "I appreciate your concern, but I sparred with a staff almost every day during the war. I'm confident I can avoid injury."

"He outweighs you by at least thirty pounds!" Tovia said.

Jason chuckled. "That makes him a bigger target."

The two women shook their heads, and the three walked to the circle Isadora had drawn in the sand.

Jason examined the two staffs. He could find no fault with either in balance or weight, so he selected the one less stained by sweat.

The two men stripped to their waists and faced each other outside the ring with their quarterstaffs poised for defense.

Jason took a deep breath, spread his arms along his staff, and exhaled slowly. He repeated the deep breathing one more time and then relaxed as he entered the void.

Galaad stood across from Jason. He was relaxed, with his feet spread, cradling his staff in one elbow, as he joked with the Defenders near him.

Each man entered the ring on Defender Clowers's announcement and faced the other.

Galaad's demeanor projected confidence, and he wore a half smile.

The crowd cheered as the two men began to circle each other, looking for an opening. Jason was taller, lean, and muscular, with a long reach. Galaad was shorter and stockier, with a robust build.

Jason struck first, swinging his staff in a side-to-side arc at Galaad's head. The huskier man ducked under the blow and countered with a thrust to the chest. The taller man parried the blow and stepped back.

They continued circling each other with an occasional clack of the sticks as they probed for weaknesses.

"Why are they circling each other and not fighting?" Melody asked Tovia.

"They are looking for patterns in each other's movements—how they stand, which leg they like to set for an aggressive blow, and how they balance and recover. Look there! See! Galaad prefers to attack off his left leg," Tovia explained.

The two men clashed again, this time with more ferocity. Their staccato of clacks increased as they continued to circle, each striving to force the other back and out of the ring. The shorter man moved more slowly than the taller, but the taller man seemed to be defending more than attacking.

They broke apart as though by agreement and circled each other warily.

Galaad no longer smiled. His lips were pressed in a straight line, and his brow furrowed in concentration.

In a sudden movement, Jason slid his grip from a defensive pose to an attack grip. He feinted toward Galaad's left knee. Galaad reacted quickly to block a blow that did not come. Jason redirected his attack high and forced the end of Galaad's staff above their heads. Jason stepped in and swung down, landing a blow on Galaad's right shoulder.

Galaad managed to avoid the full force of the blow, but it struck the muscles with a bruising impact, numbing the muscles of his upper arm. His weariness showed as he stepped back to his left and stumbled.

I have him, Jason thought as Galaad struggled.

Jason pushed his advantage, attacking with furious speed. Striving to remain inside the ring, Galaad backed up but could not regain his balance against the unrelenting attack. He toppled over the boundary onto his back.

There was a moment of silence, which was broken when Clowers began to clap. The others joined in amid cries of surprise that Galaad had lost.

Jason took a deep breath, thankful that the situation had not gone as badly as he had feared and grateful he hadn't hurt Galaad during their bout.

Maliyah brought water to the two combatants. The Defenders congratulated Jason on his victory and offered condolences to Galaad on his loss.

Jason's students huddled around him, excited by his win.

Galaad and the other Defenders left the arena and walked toward the kitchens for a snack. Most residents migrated in that direction too; breakfast awaited them.

Jason recalled his earlier conclusion that he had been set up. Clowers must have been the source since he had brought so many Defenders with him to witness Galaad's expected victory. He felt his anger rise as he thought of it, though he did not lose control. Anger was a useful tool at times.

Challenge him. Defeat him. He conspired to humiliate us. You. Xavier growled to Jason alone.

Jason turned to Clowers and stepped close to him—a distance usually reserved for intimate friends. Jason's face was flushed, his eyes were wide, and his jaw tightened. One lip was wrinkled in a half sneer, and his nostrils flared as he stared at Clowers. He did not blink.

Clowers crossed his arms and raised his eyebrows but did not respond in any other way.

"Defender Clowers, was your purpose in bringing five and ten Defenders out here to show I was not competent as an instructor?" Jason's speech was clipped.

"I suppose that was part of my reason," Clowers admitted.

"And since Galaad had won the harvest festival for several years, you expected him to humiliate me in front of your men and the residents of Terlingua," Jason said more rapidly.

Clowers paused for several moments. "I do not like your tone, young man."

"I do not like getting set up for failure by people who are ostensibly protecting me and my friends." Jason's voice rose slightly as his anger surfaced. "What is your answer, Defender Clowers?"

Clowers sighed and stepped back. "That wasn't the primary goal, but it was certainly a potential consequence."

Jason's face reddened. "What did I do to deserve that? Do you want me as your enemy, Defender Clowers?" He stood tense with his weight on the balls of his feet and his arms hanging loosely at his sides. His breathing rate increased.

"Your insult at the pub, turning your back on me in front of my men, was disrespectful."

"You accused me of being a kieff addict while I was still across the room—a direct insult, not an implied one. Had you honored the usual rules of hospitality, I would not have needed to stand for myself and rebuke your charge." Jason's anger showed in his tone and his reddened face.

"You lack subtlety, archer," Clowers said.

"Subtlety isn't for men of action. It slows gathering information and delays decisions," Jason responded. "You could've asked me to prove myself in private. You didn't. You chose a public fight against your best man with a staff. You wanted to humiliate me in front of the Defenders and my friends at Terlingua. That's not the behavior of a friend. I repeat: Do you want me as an enemy?"

"What if I say no?" Clowers asked.

"Then you must apologize for trying to embarrass me in front of my students. And you must apologize to Heather and Maliyah for disrupting life on the farm so close to harvest time," Jason said.

"What if I do not?"

"In that case, there is only one acceptable option." Jason took a deep breath. "With the sun, the sky, and the earth as witnesses, I challenge you to a duel one against one until one stands, for we cannot live in this place in peace."

Clowers's mouth fell open. He jerked his head, took half a step back, and raised his hands at shoulder height with palms outward. His eyes widened, and he sucked in a breath.

"Wait. I apologize. Beneath the sky and the sun and above the earth, I beg your forgiveness for my rash actions."

"Apology accepted." Jason took a step back and took a deep breath. His anger dissipated. "Do not neglect apologizing to Heather and Maliyah."

"I shall not," Clowers said. "Your anger seems to have vanished," he added.

"Anger was no longer relevant to our situation, so I quenched it."

Clowers stared at the younger man. "You were prepared to challenge me to the death. Why?"

"Knowing what I knew, there were only two acceptable options: I left or challenged you. When one option is untenable, the other must be taken. I have no desire to leave Terlingua.

"Once I decided, I acted. That's how I was taught."

"Would you have killed me had it come to that?" Clowers asked.

"And make the whole valley hate me? No. Once you couldn't keep going, I would have stopped. That would have proven I had the right to stay and made it harder for anyone to question my skills," Jason said.

Clowers looked Jason straight in the eye. "Were you just pretending?"

"Mostly. I wanted you to know how much I hate sabotage from people who should be on my side. I would have fought like crazy, and you would have seen how tough I am if you managed to beat me."

"I might have killed you, thinking you were trying to kill me," Clowers said.

"It is a chance I was willing to take," Jason responded.

"You are still an arrogant young man."

"If you say so." Jason nodded.

"Do you think you can take me hand to hand? As the one challenged, I would get to choose weapons. I would choose bare hands."

"Do you mean unarmed or ursine hands? I know you have two skins," Jason said.

"Ah. You listen, observe, and reason well. Which would you rather meet?"

"The bear. Then you would know you had done your best," Jason replied.

Clowers studied the younger man. "You seem confident of victory; I am almost sure you are Xavier's second skin. My bear might not fare well against the dragon, even without fire. You will be a valuable ally and a formidable opponent." Clowers raised his right hand and closed it into a fist. "And if I chose my hand?"

"Then I would choose mine." Jason mimicked the gesture.

"But not your dragon skin?"

"If I had a second skin, he was not the one insulted and did not issue the challenge."

"So pax?"

Jason visibly relaxed. "Yes. We cannot afford to be enemies here; protecting Terlingua and the valley requires we be allies." Jason offered a hand, and Clowers shook it.

"You follow the way of the warrior, do you not? It fits with what I know about how you tend to tell the truth and sometimes half truths to avoid lying," Clowers said.

"Yes. I started with the simple exercises I am teaching here, and my sensei introduced me to the way about five years later."

"That explains a few things. Like why you seem to glide when you walk and why nothing intimidates you. And you live in the moment; I recall your appreciation of Ratray's Summer Wine minutes after a death curse almost ended you."

Clowers stood in silence for a few minutes. "I now believe you will find the mage who cursed you and end him."

Clowers stepped toward the four archery targets in a row about twenty yards away. "You are teaching them the bow too?"

"Yes. Several of the boys already hunt small game with bows. I hope to have ten or twelve shooting accurately at this range within a moon. That many bows may deter a small group of invaders near the living quarters, and having a score using staffs will delay them long enough for your men to arrive and force them back," Jason responded.

"We watched you with the quarterstaff. Let us see how your students do with bows."

Jason looked to Heather and Maliyah for advice. They both nodded assent.

Jason called Farid, Eoghan, Constance, Tovia, and Heather to the shooting line. Maliyah retrieved bows and arrows from the barn. Before they started shooting, Jason huddled with his students.

"You will feel some pressure to perform because you have an audience. I know that telling you to ignore them won't work; it never worked for me either. I am not concerned with the outcome of your shooting. Do your best under the circumstances. I want each of you to take two deep breaths before you draw the arrow and aim. Then try to release after exhaling. This will help keep your body still as you let fly the arrow."

He looked around his group, catching each by the eye. "Now, step to the line, focus on the target, and exhale before shooting."

Jason reached out with one hand, and Tovia put her hand on his. Each placed one hand atop the others. When all hands were in a stack, Jason said, "All together now."

The group shouted, "Watch the target!" in unison and then clapped and went to the shooting line.

The students performed well. Heather and Tovia showed the most consistent clusters of arrows, but Farid's were closest to the center.

Clowers applauded their efforts and stated that Terlingua would soon be in much better hands to delay invaders and possibly repel them before the Defenders arrived.

The Defender chief looked at the distant target. "Why do you have a target so far from the shooting line?"

Jason answered, "That is for longbow practice. The near targets are a more likely range for defending Terlingua, while my bow is more suited to a battlefield and the hunting of animals too wary of men for a standard bow's reach."

"I have learned not to question your statements of what you can do, but I would like to see you demonstrate the longbow. Some Defenders have never seen what one can do."

"Yes, Jason, please," chorused his students.

Jason was prepared to refuse, when he saw Melody's pleading eyes. That convinced him.

"I will return in a few minutes with my bow."

He walked to his room. Once there, he extracted his bow from the staff concealing it and returned with his bow and a quiver with half a dozen arrows.

"I need a few volunteers to stand alongside the target but a few yards away to ensure no one wanders between me and the target."

Tovia and Elani volunteered. As they jogged to the distant site, he strung his bow. When they were in place, he nocked one arrow. He took two long, slow breaths, entering the void, before drawing. He held the drawn arrow for several heartbeats. The arrowhead wavered a bit and then froze.

After releasing the first arrow, Jason picked up a second arrow; he nocked, drew, paused, and released. Then he fired a third. He stood back from the shooting point and waved to the watchers. Tovia stepped in front of the target and tugged on the arrows. A few moments later, she and Elani returned to the watching crowd.

"I could not pull the arrows out of the target," Tovia said. "All three arrows are a hand's breadth above the center and would fit within my palm."

Clowers whistled. "That is some shooting. What is the range from here? 200 yards?"

"Thank you, Defender Clowers. From this spot, it is closer to two-twenty. My maximum range for a chest-sized target is 240 yards, below the 300-yard average for the king's archery squad."

A few Defenders asked to try his bow. Jason assented, and two Defenders went to the target to confirm Tovia's assessment and prevent anyone from wandering between the men and the objective.

Three Defenders tried to shoot the longbow but failed to draw the arrow fully. Each lowered the bow and unnocked the arrow without shooting. Galaad was the only one who could draw it fully, but he did not release the arrow, saying he didn't feel in control of it.

Jason chuckled. "It takes some practice before it feels like you control the bow."

"How can a skinny guy like you pull that bow?" Kyriakos, who failed to draw the longbow, demanded.

"Pulling a bow requires muscles people don't use much, and I started with an adult bow when I was about seven. I think that prepared me for the longbow. During the war, I observed several small men lifting or moving things bulkier men could not. I cannot explain better than that."

The Defenders who had fought in the Succession War mumbled their agreement.

Xavier interjected. *Watching you use the longbow, I am impressed at how formidable a foe humans can be. Your close-combat arms are no match for me, but that bow in the right hands could tip the scales on your behalf.*

Just past midmorning, Clowers summoned the Defenders and told them to prepare to return to their headquarters. While they were getting ready, he huddled with Heather, Tovia, Maliyah, and Jason.

"A few words of warning. First, for you, Jason. A man named Erlender is in Twin Rivers City, showing a drawing that looks like you and asking about your whereabouts by name."

Jason's eyes widened in surprise as he listened to the news. "Erlender? I've never heard of him. What's he want with me?" A shiver ran down his spine. The idea of a dangerous man named Erlender tracking him down was unsettling. He ran a hand through his hair. His expression was a mix of worry and anger.

"He's a lieutenant of Golgol-drath," Clowers explained. His voice was serious. "That's not good news. If he shows up here, I'll pretend I don't know anything and try to lead him away. I'll let you know when he arrives, so you can decide what to do."

Jason was silent as he tried to process the information. "A lieutenant of Golgol-drath? That's bad news. What do you think he wants?"

"All I know is he is looking for you. And that the Listener gave him a vague hint and told him to leave her city. She doesn't know you, so she did not deflect his search. He is reportedly a former battle mage and possibly a necromancer."

"As for Terlingua, I have reports of a contingent of misfits and malcontents being led by a magician living in the forest about five days' walk from here. They may come closer, and they may not. I am sure the kidnappers belonged with them."

He looked pointedly at Jason. "I do not know if Xavier flies over that

area, but I would appreciate an update on their location and number." He
paused for a moment.

Jason did not respond, but Tovia looked back and forth between the two
men. She opened her mouth as though to speak but then shut it and looked
at Jason.

Jason realized she was confused about his lack of reaction to Clowers's
comment. It was clear the Defender suspected Jason and Xavier were one
two-skinned individual.

Jason took a deep breath. "Defender Clowers, you are the only one
among this group who does not know that Xavier is my second skin. I am
sure most residents of Terlingua know after the kidnapping attempt. I will
ask him to surveil that area for you."

Clowers raised his eyebrows but did not otherwise react.

Jason chuckled. "I do not know how you and your second skin resolve
differences in opinion, but you met Xavier. He does pretty much what he
wants to, so I can but ask."

The Defender nodded and then said, "I am delighted you took it
upon yourself to train the residents of Terlingua in defense. I hope these
precautions are not tested. Farewell."

He mounted his horse and led the Defenders back to Smoky Springs.

When the mats were ready, Jason introduced falling lessons. The first lesson
was learning to roll.

"Today we start learning how to fall without getting hurt," he said to
begin the next morning's lesson.

"Why must we learn to fall?" asked Finley, one of the older boys.

"Because you *will* get knocked down at some time. I can't count the
number of times I have fallen. If you do not get up almost immediately,
defeat is your reward. Falling without injury is our goal.

"Once we have learned to fall, we can practice fighting among ourselves
without fear of injuring one another. If we don't hurt each other, we can
practice tomorrow and the next day.

"And if you are ever in a fight, knowing how to fall will keep you from
getting injured. Then you can continue fighting instead of losing the skirmish
and possibly your life."

Jason waited for that to sink in. "Are we ready?"

His students murmured their assent.

Jason demonstrated a forward roll, taking time to balance at each step.

He began with a forearm on the ground, almost perpendicular to the mat's long side, with that elbow leading and the other palm on the mat, trailing the leading hand. Then he tucked his chin to his chest and raised his butt. That automatically oriented the back of his head and shoulders to the mat; bending his arms, he completed a front somersault.

The early attempts ended with students flat on their backs; they still needed to develop the sequence of muscle actions to keep themselves tucked. A few needed more core strength to remain curled. Time and practice would cure those issues.

When it was Tovia's turn, she rolled and came up on her feet, facing back whence she'd started.

Jason's jaw dropped. "You already know how to roll. I venture that you also know how to fall?"

Tovia grinned at Jason. "Yes. My father taught me when I was younger than the children here."

"Wow! I did not realize another instructor was here. This is good news! Please help me guide the rest through the proper form in a roll and a fall."

Once a student began a roll properly, Jason emphasized maintaining a tuck and coming up on the opposite side.

"Lead with the left elbow, and finish on the right knee," he told them.

Once they reached a knee, he had them turn so they faced back along their path. Finally, he had them raise their arms, ready to defend against a kick at the end of their somersault.

As with his earlier teaching, Jason trickled life into students as they improved. In two days, half the students executed mostly correct rolls. Tovia connected with the young women better than Jason, and he was glad to have her help.

The older women had the most difficulty learning to roll. The youngest children mastered it after a few attempts.

Melody could roll off her left arm onto her right knee but struggled to complete the turn on her other knee. Jason knew she would achieve his target form as her left side strengthened.

The next step was falling. He demonstrated. From the forearm on the ground, he balanced with his feet above his head and then overbalanced; as he toppled, his opposite leg bent so his thigh and calf struck the ground simultaneously. Coinciding with those, he slapped the mat with the forearm that started hand down. He also exhaled loudly, almost in a shout.

"Doing this breaks the fall. Your impact with the ground is spread along one leg, side, and arm. The loud exhale is so you don't hold your breath and bounce.

"Remember to shout out as you contact the ground; with practice, your shout and impact become simultaneous. Bouncing hurts and takes away your breath, and it takes longer to recover from such a fall.

"Your opponent will expect you to stay down. Getting back up quickly will surprise many, giving you a slight advantage."

He helped each student to fall correctly on his or her preferred side. Extending to both could wait; he wanted them to begin randori—freestyle practice—as soon as practical.

Tovia became his demonstration partner as they began grappling. The initial randori sessions focused on tripping one's opponent. He would show them how the thasiwoda poses and transitions corresponded to positions occurring during hand-to-hand fighting later.

After demonstrating the move he wanted to teach, he and Tovia would pair with other students and help them perform more perfectly.

Heather crossed her arms and pursed her lips when Jason and Tovia randoried. She could tell Tovia was more experienced, but she didn't like how Jason paired up with the younger woman each time.

Her nostrils flared, and she glared at Tovia for a flash each time before controlling her reaction.

She took a deep breath and tried to calm down. She reminded herself that they were just practicing and that there was no need to let jealousy intrude.

She recalled Tovia sitting at his side during the full-moon celebration and running to kiss him after the quarterstaff demonstration with Galaad, and she couldn't help but feel jealous. She took a deep breath and tried to focus on the lesson. But it was hard to concentrate when envy distracted her. Watching Tovia and Jason, she could feel her anger rising.

She resolved to practice on her own until she was able to randori with Jason as he demonstrated techniques.

CHAPTER 12

It Was a Dark and Stormy Night

"Time and Magic," from *Introduction to Magic*
Master Itara
Damocles Academy of Magic

Time is an enigma. We can measure its passage but do not understand what it is we measure. We do not know why time has a direction that cannot be changed.

Time mana may exist; perhaps time is outside of magic altogether. We have no evidence either way.

However, some can see into the future and the past. The past seems fixed, meaning that all who look into it see the same things. The future is more fluid; it includes all that is possible. Trying to see the future is like looking through the fog; the further away an event is, the more difficult it is to determine details.

However, there are events whose outcomes change history. Some can accurately foretell these events but not the time they will happen. There seem to be many possible paths to these events, which makes their time and location unknowable.

For example, the gods do not care about mundane details, such as who will win a war, but they are concerned about the war happening. When and where it starts can change the outcome; thus, seers debate these certain events.

Some can trace a future event to one that will cause it—but has not happened—and attempt to change the cause and, thereby, the approaching event. These people are rare and seldom have the political power to effect the changes they want.

Seers use mana when they examine events that are not now, but the type used varies among them. Time watching is independent of the type used.

Charlatans claim they can read and change the future. Given what we know about magic and time, we should treat any such claims as imaginary.

There is an exception to this rule: the kaihana. Although they have few mages with any power as a race, they are skilled at reading the past and predicting some events. They focus on what affects them and are remarkably accurate when foretelling events, and they are effective at avoiding serious difficulties brought by floods, drought, and armed conflict.

They call their peering outside now time-walking. This describes how they travel along possible threads of events to view the future. They see the future as multiple raveled ropes crisscrossing, and they walk along one path.

The winds increased during the night. Xavier had difficulty landing at the cave due to gusty winds. He could smell the rain coming, and a faint rumbling indicated distant thunder.

Sunrise was four hours away, so the glimmerings of light near the horizon were lightning.

Xavier gathered Jason's clothing in his foreclaws and half flew and half hopped to the farm buildings.

Jason emerged, dressed, and ran to the main house.

No one was awake. Jason rang the bell at the door once. Twice. Three times.

Heather appeared at the door. Her eyes widened at seeing Jason. "What is the emergency?"

"A storm is approaching. We have about half a day before it hits in full force."

"None of the kaihana saw one coming," she objected.

"I suggest that they missed it. The winds, the lightning, and the smell mean a storm. Xavier noticed it first from high in the sky. You and Maliyah need to announce to all so we can prepare for the storm."

Heather took a few steps off the porch and sniffed. "I think you are correct. Thank you, Jason. I will take care of rousing the farm."

"Perhaps MacTíre can help," Jason said.

Heather laughed. "He certainly could. Why don't you see if he is here and willing to?"

Heather disappeared into the house.

Jason hurried to the icehouse. The outer door was open, but he could see no damage to the door, hinges, or latches.

The lack of damage meant the coming storm had not opened the door. He wondered if one of the children had entered and failed to close it properly. MacTíre might have done it, though Jason could think of no reason why the fae would've done that.

He entered, closed the outer door, and latched it in place. The latch could be opened from either side. He felt for the inner latch and carefully opened the inner door; cold air blew in his face.

"Mr. MacTíre?"

Jason entered the icy room cautiously in case something was amiss. There was not enough light to see inside the icehouse, but he could hear the wind, which was muffled by the outer door, and smell the earthen walls.

"Mr. MacTíre?" he repeated a little louder.

Hearing nothing, he relaxed a bit and turned in a circle. "If you are here, Heather has a request."

"What an unexpected visit hours before daybreak! I invited you back when you had reached your mana core, but that hasn't happened yet. So, what brings you to my parlor this windy predawn?"

The walls glowed in a soft white light, showing a room full of ice blocks and stored food.

Jason jumped and hit his head on the wooden ceiling.

"A summer storm is about to break. Heather asks your help in rousing the farm so we can prepare for it," he said.

"Consider it done. I await your return still," MacTíre said.

"One more thing. The outer door was not latched. Do you know anything about that?" Jason asked.

"Ah. Yes. One of the young living here was exploring. I startled her, and she departed quickly. I suspect she failed to latch the door," the fae answered.

"Which one? I will talk with her," Jason offered.

"No. Her magic is awakening, and it leads her here. I will instruct her on the door."

The lights went out, signaling the end of the conversation.

As Jason exited the storage room, he heard a bell clanging and a voice, seemingly from the skies, repeating, *"Wake! Wake! Storm coming."*

———— ✖ ————

Jason spent the morning checking the farm, tying down haystacks, tightening loose boards on doors and windows, putting up storm windows, and checking pen gates to ensure they would not release animals. Fortunately, the farm had a good supply of glowstones mounted in lanterns.

The sky darkened ominously, and the air was thick with humidity. The wind rustled the trees' leaves, sending dust and debris swirling through the air.

A low rumble echoed through the air, and lightning flashed in the distance. The storm was upon them.

The farm's yield would survive if the storm lasted only a day or two. If it lasted longer than that, the saturated soil would prevent almost all activity on the farm, possibly destroying the unharvested crops. Water alone was not a danger. Irrigation canals and drainage pipes would carry water to the river or through the forest, halfway to the swamplands in the south. The dwarves who'd laid out Terlingua had anticipated most contingencies.

When the storm broke soon after dawn, Terlingua was prepared. The residents gathered in the dining room while the winds and rains battered the farm. Hot tea and broth came from the kitchen, followed by bread, cheese, butter, and sliced meat.

As they started to relax, the storm hit in earnest. The rain fell in torrents, driven by the fierce wind. The trees bent and swayed; their branches creaked and groaned under the strain. Strong winds battered the building, forcing one door open. Winds pelted the building with water. Thunder followed lightning almost immediately, interrupting conversations.

Jason watched the others line up for a meal. As usual, he sat where he could see all the entrances. He would eat after all the others had, and there was always plenty of food at Terlingua.

Fionola circulated among the residents with a carafe of wine.

When she reached Jason, she filled his glass and smiled at him.

Melody's mother was the human he interacted with most after Heather and Tovia, and he felt more at ease with her than with other residents. She was quite reserved, but he decided to tease her a little anyway. He reached for the glass and sang in a low voice, intending for Fionola alone to hear him:

> *Bottle of wine, fruit of the vine,*
> *sit me down and rest my mind.*
> *I've toiled all day; I'm worn and weak,*
> *but this drink my spirit seeks.*

> *So pour me a cup, and let's raise a glass*
> *to a life well lived and too soon past.*
> *Moments big and moments wee,*
> *may we savor them, you and me.*

> *So let's raise a toast to life's sweetness,*
> *the precious moments we dare not miss.*
> *Let's savor the moments, big and small.*
> *And embrace the future, one and all.*

Fionola blushed and hurried to the following table.

"Sing us all a song!" someone shouted. He had been overheard despite his low voice.

Others took up the call. He usually avoided drawing attention to himself but recognized the call as a reaction to his choice to flirt with Fionola.

The group wanted some entertainment. He thought he had just the thing.

He stepped away from his seat and waited for them to quiet mostly. "I know a song, and I think you all will too. Join me as soon as you recognize it."

Jason cleared his throat and began to sing. He started softly, but his voice soon grew stronger.

> *Oh, the fox went out on a stormy night.*

"Chilly night," one voice called out.

"Windy night," another called.

Jason turned toward the voices, nodded at them, and continued,

> *And asked the moon to give him light.*

213

As he sang, the others in the group joined in, a dozen to complete the first verse and then all. They knew the song well, and they sang along with gusto.

He had many a mile to go that night
before he reached the town-o.
Town-o, town-o, he had many a mile to go that night
before he reached the town-o.

Jason led them through the song, ending,

They never had such a feast in their life,
and the little ones chewed on the bones-o.
Bones-o, bones-o, never had such a feast in their life,
and the little ones chewed on the bones-o.

When the song was over, the group cheered and applauded.

It was dark as the storm raged, and someone brought glowstone lanterns and distributed them. It made the atmosphere more party-like.

A group of young people started a song Jason had not heard before. He listened and joined in on the second chorus.

A bright flash and a loud crack stopped all activity.

The wind increased in ferocity, and its passing deafened all within the building.

A tearing sound came over the wind, followed by branches ripped from trees and thrown to the ground. A low-pitched, mournful creaking and groaning came next, followed by a sharp, staccato sound of crackling and snapping.

Finally, a loud thud shook the ground beneath them, producing a rumble more felt than heard.

A stunned silence descended on the room. The sound of the large tree falling was both terrifying and beautiful.

"The Grandfather Tree just fell!" one of the kaihana cried out.

The kaihana considered the Grandfather Tree sacred, and they greeted this announcement with cries of dismay. The remaining residents looked at one another questioningly.

The atmosphere in the room shifted from celebratory to sad in a few heartbeats.

Jason did not understand the kaihana's dismay; he knew of the large tree but knew nothing of its significance to them.

He noticed Akela, accompanied by two women he did not know, approaching warily. He felt anxiety, anticipation, and eagerness in the pack link; he was about to meet two pack mates he had not spent time with before.

Jason watched the three women approach as though trying to make their advance unobserved. Heather and Tovia were occupied, keeping the residents wined, dined, and entertained, but each occasionally surveyed the room.

He shifted his position so an empty seat was on each side and waited.

A few minutes later, Akela and the other two women reached him.

"Welcome, pack mates," Jason said as he reached out his hands to Akela.

She clasped them both and looked him in the eye. "Jason, you were not present at the ceremonies expanding our pack; I am pleased to introduce you to these new members of your pack.

"This is Ikigai and Reaver. They belonged to Yeruslan's pack and were freed the day we formed a new pack." She looked at Jason knowingly, as if saying, "You succeeded in renaming Yeruslan that day."

"I guess you were able to break his hold over his crew," she said, making it clear what her look meant.

Each of the women looked younger than Jason—twenty or so. Ikigai had curly red hair and green eyes; her wolf's fur was brown black. Her human form was a little shorter than Akela's and slender.

Reaver had wavy brown hair with hints of blonde streaking throughout and light yellowish-brown eyes. Her wolf, the smallest of the adult wolves, was colored like her human hair. She was slightly taller than Akela and had a more muscular build than was common among human females.

The women seated themselves on either side of Jason, and each grabbed an arm possessively; they rested their heads on his shoulder and sighed as they closed their eyes.

Jason looked questioningly at Akela.

"Wolves need physical contact with their pack kin. Ikigai and Reaver were lone wolves for almost too long. They need contact with you, a founder, the most of our extended family. A little cuddling will help bring them the rest of the way to sanity," she explained.

Jason nodded and accepted the ministrations from each of his pack members. He then extracted his arms and wrapped one arm around each wolf.

"I was surprised when you sang to Fionola. I didn't think you were attracted to her," Akela said as she dragged a chair closer for her seat.

"I was feeling relaxed and a bit like I was home and flirted a little. I hope she doesn't read too much into it," Jason answered with a little chagrin in his voice.

"I don't think she thinks of you as anything other than her daughter's savior. Hero worship isn't the same as affection," Akela replied. "If anything, you need to be careful of Tovia and Heather being jealous."

Jason's eyes suddenly widened. "What do you mean?"

"Each of them flinched when you put your arms around your pack mates. Tovia seemed to shrug it off, but I am not so sure about Heather."

Jason rubbed the back of his neck as a blush crept up his face. "Thanks for pointing that out, Akela. I hadn't noticed, but I'll keep an eye out. Heather's a great healer, and Tovia's always friendly.

"Perhaps meeting in the middle of the room was not the best choice, but I am not around in the evenings—Xavier gets the nights. You decided this was the best option for the pack. Should I worry about them being jealous over the pack connection? Should I talk to Heather and Tovia? I don't want to create a mountain out of a molehill, but I don't want to offend either the healer or the Defender."

He paused for a moment. "Perhaps if the rest of the pack join us, the explanation will be easier."

As he spoke, he saw the rest of the wolf two-skinned start to approach them. *The pack link must have told them we were thinking of them being close,* he thought.

"It's understandable, especially for Heather. You've been spending time together, partly to find your core. It's harder to say for Tovia." Akela paused. "I noticed you choose her for randori demonstrations every time and ask her advice on ways to present a move.

"I can talk to each and see if any feathers got ruffled. Tovia is two-skinned and may understand the pack's needs more readily than Heather."

He inhaled. "I appreciate your help. If any feathers are ruffled, I will need to soothe them. Somehow."

The rest of the pack settled in chairs or on the floor near the four. After a few minutes of casual conversation, Jason felt the pack link hum with contentment.

He leaned his head back against the wall and slept.

Heather, Tovia, Maliyah, and Elani met later that evening in the main house's parlor during a lull in the storm. The other residents were reinforcing tie-downs for when the storm resumed.

Three of Terlingua's guiding council members were at Sinistrad, the kaihana village. They had gone there the night before the storm but had not returned. The storm ravaged the road between the farm and the village, turning it into hock-deep mud; no one would be able to traverse it for three or four days. The eldest kaihana at Terlingua, Elowen, chose not to attend.

Heather stood and spoke, though she was not the senior council member present; Maliyah held that position. "This is the first storm during my years here that we weren't warned of at least three days before it hit. What was unusual about this storm that it avoided detection?"

Maliyah and Elani dropped their chins to their chests as they looked at each other. They pulled their arms tightly to their bodies, rocked back and forth, and moaned quietly. When they raised their heads, neither could look Heather in the eye.

Maliyah spoke first. "We are deeply ashamed of our lack. Neither of us can explain. We will return to Sinistrad when the roads are dry so the Circle of Seeing can replace us."

Heather's mouth dropped, and her eyes widened. She stared at them, incredulous. "Whatever for? I know that time-walking is prone to errors, and this is but an error. One that resulted in no damage to the farmstead."

"But we failed to protect Terlingua!" Elani wailed.

"And we failed to see the Grandfather Tree falling!" Maliyah wailed.

"Hogwash! Sinistrad also missed the storm, or else a bird would have brought a warning. Will the entire Circle of Seeing crawl off and hide in shame for one mistake in predicting the weather? Snap out of it. Help me understand what is happening!" Heather said in admonishment. "And what is the significance of the Grandfather Tree falling?"

Maliyah looked up with tears still running down her cheeks. "My failure last night was unforgivable!"

"No, it was not," Heather said. "Time-walking, when you look at the raveled tapestry of time and traverse a thread, is prone to errors. I know that faraway events can disrupt the possible paths, changing what was almost certain to almost impossible in an hour's passing. Do you have any idea what that occasion was?"

Maliyah studied Heather. "It must be the Beuman√ or at least the events that brought him."

"Jason told me you called him that when he first arrived. What does that mean?"

Maliyah hesitated momentarily before replying. "Our prophecies say the Beuman√ comes when the world is out of balance. His coming means that chaos is near. Or present.

"The falling of the Grandfather Tree is another sign." She dropped her head. "Our legends say the Grandfather Tree was here when we arrived in Smoky Springs. Even though it split and may survive, its falling could mean our time here is ending."

Elani added, "His arrival means the clouding of the future. The Circle of Seeing mentioned some uncertainty in events over a year away; near-term events—especially tomorrow's—shouldn't be affected. The arrow to the future needs some separation from now to change course."

Maliyah shook her head. "We were taught that anything we see within the next tenday is almost inevitable. We saw no storm for last night over the past tenday. Even a gentle rain brought by magic cannot appear with fewer than two days of warning. The Circle of Seeing must be having fits."

Heather thought for a few minutes as the two kaihana recovered their composure. "Is Jason this Beuman√?" she asked.

"I am certain he is," Maliyah said.

"Why?"

Maliyah closed her eyes and recited: "Sparks from his fingers fly, and in his shadow, chaos rides." She opened her eyes and said, "Jason can bring sparks to start a fire. We are seeing chaos."

She took a deep breath. "Beuman√ is literally 'the Burning Man' or 'the Bringer of Fire.' When I first saw Jason, my inner sight revealed flames dancing on his skin, just as my vision of that morning had."

Heather gasped, and her mouth fell open. She licked her lips. Then, suddenly, she felt cold and a little dizzy and sank into her chair.

Elani reached for her. "Are you OK, Heather?"

Heather nodded as she pinched her lips between her thumb and index finger.

Taking a deep breath, Heather continued. "Let us assume the chaos follows his arrival; whether he caused it or not is unimportant. What can we do to mitigate its impact?" she asked. Her voice quivered.

The two kaihana conferred in their language for a few minutes.

"I think we need to distrust our predictions and pay closer attention to what we observe each day to confirm or contradict them," Elani said. "The smell of coming rain was in the air yestereve. I dismissed it as an evening shower approaching, since neither of us saw a storm," she added.

Maliyah picked up the narrative. "The funny thing is that yesterday we each foresaw Jason singing in the dining hall this afternoon, but we didn't see him during our time-walk the day before. We just accepted his unusual behavior without question."

Heather studied the faces of the kaihana. The self-doubt in their body language at the beginning of the meeting was mostly gone, replaced with resolve.

"Well, it seems we have an approach for moving forward. Please do not blame yourselves for events of prophecy. Check with the elders, and let me know if they have more to add.

"I think we should confer more often and compare notes on what we each observe and what the two of you see during your time-walks. Using your foreseeing and what we perceive with eyes and noses will increase our confidence in our daily plans."

The kaihana agreed.

The storm continued for the rest of that day and ended that night.

The following morning, Jason walked to the Grandfather Tree. The top third of the three had snapped off, splitting the tree into two portions, one standing and one fallen part, still attached to the trunk about fifteen feet above the ground.

All the kaihana who lived at Terlingua were standing just outside the drip line of the damaged tree. Among them was a gray kaihana he had not seen before. She leaned forward as she walked, touching her left hand to the ground to help her. The youngest kaihana at Terlingua would occasionally walk in that manner when they were in a hurry. Jason concluded this one was ancient for the race, and walking upright was difficult for her.

The elder was in close discussion with four arboreals. Five more of the forest tenders encircled the tree. He had never seen two at the same time, let alone nine.

Dozens of squirrels scrambled over the fallen portion of the tree, gnawing near the broken trunk and other broken branches higher up. Jason guessed they were assisting the arboreals in emergency pruning.

After walking to the drip line, Jason removed his boots and crouched, spreading his hands on the soil, as he had done on his first day at Terlingua.

After several minutes without hearing the tree, he pushed chi—life—into the ground. Nothing happened for what seemed a long time. Jason began to feel light-headed as he exhausted his mana stores. He felt heat building in his chest, and more mana flowed through him.

Thank you, Xavier, he said to the dragon.

You are welcome. I do not see how pushing life into the ground will help the tree, but you thought it helpful, Xavier replied.

A short time later, Jason sensed a faint response. The great tree seemed confused but not in pain. Jason felt resilience and a touch of doubt from the tree. He tried to encourage the tree, emphasizing the arboreals circling the tree's base. Each of them kept one hand in contact with the trunk.

One left the group and approached Jason.

"How learned you speak with trees?" the arboreal asked.

"Acacia, an arboreal at South Haven, taught me in my youth," Jason replied.

The arboreal nodded. "Hestia, I am called. Tree into winter sleep was. Waken crucial her to live. Now she will. Thank you, we do."

Jason remembered that the arboreals referred to all trees as feminine, while the kaihana referred to the great tree as masculine.

Hestia turned and rejoined the crew surrounding the tree's trunk.

Jason stood and walked to Maliyah, who stood near one end of the cluster of kaihana standing at the drip line. "Good day, Maliyah. Who is the elder? I have not seen her before."

"She is Elowen, and she seldom ventures out of the main house," she replied.

"And what is she discussing with the arboreals?" he asked.

"It is difficult to see from this angle, but the Grandfather Tree is an amboyna. It is also called the rainbow tree. It has green, blue, and orange streaks in its yellow wood. Artists, furniture makers, and bowyers prize it for its strength, beauty, and action. She is discussing how best to harvest the fallen part without further damage to Grandfather. When the ground is dry enough, sawyers and lumberjacks will come trim accordingly."

"Very interesting," he said.

Maliyah turned to face him. "I do not know what you did earlier, but the arboreals are all more animated now. I think they are optimistic about his survival after this disaster."

"I merely pushed mana into the ground, hoping it might help."

"Well, it seems it did. All the kaihana thank you for helping keep him alive," she said, and she returned her attention to the arboreals and Elowen.

———⊱⊰———

As people were gathering for dinner that night, Heather sought Jason. It had been fourteen days since she last reviewed his attempts to reach his core. She felt a pang of jealousy over the episode with Ikigai and Reaver the night before, which she quickly quashed.

Neither of us has said anything to the other. I do not know if he has feelings for me other than as his healer, she thought.

When she found him, she said, "Jason, with all the activity lately, save some energy for our session this evening!"

"Oh. I don't remember you wishing to review my progress today," he said with his eyes widening.

"Perhaps it slipped my mind. Perhaps the storm addled my brain." She smiled playfully. "But it has been a fortnight, and that seems long enough between sessions to me."

"Very well." He glanced around and laughed softly. "I guess most of Terlingua knows of my second skin, but I developed the habit of concealing it. Shall we dine together before retiring to your examination room?"

"Of course. I see your usual seat at the far wall is still vacant. I believe all residents have decided it is yours."

He laughed, and his face exploded with humor. "Another habit I have is sitting so I can see all entrances. My sergeant would be pleased he instilled it so thoroughly."

They served themselves at the sideboard, took their plates, and sat at his table in the dining room.

When the meal was almost finished, Elani ran into the dining room. She hurried over to Heather, saying, "Defender Thaddeus fell ill at their headquarters, and it is beyond both Mi√aela's and Myla's skills. They brought him here. He is in your examination room."

Heather excused herself, saying, "When you are finished, please find me in my office. Elani can direct you to the unused room."

She hurried out with Elani.

———⊱⊰———

Jason sat in Heather's office. He did not have time to become bored before he heard her voice approaching.

"How is Thaddeus doing?" he asked when she came in.

She crossed to her chair, saying, "He is recovering. His appendix tore, but they got him here before it fully burst. That would have been a much more challenging surgery to heal. As it was, I could remove it and clean his insides fairly easily. He won't be patrolling in his eagle skin for several days, but he will recover fully."

She leaned back and took several deep breaths.

"Before we delve into slowing," Heather said in a voice a touch softer than usual, "let's see how your fire manipulation is coming along. Maybe it's changed since last time."

A hint of intrigue flickered in her gaze, leaving Jason nonplussed.

He said, "The early evening is the best time for sparking." He half smiled and then held his hands about a foot apart. A dozen sparks formed.

"Well, that is an improvement. How much are you practicing?"

Jason closed his eyes. "The same as before. I start fires twice a day. I resist the change to Xavier three out of four times and shift quickly the fourth. I am sure that speed will matter when my time here is done."

Heather frowned at the reminder that he was there to reach his core and had made no commitment after that.

Jason continued. "I will summarize. Ask if I leave too much out." He paused for a moment. "After the preliminaries, I hear a breathy voice saying, 'Diablo.' The sound is stronger now than before."

Jason visibly shuddered before continuing. "Diablo feels stronger now but also as if I could control him, but maybe I'm just getting familiar with him instead. Tess feels almost friendly.

"Then Xavier surfaces."

"All sounds like progress. You can bypass Diablo, and Tess seems to present less of a problem," she said.

"I agree," he said. "When you are ready, why don't we walk to our changing spot?"

Heather rested for almost half an hour before the two walked to the space between Jason's room and the forest.

He stepped away and turned his back. She heard him take a deep breath and let it out. She then watched as he started to remove his tunic.

She turned partway but kept glancing at him. *I am acting like a prepubescent girl.* She admonished herself as she felt her face flush. *He is well formed, though. And gentle.* She smiled as she thought of touching and being touched.

She averted her gaze until he called out, "Ready."

"Me too," she replied, and she turned to watch his change, marking time for it to complete while admiring the view of his back.

She watched for several minutes before flames began to flicker across his back and run up his arms. The flames stabilized, but then his skin changed into fog. The fog expanded until it was close to thirty feet from end to end before it began to condense.

Xavier stretched his neck and wings before turning to face her.

Lady Heather, I am glad to see you, the dragon said. *What did you observe this time?*

"Greetings, Xavier. I saw flames on Jason's upper body before he expanded into a fog. I am sure that means he is making progress," the healer replied. "Is Jason present?"

Yes, he is. Slowing no longer exhausts him. Do you wish to speak to him through me?

She shook her head. "I think we are making progress. I do not need to unless he noticed something different."

He says no. The dragon extended his head skyward and sniffed. *The air is still turbulent and not suitable for flying. I shall run a little in the forest and stretch and then return Jason to the farm.*

"Oh. That is different," she said.

This entire day has been different, the dragon said before bounding into the forest.

The following day, under gray skies threatening rain, Melody handed her crutches to her mother and walked slowly and carefully on bare feet to Jason as her mother watched with bated breath and eyes glistening with tears.

He gathered her into a hug and cried openly, soaking the back of her shirt.

"Your tears still prickle, Jason," she called out with a blazing smile.

Breaking the hug, Jason held her shoulders and gazed into her eyes.

"You are walking! And without your special shoes!" Tears streamed down his cheeks.

She wiped his face with her hands. "Why are you crying, Jason?"

"Because the Goddess has corrected your bones. You are walking straight. I never dreamed that this would happen."

The rest of the class, noticing the display of affection a few yards away, walked over and surrounded Jason and Melody. Tovia began the applause, and the others joined in, crying out in excitement and joy that the girl had walked.

Constance was the first to hug Melody, saying, "That's amazing, Melody! I'm so happy for you!"

The children and adults reacted with whispers, gasps, and excited murmurs.

"Wow, Melody, you're walking!"

"That's amazing!"

"I'm so happy for you!"

"What happened?"

"Is she cured?"

"Can she walk everywhere now?"

Finley started to laugh. "It looks like you need a new nickname! Crutches won't work anymore!"

A few adults cried in dismay, but all the children, including Melody, joined in laughter. Jason also laughed, but tears continued to run down his cheeks.

Tovia reached out and gave Finley a friendly jab in the shoulder as she laughed. "Watch yourself, or you might need them."

Tovia looked at Melody's feet and announced, "She is walking without the special shoes! Are her legs the same length?" Looking intently at Jason, she asked, "How did you do this, Jason?"

Several seconds of silence passed before Jason said, "I know of nothing I did to cause this. Perhaps it is the Goddess at work before our eyes. Heather might be able to shed some light on it."

The class dispersed and began their assigned exercises, though they kept looking at Melody.

Jason held his hands near Melody's waist as she went through the candle and cross poses she had learned earlier.

"Look, Jason," she said, attempting the raise-the-sky pose on her own. She rocked to the side, and Jason caught her.

Jason heard Fionola gasp at the girl's loss of balance.

"Not just yet, my brave one. You need to learn to balance on two feet now; then we can begin the poses the others do." He grinned and leaned close. "You will surpass them all when we start one-footed positions. But let us keep that our secret," he whispered.

He directed her to find her balance, working first side to side and then front to back. "You are trying to balance on your soles, ankles, and knees separately. Look internally, and focus on your whole body in balance, not part by part."

She nodded and focused internally.

She cried out in alarm during the front-to-back balancing as she rotated slightly. Jason's hands touched her without support as she turned.

"Your feet were slightly out of alignment, with the right in front of the left. Your internal sense of balance shifted your heels slightly to line them up to a better position. Well done!"

Again, Jason heard Fionola react. He glanced up and saw she had started to approach him and the girl. He smiled at her and waved her back.

Jason had Melody do each of the poses again, complimenting her on her progress on all.

When he walked Melody back to her mother, Fionola engulfed him in a hug and thanked him repeatedly for helping Melody.

Two days later, Melody joined the rest of the children. Even though she lagged behind them, she was proud of herself for doing the same things as the rest and excited at how much her balance had improved. However, Jason had spotted her practicing on her own with her eyes closed the day before; he deduced she would catch up when he started blindfolding them for the poses.

Next week, he thought. *Several are ready for more advanced poses. If there are enough, I will instruct the advanced students separately. I may need to hold two sessions each day to accommodate the differences in skill—or alternate days for each class.*

There was no need to consult with Heather on the logistics until he knew if he had two groups of students.

The sun had just dipped below the horizon as Jason began his evening devotions; the kalasha seemed to expand, with the statuette growing as he watched. As it grew, a translucent figure stepped down from the niche onto the floor. The full-sized female form, draped in a thin robe that covered but did not conceal, walked past Jason to the doorway of his room.

She paused there and glanced at Jason.

Jason reminded himself to breathe. He noticed his mouth had dropped open, and he closed it.

Xavier, please wake up, and tell me I am not seeing things, he said to the dragon.

After a moment without a response, he rubbed his eyes. The apparition remained in his doorway, poised midstep.

Questions jumped to his mind: *Who are you? Are you the spirit of the kalasha? What's happening? What brings you here?* But the figure finished her step and continued outside.

He jumped to his feet and followed, with any thoughts of caution overcome by curiosity. He had not observed the spectral image rise from the kalasha before.

Once outside, the glowing form walked between the kitchen and the bathhouse, directly toward the hidden area Xavier had located days earlier. When she approached the shrouded area, she turned right, walking behind the bathhouse into a wild forest. The image's soft light illuminated the ground at her feet. She walked through the few obstacles caused by undergrowth and fallen branches. Jason avoided them but did not fall behind.

The image approached a tree, which faded into a doorway at her touch. She turned to face Jason and then walked through the door.

Jason tried to open the door but could not. He shook himself and returned to his room, where the icon was still in its niche.

Jason scratched his head as he stared at the figurine. He pondered the meaning of the encounter for several minutes before concluding that the Goddess intended for him to move the kalasha to the revealed location. She had also demonstrated that he could not open its door.

He carefully wrapped it in its cover and walked to the main house despite the late hour. He entered without knocking and looked for Heather.

"Heather, there is something we need to discuss," he said when he found her.

"You are being rather free within the main house at night, Jason."

"Yes, but I believe it is warranted. I know there is a building at Terlingua with a nothing-to-look-at spell on it. Xavier first noticed it. From above, it is too large an area not to feel your eyes not looking at it. I tried to find it on the ground but learned I could not walk to it; I always got turned around. I suspect it houses a sanctuary of the Moirai, separate from the chapel."

The thought of giving the icon up after carrying it for fourteen years caused him to choke up. He continued. "It is time for me to transfer the kalasha to its next custodian. The Lady so told me by revealing the sanctuary entrance. It will serve the Lady better if it is there; that way, all at Terlingua can benefit from its presence."

Heather gasped. Her eyes widened, and she opened her mouth, closed it, and opened it again. She reached out and grasped Jason's arm before she swallowed. Tears filled her eyes as she stammered softly, "Oh, Jason! I do not know how to thank you! This is a gift beyond value. Having it here means we have the Goddess's blessings to start a temple, not just a chapel."

She took a deep breath, placed her other hand on her chest, and choked up before continuing. "I never dared to think you might offer it." She looked into his eyes and touched her lips with her fingers. "I have no idea how to thank you. I wanted to ask for it from the moment I saw it, but the Goddess entrusted it to you, and my asking would've been selfish. This offer is generous beyond words."

Jason nodded, too overcome by emotion to speak. When he found his voice, he said, "I thought the kalasha was mine. The events of tonight made me realize I just carried it. I know having it near made the war easier to endure."

He half smiled, and a tear ran down one cheek.

"Please lead the way to the entrance," Heather said.

When they reached the tree concealing it, she told Jason, "As you deduced, there are two chapels, one public and an inner one few can enter. This one is covered by a nothing-to-see-here umbrella, but you just walked straight to its entrance; this confirms that the Goddess wants the kalasha here."

She studied Jason's face. "What are you bringing to Terlingua, Jason Archer?"

Jason was bewildered by the question. "I, uh, brought only myself and an artifact for Glorinda's hands. What could I bring?"

"I am not certain, but since your arrival, things seem unsettled. You are preparing our children to fight. That would not have happened if you had not come. I do not doubt it is necessary, but I wonder if you are a harbinger of things to come. And how unsettled our future will be."

Jason's eyes widened, and his voice rose in pitch. His cheeks reddened as he said, "I do not know what to say. I am but a simple man following the warrior's path and trying to do more good than harm. I am not a prophet or anything."

Heather nodded and opened the double doors centered on the north-facing wall. The room extended five and twenty feet to the left and right, and the far wall stood almost thirty feet from them. The two entered the sanctuary, which was illuminated only by moonlight through the doorway.

Eight rows of curved, wide steps led down into the heart of the building. The steps had been placed so devotees could sit on the floor without blocking the view of those behind them. Chairs lined the wall behind him, ready for use should they be needed. Curtains blocked the view of the side walls and directed their attention to the center of the far wall. It was not clear if the side walls also curved inward or if just the curtains did.

The moonlight did not reveal the coloration of the curtains or the interior walls. The altar and columns seemed white.

At the front, three steps led up to a platform on which stood an altar. It was six feet long and about half that wide, and its top was four feet above the platform. Behind the altar, seven columns stood. The center one was a half column, slightly recessed and flush with the wall. It had a semicircular, flat top about shoulder height. The remaining circular columns stood away from the wall and extended to the ceiling a dozen feet above.

Candelabras were set in wall niches, waiting to be lit.

Standing inside the doorway, Jason felt peace like a blanket descending on his shoulders and soaking into his skin. The sanctuary was silent; not even the night noises from outside disturbed the tranquility within.

To Jason, the half column looked tailor-made for the kalasha. He reverently approached the center pedestal, knelt, and unwrapped the kalasha. Then he stepped to the stand and placed the icon upon it. It blazed into full brilliance, lighting the interior.

Heather approached and stood beside Jason. She whispered a prayer to the Moirai and bowed.

The light suddenly dimmed to that of a moonless night under the stars. The image on the statuette changed. Instead of a warm, smiling face, the visage became that of a stern woman, with eyes hard, cheekbones more prominent, and lips compressed into a line.

Heather gasped. "This isn't Hathor! She looks harsh, cruel even."

Jason remained standing. He whispered, barely breathing," Dark Lady."

"What have you brought to Terlingua?" Heather repeated in hushed tones.

Jason bowed, backed away from the pedestal, and then turned and walked to the doorway.

Heather raced to the door. "What just happened? Who was that, Jason? What did you bring to our sanctuary?" She closed the door, which faded into a tree trunk.

"I know her as Scáthach, the shadowy one. She appears on the battlefield and doesn't seem to take sides. I saw her occasionally, sometimes more than one of her, in the predawn before a battle. She gives courage to those facing death and those entering battle. When you asked me what I brought with me, I remembered seeing her during the war."

He took a deep breath. "The first time I saw her in the kalasha was the second day of the battle at Sterling." He shivered and continued with a strained voice. "The day before was brutal. A dozen battle-mage spells breached our supposed shield. Men's eyes melted first and then their faces, and they choked and drowned in the liquid. I was terrified by an enemy I could not see, let alone fight.

"The way says, 'Warriors face their fears and are not ruled by them.' But fear ruled me that morning before she appeared." Tears rolled down his cheeks.

He stared into Heather's eyes and blushed in shame at the memory. "Scáthach gave me the courage to take the first step that day."

"My! That sounds like a harrowing experience. I see you are still distressed by it, though you also seem grateful to her."

He nodded and then took a deep breath and continued. "I learned that the Goddess represents all aspects of women. Some women are harsh, almost cruel, in executing their duties. I think the Dark Lady is the face of the Mother in a role as a general who orders men to their deaths in battle. She must be different and do things that Hathor, the Mother you know, would not.

"I don't think she is evil, but she isn't gentle. She is a fierce warrior, while Hathor is nurturing. She will do what must be done, regardless of the pain inflicted, while Hathor is gentle and supportive. Scáthach is a strict disciplinarian, more likely to punish an infraction than reward desired behavior."

He turned to Heather. "To answer the question you asked twice, I fear I have brought war to Terlingua."

—⬤—

"What do you mean?" Heather's voice squeaked. Her mouth remained open. She took shaky breaths and squeezed her eyes shut.

Jason turned to face her. "Scáthach appearing here can only mean that this aspect of hers is necessary for what is coming. From what I have gleaned from talking with others, the Dark Lady is never far from a battlefield.

"That does not mean war is imminent, but it is drawing near."

"War is near? Are you sure? How near?" Heather's concern showed in her voice.

He laughed without humor. "I am sure. But war is never far in the affairs of men. I am no seer to predict it beyond that it is inevitable."

"I now understand why you were sent here and why teaching our young to fight is essential. The Goddess's hands are evident in today's events."

He heaved a sigh. "Perhaps the kalasha needs to be here to protect you and the Goddess's worshippers, and I was but a courier. I am not comfortable with thinking I am but a pawn for the gods; I like to think we forge our path in this world.

"However, I benefited from having the kalasha near. Perhaps a warning to prepare is all that is meant, but I would not assume that. I believe troops will be coming. Sooner, not later."

He took a breath and continued. "Defender Clowers needs to be alerted. I think you should tell him of the approaching hostilities. He will take it more seriously from you, especially with the vision of the Dark Lady. Do not tell him of the icon, though. She intends its location to be secret since she directed us to the private sanctuary, not the chapel."

He went to his room, and Heather walked toward the main house. The waxing quarter moon illuminated their paths.

—⬤—

Heather paused frequently on her way to the house as she pondered the revelation of Scáthach. She ran her hands through her hair, shook her head, and muttered as she walked. Her skin felt tight and itchy. Her brow furrowed, and her nose wrinkled. As she reached the door, she blew out her cheeks and released several times and then took a deep breath and let it out slowly. Upon entering the house, she walked straight to her room, avoiding the other residents and refusing to talk with those she encountered.

She sat in her room, looking out her window onto the courtyard. The moonlight robbed her eyes of color as she watched the fountain bubbling and the creatures of the night walking along the outward-spiraling tile paths bordered by flowering plants.

Heather closed her eyes and conjured an image of the Goddess. Her inner sight revealed the third-quarter moon—a half circle of light in the night sky. The Goddess was beautiful and powerful, and Heather felt a sense of peace and awe in her presence. This was the Goddess she had worshipped all her life—a benevolent being who assisted women in all aspects of their lives, especially during childbirth.

The phantasm changed. The moon shrank and took on a darker hue. Heather saw shadows gathering, and she felt a sense of dread and unease. This was Scáthach, the Dark Lady, the Goddess of the new moon. She was the embodiment of mystery and danger, and Heather felt a shiver run down her spine.

"How can I worship this aspect of the Goddess?" she asked herself. "She seems to be a manifestation of darkness and evil, one I should oppose instead of following."

Heather sat still and focused on her breath, feeling it enter and exit her nostrils, until she entered a meditative state. "Teach me, Goddess," she said. "I know you as Ashtaroth, Hathor, and Morta: Maiden, Mother, and Crone. You teach mankind about growing things and making what we need in our homes. You protect women in childbirth and comfort us when a loved one dies. I do not understand this dark aspect."

Nothing happened for a moment, and then Heather felt a comforting warmth, as if she had been wrapped in a quilt heated before a fire. The Goddess she knew appeared in a vision and split into three forms: Ashtaroth, Hathor, and Morta.

Heather witnessed Hathor move to stand alongside Jason, and Ashtaroth moved beside Melody as he taught the young woman thasiwoda tailored for her disability.

The scene shifted to the abduction site, and she watched Scáthach alongside the kaihana as they attacked one kidnapper with sickles. It moved again, and she saw a ball of fire appear in the sky, through which Xavier flew. But Scáthach sat astride his neck with her cloak billowing behind her and a sword in her right hand raised, as though leading a charge.

The vision shifted, and she saw a young woman carrying a bow, clad in armor and holding a sword beside Tovia as the Defender went from her hawk form to human and garbed herself for battle as part of the Defenders' response to MacTíre's alarm. Heather realized this was Morrigan, the warrior aspect of Ashtaroth.

Another shift occurred, and Hathor was next to Heather and the Defender Angelique as the women comforted Kaelin following her ordeal with the assailant. In a subsequent transition, Scáthach was alongside Jason as he taught the residents to use a quarterstaff and thasiwoda.

Scáthach was the defender, the warrior aspect of the Moirai.

For the first time, Heather understood that Scáthach was an essential part of the Goddess and should be included in the worship of the Moirai.

Heather took a deep breath. A sense of peace and acceptance washed over her. She knew she was ready to face whatever the Goddess had in store.

She opened her eyes and looked out the window again. The moon was still there, just past the third quarter and bright. But now Heather saw something else. She saw the shadows gathering and knew that Scáthach was there, defending against the darkness.

Heather smiled and fell into a sound sleep.

Jason sat to continue his devotions. This was his first night in a dozen years without the icon before him helping him to focus.

He missed the faint reddish light the glowing icon provided behind his closed eyes.

It took him three attempts to complete the breathing exercise that started his devotions. After that, his mind wandered; he had two false starts before settling down with a mind free from thoughts of its loss.

His devotions felt no different than they had the night before, and it did not take as long as he feared to enter a devotional state, but he got no answers beyond the feeling that he had done the correct thing.

Following his devotions, he asked himself, "Have I done all I can to prepare Terlingua?"

Teaching the residents thasiwoda would aid them in maintaining their balance during a fight. Teaching them the quarterstaff would help them defend against an armed incursion as long as they weren't significantly outnumbered. Those who learned the bow could defend and repel a small number of intruders. Hand-to-hand combat was his final contribution.

"No," he said, "I can do no more. The kaihana provided staffs for twenty; six are adequate bowmen, and the remainder know enough defensive hand-to-hand maneuvers to avoid serious harm before the Defenders arrive."

He did not sleep well that night. He kept thinking there was more he could have done.

CHAPTER 13

Terlingua Raided

Mana Shields

Notes regarding stable *mana* wards, barriers, and shields. From a lecture by Professor Isocrates of the Damocles Academy of Magic.

- If a shield surrounds you, you must let air through or make it short-term, lest you suffocate inside.
- If you need to see out, you must make it transparent; others can see in too. One-way light shields have defeated all attempts at construction.
- If your barrier needs to stop fire—magical or mundane—remember, light and heat are forms of mana. An enclosed fire barrier can cook what is inside it. Barriers against heat are also barriers against light.
- If your barrier must stop material things, your pattern must be anchored to something strong enough to withstand their impact.
- Wards for detecting an attack instead of stopping it require smaller stable patterns.
- Stronger mages can always break through your barrier, especially if they know the patterns you used to construct it.

It was a wonderful night for flying; the air was cool and still, providing neither aid nor hindrance to flight. The moon was nearly full and high; thin clouds were the only obstruction to its lighting the scene below. Xavier and Jason were enjoying the view of Smoky Springs Valley from above, far enough from Terlingua to see the high mountaintops to the north.

Despite the distance from Terlingua, Xavier heard MacTíre's clarion and gong four hours before sunrise. The dragon changed direction and raced back to the farm.

When he reached Terlingua, Xavier circled and saw the heat signatures of men to the west; he plunged silently to defend the farm.

As he got closer, Xavier distinguished a mob loosely organized into rows of about eight each. Three ranks were inside Terlingua proper; the lead men were about halfway to the barn from the boundary. Another dozen ranks ranged from the farm's border to the forest's edge. Such a group could only be interested in pillage, rape, and kidnapping, he concluded.

More were moving toward the farm from within the forest, but he could not estimate their numbers. Near the forest's edge, a mage stood within a glowing hexagonal mana pattern; the pattern had other components he could not identify from high above.

Xavier saw a line of residents strung between the barn and the bathhouse—a half dozen tenants aiming arrows at the attackers and twenty women and children armed with quarterstaffs, ready to defend. Wolves stood at the ends of the line; he couldn't tell how many there were as he flew over. The noncombatants hurried to the chapel entrance; its stone walls would hold against such a motley crew until the Defenders arrived.

As they approached, Xavier said, *I suggest I spray venom above the heads of the attackers as you slow its burning and then accelerate it. With luck, the bright blast will take a quarter of them from the battle forming below.*

I like that idea, Jason replied. *What about the mage? He has a shield; it looks like two overlapping tetrahedra plus a six-sided prism. Will it protect him from heat?*

We can see through it, so it transmits light. It surely transmits heat as well, the dragon said.

Then we'll surprise him with heat and light from above after our sortie interferes with the ground troops, Jason said.

As Xavier approached to attack from above, he saw lights like those in MacTíre's sidhe just inside the farm's limits; perhaps the fae was present. The twinkling lights engulfed those intruders who shuffled instead of walking. Those men fell and did not rise.

Xavier decided to attack the intruders about six ranks from the forest; that would minimize any threat to the residents. As Xavier planned, dragon fire could eliminate a quarter of those between the forest and the farm's edge.

'*Ware the fire, MacTíre*, the dragon broadcast as he sprayed a cloud of venom, which burned on contact with air.

With Jason retarding ignition, the mist barely smoldered, forming a red-glowing haze above the invaders' ranks.

The shining fog illuminated the farm grounds, allowing the invaders to see the defenses against them. They had expected to find the residents sleeping, not prepared to fight. They hesitated for a moment. Then the front few ranks began shouting and ran forward, raising clubs and knives.

When Jason accelerated the venom's burning, it erupted more fiercely than expected. The explosion's shock wave caught Xavier's wings at his lower back and flipped him backward. It took him a moment to regain control in the air.

Turning back toward Terlingua, Xavier saw four rows of men lying on the ground, with flames licking their clothing and the ground nearby. Six additional rows were forced forward or backward into other marauders, injuring many and adding confusion to a disorderly progression. Some fell to their knees or lay on the ground.

The wolves viciously attacked the men on the ground.

Xavier and Jason turned their attention to the necromancer.

The mage had constructed a prismatic shield to keep arrows and crossbow bolts away from himself and the six minions seated at the vertices of the regular hexagon on the ground. The shield consisted of two triangular pyramids inside a six-sided prism.

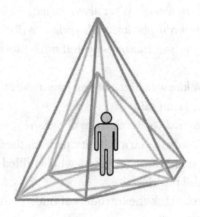

Xavier flew toward the nested pyramids. The sorcerer looked up at the sound of wings approaching, sending an energy blast at the dragon.

Xavier screamed in pain as the energy hit him on his left-wing joint and rippled down to his abdomen. The searing bolt blackened his scales and tore his skin. Despite his injury, he sprayed venom onto the shield. The mage's screen kept the venom from striking him, but it hit the top and began running down the sides.

A cold rage flared within Jason. Witnessing Xavier's agony spurred him to unleash a potent burst of heat, which he'd not channeled before. The blinding, scorching light that engulfed the shield was just as much a retaliation for his other skin's suffering as a calculated strike.

As the pair deduced, the sorcerer's defensive screen did not stop heat or light. The sorcerer screamed as radiation seared his face and eyes, blinding him.

The dragon landed nearby, and his tail lashed the shield's base.

The mage had failed to anchor his refuge to the ground. The blow moved it, which unbalanced all seven inside.

The shield crumpled against the dragon's tail without the anchor points. The prisms vanished, causing a mana backlash. The mage screamed again.

The sorcerer's defenses protected his body, but physics trumped magic. When Xavier's tail struck the necromancer, he folded forward at his knees, and his legs broke. The mage screamed again and fell to the ground with his defenses fading as his consciousness fled.

Xavier fell onto the attackers between him and the forest. His uninjured wing struck the men with devastating effect; its leading edge broke arms, legs, and necks. He bit the heads off those within range and slashed with his claws those between his torso and the end of his wing. His talons cut leather armor like a hot knife through butter. The thagomizer at the end of his tail tore melon-sized chunks of flesh from the men it hit.

He could not fly, due to his injury, but he left a trail of dead and broken men in his wake. Invaders not already closer to Terlingua turned from the dragon and fled into the forest.

"We need to return to the farm." Jason prompted the dragon. *"At least a score hostile men are still within the grounds."*

Xavier turned and ran to the rows of men slapped down by the exploding venom. Crossing into Terlingua revealed friend and foe too close together for fire, wing, or claw, so he could not effectively contribute to the defense. He shifted to their human skin.

Jason condensed out of the fog and attacked the intruders from the rear, moving with the same ferocious grace as the dragon. Years of thasiwoda training flowed through him, and his strikes were exact and relentless. He channeled his rage into precise, targeted attacks. He disarmed, incapacitated, and eliminated threats with calculated movements; his emotions fueled his focus and speed. It looked as though he danced among the marauders as they fell.

<hr />

Alicia, a human woman who mainly worked in the kitchens, heard Xavier's warning to MacTíre, glanced up, and saw a glowing cloud. She deduced the dragon was about to use fire on the attackers.

"Look at the ground!" she cried out. "Xavier is here!"

A few others took up the cry, and most of Terlingua's residents were not looking directly up when the sudden flash appeared in the sky. The *boom* and shock wave surprised all, but they could see the rows of men approaching in the afterglow. Men stumbled and fell from the shock wave. The residents taught the longest by Jason wavered slightly but lost neither balance nor weapon stance.

Xavier's aerial assault was behind the attackers closest to the farm, so the flash did not affect their vision. However, the unexpected pressure wave propelled them forward; many stumbled, and some fell. Those who did not lose their balance raised their clubs and shouted as they closed with the farmers.

The defenders swung their quarterstaffs in arcs at the assailants' chin level. The men increased the intensity of their battle cries.

Jason's students did their best to enter the void before the battle. Jason had taught them to focus on the tasks at hand and prevent the conscious mind from interfering with their muscle-eye memories. The void helped, and the deep breathing preliminaries calmed their nerves.

One man rushed Alicia, rejecting the quarterstaff she held as an ineffective defense in the hands of a human woman. She maintained the end of her staff level with his eyes. He contemptuously brushed at the staff. His eyes widened as the staff's end dipped below his hand and punched him firmly in the stomach. His breath whooshed out, and he doubled over. She struck him again on the head, and his eyes widened in disbelief before he fell unconscious. The women raised a war cry of their own for the first time.

Success bolstered the confidence of the women and kaihana with quarterstaffs. With confidence that had been missing a few heartbeats earlier, the women began to chant the steps of an attack exercise Jason had taught them and looked for opportunities to strike.

The rhythmic chanting unnerved their adversaries. What defenses they had against quarterstaffs disintegrated, and men collapsed or turned to flee.

Aishwarya, the kaihana who maintained the farm's tack, stood a little ahead of Melody and between the girl and half the wolves. Most wolves were along the edges, away from the archers and quarterstaff wielders.

The wolves shifted from their stomach-on-the-ground position to a tracking and pouncing stance and inched forward as the men walked closer in the starlight. They were ready to strike.

Aishwarya saw the rutilant cloud form as the sounds of the dragon's wings reached her. She heard the dragon's voice and Alicia's cry and lowered her gaze to the ground halfway to the nearest attacker. The flash and boom seemed simultaneous, and the pressure wave followed quickly.

Looking up, she braced herself for the attack and heard the victory cry from the center of the line, focused on Alicia.

Without warning, the wolves sounded their attack; savage growls and snarls echoed through the night. The pack hit the men from both flanks, tripping, biting ankles, knocking men down, and going for the throats of those the shock wave downed.

Aishwarya faced three, with Melody at her side, preventing any from getting within club range as the kaihana fought. A wolf dove into the midst of the three, scattering them. One went to one knee, and the wolf took him down. Aishwarya managed to get a solid stomach jab into one of the remaining. The third hooked the kaihana's staff on his knife hilt and struck a glancing blow to her head with his fist. She staggered back, and the man turned his attention to Melody.

He grabbed the girl's staff and pulled her closer. He raised his knife, preparing a killing thrust, but a white wolf charged to her aid. The wolf snarled and snapped her teeth as she scrambled over his chest, trying to find purchase on his leather armor. Unable to stop or get a hold of his throat, the wolf's teeth clamped on his left arm. The weight of the wolf unbalanced the assailant. His knife slashed the wolf, finding a target near her belly. The wolf made no sound as she fell and released him.

Melody freed her staff while the wolf kept the marauder busy, and she swung it at the man's head. She connected just as the man looked up from pulling his knife from the wolf. His eyes rolled up in his head, and he collapsed with the melon-splitting sound of a cracked skull.

Aishwarya recovered from the blow to her head, stepped forward, and kicked an invader in the groin. She was surprised as a dark wolf jumped him from the side, closing its jaws on his throat as the canine carried him to the ground, killing him.

The kaihana looked up. She could see attackers standing and some surrendering: the fighting had stopped.

"Zarya is down!" she heard someone cry out.

The avian Defenders flying to Terlingua from Smoky Springs saw a red glow at about treetop height and presumed it to be a fire. The sudden flare and boom a few moments later contradicted that conclusion. A bright flash followed, illuminating the farm buildings and the trees on the far side of the two-skinned eagles. The light did not last long enough to provide battle details, but the nearly full moon guided them where they needed to go to respond to the alarm.

As they had when responding to the kidnapping attempt, the eagles dropped the tarp and flew at head height to protect the first wave of avian two-skinned. These first landers opened the tarp; armed themselves with shotguns, shields, and short spears; and stood to defend the later arrivals.

Thaddeus landed with the second wave and donned armor before joining the first wave. When the next wave were armed and armored, they advanced on the battle scene.

The first to land saw a naked human form jump into the line of men inside the border of Terlingua from behind. They watched men fall as unclothed arms, hands, knees, and feet brushed their necks, legs, ankles, or heads.

They saw other people retreating from a line of determined women and children, each armed with a staff. Those who turned to run were dropped by arrows or attacked by wolves.

The intruders had been repelled, and the battle was almost over. After they dealt with the unknown man who fought with his bare hands, only cleanup remained.

Four armored Defenders approached Jason with short spears pointed at him. Thaddeus, a two-skinned eagle Defender, raised his voice above the groans of the wounded and dying: "Stand down, and surrender!"

Jason stopped his attacks on the invaders and turned toward the Defenders. He did not stand down. Still gripped in battle fury, he was ready to continue fighting, holding his arms loosely at his sides with knees bent, balanced on his toes. His face was relaxed, without a trace of fear that he faced four armed and armored men. He studied the four spearmen facing him for a chink or gap in their defense.

He laughed briefly and walked toward the spearmen, flexing his fingers, seemingly unaware of his lack of armor and weapons.

Thaddeus's mouth dropped open, and his eyes widened. In the muted moonlight, he saw a naked, unarmed man approaching his men as though *he* were the one in control and they were the ones in danger.

Maliyah, still holding a quarterstaff, ran between Jason and the Defenders. Seeing the kaihana interceding for him, Tovia, who had arrived with the Defenders, stepped around the line of spearmen and approached the pair.

Tovia's appearance quenched what remained of Jason's battle frenzy. He stopped and let his arms fall to his sides.

"It is Jason. He lives here and is not an attacker," Tovia announced to the Defenders.

They relaxed and began searching the downed attackers, looking for survivors.

The battle had taken less than an hour since the dragon arrived.

Jason felt a sudden sharp pain through his wolf pack link. "Zarya is down!" he cried out.

Jason's heart pounded in his chest as he raced toward Zarya. When he saw the deep gash along her side, his breath caught in his throat. The white wolf was panting but otherwise not moving.

An orange-and-brown wolf approached and shifted into Akela. "Zarya is too badly injured to shift, so she can't heal that way," she said.

Akilina and Ikigai also changed to their human skins. The three women lacked clothing, having just shifted.

Jason felt the anxiety and sadness among the swirling emotions on the pack link. After Akela's announcement, it shifted to grief as Zarya's pending death settled in their minds.

Jason cradled the white wolf's muzzle and teared up. "My wise, impetuous beauty! What happened here?" he asked no one in particular.

Melody stood beside him. She pointed to an unconscious raider lying nearby. "He attacked me with a long knife. As he slashed at me, Zarya jumped between us, and he stabbed her. I hit him alongside his head with my staff, and he fell."

Jason reached one arm out and hugged Melody. "Thank you, my brave one, for standing firm and stopping him."

A tear dropped from Jason onto Zarya's muzzle. The wolf licked it and then stretched her nose to Jason's face and licked the tears from his cheek. With a burst of energy, she licked the other cheek and eye. Jason felt her tremble. It felt as though he held an expanding bag of feathers, which condensed, leaving a sleeping woman's head in his arm.

Akela grabbed Jason's shoulder. "What just happened?" she cried with wide eyes. "Why could she suddenly shift after licking you?"

Jason looked at Akela with a slack jaw. He drew a deep breath and stuttered, "I d-d-don't kn-kn-know!"

He carefully lowered Zarya's head to the ground and stood, shouting as his voice rose in pitch, "Did you all see it?" He looked around at others standing nearby.

Nods and mumbled words of assent answered him. Akela and Ikigai grabbed him into a hug, crying tears of happiness.

"She was able to shift! It is much more likely she will heal. Let us get her to her bed," Ikigai said in a shaky voice.

Jason shook his head. "Before that, Heather should look her over to ensure she is out of danger."

Heather stood nearby. Her eyes and mouth were wide open after watching the wolf's wound improve as the canine licked tears from Jason's face.

She checked Zarya's pulse, listened to her heart, and lifted unconscious lids to peer into the woman's eyes. After watching her breathe for a few minutes, the medic said moving the woman to her room was safe.

Jason picked Zarya up and carried her to the building housing the two-skinned wolves. Zarya roused enough to wrap her arms around his neck, making carrying easier.

Akela walked alongside her pack mates to Zarya's room. "Will you stay the rest of the night with your pack?" she asked.

Jason thought for a moment. "I am not comfortable staying with you unclothed. My clothing is at Ognyen Cave; if you will get me a tunic from near the kitchens, I will stay."

Akela sent Akilina to retrieve a covering for Jason.

Jason carried Zarya to the building assigned to the wolves, surrounded by the pack, about half in human form and half in their animal skins. He settled her sleeping form on a pallet against one wall and spread a blanket over her.

He donned the raiment Akilina brought and settled on a mattress on the floor.

With Jason's attention on the fallen two-skinned wolf, the Defenders rounded up the invaders and separated them into three groups: the dead and dying, the wounded, and the whole.

As they gathered the malefactors, they found the mage's bent, burned body. It was the Defenders' first exposure to the villains, and a disabled wizard was beyond their experience.

The man lay still with his knees bent backward at almost a right angle. The man's scalp and forehead, including his eyes, were burned, with broken skin, blisters that had not broken, and patches of blackened skin extending up from his nose and along his forehead. His breath came in gasps.

Thaddeus had not dealt with a mage prisoner before but was reluctant to do nothing while waiting for Chief Defender Clowers to arrive. He asked the other Defenders if they knew how to confine him.

Sparkling lights appeared around the Defenders standing nearby. "*I will restrain him until your chief arrives,*" said a voice from the air.

All the Defenders, save Tovia, jumped and spun around, seeking the source of the disembodied voice.

"Thank you, MacTíre," Tovia said in a firm voice. "We are not prepared to hold a mage wearing a master's robe, but you can."

Her words settled the nerves of the other Defenders near the bent, burned body.

Lighthearted music played as a blanket of scintillating air settled over the mage's body and wrapped snugly around it.

———⚬∞⚬———

The wolves knew Jason belonged to the pack, but not all knew that his second skin was Xavier. Shifting from the dragon left his human form naked, so his desire for clothing made sense to those who knew. They explained to the others. Most of those in human skin donned sleep shirts before settling down for the night, while others shifted to, or remained, wolves.

The pack settled around him, each finding a part of him to touch. Jason's sleep was interrupted several times as those in wolf form shifted position among the pile of beings sharing the room.

When he awakened two hours later at daybreak, he tried to rise. A sharp pain from his shoulder to his stomach caused him to groan. All those in wolf skin were instantly awake; those in human form roused more slowly.

Akela insisted on examining Jason. Lifting his garb, she saw a half-inch-wide angry-red stripe running from the top of his left shoulder to just below his navel. She touched it gently. As she did, Jason sucked air in between his teeth. His skin was flushed and clammy, and his breathing was shallow.

"Are you in pain?" she asked.

He nodded and groaned. "Yes. A lot."

Akela turned to one of those in human skin. "Akilina, please fetch Peaiman Moonstar. Tell her our dragon was wounded last night and needs attention."

Phaedra looked at the red stripe. "This looks like the location of Xavier's injury last night. Their shift almost halted its spread, but the corruption was just too much for the change to completely heal him."

———⚬∞⚬———

The healer arrived a quarter of an hour later, along with Elani, Melody, and one human aide whose name Jason did not know. Heather looked tired, having cared for the wounded raiders since the invasion was quashed.

Heather glanced around the room. Jason was lying down in a shapeless wrap, and two women were in human skin but not yet dressed. She felt jealousy flash through her, followed by anger that Jason had been with these women.

What went on here last night? she wondered, revolted at the image she conjured. Her nose wrinkled, and her upper lip curled. She crossed her arms, hunched her shoulders, and stepped back from Jason as she turned away.

"This is Branwen. She, Elani, and Melody are my students," Heather said curtly, introducing the unknown woman. "Akilina made it sound like you were dying," she added, turning toward Jason. "Show me this wound!"

Phaedra rose with her body in a taut line, confronting Heather. "Show some respect! He was injured in dragon form while protecting you, and marks were left etched in his human flesh. Wounds mirrored between skins are the marks of grave harm. I expected more empathy from you. And, for your knowledge, Jason has not lain with any of the wolves, despite their asking him to."

Heather froze. Her jaw slackened, and her eyes widened with disbelief as they fixed on Phaedra. "What are you implying?"

Phaedra's voice sharpened, laced with possessiveness and fierce protection. "Don't pretend ignorance amongst two-skinned wolves! I saw your gaze dart about and smelled your mood shift from worry to a vicious cocktail of jealousy and rage. Why else would women near Jason set your emotions aflame?"

Heather did not step back, but she nodded. "I messed up. I'm sorry for how I acted toward you and the others. Now, let me check out the patient."

Akela lifted Jason's shapeless gown, revealing the red stripe. "It looks even angrier now than when I sent Akilina for you," she said.

Along its length, a row of pustules had appeared; some had burst, leaving a foul-smelling greenish-yellow residue.

Heather audibly sucked in her breath. "This looks serious," she said as she knelt beside Jason. "Tell me how this happened."

The wolves looked at one another before returning their eyes to the healer.

Ikigai spoke up. "We felt the dragon's warning of fire; he spoke without voice, but we understood. We saw the glowing cloud and looked down as it burned and boomed. We heard Xavier scream in pain and then saw a flare like a noonday sun. After that was the chaos of battle. None of us know details of the injury."

Jason described the wizard's counterattack on Xavier, taking several breaths to do so.

Heather shook her head. "Necromancers project a corruption of life. It eats at living tissue. I will need some help in expelling it from you, Jason."

She looked him in the eye. "You and Xavier each need to direct your life to the wound, pushing from within to expel the corruption."

Jason nodded. "Xavier is awake and heard," he said.

Heather felt a sudden increase in warmth emanating from Jason—far more than she expected from the festering wound alone. Jason began to sweat as the two-skinned wolves and the healers watched.

The healer turned to Melody. "As I taught you last tenday, when healing an infected wound, we must push the infection out using life mana. Jason and Xavier are each doing that part. The final stage of healing, though, comes from an infusion of spirit mana. Adding your strong spirit to mine will force the decay out and close the wound afterward."

Melody nodded. "Jason helped me earlier. Now it is my turn to help him!"

Heather looked up at Branwen. "Branwen, please fetch boiling water and clean cloths from the kitchens as quickly as possible."

She removed Jason's gown, took a small knife from her satchel, washed the red stripe with vinegar, and applied a layer of oxymel—a vinegar-honey mix. She made a small incision the length of the angry scar, just deep enough that blood beaded along the cut.

"We need a path for the infection to exit; this will prevent it from tearing, which would be harder to heal."

Jason gasped as Heather lanced the wound. The effect was almost immediate. The life-mana pressure Jason and Xavier applied from within caused corruption to ooze out the length of the slit.

When Branwen returned, Heather instructed her to supervise cleansing the fissure. The peaiman rolled Jason onto his right side and directed Melody to place her hands on his back, along and above his left shoulder blade. Heather put her hands on the center left of his back. Four hands glowed white as Heather and Melody directed spirit mana into Jason. The two healers closed their eyes and breathed deeply. The color drained from their faces, and beads of sweat formed on their foreheads.

Jason cried out once and then lapsed into unconsciousness. The slight ooze became a flow that smelled of burned flesh and infection. It continued for almost a quarter hour while Branwen, Zarya, Reaver, and Phaedra mopped the exudate from his torso. Finally, the wound glowed white and closed, leaving a thin scar.

Jason slept deeply following the treatment. Heather and Akela redressed Jason in the one-size-fits-all tunic without waking him.

Their red-rimmed eyes and chapped lips mirrored their exhaustion.

Heather and Melody yawned; their shoulders slumped low. Melody's head bobbed and then snapped up in a weary start. Heather's gaze lingered on her; worry was etched on her face.

Sensing the drain on both healers, Akela dispatched Ikigai and Reaver for food. The younger wolves returned with a platter of bread, cheese, fruit, and sliced meat.

"Eat before you sleep," Heather insisted, pushing food toward Melody.

When her appetite subsided, the healer sent the girl to her room with Elani and Branwen as escorts; she had only walked without a crutch for a few tendays. After a dozen steps, Melody stumbled and crumpled to the ground. Branwen caught her as dust motes swirled around them, and then she carried Melody the rest of the way. In the older woman's arms, Melody surrendered to sleep almost immediately.

Heather and Zarya sat on the porch of the wolf house after Elani and Branwen left with Melody.

Heather felt terrible. She realized she'd judged Jason unfairly, assuming he was romantically involved with the wolves. Now she was mad at herself for feeling jealous.

But a part of her still felt jealous. She had thought she'd gotten over that when Akela explained the pack bonding during the thunderstorm five days ago, but clearly not. She tried to focus.

Heather cared about Jason, but the wolves' interest in him worried her. The near-fatal attack left her shaken, and Phaedra's talk about mirrored wounds only made it worse.

Heather wondered where she fit into all this. How would the wolves, being such an integral part of his life, affect him? How could they have a relationship if she felt insecure about his being around other women, especially since he was part of the pack? She had no idea what that meant or how she could handle it.

One thing was clear: jealousy wouldn't solve anything.

The sun was two hours above the horizon when Clowers sought Jason. Elani told him Jason had quartered with the two-skinned wolves.

Just what I need—another secret about that man, he thought.

He asked for directions to the building and walked there. He saw Heather and a woman he did not know sitting on the stoop, eating.

"I am looking for Jason," the Defender said.

"He is asleep inside," Heather replied. "He was injured last night in his dragon skin and needed care. And this is Akela; she is one of his pack mates," the healer added.

"How did a two-skinned dragon end up a member of a wolf pack?" he asked.

"Jason and Xavier kindly supported us when we wanted to escape our former pack. They helped us form a new one and freed us from the influence of our former leader," Zarya said.

"I see. I think," Clowers said. He swiveled his head between Akela and Heather, unsure whom to speak to. "I have a necromancer bound in a magical net, and I need Jason's help interrogating him. He and Xavier learned Oliver Brewerson's True Name, and I hope they can help us do the same with Nizar, whose minions revealed his usename."

Heather entered the room and gently awakened Jason. "Defender Clowers needs help finding the True Name of an evil man."

Jason tried to stand but fell to his knees twice. He took several deep breaths. "I am not sure I can walk unaided, but if I am needed, I will help."

Zarya looked at Heather, who nodded. The two-skinned wolf said, "We will help you walk."

They steadied him as he rose and stood on either side to help him walk.

Clowers silently accompanied the two women as they escorted Jason to the battle site.

The battle area was almost 120 yards due north of the wolf house, but they had to detour around the chapel and between the bathhouse and the kitchen to reach it. The residents' defensive line had stretched from the bathhouse to the barn, while the area Xavier had attacked was closer to the forest than the barn.

Jason pondered the night's events as they returned to the site of Xavier's battle with the mage. From Xavier's arrival to the mage's downfall, the battle had been a whirlwind of less than an hour. Yet, in that time, Jason had witnessed violence on par with war and experienced his dragon's pain.

As they walked, his heart hardened toward the fallen man. They reached the necromancer, and Jason approached him, with Akela helping him the last few steps.

As he stood over the broken, whimpering man, his gaze steeled. Though calm, his voice held the weight of justice. "What is your name?" he asked as he knelt by the man, keeping one hand on Akela's arm.

The question wasn't a mere query; it was a demand for accountability, a first step in finding and stopping the forces that brought violence upon their peaceful home.

The man turned his face toward Jason, revealing his burns. "I can't see you. Who are you to ask my name?" His voice was low and strained.

"I am the one who burned you last night."

"How the hell did you do that? I did not see anyone coming; I heard a noise above me and saw the stars blocked. Some liquid hit my shield; then fire and light burned and blinded me," he said, struggling to get the words out.

"You first," Jason said.

"Nizar," the mage said.

Xavier, I will try to maintain the fiction that you are the one who extracts True Names. I may need to reveal you to this man to do that. Jason began the mind-to-mind conversation.

Our secret is known to many. There are too many to call it a secret anymore. One more can't hurt, the dragon responded.

"As to how I did that, I have two skins. One can fly and spits venom that burns when exposed to air," Jason said.

"What manner of being is your second skin?" Surprise colored the mage's voice despite the pain.

"I will not tell you that," Jason said.

"Why not?" Nizar asked through gritted teeth.

Jason realized he now knew—it was almost like recalling—the prisoner's True Name. He stood and turned to Clowers. "The burns have him sufficiently confused. We learned Nizar's True Name: Hashim Stonethrower."

"Thank you, Jason," Clowers said with a relieved sigh. "That will make interrogating him much easier." He continued in a lower voice. "Please remain nearby while I question him."

He paused and turned his head away for a moment before almost whispering, "I won't repeat the mistake that cost my brother his life."

He paused again before continuing. "At least Nizar will no longer bother us after today. I hate executing people, even when they deserve it. And this being surely deserves it."

"I agree with you completely, Defender Clowers. Battle mages gone rogue should be destroyed when found."

The two women escorted Jason to his room, helped him lie down, and sat outside his door. He fell asleep almost immediately.

A little more than an hour later, Clowers approached the two women sitting at Jason's door.

"Welcome, Defender Clowers. How did your interrogation of Nizar go?" Heather asked.

"I am glad to see you two," he said, glancing away from their faces. "Nizar was an associate of Erlender's, though not working with him recently. Eliminating this one does not stop Erlender's search for Jason. We still do not know why he is being sought."

He grimaced. "I know of one necromancer who managed to resurrect himself. I cut off Nizar's head, and it is burning right now. I think we will soon be safe from him." He looked each of them in the eye. "A raven from Twin Rivers City reports that Erlender claims to represent Jason's uncle and is searching for an heir."

He sighed. "That is a lie. But he is coming for Jason. The Listener's ears report that his minions are circulating Jason's sketch in Myakka, so they have traced his path that far."

"Does the Listener have ears everywhere?" Akela asked.

An awkward pause ensued. Clowers looked between the two women. "You can never tell who is an ear for her."

"That is true," Heather said.

Zarya's eyes widened. "Are each of you one of her ears?"

Clowers grinned. "We cannot answer that question. Nor can we answer what she has or has not heard from us."

Heather laughed at Zarya's expression. "Not all gets reported in any case. She knows a dragon is in Smoky Springs but not his relationship with Jason. At least I don't think she knows."

After a few moments without additional comment from Akela, Clowers shook his head. "I don't know when Erlender will arrive in Smoky Springs or what I can do about it."

Heather placed a hand on his shoulder. "You are not responsible for Jason, Clifton."

He laughed bitterly. "No, but not even his dragon can face Golgol-drath's lieutenant and win. Yesternight was, at best, a draw for Xavier, and Nizar isn't as strong as Erlender. I will do what I can to delay him when he comes, but be prepared for a disruption to the life we know. And soon."

Heather recalled Maliyah's words that Jason was the harbinger of chaos and shivered.

Jason spent the rest of that day in his room, venturing out only for a midday meal.

The following day, Jason was still recovering following his injury. He could only perform the most basic of his habitual morning exercises.

You told me that dragons were immune to human magic, Jason said to Xavier.

I believe I said almost all human magic. Necromancy is an exception. I was surprised at how seriously you were hurt. I thought shifting would allow me to heal, not that his insult would continue to putrefy in you. Perhaps we are not as separated as we thought, Xavier replied.

Half of Jason's students came for lessons, and he dismissed them with "What you did last night counts as your practice today. I'm proud of you for standing up to the bandits and really happy that none of you got hurt."

Jason paused for a moment. He knew his secret was widely known at the farm, but he had confirmed that to only a few. It is time to admit it to my students so they aren't relying on rumor, he thought.

"The necromancer hurt Xavier, and that injury affected me as well," he said, raising his tunic to show the scar. "I am fortunate that we have Peaiman Heather Moonstar at Terlingua. She was able to heal me, though I have not fully recovered. I will see you all tomorrow, when I hope I have recovered enough to teach."

Jason walked to the icehouse, limping slightly due to their wound. Changing skins would not help since the dragon was injured; they would wait until Jason felt healed enough to shift.

Jason opened the outer and inner doors of the icehouse and closed them behind him. "Mr. MacTíre," he said, "I hope Xavier's fire did not harm you the night before last."

"Well, well, well, the half-dragon visits. To what do I owe this pleasure?"

Despite expecting the voice from nowhere, Jason jumped back with widened eyes. Recovering, he said, "I saw you near Terlingua's border last night. "You stopped a few shuffling invaders, but you left others alone. I would like to know why."

There was a long pause before MacTíre replied.

"*I heard your warning of the fire. Thank you. I doubt it would have hurt me much, but I appreciate the alert.*

"*To answer your question, my queen forbade me from killing humans, dwarves, kaihana, all two-skinned, and arboreals in this realm. However, one whose soul was stripped from him and a new one injected is not strictly living. Those abominations created by necromancers should be destroyed.*

"*This may stretch the letter of her command, but I assert that a being is dead once its soul is gone. Reanimating does not mean restoring life.*

"*I am almost certain my penance will be light or dismissed should she learn of my transgression.*"

"I hope it doesn't come to that. I appreciate your assistance in defending the farm," Jason said slowly. "I am also curious that Xavier heard the alarm when well outside the farm's boundaries."

Spirited music filled the air. "*Whatever gave you the idea I was limited to the boundaries of Terlingua?*"

Jason's jaw dropped open.

"*I count you as an ally in keeping the farm and its surroundings safe. I just reached out to you where you were in your dragon skin.*"

"I thank you for alerting me. I apologize for thinking you were confined here," Jason said.

"*Think nothing of it. I want humans and others to believe that I have limits I do not. It makes it easy for them to underestimate the protections surrounding the farm.*"

The following night, the moon was full. Jason still struggled to perform the elementary poses and transitions, but he walked to the circular flower garden area and sat near the gathering for the celebration. He did not see Tovia and was not sure if she was at Terlingua or conducting Defender business.

Melody did not lead the chanting, and he did not experience the deep devotional state he had during that full moon.

The morning after, when Heather suggested they review his progress in finding his core, he bowed out.

"Nothing has changed in what I feel during the change, and Xavier and I do not think we should shift until I feel better," he told her.

She agreed.

The next day, he felt well enough to perform a sequence of twenty thasiwoda poses but could not transition between some pairs without feeling strain along his scar. He thought, *I am well enough to teach and let Xavier out.*

It's about time. The dragon spoke to him mind to mind.

Eavesdropping on my thoughts, eh?

There isn't much else I can do when I am awake and the passenger.

Jason led the group exercises that morning, walked to Ognyen, and shifted to their dragon skin.

Xavier could see a black streak about a palm's width running down the left side of his abdomen. His neck was not flexible enough to see the full extent of the scar, but he expected it to correspond to Jason's, extending from the wing joint to the center of his abdomen, above his pelvis. He opened his wings carefully and stretched, finding his left wing joint stiff.

He took a few practice flights, more a hop and a glide, before launching himself into the air. Climbing to his cruising height took longer than usual, but his wing loosened as he flew.

Jason, can you carry a half deer to the kitchens from Ognyen? Xavier spoke to his passenger.

The human replied, *I am not certain. I would not like to find out after you eat when there is a carcass ready to haul.*

I shall drop the uneaten part as close to the kitchen as possible, Xavier said. *I have no qualms about leaving it at the cave, but it could attract scavengers.*

Xavier landed and set the half deer near the kitchen doorway at midnight. He returned to Ognyen and molted. Again, he left one wing's shedding for Maliyah at Ognyen. Jason would return later in the day with a cart to carry the cast-off skin back to her.

CHAPTER 14

The Fire Awakens

"Elements of Magic," from *Introduction to the Foundations of Magic*
Master Yona
Damocles Academy of Magic

You may have learned that there are four elements, each with its mana type or magic: air, earth, fire, and water. Since you are here, you were likely told you have an affinity for one or more of these.

This old-fashioned view is good enough for many purposes; it is often all the hedge wizards know, and they serve their villages well.

However, these four are insufficient to describe all mana. For example, lightning, lodestones, light, life, and spirit all are, or have, a type of mana but do not fit the four-element model.

T wo tendays later, Isadora, a two-skinned hawk, flew to Terlingua from Defender headquarters in Smoky Springs. After landing at the kitchen entrance, she shifted to human form before donning a shapeless gown from the supply in an adjacent storeroom.

She ran to the main house and insisted that she speak with Maliyah.

"Tiernan is a spy for Golgol-drath; he told Erlender that Jason lives here. They will come here tomorrow. Erlender has three and twenty men with him; Defender Clowers can't delay them!" she exclaimed when the kaihana arrived.

"Thank you for bringing the news," Maliyah said.

Maliyah called into the house, "Elani, send Heather to the kitchens as soon as you find her. Then find Jason, and bring him there as well. It is urgent." Taking Isadora by the arm, she escorted her to the kitchens and served her.

Elani first found Heather and then ran to find Jason in the fields.

Jason hurried to the kitchens.

"Elani told me my presence was required," he said when he found Heather.

"Erlender is in Smoky Springs and headed here tomorrow. He spoke with Tiernan; you were right about that man. You should leave today and return after Erlender has decided you are not here."

"Leave? Just because a man has found me?" Jason raised his eyebrows.

"Erlender is a necromancer with a twenty-three-man retinue. Glorinda might not choose to face Erlender alone; she would not face him with twenty-three supporters. And she is a university graduate with years of practice, while you are—pardon me—an uneducated neophyte."

"That is a fair assessment." He nodded. "But I have defeated others when I was the underdog. Remember Galaad and the quarterstaff bout."

"But you did not pick up a staff for the first time that morning and are an experienced fighter. Your magic is still as weak as a child's, and you have no weapons or experience for a magical duel." Her voice broke as she looked him in the eyes. "Remember what Nizar did to Xavier, and that was but a single death dealer. I want you to leave; I don't want to bury you."

Jason looked toward Smoky Springs for a moment before speaking. "I think your advice is sound, though I dislike it."

Her cracking voice alerted him to a possibility that had escaped him: she cared for him more than as a mere friend. He did not know how to react.

He sighed. "I don't need to leave immediately, do I? Do we have time for a final attempt to reach my core magic before I leave?"

Her eyes widened; her gaze flickered downward for a moment. "You must leave today." Her voice trailed off, and then she looked him in the eye. "And no, you do not need to leave immediately. We have time for another attempt."

Her eyes watered, and she blinked rapidly. A half smile played across her lips as she continued. "How have your transitions to Xavier been going? Are you slowing down? Do you feel your inner magic core?" she asked.

"Better, yes, and no," Jason replied.

It seems she has feelings for me. She is battling tears, he thought.

Heather nodded at him to continue.

"I can slow the change. It now takes several minutes. I haven't noticed any differences in what I see or feel during the transfer since we last spoke. The larger space I detect at the end hasn't changed."

Heather paused before adding, "I know you are resisting the change to reach your core. Is Xavier also resisting, or is he just doing whatever he does when he is next out?"

"He watches, I believe. I haven't asked him, and he hasn't volunteered any action."

"Well then, you and he have something to try today. Let us resume behind the barn, near your room."

They walked the hundred feet separating the kitchen from the space beyond Jason's room, surrounded by the barn, the hot-spring field, the forest, and MacTíre's sidhe. He paused, studying their surroundings.

It may be a while before I can return to this place, he thought. *Leaving South Haven was easier than this.*

He stepped to his usual spot and turned his back to her. He took a deep breath and let it out. After he folded his clothes, he squatted and called out, "Ready."

"Me too," he heard.

With another breath, he entered the void. *Xavier, wake up if you are not awake.*

I am here, Jason.

Please resist the shift this time, Jason told the dragon.

Yes. I overheard your discussion with Heather. I will not allow the shift.

Thank you.

The familiar sense of a hot, dry wind blowing and the desire to destroy that was Diablo came and went. The smell of rain and the sensation of rain falling arrived and faded.

With Xavier resisting the change, Jason felt suspended in space and pulled in two directions: one led to a red-orange glow and the other to the familiar body shape.

He focused on the glow, which resembled a fire.

He felt a tingling on his skin, similar to the frisson when he created a spark. That prickling spread to his entire body and intensified, past comfort to the point of pain.

He saw a sphere formed of intertwined streams or rivers before him, looking like ribbons twisting and circling. One consisted of winding cords of white and royal blue, and one was multicolored, changing from colorless to red to purple to violet to blue and then back to colorless. One consisted of three thin threads of blue, yellow, and green, twisting, fraying, and reweaving as he watched. One was clear like water. One was black or a dark color for which he had no name. One glowed the orange, yellow, and red colors of a fire. He reached for the fiery stream.

He seemed suddenly immersed in a river at flood amid boulders, so the current yanked him in all directions. He tried to resist it but could not hold the torrent back.

Just as it seemed to break through him, Jason jumped up away from Heather and waved her back. As she stepped away, he was engulfed in flames, and the sudden heat caused her to jump back several steps.

The flames mostly subsided, leaving Jason inside a glowing red-orange cloud extending three feet from him—the ground beneath him and within the plume burned. The red-orange halo grew upward, reminding Heather of a massive fire, with sparks extending some distance above the flames. White smoke formed above the blaze.

A klaxon sounded, and a stentorian voice called, *"Fire behind the barn! Fire behind the barn!"*

Heather spun in place, swiveling her head to each side as she turned. She yelled, "MacTíre! Fire under control! Fire under control!"

An all-clear whistle sounded, and the voice repeated Heather's words.

The fire stopped, leaving Jason in the middle of a charred ring. He hugged himself and stuttered, "C-c-cold. C-c-cold!"

She hurried to his side and grabbed his arm. "I will take you to the hot spring," she said.

"N-n-no. N-need f-f-fire."

She turned around and helped him stagger to the kitchen firewood stack.

Once there, Jason pulled down split logs and arranged them in a circle around himself, placing them three pieces deep and two high. He crouched down in the center and touched the ring with each hand. All the wood burst into flame—a fire with no smoke.

Jason stood, and the flames followed him, swirling around and into his skin.

"Oh my!" Heather cried out as his hair and beard burned away.

Half a dozen kitchen staff came out and watched the inferno surrounding Jason.

The wood burned to ashes in less than ten minutes, leaving Jason in a white ring. All hair was gone from his body except his eyelashes, and soot streaked his skin.

Turning to the woodpile, he selected a piece of kindling about the diameter of his thumb. He gazed at it a moment, and fire suddenly engulfed it. The flame turned blue and leaped upward.

After a moment, he extinguished the flame and set the cooled stick back on the pile whence it had come.

He turned a slow circle with his mouth agape. "Everything glitters! The colors are all so bright! It is like I was blind and now can see," he said.

He stepped to the end of the woodpile, knelt, and touched a drab summer wildflower. "Wow!" he burst out in a voice tinged with awe. "The leaves are practically glowing! And that flower—it's like a thousand tiny jewels! This blossom is absolutely gorgeous! It's white and blue and has streaks of red."

He looked up at Heather. "Do you see?"

"I can only see a small gray-white flower," Heather replied, knitting her brows.

Standing, he turned to face her. "You are glowing white," he said, approaching her. "It is as if light is leaking out of your skin."

He reached out and touched her arm with a look of wonderment on his face.

She shivered at his touch and then ran a finger down his arm, leaving a clean streak along it. "You are covered in soot, Jason. You need to bathe."

He nodded absently, turned toward the bathhouse, and walked beside her.

As they walked to the bathhouse, Jason stumbled frequently. He swiveled his head continuously and exclaimed, "Everything looks so bright! So colorful!"

He often stopped to examine a branch, a leaf, a flower, an insect, or just the ground.

His foot caught on an exposed root during one of his partial turns. He tripped. He tried to fall correctly, as he taught in the mornings: striking the ground with both forearms and holding his head up as he shouted to empty his lungs. However, he landed on his chest first and then his left hand, his head, and, finally, his right forearm. His head hit the ground as his body bounced from the air still in his chest.

Stars danced at the edges of his vision, slowly resolving into the blurry shapes of trees and sky. A metallic tang, thick and coppery, filled his mouth. Each breath was a struggle.

He lay there unmoving for a moment. Slowly, his lungs began to cooperate. Shallow gasps turned into ragged breaths, each one a victory. The metallic tang receded, replaced by the sharp sting of scraped skin.

He pushed himself to his knees and looked at Heather. "I fell!" he exclaimed. "And I did not fall properly!"

He looked at the beads of blood collecting along the scratches and said, "I seem to have lost some balance and reaction speed. I wouldn't have fallen yesterday, and a fall like this would not have knocked the wind out of me either."

He tried to stand but had to place his hands on his knees to avoid another spill. He stopped, unable to proceed, until Heather helped him to his feet. He stood there with his legs shaky beneath him for a moment and his eyes closed; each breath was a victory against the pain. The world was no longer a terrifying blur but a canvas painted with sharp edges and vibrant details, immersing him in awe with his new sight.

The two stood there for a minute while Jason performed the standing tree until he felt centered again.

At first, Heather thought his distractions caused him to stumble. However, during one of his stare-at-the-treetop moments, she was surprised to observe he was at least six inches taller than before.

It is like a teenage boy's growth spurt in an hour. No wonder he is so awkward!

She was acutely aware of his every move, noticing everything, from the way he walked and talked to his entrancement with the everyday things they passed.

Heather started the water flowing from the bathhouse's cooling tank, which was fed by the hot springs, and guided him beneath the water from the shower's overhead nozzle.

Heather returned to his room and gathered his clothing. *I wonder if anything will still fit him*, she mused.

When she returned to the bathhouse, she found Jason sitting beneath the flowing water, entranced by the spray hitting the wall and making rivulets along the tiles.

His curiosity is as intense as a two-year-old human's, she thought.

"Hi, Jason. I have your clothing. Are you finished bathing?"

Jason jerked with surprise. "Hello, Heather. I believe I am." He looked up at her and said, "Have you watched droplets collect and start traveling down the tile? I am sure I must have at some point, but their flow is fascinating!"

I am glad there isn't a sunbeam creating rainbows on the wall, she thought.

He rose from his seat and stopped the water from flowing. Heather handed him a towel, and he dried himself as she watched.

When he was dry, he approached Heather. "Thank you for your help in accessing my magic. I did not know there was so much I had not seen before!"

He took her hands, looked at them, and said, "They are so beautiful." He raised them to his mouth and kissed each fingertip and then moved on to the backs.

When he kissed her hand, her heart skipped a beat. His lips were soft and warm, and she felt a warm flush spread through her.

He stood, held her face gently in his hands, and kissed her forehead.

She felt as if she were going to faint. His lips were a warm caress, and a shiver ran down her spine.

Heather grabbed his head, pulled it to her, and kissed him fiercely.

He flinched slightly before wrapping his arms around her and returning the kiss. She began undressing while their lips were busy. Once unclothed, she pulled him to the ground, pushed him onto his back, and straddled him.

Grasping his erect penis, she guided him to her opening, rubbing the end against her to widen her entry. She began easing him in slowly but then stopped. She paused and then pushed down hard with a slight cry of pain. She continued slowly taking him until all of him was inside. She rocked forward and backward with some circular grinding and began to pant.

After a few minutes, she moaned, "Ahhh. Aaahhh." She stopped moving and leaned forward, resting on his chest.

He grabbed her hips and thrust until he moaned and stopped moving.

They lay on the bathhouse floor for several minutes with Heather's face on his chest. He heard a long, drawn-out exhale before she raised her head and looked at him. She had a gentle, relaxed smile and brow and slightly closed eyes.

She heaved a gentle sigh and then sat up and climbed off Jason. "I think I need to bathe now."

She stepped into the shower area, started the water flowing, and washed.

She took a step back and finished drying. Glancing at Jason, she observed his member swelling.

"Not now. Later," she said. Impulsively, she bent down and kissed the tip.

She cried and jumped back a little as it sprang fully to attention. She kissed the end again, and he sucked air between his teeth. She experimented with her tongue and was rewarded with a moan.

"Oh my!" she exclaimed. "No one ever mentioned this as a possibility! This is going to be more fun than I imagined. I can't wait for you to return!"

She dressed.

Jason dressed. Heather observed his trousers fit his waist but stopped well above his ankles, and his tunic was tight across the shoulders, with sleeves two inches above his wrists.

She watched him struggle with his boots.

"My feet are too big now. This is going to make travel difficult." He looked up at Heather. "I cannot leave Terlingua now."

"But you must."

"You could be with child."

She turned on him. "And what difference does that make?"

"I should be here for my child."

"It is not just your child; I may not be pregnant, and if I am, it will be my daughter to raise," she declared.

"But I should be here for you. I should be here for my child. Wait—did you say *daughter*? How do you know?" His brow furrowed as he asked.

"You have no choice. You must leave. Erlender will come here tomorrow and kill or capture you if you are here. And I cannot tell you how I know it would be a girl."

"But what about you?" Jason's lips tightened, showing wrinkles at the ends, and he reached out to touch her.

"I will be fine. He has no reason to harm me but will hunt you," she said.

"I don't want to leave you," he said.

"I know. But you must," she said firmly.

Jason inhaled and exhaled loudly. "I planned on leaving before we, um—"

She laughed. "Yes, before we joined."

He bowed. "I will do as you wish, Priestess."

She spun to face him. Her eyes were wide, and her face was red. A vein on her forehead stood out. "What did you just call me?" she demanded with anger coloring her speech. "Who told you? Xavier did, didn't he? I should have known he would not keep secrets from you!"

Jason stumbled back a step and sat suddenly as he backed into a bench's edge. He looked quizzically at Heather before his eyes lost focus.

As she watched, his eyes regained focus.

He shook his head slightly. "Xavier tells me that conversations between you and he are none of my business."

He took a deep breath. "I know some details of people I meet without being told. It extends to knowing some True Names."

"That is impos—"

"Silent Song of Peace," Jason whispered.

The color drained from Heather's face. She seemed to melt into a cross-legged sitting position in front of Jason.

"Y-you know my True Name?" She gasped.

"Yes," he answered.

"How?"

"I recently discovered this ability. You were present when I identified the True Names of Nizar and Oliver."

"Who else knows? And I thought Xavier found those," she said.

"Three wolves from my pack. I broke the pack link to their abusive leader by changing their True Names.

"And I provided Xavier with Oliver's True Name and implied he had read Nizar's. The dragon hid my involvement with Oliver with a, uh, deceptive statement."

"Why can't you use Erlender's name against him?" she asked.

"Well, for one thing, I do not know his True Name. It takes me some time around someone to learn what he or she hasn't offered, which isn't always the True Name. I learned you were a priestess some time ago, but I just learned your True Name today.

"And from the little I know of name magic, knowing a True Name is like having a weapon; it does not make the battle even. Relative skill and strength—mana and will mostly—come into play after a True Name is known."

"I see," she said quietly. "Now back to practical matters. You are leaving today and will return when it seems safe. Correct?"

"I cannot return as long as Tiernan is here. He will recognize me and notify Erlender."

Heather laughed. "You don't know all that happened today! You are taller. Stand up, and see how much."

He stood. The top of her head was no longer at his nose; it was now well below his chin. His face showed bewilderment.

"You know you are seeing things differently. But you don't know your eyes are different: the left is half green and half blue, while the right is orange amber, with a cat's pupil."

Jason's head snapped back, his eyes widened, and his mouth fell open. He sank back onto the bench and put his face in his hands. "What kind of freak am I?" he said. His voice cracked. He looked up at her. "Three moons ago, I learned I had two skins. I did not know two-skinned people existed.

"I am glad I have two skins. I like Xavier. He and I can talk—unique among two-skinned. He is smart, and we fly. I was not comfortable flying at first, but now I enjoy it.

"We are the first human-dragon two-skinned ever seen. I know other humans, but we are not sure other dragons exist. Dragons haven't been seen in over 200 years. Xavier doesn't say it but is concerned that he is the only living dragon. Two-skinned or not."

He laughed as he raised his head, but his laughter lacked humor and bordered on hysteria. "Today has shaken me to my core. My inner fire abruptly expressed; I resembled a giant fireball. Now, I am *really* different. I can summon a bonfire, not just a spark. But I hoped that would happen.

"You tell me I am six inches taller than I was an hour ago. My hair and beard are gone— burned off. My left eye is half blue and half green, and my right eye is orange amber, with a pupil like a cat's. I see colors I could not see before. Every living thing glows, and I do not understand it."

Heather sat beside Jason and took one of his hands in hers. "Jason, take a deep breath. You're OK. I'm here with you. More importantly, the Goddess is here with us. She trusted you with her kalasha, so you should know she favors you.

"You're the only known human-dragon two-skinned, and that's amazing. You're showing the world there's more to life than we can see.

"Today brought unexpected changes; you can now access your fire, and it is strong.

"You can't control what's happening, but you can control how you react to it. You introduced me to the Dark Lady, and I am still not used to the idea of her. You will accustom yourself to your situation in time." She smiled at him.

"Take a few deep breaths. Inhale slowly through your nose, and exhale slowly through your mouth. Focus on your breathing. Let the tension in your body melt away," she said. "We will figure out what to do next. But for now, just focus on breathing."

Bitterness tinged his laughter. "You think entering the void will help?"

"I didn't mean for you to go that far, but the breathing exercise might help you gain some perspective. You're still the person you were before, with some new abilities, and as with all things, controlling them will be hard before it is easy," she said tenderly.

Jason performed the breathing exercises preliminary to entering the void. His ragged breathing settled, and his breaths slowed and became deeper. He took a deep breath and visibly relaxed. "OK. Thank you. I should have remembered to do that."

"OK, now that you're feeling better, let's talk about what happened," Heather said. "You reached your inner fire. You're now six inches taller, your eyes have changed color, and you can see things you couldn't see before. That's a lot to take in, I know. But this is just a change, and growth requires change."

She took a breath. "You're still Jason, the man who went out of his way to help Melody and who went out of his way to train us—to prepare us for what is to come.

"You told me a few days ago that war was coming. Perhaps your new abilities manifested now to prevent that. Or to prevail in it.

"You are the bravest, gentlest man I know. You're stronger than you think you are. I know you can handle anything that comes your way, and I will face the future at your side."

Jason took another deep breath. "Thank you. But how can you face it with me if I must leave?"

Heather punched him lightly on the shoulder. "I don't think you should stay," she said. "Jason's leaving and your arriving on the same day, even in your new form, is too much of a coincidence. You should still leave but can return after some time passes; I believe you will be safe.

"You will need a new name. And perhaps a new look. Your hair and beard are gone; you could shave now as your new look."

Jason responded, "I will leave. I want to visit South Haven and see my mother again. Xavier needs to find a roomier cave and wants to search for other dragons. I do not know how long those will take."

Heather nodded. "Now a name."

They sat in silence for a few moments.

"Drake," she said. "I think Drake will do. It is an old word for a wingless dragon but isn't used for that now."

He nodded. "And I will take a surname from my journey. I will be Drake Doingolla. Starting fires set my feet on this trek."

Heather rubbed her chin. "Doingolla. I think that is the Arrokothokoth words for 'hot' and 'carry' combined."

"I did not know you spoke the Dwarvish language," Jason said.

"I know a few words. I wasn't sure I had the right ones, though." Her eyebrows rose. "Did you just embrace Maliyah's claim that you are their fire bringer? The Beuman√?"

He blinked several times. "No, that is not what I intended, but it is what I have done. I think I shall keep it."

Heather laughed. "That sounds good to me." After a moment, her expression sobered. "I am sorry that you must leave, but I think it is necessary for your safety."

They heard a knock at the doorway and chorused, "Come in."

Maliyah and Aishwarya entered the bathhouse. Maliyah carried a package, and Aishwarya held a pair of half boots.

Drake stood to greet their visitors.

Maliyah began. "Greetings, Heather and—" She stopped. "Who is this with you? It is not Jason! He is not as tall as this man. And his eyes are green, not—what color are your eyes? They are not the same! Who are you?" she demanded.

Drake looked at Heather, and she looked back and nodded. He settled back down.

Heather spoke. "Jason came to Terlingua to learn to reach his core magic. He touched it today and then started a bonfire and stood in it, which burned the hair from his head. And when he stepped from the fire, he was taller, and his eyes had changed. He and I discussed changing his name rather than trying to explain his transformation. This was Jason, now called Drake."

Maliyah studied Drake for a moment. "Are you well? Other than missing hair, you don't seem badly injured—just some scrapes and scratches on your hands and knees." Concern was evident in her face and tone.

"I feel fine. It seems that a simple wood fire doesn't hurt me," Drake said. "Though I fell walking here and skinned my elbow and forehead. I haven't fallen like that since I was ten years old."

He took a slow, deep breath and continued. "I will return to Smoky Springs in the future, and I hope I am greeted as a new arrival."

The kaihana talked to one another in their language.

Aishwarya spoke. "Your bonfire confirms that you are the fire bringer, the Beuman√, the herald of chaos. We will do as you wish."

Drake's eyes widened, and his mouth fell open. "Herald of chaos? What does that mean?"

Maliyah spoke up. "Our prophecy says that chaos follows in your shadow, not that you serve chaos. Your coming means the world is about to change. The kaihana's part in the prophecy is to help the Beuman√, and we shall."

Aishwarya asked, "The Circle of Seeing directed us here, but why are the two of you in the bathhouse at midday?"

Heather blushed before replying, "When Jason stepped out of the bonfire, he was covered in soot. We came here so he could wash."

"But why is your hair wet?" Maliyah asked.

Heather's face turned beet red. Drake also blushed.

Aishwarya looked at each human in turn. She also blushed.

Maliyah looked at Aishwarya, and her eyes widened. She mouthed, "Oh," and looked away.

Heather swatted Maliyah playfully. "I think you are imagining things!"

An awkward silence followed.

Maliyah nodded, half smiled, and said, "Our purpose today is to deliver this package from the Council of Elders. They foresaw your need to travel and provided some clothing for your trip. I can see that your clothes do not fit, so this is a timely presentation."

"How did they know I needed—no, never mind. I am sure some time-walking by your Circle of Seeing," Drake said.

Maliyah nodded, smiled, and gave him the package. He opened it and found two tunics, one heavier than the other, and one pair of trousers.

Drake was speechless.

Heather thanked Maliyah and the council for their generosity and timely gifts.

Aishwarya handed him the half boots. "I made these three moons ago, based on a vision. I did not think they were for you; your feet, I thought, were too small for them, but Elder Sabah said I should offer them to you."

Drake stood and took the boots from her.

"You are taller! These might fit you perfectly! When did you grow?" she exclaimed.

The healer answered, "He was taller when he exited the bonfire. The Goddess must need a taller man."

The kaihana looked at each other, spoke in their language for a moment, and then remained still. They stepped closer, and each tentatively reached out to touch him. He allowed them to.

"We are happy to help you, Beuman√," Maliyah said reverently.

He embraced the two and thanked them; he choked a little while getting the words out.

They bowed and left the bathhouse.

Heather looked at Drake. "Well, your footwear concerns are moot. The Goddess's hand is involved in today's events. Now you need to pack and leave Terlingua."

He nodded. "I have an appointment with MacTíre before I go. I shall say farewells to my wolf pack; it will seem to most others that I just walked away. I will lie low for the rest of the day and leave when it is dark to avoid being seen.

"I will write a note for Tovia, but I ask you to encourage her to continue teaching quarterstaff and hand-to-hand combat and leading the thasiwoda." He paused. "Her Defender duties may not allow her to do all these."

He looked at Heather again. "I apologize for leaving a mess for you to clean up."

Heather smiled. "That is just some of the chaos that follows you." She turned and left.

Drake watched her leave. A hollowness settled in his chest. Was there something else he should have said? How strong were his feelings for her? Today's events had surprised him, and he was still reacting to them. He changed into his new clothes and walked stealthily to his room.

His new boots felt like a well-broken-in pair. Neither pinches nor hot spots showed during his trek to his room. As he crept the short distance, avoiding being seen by other Terlingua residents, he felt tension in his pack link.

I must visit them, he thought. *Something has agitated the pack, which could be what happened to me. I must set them at ease before I go, but first, MacTíre.*

Drake slipped the twenty yards separating the icehouse from the bathhouse, careful to avoid being seen by other residents. He knew he was taller than before, clumsier, and clothed differently, and he did not want to be mistaken as an intruder, nor did he want to discuss his new appearance. He had visited MacTíre twice since his first day at Terlingua and had promised to return when his inner fire awakened.

He was suspicious about working closely with a fae, but MacTíre was the only skilled magic user he knew, and MacTíre had offered to teach him. Taking a deep breath and letting it out slowly, he opened the outer door of the freezing room; his breath showed even in the warmer antechamber.

Closing the outer door, he entered the storage area. "Mr. MacTíre?" His words were slow, low, and tenuous.

"Welcome back, Jason Xavier—and with a new name! You are full of surprises; what was the occasion?"

As before, MacTíre's voice surrounded him. It was not accompanied by the flickering lights that Drake remembered from his visit as Jason.

Drake explained the events of the day.

"Outstanding! I have expected you since the fireworks behind the barn earlier today. What other changes have you noticed?" the fae asked.

"Everything seems brighter, more colorful, shining, and glittering. And this form is clumsy," Drake said. "I am not used to stumbling and knocking things down unintentionally. I hope daily thasiwoda will remedy these soon."

MacTíre said, *"Your wizard sight emerged on the day you touched your core! You are seeing reflections of mana, and you will soon be able to see if someone is manipulating mana. That will come with time. Progress in magic is much easier with wizard sight.*

"And I am pleased with your outlook on your … reformation! I am sure every

mage within fifty miles knows precisely when you touched your source. We can discuss that later.

"Now, what is your new name, if I may know it?" the fae asked.

Drake laughed. "You mean you aren't going to coerce it out of me this time? It is Drake. Drake Doingolla is the name of this form. Lady Heather suggested it."

"An excellent name. You have taken a name that means wingless dragon who carries fire, and that fits nicely in a changing world. It suits you better than Jason Archer did."

"I did not tell you I was called Archer," the human said.

"Indeed, you did not. But you are not my only source. Your aura is different today. Where is Xavier?" MacTíre asked.

"Xavier is sleeping right now. We each sleep for part of our passenger time—when our other skin is in control," Drake answered.

"Ah. His presence is more difficult to see. I might have missed it on our first meeting had he slept."

Drake took a deep breath. "I somehow think you would have noticed him anyway. Now I have a question for you. Are questions about your form and your residence insulting or offensive?"

"I can take many forms, oh man of two skins and two—no, there may be other forms yet to express," MacTíre said.

Drake laughed. "You told me I was evasive with my answers during our first visit; you are at least as adept as I. And what do you mean there are more forms?"

Joyous music filled the air, and the flickering lights he remembered from the first visit appeared. *"Your race is short-lived and hasty. You seem more patient than many; you might have a dragon's lifespan. That would make you more interesting than any human or shifter I have met."*

"I see the potential for more forms, but they will happen when they happen. Or not. Time-walking is not a strength of mine. I catch glimpses occasionally, and sometimes they are accurate," MacTíre said.

The lights flickered and faded to nothing. It seemed to Drake that the icehouse relaxed a bit.

"Well, you deflected my question about your form. However, I would like to know if you reside here or if this is merely a meeting place," Drake said slowly.

"Ah, another personal question. I do not live here. This place is one where the fae realm and yours are close, and crossing is not difficult. I have wards on the doors

to alert me when someone enters, and a member of my house is often here to identify visitors. I can usually be here quickly should events require it," MacTíre said.

Drake inhaled before saying, "When I was first here, you suggested I return after Lady Heather awakened my magic, so you could teach me about patterns and symmetry."

"So I did. And so I shall. I watch you teach your young; you are a gentler instructor than the fae. Are you prepared to begin? Once you start on this path, you cannot turn back," MacTíre said.

Drake laughed. "Life is a series of choices. Each of us must live with what we choose. Yes, I guess I am ready."

"Excellent. You must learn to control your magic and use patterns before facing Erlender and other senior wizards.

"First, some preliminaries on mana and magic," MacTíre said. "Ask questions when you have them."

Drake nodded.

"The first thing you must accept is that mana is energy. It surrounds and permeates us. It comes in different forms. Humans, fae, and, to a lesser extent, dwarves and kaihana manipulate mana. This is magic. All magic reduces to mana control."

"What of names?" Drake asked.

The music stopped before MacTíre replied. "A remarkable question! True Names allow some control over beings, with the amount of control related to strength. But mana has no direct effect on Name compulsion. Relative mana capacity is one form of strength to consider when using Names. If I am stronger than you physically or politically, the Name influence will wane with distance and time. If I greatly exceed your mana ability, the influence is less affected by separation in space or time.

"Keep in mind, though, that regardless of how much power you have, you can't overcome another's true nature; you can't force others to kill themselves or turn on a loved one."

MacTíre paused for a moment before continuing. "I can teach you nothing else about True Names; I do not know yours, but as my student, I expect your obedience without a binding."

Soothing music began as the fae added, "Let us return to the lesson. As you practice with mana, your ability to control it increases. Think of mana as your muscles; the more you use them, the stronger they become. For heat mana, this means both bigger, hotter fires and fine control, such as maintaining alternating bands of fire and ice on a log or board. Controlling heat includes the withdrawal of heat.

"*Now consider digging a hole. You can do it with your hands and muscles alone, but a shovel makes the task easier. Patterns are the tools you make from mana.*

"*Hidden in the patterns you construct is the true expression of who you are.*"

After a moment, the fae continued. "*I will not teach mana theory; surprisingly, humans are better at that than the fae. But know you do not control fire; fire combines heat, burning air, and fuel. You can summon and direct heat—raw mana—but only one portion of fire.*

"*Your life mana control is quite strong too,*" MacTíre said.

Drake pondered that information briefly before saying, "I thought air and fire were two of the four elements."

A melody like wind chimes in a summer breeze and lights like fireflies accompanied MacTíre's response. "*Four elements? My dear Drake, that's like trying to paint a rainbow with just four colors. The world is a kaleidoscope, and mana dances to a symphony far grander than a quartet.*

"*Four is neither the number of elements nor the types of mana. Elements, to mages, refers to the mundane. I know not the number of elements. The human naturalist Dimitrios listed sixty-three in his innovative table. It describes the characteristics of four unknown elements, and others search for them.*

"*The number of types of mana changes as men and fae explore the limits of mundane stuff and magic, getting smaller or larger as the theories change. Our races are the only ones consistently exploring these boundaries.*"

MacTíre continued. "*To understand using patterns, you must understand symmetries. Tell me what you know of symmetry.*"

Drake's eyes narrowed as he furrowed his brow. He felt tension in his stomach, and his breathing paused. He opened and closed his mouth. "Um, let me see. Symmetry is when something looks repeated but flipped. A face is one example. The eyes are the same shape, but the outside corners match each other, while they do not match the inside corners. The lips, nose, and eyebrows match as you move from the center of the face to the outside."

He continued. "This is true for people, dwarves, kaihana, dogs, cats, horses, birds, and insects."

"*Excellent! You described what we call reflexive, or mirror-image, symmetry. Now consider this wild rose image.*" MacTíre created an image of a pink wood rose before Drake's eyes. "*Nature is seldom perfect in its symmetries, but it contains examples. My image lacks the minor imperfections of a living flower.*

"*This flower has a mirror symmetry. Imagine folding about the line I show here.*"

A black line appeared, bisecting one petal and between two others.

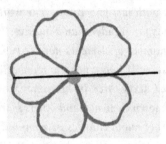

"*However, it can be rotated as well. Observe.*"

The rosette with the line turned before Drake's eyes, revealing an identical blossom.

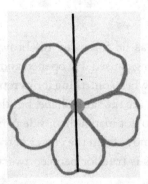

"*Stable mana patterns all have reflections, rotations, or both symmetries,*" MacTire said. "*I will teach you how to form stable mana patterns alone. There are other methods to concentrate the power of many for one to wield. You will learn about those at the university.*"

"What university?" Drake interrupted.

"The Human's University of Engineering and Philosophy. Their college of philosophy includes an academy of magic. They have faculty dedicated to expanding the theory of mana. You shall go when you can control all seven forms of mana."

MacTíre hummed for a minute, then resumed: *"Briefly, there are seven types of mana and two hypothetical ones: light; heat; lodestone; lightning and electricity, one up and one down; life; spirit; the conjectured strong binding, enabling matter constructed from mana; and spellbinding. Theory predicts the last two to explain how primary forms combine. Neither is directly useable by mages.*

"You will observe this when you infuse your heat patterns with life to stabilize them."

"Why only one lodestone? Doesn't a lodestone point north–south, and two attract or repel based on orientation?" Drake asked.

"An insightful question! You may develop strong theory skills during your studies. There may be two types, but we can't separate them, so we call them one."

"Heather told me that Nizar struck me with a corruption of life mana on the night of the raid. Is that a different mana?" Drake asked.

The music ceased for a moment. *"I am not prepared to discuss this aspect of mana now. There is an arithmetic for mana types, and each type has its opposite. Heat seems to be its own opposite since you can make things cold by withdrawing heat from them. Necromancers can create the antithesis of life mana. You will learn how to combine mana in due time."*

After a moment, the fae added, *"I will teach you to stabilize patterns by mixing types as needed but not the theory behind those acts.*

"Enough lecturing on background. Now your real training begins."

"What do you mean?" Drake asked, but blackness descended suddenly.

When Drake regained consciousness, he was on his forearms and knees on the icehouse floor. By the smell and taste of bile, he knew he had vomited. The icehouse floor felt rough and cold beneath his hands. He coughed and spat.

"How long was I out?"

MacTíre's voice danced with humor. *"About ten minutes. Future lessons will be longer. I instilled knowledge directly into your brain. Doing so tends to disrupt the human brain, causing nausea, vomiting, and, sometimes, falling sickness.*

"Now, answer some questions for me. Who are you?"

"I am Drake. Formerly Jason, the human skin of Xavier the dragon," he said.

What did he do to me? Drake thought. *Why didn't he give me some warning? Is my magic so important to him that he decided the risk to me was worth it?*

"Good. Why are you here?" the fae asked.

"To learn about patterns in magic." Drake coughed again while speaking. His thoughts spun as he tried to understand what had happened.

"*Excellent. You are aware and can speak. Your memory seems intact. The lesson did no permanent damage.*" MacTíre seemed satisfied.

"What did you do to me?" Drake asked.

"*I imprinted your subconscious with the first steps in forming patterns with your magic. It is the quickest way. Some do not survive. Many survive but with some impairments. You seem to have come through unscathed,*" the fae replied.

I was right to be wary of the fae, Drake thought, *but not cautious enough. Should I have protested earlier or asked beforehand? What kind of impairments is he talking about? I suppose if there were another way, he wouldn't resort to such forceful methods. However, I am a warrior and deal with events as I find them. I will survive this.*

"You said that the fae were not gentle as instructors. Is this all you have?" Drake, relieved that the brutal knowledge transfer hadn't caused damage, asked as his sense of humor returned.

The lights twinkled and danced about Drake. "*I like your spirit. It will sustain you through your apprenticeship.*"

"Oh! I am your apprentice now?" Surprise colored Drake's response. He flinched, and a cold dread crept into his gut as MacTíre began his explanation.

"*Yes, yes! Oh yes! I haven't had a disciple in twice a century. I am looking forward to it.*" MacTíre sounded excited. "*You can call me Maestro, a term associated with one who mastered his art.*"

Drake gasped, and his eyes widened in disbelief as he stared at the floor. He was sure he had made a huge mistake. *Apprentice?* he thought. *What brought that on? I came here to learn patterns, not to sign up for an indenture. MacTíre is fae, and I shouldn't trust him. Maybe that's why he's so excited. Is the excitement in his voice genuine or just an act? He shoved knowledge into my head without asking. I can't trust him, not after that.*

As he stood up, he felt dizzy; he bent and put his hands on his knees until it passed.

He had been tricked; he was now under MacTíre's tutelage. He didn't know the future but knew he would have to be careful. MacTíre was a powerful fae, and he was unsure of the fae's intentions.

"How did I get to be your apprentice? That usually involves some negotiations. Did you trick me for some purpose?" Drake spoke slowly, as if searching for the right words.

"*I offered, and you accepted. Apprenticeships are less formal among the fae. I intended no deception,*" MacTíre said as the lights in the icehouse faded.

"I did not realize what I agreed to. What does apprenticeship entail among the fae?" Drake's voice quivered a little with uncertainty.

"*I instruct, and you practice as you do your devotions. I am only interested in your magic, not where you reside or other aspects of your life. I have no need for servants. Return here when you have questions or when you think you are competent. You may also ask questions when I contact you. When I find you competent, I will provide the next lesson,*" MacTíre said without emotion.

"How do you contact me? And what happens if I am not competent when I return?" Drake asked.

"*You will hear me as you did when Nizar invaded Terlingua. I can hear your mind speech when I initiate contact. And if you are not competent, you will get a remedial course in meeting expectations. You will not find it pleasant,*" MacTíre stated firmly. "*Now we will review parts of your instruction.*"

Playful, spirited music filled the room. "*You must use your new knowledge to ensure it has taken hold. Else you must repeat this session. Repeat lessons are less pleasant but inflict no additional damage.*"

The music in the room turned somber. "*Now, initiate, I will guide you through creating a durable mana pattern. This will cement the lesson into your conscious brain, and you can henceforth use what I impressed on you.*

"*Stable mana patterns all have reflections, rotations, or both symmetries. How many symmetries are in this pattern?*" A line with a ball on each end replaced the flower's image.

Drake studied it for a moment. "Two," he said. "The ends can be switched to form a second identical form."

"Splendid!" MacTíre said. "*Now, how many are there for this pattern?*"

Another ball appeared, and lines connected it to the other two.

Drake answered immediately. "Six," he said. "Wait—how did I know that?"

"*Magnificent! Yes, six. You retrieved one of your lessons!*" MacTíre said. "*You can count them too. Any of the three corners can be on top, and for each one on top, the bottom will have two like the line, for a total of six.*" MacTíre sounded pleased.

"*Now you will construct a stable triangle of heat mana. This has no practical use, but it is a place to start. First, bring a spark into being.*"

Drake created a foot-long flame, surprising himself.

MacTíre laughed. "*You are stronger than you were, having touched your core. Recall what starting fires was like yesterday, and repeat that.*"

Drake nodded, extinguished the flame, and struggled a little to create a lasting spark. "It feels like I am trying to hold back fire. It is like aiming a bow while balancing on one foot on a ball."

"*Excellent! Now extend it into a line,*" MacTíre instructed.

Drake struggled briefly before the fae added, "*Try creating another spark and connecting them. Excellent.*

"*Finally, add a third spark, and construct an equilateral triangle like I showed you earlier.*"

Drake's third spark winked out as he positioned it the first time. On the second try, the new one connected to the other two, forming a triangle. Its interior glowed and then dimmed; the glowing continued to pulse.

"*It will waver if you don't stabilize it with a touch of life mana,*" MacTíre said.

The triangle winked out as Drake's attention shifted to his teacher's words. "How do I give it a touch of life?" he asked.

"*Direct a tiny bit of life mana—you know it as chi—into the construct. I told you your life mana was also strong; you can already control it a little. Touching the triangle with life will feel like chi flowing from your hand instead of into your feet, as when you perform thasiwoda,*" the fae explained.

Drake recreated the equilateral triangle with three sparks as vertices and sent chi into it by reaching toward it with his right hand and directing the tingling he felt during thasiwoda to the triangle. When he relaxed, the figure persisted, floating before his eyes; its sides and interior glowed red-orange.

"This is the minimum stable form, but it is easily broken by pressure from outside its plane. Observe." MacTíre put tension on the center of the triangle. It bulged slightly before popping out of existence.

Drake yelled, "Ouch! That hurt!" He rubbed the fingers on his right hand.

MacTíre said, *"Yes. The pattern was yours, held in place by mana you sent. When I disrupted the pattern, you felt the backlash. More complex patterns and those with more power will hurt more if someone breaks them.*

"Now I will teach you a more durable pattern. Breaking it will hurt four times as much. Observe."

A green equilateral tetrahedron appeared before Drake's eyes, with its edges more prominent and its interior translucent.

"This is the shape I require you to form connecting sparks, just as you did for the triangle. This one is life mana; fire mana is red, orange, and yellow."

MacTíre walked Drake through the construction using fire mana. As with the triangle, he touched it with life, and the pyramid floated before his eyes. The edges were redder, and the center was more yellow; orange filled the space in between, fading from red through red orange and yellow orange to yellow.

"Impressive. This pattern is useful to store and redirect mana. As mana touches one face, the pyramid balances the mana among all four faces," MacTíre said.

"Where does the mana come from to touch each face?" Drake asked.

MacTíre's response was light with humor. "Mana arrives on Earth as sunlight, moonlight, and falling stars. All mundane matter was, at one time, mana. Some mana rebounds from matter, some is absorbed, and some passes through. You are surrounded by mana. You will learn to tap into it as a source in time."

MacTíre's tone shifted back to instruction. *"Now dissolve the pattern yourself. Pull the life mana from it first, reversing how you pushed a bit into it for stability. Then you can absorb the heat mana."*

Drake did so. He felt both forms of mana on his skin as he reabsorbed the energy.

"Maestro, why does adding one vertex to three result in four times as much backlash?"

The music resumed a light, humorous tune. *"A delightful question! It has to do with the number of symmetries of the construct. The equilateral triangle has six symmetries. Guess how many the pyramid has."*

Drake's eyes narrowed, his eyebrows wrinkled, and he pursued his lips. He rubbed his chin for a few moments. "You must have given me clues to find the answer. It hurts four times as much, and that is related to the symmetries. I answer four and twenty symmetries for the tetrahedron."

"You did well, apprentice! Yes, the tetrahedron is the smallest of the strong patterns. With one mana type, the symmetries are difficult to see. It has twenty-four, as you deduced, and is extremely stable." Approval was evident in MacTíre's voice. *"You can count them, as we did for the triangle. Choose any of the four vertices as the top: the remaining three form the base, an equilateral triangle with six symmetries. Four sixes total four and twenty, as you deduced. Generally, the more symmetries, the more stable, but there are exceptions. Some highly symmetric patterns spin and break apart. I will teach you how to construct stable patterns."*

The fae continued. *"My strength is in practical manipulation, and I will teach you that and a little theory as needed. You will also learn to stabilize patterns by mixing types."*

The music resumed, but the tone was tranquil, and the tempo was slower. *"Light and heat are related and could be a single form that appears as two. With heat as your strength, manipulating light should come easily.*

"Some types can't remain in a pyramid without constantly feeding them energy but are stable in other shapes.

"You are used to the feeling of life mana flowing through your body. Heat mana will not feel the same. I do not know what either feels like to you," MacTíre said.

"Chi—life mana—feels like hitting my elbow, a tingling sensation without the burning sensation," Drake said.

"Expect whatever you felt when starting a spark but stronger when you direct heat mana," the fae said. *"Now, create a stable heat pyramid, and lower it so its base is parallel to the floor and about two fingers' width above the former contents of your stomach."*

When Drake completed that, the fae continued. *"Feed it energy; push heat mana into all three triangular faces pointing upward simultaneously."*

Drake raised his head and stared, momentarily forgetting that MacTíre did not take a form in the icehouse. "How will I get it into all three at the same time?" he muttered.

"By focusing, my disciple. By focusing," the fae answered.

Drake created another tetrahedron and lowered it as directed. He tried to create a large spark. Heat mana flowed along his forearms, running in streaks along his veins. The sensation startled him, and he lost focus on the construct, which dissolved before his eyes.

"Even the most stable pattern fades over time; this seeming failure is nothing to worry about."

Drake took a ten-minute break before resuming. After his break, he reconstructed the triangular pyramid, lowered it, and pushed heat in a wide arc covering the object. The stripes running down his arms did not interfere with his concentration.

The vomitus began bubbling, and flames formed above the construct. After a few minutes, the stain was gone, leaving a dry patch on the icehouse floor.

"Well done, Drake! You are leaving Terlingua for a while. Practice forming triangles and pyramids with heat. Reach for light mana. It first manifests as a glow between fingers, like a glowstone. Return here when you can construct tetrahedra of light or if you have not succeeded past a light triangle for two tendays."

Drake cleared his throat. "How did you know I am leaving Terlingua?"

Silence filled the room for a moment. *"Erlender is coming here soon. You must not face Erlender now. He has been a necromancer for twice your years. You may exceed his strength, but he has decades of experience, and you do not know how to defend against him."*

After a short pause, he added, *"Yet. You are strong, but you can only project heat now, like flowing water.*

"You have seen the six-man water pump in action, producing a stream of water capable of reaching the top of the barn. Your magic is similar to that. Erlender knows patterns to deflect mana streams, and he can propel mana patterns in the form of spears, as Nizar did. When you can create a weapon from patterns and a shield against mana weapons, then you can train for magical conflict."

The icehouse fell silent for a short time.

"And I almost forgot: tomorrow is an unusual day. The sun will darken at midday. Looking at it for long can damage your eyes. Avoid doing so."

"What causes it, Maestro?"

"The moon will obscure the sun for a few minutes. This happens about once a

decade. *The natural philosophers have found a way to predict their occurrence very accurately. You may learn more at the university, should you desire."*

"What does it mean, though?"

"Some prophecies refer to an eclipse of the sun. I know no way to tell if any particular eclipse relates to a specific prophecy, though."

Drake nodded, though he did not understand. *Avoid looking at the sun. That should be easy to do,* he thought.

The lights dimmed for a moment; then multicolored sparkling lit the chamber.

"Return after you and your dragon have found what each of you needs," MacTíre said dismissively.

"I am concerned about the safety of Heather and the other residents. I know my presence alone would not protect them."

After a moment, the fae responded, *"Be assured I will protect all residents of Terlingua from Erlender during your absence."*

With that, Drake rose. "Farewell, Maestro."

"Before you leave, do you wish to discuss finding your core?"

"Based on your question and its timing, I think you want to discuss it." It was Drake's turn to be amused.

"Yes, I am intrigued by your transformation. Tell me what happened, what you saw, and what you did."

Drake took a deep breath. "I saw a sphere of colored bands that swirled around, interweaving but not mixing. One consisted of the colors of fire, mostly reds, oranges, and yellows but some blues and greens. One was clear like water, and one was multicolored, changing colors from colorless to red to purple to violet to blue and then back to colorless. One was made of three braided threads: blue, yellow, and green, twisting, fraying, and reweaving. One was a bluish white, and one was dark; I would call it black, but that doesn't fit. It is more that I could not identify the color beyond very dark."

He looked around the icehouse, seeing only the food stored there. "I reached for the fiery one. I felt heat, and it smelled like a blacksmith's shop. When I touched it, I felt overwhelmed and returned to my human form, and the fire seemed to pour out of me."

"Oh my! You continue to surprise me. You are much more dangerous than I imagined!" MacTíre exclaimed.

"And what do you mean by that?" Drake asked, surprised at the fae's words.

"You are a two-skinned dragon—the first, to my knowledge. You are a mage, but

all know that two-skinned can't wield magic. Your magical core indicates all seven of the mana types and is strong, since a mere touch caused such a reaction.

"An adult dragon can destroy a small city, but with the control of his fire you demonstrated against Nizar, you can threaten kingdoms by yourself."

"Does this change anything between us?"

"Yes. And no. I chose to teach you magic, and I shall. Your spectacular transformation changed nothing about that. But your future—I can't wait to see what happens next!" MacTíre sounded happy about the exchange. "Be sure you practice getting close to your core without touching it while you are gone. You must learn to get to your core in less than a heartbeat to defend against Erlender and his ilk. I want to be with you when you touch it next, to teach you to control the onrush of energy instead of letting it go free. You cannot leave mana uncontrolled; it will destroy you."

"I will leave now, Maestro, and return when I think I am ready," Drake said.

"May your travels take you where you need to be, and may you return with the knowledge you seek." MacTíre dismissed Drake by dousing all the lights.

Drake exited the icehouse two hours after entering it.

No wolf just abandoned its pack, nor could he. Though lacking a wolf form, he belonged to the pack with Akela, Zarya, Phaedra, and the others. His proximity to the wolf pack over the past few months had cemented his connection to them. If he left without their consent—no, that was not the right word; *acceptance* was better—he would drift into insanity, as any lone wolf would have.

He was sure that the anxiety he had felt earlier in the pack link was due to the changes he had gone through earlier that day. It had increased during his time with MacTíre. He had to visit them as soon as possible without alerting other Terlingua residents.

He took a circuitous path through the woods, vanishing into the maze of trees near the sidhe, avoiding the direct route to the pack's residence. He skirted the sanctuary's edge, providing more coverage from sight. He wanted to leave Terlingua without fanfare, with as few people knowing of his exit as possible. That way, Erlender could not gain information about his departure from the residents when the necromancer arrived.

He walked stealthily, moving like a hunter of skittish game, to avoid snapping any small twigs he did not see.

When he reached the closest approach from the forest to his pack's quarters, he realized his new boots were better than he had thought. They seemed to conform to the ground's contours, helping him identify small branches that might break and announce his passage.

As he neared the house, Drake saw Aghi, one of the children in human form, enter. He saw no other pack members.

Drake continued his cautious gait as he approached the door. He heard voices, which indicated that at least some were in human form. He knocked, eliciting cries of surprise from within. Two-skinned wolves, even in human form, were not used to someone arriving unheard; their hearing was much better than that of single-skinned humans. He was pleased his arrival was not detected.

Phaedra opened the door and, seeing a bald, clean-shaven face she did not recognize, said, "Who are you, and how did you sneak up on our dwelling?"

Drake replied, "You know me as Jason."

Her eyebrows knitted as she exclaimed, "You don't look like Jason!"

"But it is I." He smiled at her.

She sniffed cautiously. "It is you!" she cried out with a wide-mouthed smile. "We were worried about what we felt through the pack link today. What happened?" she said, laughing. "Your hair and beard are gone, your eyes are different, and you are taller! I would not have recognized you if I hadn't smelled you." She pulled the door open, stepped outside, and hugged him.

She escorted him into the dwelling, saying, "Jason is here! Helios, run to tell Godiva and Melite that Jason is here; they no longer need to wait for him at his room."

Akela, Akilina, Zarya, and Ikigai crowded around Drake as he entered.

"What happened to you today?" Akela asked. "Your emotions bounced all over the place. They went from acceptance to apprehension to euphoria to anguish and then to excitement."

"And soon after that, you were acting like a kid going out into the snow for the first time," Yaritza, the mother of one of the children, said.

"That was followed by hysteria and self-pity," Akilina added.

"And then—" She sniffed.

Each of the others did also.

Almost in unison, they said, "You were with Heather this afternoon."

That got the attention of the rest of the adult wolves.

"But she isn't pack," Zarya complained.

"That isn't important," Akela replied. Then she frowned and said with disapproval, "Whom he chooses is not a pack decision, however much it may pain us that it wasn't one of us."

"Wait," Godiva said quietly. She seldom spoke, so her interrupting Akela, the pack leader, was unusual. "Mah wolf doesn' un'erstan' why y'all are reactin' like ya are. We know tha' single-skin women desire Jason, and none of us commi'ed to the pack for partners." She looked at Drake, and her eyes opened wide as the thought occurred to her. "But tell us this is no' a marriage wi' her!"

Drake looked at Godiva, open-mouthed. "No," he said quietly. "We did not commit to each other after the incident today."

Silence followed the exchange. Akela and Zarya looked at each other before each nodded.

"Thank you, Godiva, for reminding us we are wolves and humans," Zarya said. "And we know Jason is as close to a wolf as any human can be."

"Tell us what happened to you today," Phaedra said.

Before Drake could speak, Zarya said, "He is preparing to leave Terlingua."

"Leave?" Phaedra's gasp echoed in the cabin.

Drake felt a pang of guilt at Zarya's bluntness. "Yes, I am," he said. The words were heavy on his tongue.

Once filled with joy at seeing Drake, Phaedra narrowed her eyes with concern. "But why? What happened?"

"It's not what you think." He hesitated.

His gaze flitted around the room, avoiding their questioning eyes. He didn't want to alarm them with the news that Erlender was looking for him, but he could not lie to them. The wolves would detect any deception.

Zarya placed a comforting hand on his arm. "Tell us, Jason," she said. Her voice was gentle yet firm. "We're here to listen."

Drake looked at the faces of his pack surrounding him and saw the concern on their faces. He took a deep breath and began. "The short story is that another necromancer is coming. This time, he is looking for me instead of raiding the farm. He is not alone; three more wizards are with him.

"You all know how my dragon and I fared against one of these evil men. We cannot face four. I must leave and hope they follow, leaving you unharmed. They will arrive tomorrow."

"You can't leave," Akela growled. Her voice was laced with disapproval. "You belong here with us."

"Thank you, Akela," he said. "I plan on returning, but I do not know when."

"That does not explain the yo-yo of your emotions on the pack link," Zarya said.

"Ah, yes. That story will take a little time." Drake sat on the floor and motioned to the others to get comfortable. He described the day's events, omitting his encounter with Heather in the bathhouse and how that encounter had affected his emotions.

The pack listened intently; their expressions shifted with each turn of phrase. Akela frowned; her skepticism was evident. Akilina, ever perceptive, seemed to sense the hidden layers of his story. Zarya, with her uncanny intuition, remained silent as her eyes bored into Drake, seemingly searching for the truth.

"This doesn't explain our smelling Heather on you," Zarya said. "That must have happened in the bathhouse before you visited the fae."

Drake nodded. "Yes. That was when we, um—" His face reddened.

The women laughed at his discomfort, which caused him to redden more.

"So you are now apprenticed to MacTíre," Akela said, changing the subject. "And he ordered you to leave. There isn't much you can do except obey."

"He promised to ensure no one at Terlingua would be harmed by Erlender," Drake said.

"And you trust him to do this?" asked Akilina.

"Yes, I do," he answered.

"But why d' y'all trust 'im?" asked Melite.

Drake paused for a moment before responding. "First, Heather and the kaihana trust him to raise alarms when intruders come. Second, he stopped the reanimated from entering Terlingua during Nizar's raid. And finally, he held Nizar bound in a magical net after his downing. He is invested in the security of the farmstead. I am his apprentice, and I requested it. He promised. I am sure he will honor his word to me."

He looked around the room before adding, "I ask that all of you be in your wolf skin and some distance from Terlingua tomorrow."

Godiva said quietly, "I shorely do 'preciate yer lookin' out fer us and all. But y'know, this 'ere decision 'volves the whoo-ole pack. Gotta get the wolves in on it too."

The pack exchanged glances as their worries flowed over their faces.

"If you must leave Terlingua, may we come with you?" Reaver asked. "A pack should not separate like this."

Drake looked the woman in her eyes. "I don't think my trip is one for wolves," he said slowly. "Xavier wants to look for other dragons, so we will fly longer distances than a wolf can travel in a day."

"Wolves are stronger than you think," Helios, one of the young, said with some heat.

"You haven't seen how far a dragon can fly in a day, though, young wolf," Drake responded with a slight smile. "Xavier flies over as much ground in an hour as you usually cover in a day. There are no hills to climb and fewer obstacles to avoid in the air."

The adults exchanged glances before Phaedra said, "Well then, farewell, Jason. Come see us as soon as you return."

Drake smiled. "I shall. And due to the changes in my form and eyes, I wish to go by Drake now."

"Naming yourself Flightless Dragon isn't a subtle way of hiding your second skin." Akela laughed. "As much as we wish you to stay or let us accompany you, go with our blessings."

The others echoed that last phrase.

He hugged each of the women and the children who allowed it and left as stealthily as he had arrived.

He was used to having the pack nearby, though he seldom spent time with more than one at a time. He was sure he would continue to feel them through the pack link and was only a little concerned about feeling lonely during his journey.

I still have Xavier, at least until we return, and I call him Aiden.

CHAPTER 15

Drake Departs

Notes on Spellcraft
Sister Ismat of the Temple of the Moon
Damocles Academy of Magic

"Before Évariste the Gaul developed the theory of groups, before Euclid wrote his geometry and laid the foundation for patterns, and even before women learned to spin thread from cotton and wool, magic blossomed across the land. Patterns are late in the history of magic, though many act as if patterns are all there is to advanced magic.

"Your earliest expressions of talent most likely did not involve patterns but very likely used rituals learned from your friends or household staff or songs. You were crafting minor spells with just the energy of *mana* and your will."

She raised a hand, and six candles on the table ignited.

"That magic did not involve patterns." She surveyed the room before continuing. "Spell crafting is the art of weaving mana to accomplish a goal. You will learn to weave mana, accomplishing more than just summoning heat or lightning or life. Once you know how to weave mana, you can combine patterns and raw mana to accomplish greater tasks than with either alone."

She raised a hand, opening the doors and windows. "Your first task is to create a breeze to freshen this room."

The room was suddenly very warm.

Drake reached his room without being seen. He folded his bedding and spread his belongings out, organizing them to pack for his trip.

He heard a knock on his door. He opened it to see Elani.

"Jason, I bring an invitation from Elder Althea to visit her at Sinistrad," she said. She then stopped and stared at his bald head. "Your hair is gone!"

Drake turned aside, inviting her in, but kept his gaze on the ground, shielding his changed eyes from her view. "Good evening, Elani. Yes, Peaiman Heather succeeded in guiding me to my core magic." He related his transformation to her, as he had to Maliyah and Aishwarya.

"What does Elder Althea wish of me?" he asked when finished.

"I do not know. She told me to bring you this pack; it has a band that you can put over Xavier's neck and arm loops that adjust so it can hang from the shoulders of each of your skins," the kaihana replied.

Drake nodded, took the gift, and thanked her. She showed him how to drape the strap over his neck and put his arms through the loops to prepare for Xavier's chest.

He adjusted them for his back when in human skin and practiced changing from one configuration to the other.

"I do not know how to thank the elder for her gifts. I was worried about how we could travel with my belongings. I will visit her tomorrow morning," he said.

As Elani left, Heather arrived.

He greeted her with a big smile. "I wasn't sure I would see you again before I left." He opened his arms for a hug, and she stepped into them. She handed Drake a small piece of cloth with some ties attached. "I thought your mismatched eyes might attract attention. I stitched this eye patch for you. I believe your amber eye will attract more attention than your two-colored eye, so I suggest you cover it."

Drake took the eye patch, put it on, and then hugged her again. "I don't know if I can repay all you have done for me," he said.

"Just come back after your journey is over," she said with a tear running down her cheek. She turned and fled his room.

Drake prepared notes for Maliyah, Tovia, and Melody. Each letter was brief, stating, "MacTíre sends me away," with a personal message.

He thanked Maliyah for all her assistance and help in adjusting to life at Terlingua.

He asked Tovia to continue leading the hand-to-hand combat and thasiwoda classes and work with the students to improve the quarterstaff and bow.

The message to Melody took him longer. Though not the best, she was his favorite student, and he apologized for not continuing to teach her to balance and fight.

He did not sign the notes, for fear Erlender would find them and harm the women. He waited for full dark before taking the notes to the main house and placing them in a basket near the front door provided for that purpose.

He walked to Ognyen. At the pond, he packed his clothing and staff into the kit bag and configured it for dragon use. He prepared for a shift to the dragon, leaving the bag around his neck, with his arms threaded through the shoulder straps.

After the shift, the band looped around Xavier's neck, and the two armholes encircled the dragon's front legs. Stretching and flapping his wings gently showed no significant restrictions on his movement.

The duffel rests firmly against my chest. I suspect I can feel it loosen and land before anything escapes. It is a lovely gift from the kaihana, he said to Drake mind to mind.

I agree, Drake said. *I am unused to such generosity. I can't help but think there is something more. Perhaps we will learn that at our meeting tomorrow morning. Leaving Terlingua saddens me. We made some good friends here. I look forward to our return.*

The dragon jumped into the air and began climbing.

A few minutes later, Drake continued. *Xavier, changing my name to avoid Erlender is not enough. You are connected to me, and we also need a new name for you.*

The dragon flew in circles for a while. *Aiden Stormrider of the Cliffdwellers. I choose that name for when we return. Until then, I shall remain Xavier Kahuruan.*

So be it, Xavier, who will be Aiden. Why Cliffdweller? Drake asked.

When I think about searching for dragons, I sense that an opening in a cliff face is important.

After a moment, Drake replied, *No one at Terlingua will know your new name when we return. I don't expect that to be a problem, though. Only Heather, Maliyah, Aishwara, the wolf pack, and MacTire know that I have changed mine.*

Now that I enumerate them, that is a lot to keep a secret. We shall see what happens on our return.

And, Drake, Xavier said, *I still want the athamé. A desire that sits like a restive lump in my stomach, churning angrily the longer it is not in our possession.*

As do I, Xavier. As do I. We will find it when we return and convince Glorinda to give it to us.

Xavier flew through the night, reaching the outskirts of Twin Rivers City before turning back. As he approached Smoky Springs Valley, the sky began to pale and soften with a subtle luminosity; the eastern horizon glowed faintly, and colors began to race across the dome above.

The hour was close to the time when they shifted to human for the day. Drake began to stir as he awakened.

Are you ready to talk about what happened yesterday?

Not quite, the human responded. *Touching my core has changed how I view the world, and my interactions with Heather, MacTíre, and my wolf pack are still somewhat confusing.*

Should I continue to Sinistrad to meet with Elder Althea? the dragon asked.

Yes. I see no reason to delay finding out what the kaihana have in store for us. However, we should wait for the sun to rise before landing there. No reason to disturb their early mornings.

The dragon flew toward Sinistrad as the sun continued climbing above the horizon.

When Heather awoke the day after Jason—Drake, she corrected herself—left, she noticed the house was quiet.

After rising, she searched the house. All of the kaihana were gone. That explained the silence but created another mystery: Where had they gone?

She continued searching, finding no kaihana. Jason's room—Drake had not stayed there, she reminded herself—was back to the storeroom it had been, full of farm tools and supplies. The kaihana had been busy during the night.

As she walked around the residents' dwellings, all else seemed normal. She reorganized the human women to start the day's activities in place of the missing kaihana.

Breakfast and task assignments took longer than usual. Any process change disrupted until it became a habit, so Heather was unconcerned. The humans dispersed to their work areas, and their activities continued as usual.

✺

The sun rose to partly cloudy skies and a moderate wind from the southwest. Xavier timed his arrival at the kaihana village for one hour after the sun broke the horizon.

From above, Sinistrad appeared like a block letter *K*, with the back abutting cliffs and the legs extending along the roads—one southwest to Smoky Springs and one east toward Lion's Tooth Canyon. The pottery works and kilns spread out a mile west of the *K*, and kaihana were working there. Not far from the kilns, vats of dye simmered over open fires, though neither weavers nor spinsters were visible.

A stone culvert carried water from Upper Lake to a pond beside a brick building housing a water mill. Water from the pond spilled, forming the headwaters of a stream flowing toward Stairstep Falls.

The legs and spine of the *K* formed a quadrangle where they met—a space lined by regularly spaced brick buildings. Each building sported a brightly colored cloth canopy extending ten feet into the square. It was early in the day, and most of those in the square were still setting up for commerce.

With his forty-foot wings tucked tightly, Xavier angled for a graceful, spiraling descent into the square. Below, details of Sinistrad materialized: a breathtaking paradox of carved stone and sunbaked brick. Ancient cave dwellings honeycombed the sheer cliff face, while quaint buildings adorned with thatched roofs spilled like a waterfall toward the valley floor.

Flights of weathered stairs carved into the rock led from the valley floor to shadowy entrances in the cliff face. Carved paths spread between the natural ledges, forming a grid. Poles and ropes extended from the precipice to the ground and were used by the young and some old.

The backdraft from his wings whipped the canopies into a frenzy. Merchants leaped into action to secure their coverings and wares. Despite that disruption to their morning routines, few did more than glance at him and return to their tasks. When he landed with a gentle thud, a hush fell over the crowd for a moment. A single child pointed, momentarily forgetting his game, before the usual marketplace sounds resumed. It was as though a dragon's arrival were a commonplace event.

Time-walking, Drake murmured. His mental voice was tinged with amusement. *It seems they expect us.*

Indeed. Not even the children cared that a creature from myth landed in their city. Curious, the dragon responded.

Xavier smelled typical village odors: kaihana, goats, chickens, vinegar from the dying vats, and fish drying. Kaihana seldom ate flesh except fish, so their location near Upper Lake matched their needs.

A cavernous archway, a quarter of a sphere hollowed from the cliff face, opened onto the town square. Large enough to accommodate even Xavier's almost twenty-foot height, its mouth seemed to bite into the central square. Gnarled branches of two ancient trees intertwined overhead, creating a natural archway that flanked the entrance.

At the western end of the cave's entryway stood a kaihana—not just any kaihana. Her fur glowed a radiant white like a pearl or a seashell—a stark contrast to the city's dark, earthy tones. She was surrounded by four imposing figures clad in eggshell-white armor that gleamed like polished bone.

The white-furred kaihana and her entourage approached Xavier.

I am Xavier Kahuruan of the House of Fire. He broadcast to the five kaihana. The arrogant, commanding tone from his encounter with the Defenders was back. *I am here to speak with Elder Althea. Bring her to me.*

When Althea was a few feet from the dragon, she sat on her haunches and looked him up and down. "I am Eldest Althea and not accustomed to being greeted with a summons. Further, I am not comfortable with mind speech, oh beast from long ago. I want to speak with your human skin."

Two of her guards approached, carrying a blanket, which they held to hide Xavier from view as he shifted. One of them also brought a cotton kilt.

Xavier changed into Drake, who donned the clothing the guard provided.

Drake bowed. "Greetings, Eldest Althea. I am Drake Doingolla. How may I help you?"

"Jason Archer, where is your bow?" Althea asked without any preamble.

"I no longer go by Jason, Eldest," Drake said.

"It matters not. Where is your bow?"

"Why is my bow important to you but my name not?" he asked.

"I must see it to confirm my suspicions."

"And what do you suspect me of that my bow can confirm?"

She waved a hand dismissively at him. "It is what I require," she said imperiously.

Drake retrieved his staff from his belongings. He turned it over, running each hand along its length. When he finished, he held an unstrung longbow with a small quiver containing six arrows.

Althea nodded. "I expected this. Come. Let us find a more comfortable setting than the middle of Market Square to converse."

Drake returned his bow to his hiding place in his staff and followed the kaihana.

The elder and her four guards walked to a ring of chairs beneath the great tree to the west. Once they settled, she spoke again.

"Maliyah spoke truly when she called you the Beuman√, the burning man, the fire bringer. One of our prophecies begins, 'From the west, a warrior walks. / In his staff, a longbow hides. / Sparks from his fingers fly, / and in his shadow, chaos rides.'

"We know you fought in the Succession War. You are a warrior. We know you walked from O'otoka, which is west of here. 'Sparks from his fingers fly' describes your fire talent.

"This bow was the final piece of the puzzle. You are the Beuman√, the herald of chaos, the harbinger of great change."

She adjusted the blanket about her shoulders. "The chaos that follows you has already reached us. Elder Gabrielle died in her sleep with no warning from our time-walks. Unheard of!" She shook her head vigorously. "Then a worse calamity: Eldest Yastreb committed suicide fourteen days ago. That makes two of our Council of Elders dead without warning in three moons! None in our Circle of Seeing saw either event coming! Furthermore, taking one's life has only happened three times in our history. Chaos is upon us if we cannot predict the suicide of an elder." Age did not dilute the strain or doubt in her voice.

"Gabrielle's death occurred the night you arrived at Terlingua. In hindsight, this was the first indicator of chaos. Did something unusual happen to you a fortnight ago, Jason?"

"I no longer go by Jason—"

"It doesn't matter what you call yourself. You are the Beuman√, and that is all that matters to me," she said.

"I can think of nothing that happened fourteen days ago," Drake responded.

Althea nodded, extending to a rocking to and fro. "I suppose something happened in her time-walk that frightened Eldest Yastreb, so she fled her life instead of facing it. I do not know what she might have seen."

Althea calmed down and sat quietly after a short time.

"What else does your prophecy say?" Drake asked from his seat across from her.

Althea studied Drake's face and then quoted the prophecy:

A stranger in this land,
a wanderer from a far-off place.
Within him, a power, ancient and dangerous,
a power he must embrace.

A man of mystery, in lore well read.
Secrets within he shrouds.
Feared and respected, loved and hated.
For seers, the future he clouds.

Althea paused and then continued. "The elders and seers disagree on what this means. We aren't sure if it describes a single person or one for each verse. Prophecies are seldom clear except in hindsight."

Drake frowned, and a crease appeared between his brows. "So I'm a harbinger of chaos, but you're not sure if the prophecy refers to me? Does the prophecy say anything about my dragon or his role?"

Althea chuckled. Her voice was dry and rasping. "Exactly. It's maddening, isn't it? We kaihana pride ourselves on our foresight, yet here we are, blinded by your arrival."

Althea shook her head, and the white fur on her chest rippled slightly. "The Beuman√ brings change. That much is clear. How that change manifests—well, that's the mystery, isn't it? There's no mention of a dragon. As I said, prophecies are rarely clear. But its presence being unseen by my time-walks is troubling. It reinforces the idea that you and perhaps the dragon are anomalies."

"Anomalies? You mean we don't belong here?" Drake's eyebrows rose as he asked.

"Oh no, I am sure you belong here, but you disrupt the flow of time, making it harder to see the future. Think of it like throwing a pebble into a still pond. The ripples obscure what was once clear."

"So I'm a walking paradox?"

Althea smiled slightly. "You seem to handle paradox well, young man."

"And what about this ancient and dangerous power the prophecy says I possess?" Drake tapped his staff thoughtfully against the ground.

Althea leaned forward. Her eyes gleamed with a strange intensity. "That, young Drake, is a mystery. The prophecy hints at a power you haven't fully grasped yet. Perhaps your fire magic is just the tip of the iceberg."

"What am I supposed to do?" Drake asked.

She reached out and patted his knee. "Ah, young man, none of us is wise enough to answer that. Your presence means change is coming; it has already arrived. Whether you do anything or nothing, we are all caught in the turbulence following you.

"Our Circle of Seeing are panicked. What was once certain is now unlikely or almost impossible. Circle members no longer see the same thing; each has a different vision of what will be and when it will happen."

After a few minutes of silence, Drake asked, "Why did you not warn Maliyah that my dragon would be at Ognyen Pond?"

Althea studied Drake's face for a moment. "Your big blue beastie does not show in my walks along the threads of time. I looked forward on the pond and watched you and Heather approach, then Heather alone and harvesting, and then Maliyah arriving; then you were back in the scene. Looking back was no different from looking forward."

She sighed deeply and continued. "I do not understand it. I think the dragon may be a creature from another time and, thus, not one we can observe."

Drake let out a frustrated sigh. Meeting Althea's gaze, he said, "So I am but a pawn of prophecy. What do you want from me?"

Althea gently touched his arm. "Nothing, young one. We want you to survive it. We crave stability, Beuman√. The seers are the foundation of our society, but our visions are in disarray. Please help us understand what's happening. Perhaps you, the harbinger of chaos, can deflect the storm that follows you."

She frowned. "I suspect the dragon you carry may be the actual instrument of chaos."

She insulted me. Slap her! the dragon demanded.

Drake felt muscles in his arm twitch as the dragon tried. *I think your recommendation is too strong a reaction,* he replied.

Drake's eyes widened, and his mouth dropped open. "How can you possibly think that?" he said aloud.

"I explained that I cannot see your dragon during time-walks. That also happened 400 years ago with Grubogonik, another fire dragon. She *was* an agent of chaos. I am sure that the inability to see them connects them with chaos," the elder explained.

Drake studied the elder's face as anger prompted by his dragon's reaction flowed over him. He stood and closed his fists. He spoke slowly. "This does not explain why every kaihana surrounding the square seemed to expect us; some kaihana can see Xavier, even if you cannot. Xavier, by the way, is present. He hears through my ears and sees through my eyes when my skin is out. This conversation is over. Neither my dragon nor I serve chaos. We are leaving; the affairs of the kaihana are not our concerns." He stood, gathered his staff, and turned away from Althea.

One of her guards stepped to block his passage.

"Step aside, O'omah-Zid," Drake ordered.

Surprise showed on the guard's face as he jumped out of Drake's way.

"Eldest!" the guard cried out. "He knows my True Name! I could not resist him."

"I saw, Montagga. It is not your fault."

Drake walked to the town square. The dragon flew south a few minutes later.

—— ∞ ——

Another aged kaihana approached Althea. Her fur was half gray and half orange brown. Her four guards melded with Althea's to form a tight circle, looking outward.

Althea looked up. "Come to gloat, Sabah? I lost him, as you warned."

Sabah sat beside Althea and looked intently at her. "Eldest, I tried to tell you. He is young for his kind and but an infant to us. The prophecy is too deep for a youngster to confront so abruptly. A slower approach might have met with more success."

"I told him I thought the dragon was the agent and he was but the carrier."

Sabah sighed. "I imagine that did not go well."

"No. He left, affronted, saying our affairs were not his concern."

"I tried to warn you that your fixation on the dragon clouded your time-walks. Otherwise, you might have foreseen his reactions," Sabah said. "Does he still carry the bow in a staff that marks him as Jason Archer?"

"Yes. He took insult to my words and left before I could offer to change his bow for one better suited for his new body," Althea answered.

They sat in silence for several minutes.

Two more graying kaihana exited the cave and approached Althea and Sabah. Four guards accompanied each. The kaihana seated themselves. Their protectors melded with those already present. The sixteen arranged themselves in concentric ranks, using gestures and nods.

Althea watched the two approach. "Why are two members of the Circle of Seeing joining us? What is up, Sabah?"

Sabah took a deep breath and began with a slight quiver in her voice. "Eldest, I fear your obsession with the dragon has led you to overemphasize his importance in the coming events, to the exclusion of more prominent threads in time."

Taking another breath, she continued without quivering. "We three took a moonstone last night and performed the moon ritual. The dragon is visible to our seeing, provided no one is interfering with time-walking."

"How dare you! I did not authorize a moon ritual; I am Eldest and will not tolerate this disrespect!"

Sabah continued, encouraged by the exchange. "In this case, I fear you must. Your view of the outcome of your meeting with the Beuman√ did not match the facts, and it was so near in time that a discrepancy so great should not be possible.

"And when Candace, Nuraya, and I look back on Ognyen Pond, we always see the dragon with Heather the day Maliyah joined her there. Your sight is clouded and affecting our younger members' visions."

"I also see the dragon on my time-walks, Eldest. I hesitated to speak during the circle, because you insist he cannot be seen," Candace said.

"I will have you removed from the circle and the council, Sabah!" Althea said with authority. She turned her gaze to the other two. "The same goes for each of you, Candace and Nuraya."

"I will challenge that. You do not have the votes to make it so," Sabah responded. "We are at a point of crisis. You have two options. You can retreat from your position and spend time in seclusion until your vision clears, or you can face a challenge in the circle and the council. Should you lose there, you know the penalty."

Althea studied Sabah's face. "You are serious! You would have me expelled?"

"Yes, I will. We cannot afford to remain wedded to the fallacy that the dragon is the agent of chaos, and you can't rid yourself of it. This young man and his second skin are not Grubogonik from 400 years ago. You should not let your memories cloud your time-walks. Your prediction for today was false, and your clinging to it is a sign that you are lost, or almost lost, in a time loop.

"And we must support the Beuman√ if he is to prevail against the dark, not antagonize him."

Tears formed in Althea's eyes. "But we are sisters in the circle!"

"Yes, we are. Were. You must step aside during this period of uncertainty," Sabah said firmly. "We need dragon fire to light the forges; without them, we have no white steel. We must cultivate this young man, not alienate him."

"The Council of Elders backs you in this?"

"Enough do. This does not please me, Althea. You have served us well on the council and in the circle until recently," Nuraya said.

"You would eject me as eldest after less than twenty days? Why did you not object when the council met after finding Yastreb's body?" Tears ran down the kaihana's cheeks.

"The main reason, Sister, is that would have created a crisis visible to all kaihana. If you withdraw, however, the second eldest steps in to fill your position, and all will sadly agree that taking the appointment so soon after her suicide was too stressful for you. And you can return when a more private existence has cured you of your obsession with dragons," Candace said.

"We all agree with Candace," Nuraya added.

"I must meditate on this," Althea said, wiping the tears from her cheeks.

Sabah nodded. "It is as it must be."

They separated, with each going her own way. Their guards took posts around each without comment or gestures.

Terlingua's workday was interrupted when twenty-four men on horseback approached the farm's front gate a little past midmorning. The leader was dressed as a minor nobleman, and Tiernan was alongside him, as though he was important to this visit.

297

Three in the party wore wizards' robes, two with the black armbands of battle mages. Ten men wore knights' armor; the remainder wore chain mail. Two knights dismounted and helped the leader down.

He approached Heather with a big smile, exuding goodwill. "Good morrow, lady. I am Baronet Erlender Uzani. I am looking for a man—Jason Archer. I was told he lives here."

"Good morrow, Sir Erlender. I fear you have wasted a trip. Jason did live here. He left yestereve to visit his family in South Haven," Heather said.

"Did he now?" The goodwill vanished from his face. "You won't object if I verify he is not here?" His tone promised that any objection would be ignored.

"Please search, but honor my request that one of my people accompany your men. We will open doors as you request and ask that you avoid damaging property and animals."

Tiernan, who had driven Jason to Terlingua, walked up. "Kaihana I see not. At least a score I saw when last here I was."

Erlender looked questioningly at Heather.

"There are usually kaihana here. I do not know their whereabouts today," she responded to his look.

The man nodded and directed his men to search for Jason.

They searched until midday. There were a few instances of a man slapping a woman for not answering quickly, and each man reported getting an electrical shock temporarily disabling that hand the first time. There were no second times.

Ultimately, Erlender's companions reported that they had found no evidence of a man living at Terlingua and that all the residents interviewed agreed he had not been seen since yesterday afternoon.

Erlender turned to face Heather. The man's face changed from open and friendly to cruel in the blink of an eye. His smile disappeared. The warmth and friendliness that had been there moments before were gone, replaced by a cold, calculating malevolence.

She shivered visibly. Never had she seen such a sudden and dramatic change in someone's expression. It was as if the mask of civility had slipped, and the real man was revealed.

The change was so dramatic that it was almost like looking at a different person. The man's features seemed to sharpen and contort, as if some unseen force were twisting them. His skin paled; then his cheeks flushed with color. His nostrils flared, and his breath came in short, ragged gasps.

The man's eyes were the most striking part of the transformation. They had been a warm brown before but were now cold and dark. They seemed to glitter with malice and bore into her piercingly.

The man's lips were also different. Before, they had been curled up in a friendly smile, but now they were curled down in a sneer. The sneer revealed the man's teeth, making him look like a predator about to attack.

When the man's eyes met hers, a wave of hatred washed over her.

"You will identify three of your young women for me to put to the question. If you fail, I will start with that one"—he pointed at Melody—"and continue until I am satisfied that no one knows more about Jason's whereabouts."

"I told you he left here yestereve. That is all you will get," she replied.

He laughed with an edge of mania. "Whether I find more or not is not the purpose of the questioning; extracting life under torture is the reason, not the answers. Pick your three—now!" he commanded.

"*No.*" MacTíre's voice from nowhere was firmer than Erlender's command.

"Who said that? Who dares contradict me?" Erlender spun in place, looking for the source.

"*I dare.*" A spiral of dust formed a few feet from Erlender and reached above the eaves. "*You and your retinue will leave Terlingua now and exit the valley at your greatest speed.*" A lightning bolt from the clear sky struck the ground a few feet from Erlender. "*And I enforce my will here!*" A fist-sized hole burned where the bolt hit, and the smell of ozone permeated the area.

Erlender jumped back, and a smaller bolt struck where his feet had been, leaving a bull's-eye-sized scorch mark.

"*I advise you to hurry; I am not known for my patience,*" MacTíre added.

Erlender heard a dozen electric *cracks* behind him and turned to observe his men closing ranks. Two rows of dust devils stood between them and the farm.

"Mount, we leave immediately!" he shouted. He turned back to face Heather. "But I will be back!" He sneered.

Something struck him, knocking him to his knees.

"*Mind your manners in the presence of your betters!*"

The necromancer stood, brushed at his clothes, and raised a hand toward the circling dust. An energy bolt jumped out of his hand—and dissolved halfway to the swirling dust.

This time, Erlender was lifted off his feet and propelled backward toward his men. He landed on his back with a dull thump and didn't move for a moment.

Four of his men ran to assist him. Once he was on his feet, three tree-high whirlwinds formed and approached the necromancer and his men. Small lightning bolts that struck the ground near the men's feet herded them out the gate.

Once out of Terlingua, the departing men increased their horses' speed to a trot.

Heather watched open-mouthed as Erlender and his entourage exited the farm.

MacTíre spoke to Heather. *"I loosed several nameless lesser fae to escort them. They are simple creatures but know the boundary of the valley. If none of those men try to break away, they will not be harmed."* The fae paused. *"If any men try, battle lust may overcome the fae. Erlender will, I think, survive that event, but I am not confident that more than four of his party will."*

Heather said, "Thank you for your help, MacTíre. I have never seen you out of the icehouse."

Laugher greeted her words. *"Surely, you did not think me bound to that location?"*

"I never thought about it, except when Jason asked about your living there. I am glad you were here today." She paused. "What will happen when Tiernan tries to turn to Smoky Springs at the crossroads?"

The fae replied, *"Drake, my apprentice, asked me to protect Terlingua's residents today. Ah, I did not consider Tiernan lived in Smoky Springs. I must make haste to ensure his escorts behave while ridding the valley of them. My queen will not be pleased if humans are killed due to my actions. Farewell for now."* The whirlwind stopped, and the dust, leaves, and barnyard debris fell.

Heather stared at the small pile where the fae had been or might have been. *Was that his form or a conjuring?* she wondered. If she was surprised that Drake was now MacTíre's apprentice, she did not show it.

The lesser fae MacTíre had summoned drove Erlender and his entourage through Smoky Springs Valley to its southeastern point.

The fae, invisible but potent, whipped sand into a frenzy. Dust devils danced across the road, merging and scattering with an unsettling intelligence.

Once Erlender was gone, Maliyah and Elani appeared.

"What happened to you?" Heather asked.

"We and the other kaihana hid in the forest early this morning. We did not want to face a necromancer; the animosity between them and our race goes back lifetimes," Elani replied.

"Our midnight time-walk showed him leaving when the lightning began. We heard the sounds of lightning strikes," Maliyah added.

"The vision was so clear that we decided to act on it. I apologize for not awakening you and sharing our plan with you. When the lightning ceased, we came out to ensure it was safe before telling the rest to come out of hiding," Elani said.

"It is as safe as it usually is," Heather said.

"Then we will tell the others to return," Maliyah said.

The pair returned to the forest to retrieve the remaining kaihana.

Tiernan tried to leave the group when they reached the crossroads leading to Smoky Springs. Half a dozen spirals appeared along the road, blocking his path.

"Very strange, these winds are," the blacksmith said as Cathán rode up along his side.

Cathán was the youngest of the wizards accompanying Erlender, having graduated to journeyman a few months ago. He was clean-shaven, with sharp cheekbones, and his eyes crinkled when he smiled. A silver ring adorned with a swirling rune, a family heirloom passed down through generations of mages, hung around his neck.

"Very strange indeed," the mage agreed as the whirlwinds approached the pair with tiny lightning bolts appearing. "I cannot see the mana they yield until they become strikes. Speaking of that, we should return to the course they set for us, lest we get shocked into obedience."

The two returned to the group, which had slowed but not stopped, to find more of the dust devils had formed and forced them to increase their speed.

Fortunately for their horses, the winds stopped their advance every few hours but resumed once they rested. During their first rest period, Erlender and the other three mages clustered.

"Who or what is sending this magic after us?" Erlender asked.

The journeyman did not know, nor did the two battle mages.

"They act much like normal dust clouds, starting across the road and then vanishing or growing," Pitrambra said. "One difference is that two will merge and later separate. Another is that one will split into several, with each moving independently."

Pitrambra was the oldest mage in the troupe, save Erlender. Despite being past his forties, his eyes still held the spark of an adventurer. His brown hair, streaked generously with silver, was pulled back in a no-nonsense braid that threatened to come undone at any moment. A thin beard, flecked with the same gray, cascaded past his neck, partially obscuring a jagged scar that ran along his jawline.

Darkness suddenly descended on the group. The horses huddled together with eyes widening and stamped their feet as though unsure where to go.

One of the men-at-arms looked up. "The sun is black! Apophis, save us!"

Erlender glanced at the sky. "It is merely a solar eclipse. Do not stare at it for long; when the sun begins to emerge, it can blind you. Accept the coolness of the day."

"But what does it mean?" the man asked. His voice was shrill and cracked in panic.

"For us, nothing. Some prophecies mention eclipses. If it is an omen, I do not know what it portends," Erlender replied.

Light returned just before the horses were rested. The winds grew in velocity, and the dust rose to tree height and approached the group. Lightning bolts encouraged the humans to move.

A guttural roar escaped Erlender's lips—a sound born of both pain and fury. His wild eyes darted around, seeking a target for his rage. His gaze fell on the nearest of his men-at-arms, a hapless soldier who had wandered in range. Without a second thought, Erlender lashed out, and his fist connected with the man's jaw.

The man fell. When the wizard turned to seek another target, two soldiers approached and took their comrade to safety.

Erlender swore under his breath as the funnel clouds forced them to abandon their half-cooked meal and the cooking gear they had used. The winds howled like banshees, carrying the crackle of lightning unseen.

The winds stopped at sundown.

During the night, the wizards consulted. What was herding them? How were they summoning lightning?

Cathán said, "I can see no mana patterns. How can they conceal mana manipulation from our wizard sight?"

The journeyman mage stood beside Erlender; his face was etched with a mix of worry and resignation. The two master mages, aloof and enigmatic, seemed as puzzled as the young man.

Erlender's face became a mask of crimson fury. "You useless, gutless curs!" he bellowed. His voice was a hoarse rasp. "The only way is direct mana control without patterns. Untrained mages from small villages usually do that, but those never achieve such fine control over lightning. We are dealing with entities for whom mana is like air to us."

"What race does that?" Arkadios asked.

"Elementals do that, but these are more intelligent than elementals," Pitrambra said.

"I do not know!" Erlender screamed, turning his head, seeking an outlet for his rage.

The trio backed away and waited for his rage to diminish.

Erlender's breath came in short, ragged gasps as he paced in a tight circle. His breathing slowed, though his chest heaved with each inhale. His hands opened, but his fingers twitched involuntarily. The color drained from his face, replaced by an ashen pallor. He wiped a bead of sweat from his brow and forced himself to take slow, deep breaths. A cold, detached clarity began to seep into his mind.

Once he had calmed, they discussed constructing wards to protect themselves and their guards. They decided on layer wards—one against the sand, one against lightning, and one against magnetism. They spent much of the remaining night forming them.

At sunrise, the winds stirred again but remained a furlong away from the men and horses. The men saddled horses and packed quickly while the wizards waited within their shields. Small, conical winds approached and surrounded the mages, then paused.

The wizards heard the sounds of sand striking metal. Sparks appeared at the outer edge of their defensive screen. All four mages sighed in relief, but then clouds of dust appeared within the shielded area as if they were climbing out of the ground.

While that happened, one of the younger men-at-arms extracted a grenade and matches from his belt.

"You fool," an older soldier said as he struck the grenade to the ground. "There is a reason rifles and grenades are not used in warfare. I watched the mages cause all gunpowder to explode, killing a regiment during the battle at the Gulf of Tears. If they could do the same with arrows, they would. If you detonate one, ours would likely follow soon, killing us all."

"Then why do we carry them?" the young man asked.

"To use against bandits and in small skirmishes. If we know where the only mage is, we can use them with a sure kill shot. Do you know where the wizard is?"

The young man shook his head and retrieved the grenade, adding it to his bandolier.

The small dust clouds struck the wizards with lightning, forcing them to drop their perimeter. Erlender and the other wizards hurried to join the men-at-arms as they started the day walking ahead of their escort.

The valley was farmland and mostly flat, so the walking was not strenuous for the horses, especially with the rest stops.

Erlender was not used to the regimen of a forced march and complained loudly to any who would listen.

Each catch of his horse's hooves on the roughening ground intensified his rage. His mind, clouded by the pain of the unaccustomed rigors of the march and the humiliation of being herded, was a maelstrom of fury. Each new event added to his burning humiliation that now surpassed any physical pain.

He wasn't sure if he was angrier at being escorted out of the valley or at being ejected from Terlingua. He replayed the events in his mind but could find no hint of danger before the speaking wind had appeared. He'd detected no mana expenditure or signs of recent magic use beyond a burned circle behind the barn. That spot had reeked of heat, with traces of life but no lightning. Where had his assailant hidden?

Try as they might, the wizards in the group could not identify the magic driving the dust devils or the patterns they employed to direct the lightning. They couldn't defend against their wardens, let alone counter their prods. The master mages were not accustomed to such restrictions and bickered among themselves. The twenty men-at-arms separated themselves as best as they could from the irritated wizards.

It took them three days to reach the valley's boundary. There were shorter paths, but whatever kept the winds on their tails did not allow for deviations in course. The winds directed the two dozen men toward the mountains to the southeast, dropping them near Long Lake.

The winds herded them to the mountaintops surrounding the valley. They stopped at the ridge but remained there until the men could no longer see the mountain's spine as they descended the steep mountainside.

Three more days of walking through the virgin forest led them to Pitman's Place, a village where Step Falls River emptied into Lower Lake. There they could rest, eat their fill, and provision for a trip to Dwarflocks.

Tiernan left them to return to Smoky Springs along Step Falls River. He hoped the winds would not harass him further.

From the mouth of Step Falls River, the group hired a ferry to Dwarflocks and continued on the Tapti River to Twin Rivers City.

At Twin Rivers City, Erlender found a message from Golgol-drath waiting for him. Opening it, he read an innocuous message. He saw the inner envelope. Golgol-drath's glyph, in a purple black, sealed the enclosure: the symbol of Apophis, the moon serpent, who consumed the moon each month. It ensured no one other than the intended recipient could open and read the message.

The message was simple and direct: "Come to Dämmerung. Now."

He reread the stark directive. The parchment crackled in his grip, betraying the tremor in his hand. His face, once a light shade of olive brown, flushed crimson, with veins pulsing like angry worms beneath his skin. His blood pounded in his ears. A scream clawed at his throat, but he choked it back, and the sound morphed into a guttural growl.

He stood there, shaking from head to toe. He had not been summoned in four score years, and at that time, he'd killed the man who ordered him to appear. That had been before he joined Golgol-drath's company. He could not defeat the dark one, so he was denied that outlet this time.

He moved slowly toward Cathán.

Cathán watched the parchment writhe in Erlender's grip and heard the ragged growl that escaped his lips. Fear prickled his skin as he stepped away. "He's a storm about to break! Get back, all of you!" he warned the other wizards.

That was enough to dampen Erlender's rage. He sucked in a ragged breath, and the air hissed between clenched teeth as he smothered the inferno within. He slammed the crumpled parchment to the floor and stomped it.

When it finally emerged, Erlender's voice was a rasping whisper. "Golgol-drath summons me—after all these years!" He met Cathán's gaze with a flicker of fear battling the rage in his eyes. "We leave tomorrow. Rest tonight. What awaits in Dämmerung is uncertain."

CHAPTER 16

Endings and Beginnings

The gentle breeze whispers of Xavier's flight,
my heart, a fragile dove, lost in the night.
Erlender, vanquished by MacTíre's hand,
left broken, chased by golden sand.
MacTíre, a blur, in whirlwind's swift flight,
a guardian's promise in fading light.
Will Drake return through mists that divide?
Or am I bereft, with hope cast aside?
—"Heather's Lament"

Night fell, and Heather sat in her room, looking out at the moonlit gardens. She saw only shades of black and gray; the landscape was colorless, just as she felt.

Eighteen days had passed since Drake was forced to leave because Erlender arrived at Smoky Springs.

Erlender was gone, thanks to MacTíre; she needed to see him to express her gratitude again. The unease among the Defenders had not abated. They remained on high alert and were exhausting themselves.

She shook her head.

Why did she feel so deflated, with so much heaviness in her chest and arms?

He had said that he would return but not when. He wanted to see his mother again, while Xavier wanted to look for other dragons. Dragons had not been seen for more than 200 years, so she knew that finding more could take some time. Still, she expected some word.

She berated herself. If he sent word, it would be challenging to maintain the story that Jason's whereabouts were unknown. Sending a message would indicate he had not cut ties when he left, and it might leave a trail for another of the Black Sorcerer's minions to follow. She hoped his reformation and his taking the name Drake further obscured his trail.

She moved from her chair to her bed. Reclining, she spread her fingers on her stomach below her naval. *Useless*, she thought, scolding herself.

A healer using spirit could not detect life in herself. More concerning was that her menses was two days late.

Blinking back tears, she thought she hadn't received clear direction from the Goddess in some time. Three times, she'd received irrefutable directions from her. One had been to search for Terlingua, though not by name; the Goddess was seldom so direct. One had been to stay there when she found the place. One had been when Jason gave her the kalasha.

She summoned light to her fingers. First, she formed a translucent image of the kalasha; it was safe in the inner sanctuary.

She morphed it into an image of Jason. She rotated it slowly, examining his visage from all angles.

Finally, she removed the beard and hair. Jason had looked like that as he stepped out of the fire. Drake had become his name that day.

She let the tears flow this time, and she brought her hands, glowing with his image, to her face and kissed its forehead.

A strong feeling of peace and belonging filled her as the image changed into the Goddess as Hathor.

Heather smiled—four irrefutable messages.

Someone knocked on her door.

Who could come here this time of night?

Tovia stood in the doorway, holding two glasses and two bottles of wine. "Buck up, girl. You have been moping the better part of two tendays over Jason. No man is worth that much. I bring the cure, courtesy of Ratray." She raised the two bottles. "Summer Wine. He usually pretends he doesn't hear you if you ask for it. When I told him you needed to get over a man, out came these from wherever he keeps them." She grinned and tilted her head to one side. "Well, aren't you going to invite me in?"

Heather wiped her cheeks and laughed. "Jason once referred to you as a force of nature. I hadn't observed it before. Please do come in."

Tovia scowled. "Our task tonight is to forget him. But I suppose we can first remember him and then drink him away."

She opened one bottle and poured some into one glass, stopping when there was about a swallow. "This doesn't look like Summer Wine. This is thick and a little oily looking. What is Ratray trying to pull?"

She smelled it, frowned, and then tasted it. "He sent his midwinter Forget the Past fortified wine. This won't do to start a man purge but will end one perfectly."

She opened the other bottle and poured a taste into the other glass. "Ah, this is more like it—bright red and clear. I suspect Ratray intended we drink them in order but neglected to tell me the order." She paused for a moment. "Not that I waited around once I had them in hand." She giggled.

She drained the first glass and filled both with the Summer Wine.

Tovia handed Heather one glass. The Defender took a swallow from hers and closed her eyes. "This is really good. My only other time tasting it was when Clowers called for it to toast Jason—I forget why.

"I remember him smelling it, tasting it, and announcing, 'Strawberries, cherries, and angel's kiss.' Ratray was impressed by his nose and tongue.

"Oh, you should have seen Clowers's face when Jason turned on his heel to leave! He turned purple, his mouth dropped open, and his eyes bulged. It was priceless!"

Heather took a sip of her wine. Her eyes widened. "This is exceptional! Ratray is a genius!"

Tovia continued. "I first saw Jason on the road from Wolverton Mountain. I knew he was a warrior from his walk; he never let his weight remain on a heel for any time, always poised to step in any direction. Graceful in movement and no wasted motions.

"He is extremely confident. He turned his back on Clifton and faced Galaad." Tovia continued her reverie. "You didn't see Galaad's face when Jason said, 'Do not stand between me and my path.' Jason exuded confidence that he would prevail. Galaad, for sure, did not expect that. Badgers never back down, so it was like an irresistible force against an immovable object until Clifton called Jason back." Tovia giggled at the memory.

Heather smiled wistfully. "I first saw him in the infirmary. I remember that day; I was so distracted by the kalasha that I didn't notice him at first. But then I saw his eyes, and I knew he was someone special." Her eyes filled with happy tears at the memory.

Heather took a deep, cleansing breath. "He is arrogant. Perhaps that is too strong. He is sure of himself, confident that he is living as he should. It wasn't until his dragon prevented the kidnapping that I was sure his coming was part of the Goddess's plan."

"Don't forget Melody," Tovia said. "And teaching us to defend ourselves."

Heather laughed. "Or the quarterstaff demonstration. I am sure he confronted Defender Clowers after it ended, but they seemed on good terms."

"Nothing seems to fluster him," Tovia added.

"He was so sure of himself. Yet he was somehow vulnerable; it showed most when he taught Melody," Heather added. "He seemed to be almost too comfortable in his skin. Xavier shook that up, though! Xavier Kahuruan of the House of Fire. I thought I would wet myself when he demanded the prisoners." Heather paused and then continued pensively. "It seemed a royal pronouncement at the time."

They finished their second glasses of wine, which Tovia refilled as she said, "He is a fine figure of a man; I felt myself tingle whenever I spoke with him."

"He affected me that way too." Heather paused. "I am not sure if I am pregnant or not."

"Just like a man!" Tovia exclaimed. "Have his way with a woman and leave!"

Heather laughed. She then laughed harder until tears ran down her cheeks. "It is more like I had my way with him and then sent him away," she choked out through laughter.

"No! Tell me more!" Tovia exclaimed. "Tell me of your last encounter with Jason, the man of mystery."

Heather blushed. She then described her encounter of eighteen days ago.

"Did you know that if you kiss a man's penis, it jumps to attention? And if you lick it, he will moan?"

"Heather! What a strumpet you are!" Tovia paused, and her expression turned thoughtful. "I wonder on whom I should try this."

"Tovia! And you called me a strumpet!"

The women drained their third glasses of Summer Wine, emptying the bottle.

"Before we finish remembering, do you think he will return?" Tovia asked, covering a burp.

Heather's face was troubled, and she took a deep breath before she spoke slowly. "We will not see Jason again. But I expect we will see Xavier."

Tovia's eyes widened, and her eyebrows rose. Her mouth fell open, and she gasped. "Why do you speak in riddles, Heather Moonstar?"

Heather's eyes filled with tears as she thought about Jason—Drake, she reminded herself, but Tovia did not know that. "Maliyah said Jason is their Beuman√, and chaos is in his shadow. Mysteries surround him, and hope is all I have, so I rely on riddles." She laughed. "And I am talking nonsense. Too much wine, I think."

Tovia hugged the other woman.

When they separated, Tovia poured each a glass of Forget the Past fortified wine and said, "The time for reminiscing is over; now we drink to forget."

She held both glasses up briefly; her jaw tightened, and her cheeks flushed. She looked away from Heather and blinked several times before saying, "Before we start to forget, I must admit I have a crush on Jason. I always imagined being with him, but I am glad for you. You have something to remember."

It looked as if she were about to say more, but she shook her head and fluttered her eyelids several times before she laughed and handed a glass to Heather.

Heather sipped the wine. It was sweet and spicy, with a slightly bitter aftertaste, like her memories.

The rest of the night was a blur. Heather remembered sitting on her bed in the moonlight with Tovia beside her. They talked and laughed, but she couldn't remember what they said or how she felt. All she knew was that she felt safe, warm, and contented. And she had a close friend in the Defender.

The following day, Heather woke with a headache. She got out of bed and went to the window. The sun was shining, and the birds were singing. Two empty wine bottles lay on her small desk. It was a beautiful day, but Heather would need an infusion of willow bark to perform her duties.

She dressed and went to breakfast. Drake would return on his schedule; she would worry about that tomorrow.

Erlender squeezed his palms against his eyes, with the heels digging futilely to block out the assault. Golgol-drath's antechamber reeked of brimstone, hot metal, and blood—a caustic cocktail that burned his sinuses. The constant hum of heat mana radiating from the walls mocked his diminished reserves. Unable to tap into this energy to ease his depletion, Erlender only felt the pain intensify.

For the past tenday, he had come each morning and waited, with his headache worsening. For the past three days, he'd needed assistance to return to his quarters. His frustrations increased each day, as did his fear of what Golgol-drath would mete as punishment. He was sure that anticipating his penalty made his migraines worse each day.

He had watched Golgol-drath remove the skin from a man's fingers using magic alone before dripping vinegar onto the exposed nerves during an interrogation. He shuddered at the memory.

Dämmerung Castle had been carved out of a mountainside, and the outer wall had been constructed from stones removed during the excavation. Glowstones provided all the interior light; only a few were in the antechamber. Bright lights and loud sounds exacerbated his headaches.

When he had first arrived, he'd rushed to the castle and told the herald he had arrived. He'd expected immediate admission, not being shunted off to the antechamber to cool his heels. He had tried to bluster past the guard at Golgol-drath's receiving room, but to no avail.

He heard footsteps approaching and looked up. The castle's dim lighting allowed him to see what happened in the room, but the room's dreary arrangement drained him. The only thing that broke the stark emptiness of Dämmerung's walls was a fifteen-foot-tall statue of Apophis, the god of darkness, in serpent form, rising menacingly above his head.

A footman escorted Arnock and Tiernan into the room. They took seats on the opposite side and avoided looking at the necromancer. Tiernan's presence confirmed to Erlender that the events at Terlingua were the subject of this interview. He could not fathom why his cousin was at Dämmerung.

He heard the sound of silk swishing from the doorway to the receiving room. Turning to look in that direction, he felt a push from the mana wave that preceded the person coming.

A tall woman with long jet-black hair sporting a white streak at her right temple stood there for a moment so exquisitely timed it had to have been deliberate. Every eye turned to her, gauging and appraising.

She glided into the room, wearing an elegant purple silk dress. The dress hugged her slender frame and featured a plunging neckline, an ankle-length hem with a thigh-high slit, and black trim that accentuated her beauty.

There was an energy in her posture, a coiled tension that vibrated through the air. She stood ramrod straight with her head held high, and her gaze swept the room possessively. It wasn't arrogance; it was focus, the unwavering concentration of someone who knew exactly where she was going and what she could do. The three men knew where the power in the room resided, and it wasn't up for debate.

Her pale skin shone like oiled alabaster, highlighting sharp features. Vivid green eyes flashed, and a cruel amusement flickered within their depths as she finished her appraisal of the room.

She moved across the floor with the grace of a dancer, exuding authority. Stopping before Erlender, she narrowed her green eyes to slits; a hint of a smile played on her lips, revealing a glint of canine. Tilting her head slightly, she let her gaze linger on him a moment too long before she spoke.

"Drink this, Erlender. I need you clear-headed as the four of us discuss the Smoky Springs debacle."

She selected a glass from the four on a tray carried by a steward at her side.

Erlender observed her unevenly dilated pupils. *I wonder which mushroom she ate today.*

He took the glass with trembling hands. "Thank you, Golgol-drath."

Vapor wafted from the rim of the glass as he brought it to his lips with quaking hands. The foul smell made his stomach churn, but he forced himself to take a small sip. The liquid burned his throat and spread heat across his abdomen, easing the throbbing behind his eyes. Grimacing at the bitter taste, he managed a second searing sip, further dulling the pain. He finished the noxious drink with great effort, leaning back in relief as the ache slowly receded.

With a smooth, practiced motion, she turned, and her presence filled the room like a tidal wave.

She walked across the room and kissed the other two men on the lips.

Erlender saw her emanate an intricate mana pattern that sank into each man's skin during her embrace. *She has them enthralled but not to the point of slavish adoration. I did not know she had such skill.*

Each man's eyes softened, and they looked at her lovingly. She handed each a glass from the tray, took the fourth, and dismissed the steward.

My cousin and the blacksmith are under her sway. I knew Arnock had loyalties to another, but I had not dreamed it was she. Tiernan is, or was, her agent in Smoky Springs. I wonder what she brought them here for.

She sat and directed her gaze at Arnock. "Tell me what brought Erlender to Smoky Springs."

---⊶⊷---

Arnock looked at Erlender and then back to Golgol-drath.

Erlender crossed the room and took a seat at the table with the other three as his cousin spoke.

"It began over five years ago," Arnock said. "We were in a tavern after the Battle of Ouray, where both sides suffered horrendous losses. One of the men mentioned seeing a man carrying a small, glowing statue. That man, he said, led a charmed life. His wounds were always slight, and the insects did not bite him at camps."

He paused before summarizing their search, which had ended with Erlender's torture of the healer who knew Jason and the discovery of a man who both knew Jason and could sketch his likeness. The search had led to Smoky Springs, where Tiernan had identified a man living at Terlingua from a sketch.

Golgol-drath turned to face Tiernan. "Continue, please."

Tiernan told the story of taking Jason to Terlingua. Three months later, Arnock had brought a sketch to identify, which he had. When Erlender had arrived, he had insisted that Tiernan accompany him to the farm.

Erlender's entourage had not found Jason there. Tiernan told of Erlender saying something to the human woman who seemed to be in charge, and then the funnel clouds and lightning had started.

He began describing the trip out of the valley, but Golgol-drath raised a hand, saying, "I know enough about that for now."

Golgol-drath turned to Erlender. "First, why did you decide to follow this Jason to Smoky Springs?"

Erlender said, "As Arnock explained, we overheard soldiers talking of a man unbothered by insects, dysentery, and other maladies of a foot soldier. There are always rumors of special soldiers, so that is not remarkable. However, the tale continued that this man carried a glowing statue, and the figurine's presence kept him from injury. It was a kalasha of the Moirai."

"A kalasha of the Moirai in the hands of a man? What led you to such an extraordinary conclusion? Most men will not or cannot touch one when given the opportunity." Golgol-drath's gaze bore into Erlender.

Erlender shifted on his chair as his gaze darted away from the steely glint in Golgol-drath's eyes. He cleared his throat; the sound was scratchy with apprehension. "I admit it was a long shot, but I thought it worth investigating. I thought you might appreciate having a second one in your hands."

Her laughter, void of mirth, greeted his comment. "That explains your not telling me but not your conclusion. Continue."

He resisted the urge to squirm under her intense look. "I questioned one of those soldiers out of Arnock's view and found some details he had not divulged in the public house. At one time, the camp was overrun with rats following a heavy rain. Most of the men were bitten by rats and by their fleas. The army's healers struggled to prevent the plague, but Jason was not bitten by either pest. It was during that time that my quarry began visiting the healing tents with his icon. It seemed the fleas would hide from the glow it emitted."

"That could be explained by other artifacts, though." Golgol-drath's brows knitted as she analyzed Erlender's words. "Continue."

"We tracked our informant back almost a year to a battle at Sterling. The king's forces outnumbered Zephyrus's and held the high ground but almost lost. One of Zephyrus's battle mages had a spell that melted flesh. On the first day, one-third of the king's army was lost. On the second day, their morale was destroyed; an entire army sat with their heads in their hands, waiting to be captured or killed, until one soldier stepped out of his tent carrying a glowing stick. Everywhere he walked and talked, men picked up their weapons, took their positions, and pushed Zephyrus's army back. And that is clearly a god's involvement." Erlender paused, letting the weight of the story hang in the air.

Golgol-drath sat still for several minutes, drumming her fingers on her thigh, and then spoke. "If it weren't a man, Erlender, I'd agree." Her voice held a hint of frustration. "Why not bring this to me sooner?"

Erlender straightened in his chair. "I haven't reached the final evidence," he said, glancing at her before looking away again. "I found a healer from the king's army who witnessed the icon in use. Somnath told me that Jason brought the glowing icon to the surgery tent and that the survival rate from surgeries was much higher with the statuette present. Somnath recognized Hathor in the statuette."

Golgol-drath's expression remained thoughtful. "Your work identifying the kalasha is exemplary. Now finish your story."

Erlender told of the search, beginning with examining army records at the capitol and concluding with his ejection from Terlingua.

Golgol-drath rubbed her right ear and wrinkled her brow. "What did you say to the woman—Heather—before the funnel clouds appeared?" she asked.

The air crackled with the unspoken tension that followed. Erlender fumbled with his cloak as his face paled. He sat fidgeting with his hands, looking at the floor.

Her posture stiffened, a testament to her simmering anger. When she finally spoke, her voice was a low, dangerous purr. "Erlender, answer me. Now!"

He looked up but could not meet her gaze. "I—" He tried to swallow. It took several tries to get enough saliva. When he spoke, his voice was barely a whisper. "I asked her to identify three young women for me to—"

He swallowed again. "For me to drain." Shame flushed crimson on Erlender's face. He looked away, unable to meet Golgol-drath's blazing eyes.

Golgol-drath stood and stalked a circle around him. Her movements were those of a predator closing in on its prey. "You fool! You had him in your hand, a mere day ahead of you and twenty-three men. But you decided to sate your obsession instead of finishing what you started, and in doing so, you awakened Smoky Springs' protector, who drove you out. Now you know neither where this Jason is nor where to start looking. He knows you pursue him, and he will be more difficult to track. And due to your bumbling, it will be even harder to plant an agent in Smoky Springs now."

Tiernan spoke up. "The dragon, the protector of Smoky Springs is?"

Golgol-drath turned to him. Her mood suddenly changed to cheerfulness. "I do not think so. I suspect the dragon is his companion or maybe his associate."

Turning back to Erlender, she donned the mask of royalty passing judgment. "You have failed me, Erlender," she said. Her voice was low and filled with icy finality. "Service to me requires a certain level of astuteness, a quality you seem to lack. Perhaps a new position, something less demanding, would be more suitable for your talents."

Erlender stammered a desperate plea, but she held up a hand, silencing him.

She pursed her lips before continuing. "You will remain at Dämmerung.

I will break your fixation on torturing men to death. You are of no use to me now; you've disrupted operations in place for almost twenty years. Replacing Tiernan in Smoky Springs will take me at least another decade."

The blood drained from Erlender, and his vision blurred for a moment. A tremor ran from his neck to his toes, and cold sweat prickled his skin. Her mask of royalty had slipped, revealing the predator toying with its prey. His face remained a mask, but a flicker of icy rage ignited in his eyes. His jaw clenched, with the muscles bunching beneath his skin, betraying the storm brewing within.

The fury in his chest threatened to boil over—a pressure that battled the need to maintain composure. His hands balled into fists at his sides; his knuckles turned white. He took a slow, measured breath, attempting to control the rising anger, restraining the primal roar threatening to erupt from his throat. A white-hot inferno of betrayal and humiliation threatened to consume him.

"As you wish," he managed to say, though the words cost him; his skull pounded as his migraine returned.

She paced the room, ignoring Erlender. "The disrupter is walking the earth. I suspected he'd been born; my time-walkers cannot see further than a tenday. A *man* brandishing a kalasha of the Moirai confirms it.

"This Jason could be the disrupter, or it could be the priestess who gave it to him. I suppose he could be a confederate of the instigator, but that makes tracking them down impractical." She stopped and hummed for a moment and then sighed. "When the gods play games, the pieces are never what they seem."

A footman entered the room, clicked his heels, bowed, handed her a note, and left.

She read it. Her back straightened, her eyes widened, and she gasped. "Well, it seems the game is afoot." She tapped the note against her teeth.

She turned to Tiernan. "What is the name of the dragon seen in Smoky Springs?"

Tiernan's eyes widened. "His name recall I not. With a Z his first name begins, think I, and a K his surname."

Golgol-drath laughed. "I thought the man carrying a kalasha was the disrupter, but perhaps it is this dragon. Xavier Kahuruan of the House of Fire acted against Nataraja five days ago, destroying with fire both the temple and the garrison at the border town of Lyrabog."

She turned to her henchmen. "It seems the dragon is resisting the temple's expansion into Rutendo. This is interesting." She spun around in the middle of the room. "Perhaps the gods themselves will join in war on earth again. You are all dismissed. I must think on this."

As they left, Erlender heard her say, "A war with dragons again! How exciting! Should I amass troops on each border …" Her voice faded as they exited the room.

—⚬⚭⚬—

Erlender simmered as he watched knights exercise in the yard below. He had a semblance of freedom within Dämmerung's walls, except for Golgol-drath's apartments, but was always watched. Every move was reported—a constant reminder of his punishment.

It was Jason's fault. Jason and that woman I met at Terlingua. Moonstar, was it? He was sure she knew where to find him. And he was an expert at extracting information from reluctant confidants.

He thought only about revenge on those who had led him to this; the kalasha was forgotten.

Once he found a way to leave Dämmerung or Golgol-drath released him, he would return to Smoky Springs and pick up the trail. Payback consumed his thoughts.

The memory of being forced out of Smoky Springs, escorted by funnels of dust flinging lightning bolts, still left a bitter taste in his mouth.

Never again.

Each day, he practiced using raw mana without patterns. He turned away from the window and held his hands up with the palms facing. He concentrated on his internal stores of lightning mana, conjuring a foot-long bolt that was sizzling, raw, and untamed. Sparks continued to dance in his palms—a flicker of defiance in the oppressive castle.

He grinned in pleasure and pride at his progress. *I am coming, Jason Archer. I will be ready for you and the protector of Smoky Springs.*

PRONUNCIATION GUIDE

Acacia	UH-kay-shuh
Adina	UH-dee-nuh
Aghi	AHG-he (the *g* is barely sounded, almost a guttural stop)
Aiden	AI-d-un (*AI* as in *pain*)
Aishwarya	AI-sh-war-ya
Aiolis	AI-ol-is
Akela	ah-KEY-la
Akilina	Ak-ah-lee-na
Alicia	uh-LISS-ee-uh
Ashtaroth	ASH-tuh-reth
Althea	ael-THEE-uh (ae as in at)
Angelique	an-JUH-leek
Arkadios	ARK-aid-ee-os
Arrokothokoth	ARE-uh-koth-uh-koth
Aurvang	OR-vange (as in *Orange* with a *v* in the center)
Beuman√	Bow-MAN-*click* (the click made with the back of the tongue)
Branwen	br-AHN-wehn
Camille	kah-MEEL
Candace	CAN-dass
Cathán	KHA-thân
Conchobar	KONK-o-bar
Degataga	DAY-gah-tah-gah
Diablo	DEE-aw-bloh
Elowen	e-LO-wen
Eoghan	OH-un

Erlender	ERR-len-der
Farid	fah-RID
Fedlimid	FED-lim-id
Finley	FIN-lee
Fionola	FEE-uhn-o-la
Fundin	FUHN-deen
Galaad	GAH-lad
Glorinda	GLO-rin-da
Golgol-drath	GŌL-gōl-drath
Godiva	ga-DIVE-uh
Grubogonik	GROW-bog-o-nik
Hashim	HASH-eem
Hathor	Hah-thur
Helios	HĒ-lē-ōs (*o* as in *no*)
Hestia	HES-tē-uh
Hildingr	HIL-ding-jer
Ikigai	ICK-ah-gi
Isadora	Ih-sah-doh-rah
Isocrates	I-SOCK-ra-tees
Itara	Ē-tar-rah
Iudgual	I-YOU-djual
Jojotessantana	Joe-JOE-tess-antenna
Kahu	CAH-who
Kaelin	ke-EH-lihn
Kaihana	KAI-hana
Kaihana'sa	KAI-hana-sa
Keshia	KEE-sh-yuh
Kyriakos	ki-RYE-ah-kess
MacTíre	mac-TEER-uh
Maliyah	mah-LI-yuh
Melite	MAH-leet
Mi√aela	ME-*click*-aa-luh (the click made with the tongue at the back of the mouth)
Moana	MO-ahn-ah
Montagga	mōn-TAG-ah
Morrigan	mōr-EH-gan
Morta	MORE-tah

Myla	MAI-luh
Nataraja	nah-TUH-rah-jah
Niamh	NEE-ehv
Nizar	NĬ-zar
Nuraya	NOOR-eye-ah
O'omah-Zid	O-o-mah-zid
Padraic	PAH-rick
Phaedra	FAI-dr-uh
Rashad	RAH-shad
Ratray	RAT-ray
Reaver	REE-ver
Sabah	SAH-bah
Scáthach	SKAH-thaach (the final *ch* is guttural, similar to the Scottish *loch*)
Sensei	SIN-say
Somnath	SAWm-nath
Thaddeus	THAD-e-us
thasiwoda	THA-see-wode-uh
Tiernan	TEE-er-nan
Tovia	TŌ-vē-ya
Xavier Kahuruan	EX-zav-ee-ur ka-HUR-ooh-an
Xochitl	SEW-sheetl (the *t* is chopped short)
Yaritza	yar-ITZ-uh
Yeruslan	YAR-oo-slan
Yiska	YIS-ka
Yona	YO-nah
Zarya	ZAR-ya
Zephyrus	ZEH-fruhs

GLOSSARY OF NAMES

Acacia (F) is the arboreal who lived near South Haven. She taught Jason how to identify plants, including those to avoid, those to eat, and those eaten by different animals; how to recognize signs of recent animal activity; and how to leave little evidence of his passage. She taught him to listen to the unspoken speech of trees.

Adina (F) is a human. She is Farid's mother. She accompanies Heather and Elani to the kidnapping site.

Adversary is a pseudonym of Golgol-drath used to discuss the evil sorcerer.

Aghi (M) is a two-skinned wolf. He is a child in Jason's wolf pack.

Aiden Stormrider (M) is an alternate name for the dragon Xavier. The dragon adopts this name when Jason becomes Drake.

Aishwarya (F) is a kaihana at Terlingua who manages their tack room.

Aiolis (M) is a battle mage who destroyed the mind of Jason's friend.

Akela (F) is the name Jason gives to the timber wolf who joins him in the cave the first night he spends there. Storm is two-skinned. Her second skin is an orange-and-brown timber wolf—she and two other two-skinned form a pack with Jason.

Akilina (F) is a two-skinned wolf in Jason's pack.

Alicia (F) is a human who mainly worked in the kitchens at Terlingua.

Ashtaroth (F) is the face of the Maiden aspect of the Moirai. She is a poet and musician.

Althea (F) is the kaihana elder residing at Sinistrad.

Angelique (F) is a human Defender.

Apophis (M) is the god of chaos and the embodiment of darkness and disorder.

Arkadios (M), a human, is one of Erlender's trusted lieutenants.

Aurvang (M) is the king of Rutendo.

Beumanᐯ is the kaihana name for the prophesied bringer of change, the burning man, or the bringer of fire, the harbinger of chaos.

Branwen (F) is a human student of Heather's.

Camille (F), a human, is one of the attempted kidnapping victims.

Cathán (M) is a journeyman mage (necromancer) traveling with Erlender, acting as his valet and general factotum.

Claudia (F) is a human working in the kitchens at Terlingua.

Constance (F) is one of Jason's students. She demonstrates her archery skills to the Defenders.

Clifton Clowers (M) is chief of the quasimilitary organization known as the Defenders. They maintain peace within the valley of Smoky Springs. He is two-skinned, with his second skin being a great bear.

Diablo (unknown sex) is a destructive air or wind entity, like a sirocco, haboob, or derecho. Diablo has a sense of identity and wants things to burn up and blow away.

Drake Doingolla (M) is Jason's name following his transformation.

Elowen (F) is an elder kaihana who lives at Terlingua. Jason learns of her following the storm.

Eoghan (M) is one of Jason's students. He demonstrates his archery skills to the Defenders.

Erlender (M) is the necromancer who pursues Jason to obtain the kalasha.

Farid (M) is one of the boys at Terlingua. He lives with his mother. He is Jason's first student in thasiwoda.

Fedlimid (M) is the king's mage adviser. He death-cursed Jason and placed a geas on him not to talk about his involvement in the end of the war.

Finley (M), a human, is one of Jason's students.

Fionola (F) is Melody's mother.

Fournival (F) is the high priestess of the Moirai and Heather's mother.

Fundin (M) is a human Defender. He is shorter and heavier than Jason, with unkempt medium-brown hair and brown eyes.

Galaad (M) is a Defender and a two-skinned badger. He is Jason's age and a little shorter, with a heavier build, black hair, and a thin beard.

Glorinda the Green (F), a human, is an earth and water mage and also a Defender.

Golgol-drath (F) is the dark sorceress, a necromancer who holds sway over one-third of Rutendo.

Godiva (F) is a two-skinned female wolf. Storm, Snow, and Phaedra added her to Jason's pack.

Green Star on a White Sky is Glorinda's True Name.

Grubogonik (M) is a dragon from long ago.

Hashim Stonethrower (M) is Nizar's True Name. Nizar is human.

Hathor (F) is the face of the Mother aspect of the Moirai. She is the goddess of hearth and home, especially of childbirth and raising children.

Heather Moonstar (F) is a human healer living at Terlingua. She is the priestess of the Moirai, daughter of the high priestess, and heir to the temple leadership. Her title is peaiman (a prescience healer).

Helios (M) is a young two-skinned wolf in Jason's pack.

Hestia (unknown sex) is one of the arboreals who works to heal the Grandfather Tree after the storm splits its trunk.

Hildingr (M) is the other surviving kidnapper.

Ikigai (F) is a two-skinned wolf. Storm, Snow, and Phaedra added her to Jason's pack.

Isadora (F) is a two-skinned Defender. Her other skin is a hawk.

Isocrates (M) is a professor of magic at the Damocles Academy of Magic.

Master Itara (M) is a professor of magic at the Damocles Academy of Magic, a college within the University of Engineering and Philosophy.

Iudgual (F), or Grandmother, is a mage who appears to be an old woman. Respected for her skills and wisdom, she is a principal resistor of Golgol-drath.

Jablochkov, Davy, and Messer Trinidad Atkin are the three who installed the captured lightning at the docks at Biblola.

Jason Archer (M) is a longbowman seeking a place to live in peace. Tasked by Iudgual to deliver an athamé to Smoky Springs, he learns he has two skins. His other skin is Xavier, a dragon.

Jojotessantana is Jason's True Name.

Kahu (M) is a bowyer in Smoky Springs.

Kaelin (F) is a human, one of the attempted kidnapping victims.

Keshia (M) is a kaihana at Terlingua and is present during the kidnapping attempt.

Kyriakos (M) is a human Defender.

The Listener (unknown sex) is an individual of unknown race and sex (thought to be female) who has agents listening throughout Rutendo.

MacTíre (M, presumed) is a major fae (see *fae* under "Glossary of Words and Places"). He can be found in the icehouse at Terlingua. He becomes Jason's teacher in magic.

Maliyah (F) is a kaihana at Terlingua, a member of the guiding council, and Jason's foreman at the farm.

Melody (F) is a young human living at Terlingua. Her left leg is shorter than her right. She is the girl with the golden voice.

Melite (F) is a two-skinned wolf in Jason's pack.

Merrill (M) is a human and one of the Listener's agents.

Mi√aela (F) is a kaihana Defender. The day Jason arrives, she mans the desk at Defender headquarters.

Moana (F) is the first kaihana Jason meets along the road from Wolverton Mountain.

Montagga (F) is the daily usename of O'omah-Zid, a kaihana.

Morrigan (F) is the warrior aspect of the Moirai as the Maiden.

Morta (F) is the Crone aspect of the Moirai. She appears as a kindly grandmother.

Myla (F) is a kaihana healer.

Nataraja (M, Lord of the Dance) is a deity in Rotunda. His cosmic dance represents creation, preservation, and destruction. His priesthood uses song and dance to focus *mana* for their magical acts.

Niamh (F) is a kaihana at Terlingua. She is present during the kidnapping attempt and kills one of the kidnappers.

Nizar (M), a human, is the leader of the group of brigands the kidnappers belong to.

Oliver Brewerson (M), a human, is one of the kidnappers. His True Name is Alberich Waterwalker.

O'omah-Zid (F) is the True Name of one of Althea's assigned guards.

Padraic (M) is a human Defender.

Phaedra (F) is a two-skinned wolf. She is black brown in wolf form and a brunette with brown eyes in human form. She is one of the three who form a wolf pack with Jason.

Duke Rashad (M) has a castle at Two Rivers Bay.

Ratray (M) is the innkeeper and brewer at the Laughing Owl. His race is not evident from looking at him.

Reaver (F) is a two-skinned wolf. Storm, Snow, and Phaedra added her to Jason's pack.

Sabah (F) is a kaihana. She is the second eldest of the Council of Elders at Sinistrad.

Scáthach (F) is the warrior aspect of the Mother, one face of the Moirai. She is a strict disciplinarian, more likely to punish an infraction than reward desired behavior.

Sensei is an honorific for a teacher. It is usually used for a martial arts expert.

Somnath (M) is the healer whom Erlender tortures to find Jason's name.

Thaddeus (M) is a two-skinned eagle Defender.

Tiernan (M) is a journeyman blacksmith. He gives Jason a ride from Smoky Springs to Terlingua.

Tovia (F) is a two-skinned hawk Defender. Her hair is between silver and white. She has amber eyes, is slightly built, and comes up to about Jason's nose.

Xavier Kahuruan (M) is Jason's other skin, a fire-wielding dragon.

Xochitl (F) is a priestess of the Moirai from Jason's childhood home at South Haven.

Yaritza (F) is a two-skinned wolf in Jason's pack.

Yeruslan (M) was the pack leader for Yiska's (Storm's) wolf pack.

Yiska (F) was Storm's name before Jason changed it using name magic.

Master Yona (M) is a professor of magic at the Damocles Academy of Magic. Her race is not stated.

Zarya (F) is a two-skinned wolf. She is gray white in wolf form and a silver-white blonde with hazel eyes in human form.

Zephyrus (M) is King Aurvang's second cousin and the usurper during the Succession War.

GLOSSARY OF WORDS AND PLACES

....

A

Amboyna is the name of the rainbow tree. It has green, blue, and orange streaks in its yellow wood. It is prized for carving, bows, and furniture. The Grandfather Tree is an amboyna.

Angel's kiss is a medicinal plant used to induce sleep (its leaves), induce a coma (its roots), or relax (its blossoms). It is not addictive.

Athamé is a dagger imbued with *mana* (magic energy) used in rituals.

Arrokothokoth is the language of the dwarves.

B

Babirusa is a city some distance away. It is referenced by Arnock but not visited.

Biblola is a shipping hub of Rutendo and is one of the places Erlender tracks Jason to.

Black jelly is the monster that attacks Jason on the first night of this tale.

Blackwoods is a community on the other side of Wolverton Mountain from Smoky Springs.

C

√ is a clucking sound made by the tongue at the back of the mouth. This sound is present in kaihana's speech.

The Circle of Seeing is the religious leadership organization among the kaihana. Those with the strongest foresight are selected for the circle. Thirteen women sit in the circle. Some kaihana serve on both committees.

The Council of Elders is the political leadership of the kaihana. The oldest twenty serve unless they retire, refuse to serve, or are expelled for cause. Expulsion requires fourteen votes among the council. The council can eject members of the circle, but the reverse is not true.

D

Dämmerung is the name of Golgol-drath's castle and the surrounding area. A drake is a wingless dragon.

F

Fae are one of the races in Rutendo. Their caste system, from lowest to highest, is as follows: least fae, lesser fae, minor fae, major fae, great fae, greater fae, and grand (or oldest) fae. MacTíre is a major fae.

G

The Ga'aton River is a narrow, rapid river too shallow for navigation except by small, flat-bottomed boats called wave gliders. Trade in fur keeps the river busy.

K

Kaihana are the race of humanoids derived from orangutans. This term is used for a generic person or a female.

Kaihana-sa is the name for a male kaihana.

A kalasha is a holy artifact of the Moirai, a container of her blessings. Six exist, but only three are commonly known.

Kieff is an herb with mildly narcotic effects when used sparingly. It can be addictive.

L

The Laughing Owl is a pub at Smoky Springs.

M

Mana is the energy of magic.

Moirai is the collective name for the Triple Goddess (the Maiden, the Mother, and the Crone). Each aspect has multiple names.

Myakka is a city along the Ga'aton River. A road from Myakka leads to O'otoka.

O

Ognyen is the location of a cave and pond about a half-hour walk from
Terlingua. It is a stone bowl fifteen feet in diameter, filled with hot liquid
mud. The pond stinks of burning sulfur, rotting vegetation, and rotten
eggs. The cave overlooks the muddy pond.

O'otoka is a trading center to the west of Smoky Springs.

P

Pemmican is a compact, calorie-rich food made from dried meat, fat, and
dried fruit.

R

Rutendo is the kingdom in which the story takes place.

Rutilant refers to illuminating or reflecting light or having a reddish
complexion or color.

S

A sidhe is a hill or mound with a doorway into the land of the fae.

A snool is a cowardly or mean person, someone who submits easily to others.

Sinistrad is the kaihana village—part cave complex and part simple buildings
of clay brick and wood.

Smoky Springs is a city named so because of the abundant hot springs in the
area. Some are mineral springs, and some are just hot water. The city is
at the entrance to the valley of the same name, along the Step Falls River.

South Haven is the farmstead where Jason was raised. It is owned and
managed by the priestesses of the Moirai.

T

The Tapti River is a river navigable to the lock system (built by the dwarves)
leading up to Lower Lake. Cotton, spider silk, cut stone, timber, finished
wood, and agricultural products flow along the river and Lower Lake.

A tenday is a unit of time between a day and a month—ten days in duration.

Terlingua is the farmstead where Jason settles following his journey to
Smoky Springs.

Thasiwoda is a system of exercises to improve the balance and flexibility of
its practitioners. Advanced students learn to fight using the positions and
transitions, which mimic movements in hand-to-hand combat.

Twin Rivers Bay and Harbor are at the mouth of the Ga'aton and Tapti rivers and are a major trading center controlled by Duke Rashad.

Twin Rivers City sits where the Ga'aton and Tapti rivers merge at the bay. It straddles the Ga'aton River and the north shore of the bay.

A two-skinned is a being with both a human form and an animal form. The human is aware when the animal is on the surface and can influence the animal's actions. Similarly, the animal can affect the human when their roles are reversed. All known two-skinned are predators in animal form.

V

The void is a state of consciousness in which a person is aware of his or her surroundings but focused almost exclusively on a goal. The person is barely aware of the passage of time, being focused on the present time.

W

A wave glider is a small, flat, shallow draft water conveyance powered by magic and used to move small packages or a person on fresh water.

Wolverton Mountain is a mountain to the north of Smoky Springs.

Y

A yepsen is a unit of measurement denoting the amount that can be held in two hands cupped together.

Printed in the United States
by Baker & Taylor Publisher Services